The ARMCHAIR DETECTIVES

The ARMCHAIR DETECTIVES

MATT DUNN

Bookouture

Published by Bookouture in 2025

An imprint of Storyfire Ltd.
Carmelite House
50 Victoria Embankment
London EC4Y 0DZ

www.bookouture.com

The authorised representative in the EEA is Hachette Ireland
8 Castlecourt Centre
Dublin 15 D15 XTP3
Ireland
(email: info@hbgi.ie)

ISBN: 978-1-80550-097-1
eBook ISBN: 978-1-80550-096-4

For Katie and Simon
If you've ever wondered whether you've appeared in one of my books, now you have!

1

You see a lot of dead bodies when you do what I did for a living. Some of them you're responsible for. Which is why the moment I lay my eyes on Elsie's, I can tell there's nothing 'natural' about the causes of her passing.

News of her death has spread like wildfire round Twilight Lodge, the seafront nursing home in St Leonards-on-Sea where I'm currently ten days into a month's post-operative stay, casting a shadow over the normally jolly thrice-weekly singalong currently underway in the Garden Lounge. Perhaps as a consequence, the staff have been doing their best to lead the room in an enthusiastic version of 'I Will Survive', an interesting choice of song given this morning's developments. As I'd made my surreptitious exit, they'd segued seamlessly into 'Staying Alive', as if attempting to impart some sort of subliminal message. Though if so, it's a little late for Elsie.

The crime scene – Elsie's room – is on the ground floor at the front of the imposing Victorian red-brick building, at the furthest end of a long, blue-carpeted corridor lined with tracks from years of walking-frame traffic, and perfectly located for any villainous activities. Though I'm eighty-four and nursing a brand-new hip, I appear to be one of the younger and more mobile 'Lodgers' – as we affectionately refer to one another here – so I'm the first to make the journey, both to pay my respects and check whether anything untoward has happened. And while I'd like to go in and examine the body for clues, Miriam's presence by Elsie's bed makes that impossible. Miriam's one of the good eggs – a carer at Twilight Lodge who actually lives up to her job title, as opposed to certain other members of staff who treat us as if we're a bit of an inconvenience.

Not one to be thwarted so easily, I decide to invoke a skill I learned on day one of surveillance class at 'the Company' – which was how new recruits were encouraged to refer to the covert organisation I once worked for – utilising my expert muscle control to stand statue-still and silent in the doorway, consequently allowing me to scrutinise the scene. There are no signs of a struggle – though that's perhaps not a surprise given Elsie's age and frailty – and nothing appears to be missing, given how every available space is chock full of framed family photographs or porcelain knick-knacks. In fact, to my trained eye, the complete lack of any indication of anything untoward seems suspicious in itself.

Slowly, stealthily, careful not to alert Miriam to my presence, I reach for my cardigan pocket and retrieve the notebook I've begun carrying with me as an *aide-memoire*, intending to record my observations before I'm shooed away. But before I even get as far as uncapping my pen, I'm reminded how at my age my expert muscle control doesn't quite extend to *all* my muscles, in particular my sphincter, as I can't prevent myself from unexpectedly breaking wind. Rather loudly.

Miriam jumps, peers accusingly at Elsie, then finally notices me in the doorway. 'Martin!' she says, as if I've caught her *in flagrante*, so I give her my best full-beam smile.

'Any idea what happened?' I say, and Miriam frowns.

'Happened…?'

I point at the bed with my walking stick, a necessary – though hopefully temporary – accompaniment given my newly installed titanium joint. 'To Elsie.'

Miriam looks surprised at my question. 'She died, Martin.'

'Yes, but how?'

Miriam looks even more surprised. 'Old age, I suppose.'

I widen my eyes, in disbelief rather than shock, and Miriam appears mortified, as if she's just realised attributing Elsie's demise to a condition all Twilight Lodge's paying guests suffer from to a varying degree might not be the most tactful of observations. 'Sorry, Martin. I didn't mean to imply...'

I wave her apology away in a 'no offence taken' way, adding a friendly, 'No offence taken,' for good measure, and Miriam looks relieved, though I wish *I* was. First George, then Diana, now Elsie, all three departed since I arrived. To paraphrase a line from *Goldfinger* – one of my favourite films, and not just because of my keen professional interest in the genre – once is an accident, twice is coincidence, three times is evidence there's something fishy going on.

And while you might argue there's nothing more to worry about, that these things come in threes – if only that were true. Because then I could be sure that'd be the end of it.

From what my intuition tells me, I'm surer that it isn't.

2

'It's the best way to go, in your sleep,' Miriam says, brushing her fingers softly against Elsie's cheek.

'It is,' I say, though it occurs to me to point out how people who die in their sleep generally look like they're still deep in the Land of Nod – minus the breathing, of course – as opposed to Elsie's apparent surprise during her final moments. But then I realise if I did, Miriam might ask how I know this, and clueing anyone in on my background is *verboten* – or at least, seriously frowned upon – courtesy of the Official Secrets Act. 'Was anyone with her?' I ask instead, and Miriam shakes her head.

'That's the tragedy,' she says. 'Normally if we fear someone's coming to the end we'll let one of the relatives know so they can be here to say goodbye. Or at least, one of us will sit with them until... Well, you get the idea. But we didn't know anything was wrong until Shane found the bod— I mean, found *her* this morning.'

'Shane, you say?' I raise one eyebrow. The antithesis of Miriam, Shane's an insensible bully who everyone dislikes, and the feeling's evidently mutual given the way he approaches his job.

Uncapping my pen, I jot down his role in this sorry affair, mentally promoting Shane to the top of my list of suspects even though his is the only name on it. As I hover in the doorway, Miriam evidently mistakes my professional interest for self-concern, because she gives me a kindly look.

'She was *ninety-three*, Martin,'

I do a quick bit of mental arithmetic, then clutch a hand theatrically to my chest. 'You mean I've another nine years of *this* to look forward to?'

Miriam smiles, which is good, because I'm joking. Assuming my new hip holds up through the rest of my daily physiotherapy sessions here with Olga – which on occasion are so torturous I almost suspect she might be ex-KGB – I'll be out of here and back home by the end of the month, never to darken Twilight Lodge's doors again.

'Elsie didn't have it so bad,' she says. 'A comfortable room, and with such a lovely view of the sea.'

I peer out through Elsie's window at the perennially grey English Channel. In the distance, and though I'm sure it's just an optical illusion, a cargo ship looks like it's about to sail over the horizon and fall off the edge of the world.

'Maybe,' I say, and Miriam looks at me for a moment, perhaps unsure how to respond, then walks over to where I'm standing in the doorway and rests a gentle hand on my arm.

'You know you shouldn't be in here?'

I'm about to remind Miriam I'm only at Twilight Lodge to convalesce and that otherwise I'm much too 'with-it' for a place like this, when I realise she probably means I shouldn't be in Elsie's room, so instead I nod down at my slipper-shod feet, which are clearly still on the blue corridor carpet rather than the beige in-room one.

'I'm not.'

'You know what I mean.'

'I wanted to pay my respects,' I say, hoping that'll afford me a closer look at Elsie's body. But Miriam's not small, and she's effectively blocking both my view and my route to the bed.

'That's sweet of you.'

'But now I'm here...'

'Yes, Martin?'

I point my stick towards Elsie's bed again. 'You don't think there's anything... suspicious?'

'*Suspicious?*'

'About Elsie's, you know...?' I stop short of calling it 'murder', as I suspect doing so might shut Miriam down before I can get anything useful out of her. Instead, I cross my eyes, stick my tongue out and mime being dead on the end of a hangman's rope, and Miriam sighs.

'I think someone has a rather over-active imagination,' she scolds, locking the door behind her, before escorting me from the doorway.

'But Elsie's the third death since I got here!'

'I very much doubt that's—'

'It's true!' I flip back in my notebook to where I've written this down, holding it out so Miriam can see the relevant page. 'I arrived on the first of June. George died on the second. Diana on the seventh. And now Elsie, and it's only...' I glance at my wristwatch, a retirement present from the Company, though very different to the ones my fictional counterparts on the silver screen sported, given the lack of built-in gadgets. All this one does is tell the time and date. 'The eleventh. That's more than one a week!'

Miriam grimaces, perhaps as if this somehow reflects badly on her, then squeezes my arm gently.

'You do know where you are, don't you?'

I'm a little affronted at the implication I might be so far gone as to *not* know. 'Twilight Lodge,' I say confidently, adding, '"St Leonards-on-Sea's number-one nursing home".' It's a quote from the brochure, though given this place is hardly the most luxurious of residences, I assume it refers to the fact it's been here the longest.

'That's right!' says Miriam, as if I've just correctly answered the final question on *Who Wants to Be a Millionaire?* 'And I'm afraid this is what you get in places like this.'

'A serial killer systematically bumping off the, you know...' I hesitate, not knowing whether the term is 'residents', 'guests', 'patients', or 'inmates', then settle for a pointed glance back towards Elsie's room.

Miriam rolls her eyes. 'No one's bumping off the residents!' she says, putting me out of my vocabular misery. 'What I meant was, everyone who moves in... eventually...' She squeezes my arm again. 'Well, you know, at some point, they're going to...' There's a pause as Miriam looks at me as if it's my fault she can't say the word. 'I mean, that's why most of them are here.'

'What is?'

Miriam lowers her voice, though I don't know why. Given the widespread reliance here at Twilight Lodge on hearing aids, coupled with an apparent proclivity for losing them on a regular basis, she could shout at the top of her voice and still not cause alarm. 'To *die*.'

Though my memory might not be what it was, I'm almost positive it doesn't say *that* in the brochure. Even in the small print. 'I see,' I say, then I make a face, and for the second time in as many minutes, Miriam looks mortified.

'Not you, obviously, Martin,' she says hurriedly. 'You're here to get better. But the rest of them...'

'Phew!' I say, then realise that might sound rather selfish, but Miriam doesn't seem to mind.

But later that afternoon, as I watch them wheel Elsie out to the undertaker's van, I think about Miriam's reassurance and realise something: Even though I'm not actually staying here for the duration, if there *is* something suspicious going on at Twilight Lodge, then getting to the bottom of Elsie's death – not to mention George and Diana's – might well be my only way of making sure she's right.

3

Though I don't have a sea view like Elsie's, my room's pleasant enough: about the size of a standard prison cell, though equipped with an actual separate 'en suite', as opposed to the kind of stainless steel in-room stand-alone lavatory you might find at Pentonville or Strangeways. There's a bed against the far wall – a single, but that's all I've needed since my wife Madeleine's untimely passing last year. Sleeping in a double only reminds me of her absence, and I can do without that while I'm here.

On the left, just as you come in through the heavy fire-and-soundproofed door, there's a wardrobe and a chest of drawers. My daughter Dionne's dutifully stocked them with garments designed for post-operative comfort and ease of access rather than, say, a night playing high-stakes baccarat at a Macau casino or an impromptu abseil down the side of a Shanghai skyscraper – though the realities of my job at the Company were usually more mundane than that – and instead of labels bearing the names of the best Savile Row tailors, my clothes are tagged with *my* name, Martin Maxwell, so as not to get lost in Twilight Lodge's communal laundry.

I've intended to spend the rest of the day holed up in here, trying to work out the motive for Elsie's murder, though the combination of a lack of background information, the radiator in my room being on its default setting of 'volcanic' despite the pleasant June temperatures outside, and the comfortable armchair I've sat in to have a think, means 'dozing' is a more accurate description of my afternoon's activities. Besides, Shane's gone home for the day, and while I'm probably a good few years past being able to beat a confession out of him, I console myself with the fact that if I'm right about who the murderer is, at least no one else will get bumped off in his absence.

Come the evening, I've done my exercises, had my dinner, then surreptitiously checked the visitor's book at reception for any suspicious recent comings and goings, before watching the local news on the ancient television perched on top of my chest of drawers – though, perhaps not surprisingly, there's no mention of Elsie's demise on there – and I'm just enjoying a postprandial nap when Dionne appears at my door. In my semi-conscious state my first thought is that she's here to investigate the murder, although she's not in uniform, which, unless she's been recently promoted to Sussex Constabulary's plain-clothes division – and that's an achievement I'm sure I wouldn't have forgotten – would suggest not. Plus, she's brought Custard, my late wife's beloved pug, and I can hardly see *him* getting a job with the force unless laziness and obesity have become recruitment prerequisites.

'Dad?' she says, quietly yet insistently, perhaps to make sure I'm awake – or even *alive* – before marching over to where I'm sitting and kissing me on the cheek, and I beam proudly up at her. With the whole of my career shrouded in secrecy, Dionne's the one thing I've got to show for my life – the only thing I have left after cancer cruelly took her mother from us. She's also my main reason to keep going – after all, she's got no one else to look out for her. Custard certainly isn't going to do it. And at forty-two years old she's not yet managed to meet a man who deserves her. Despite my best – and often unappreciated – efforts.

'Hello, love.'

'Look who I brought!' she says, though Custard seems reluctant to move from his position in the doorway. Perhaps he remembers visiting Madeleine in the hospice – a similar environment to Twilight Lodge – and we all know how *that* turned out. And even though I'll be home in a few weeks – assuming I don't get murdered in my bed like Elsie – you can't blame him for being suspicious.

With an excited, 'Here, boy!' I pat both thighs enthusiastically, though I don't really expect Custard to run to me and leap up into my lap. He's hardly the most athletic of creatures, unless either food or a cat are present. Instead, he lets out an aggrieved sigh, then – as if he's doing me a favour – trots over and allows himself to be petted for a moment or two, before ambling off to lie by the radiator.

Dionne makes a 'what can you do?' face, then perches on the bed, her feet not quite able to touch the floor, and I'm suddenly reminded of her as a little girl. Something I saw too little of, given my regular far-flung postings courtesy of the Company.

'How was your day?' she asks.

'Can't complain,' I say, and Dionne smiles, perhaps with a hint of relief. She's a worrier, especially when she can't keep an eye on me, but a recent hip replacement and living in a house without a downstairs toilet aren't good bedfellows, which is why I checked myself in here until I'm firing on all cylinders again. 'Yours? Catch any bad guys?'

'Not today. Paperwork mostly. You know how it is.'

I nod, even though I don't. Paperwork wasn't something I had to particularly bother with back in the day. Shoot first and ask someone back at Company HQ to fill in the forms later. Besides, in my line of work, you didn't want to leave a paper trail.

'There's always tomorrow,' I say, reaching across to give her hand a squeeze, proud that she's following in my footsteps, in a way.

'There is,' she agrees, and we sit in a comfortable silence for a moment or two, then I remember what I've been meaning to tell her.

'Oh – there's been another one!'

'Another what?'

'Death. Elsie.'

'Oh, Dad.' Dionne's face falls. 'I'm sorry. Did you know her well?'

'As well as I could after a week and a half.' And that's true – as the 'new boy', I've tried to fit in as quickly as possible, so I've thrown myself into the group activities in order to meet and mingle with my fellow residents. 'She wasn't that mobile. Spent a lot of time asleep in her room. Too much time for her own good, if you ask me.'

'I don't...?'

'I think she might have been...' I draw my index finger across my throat, and Dionne's jaw drops open.

'Seriously?'

'*Yes*, seriously! Just like the other two.'

'*Dad...*'

Dionne's sounding a little exasperated, so I fold my arms defiantly. 'You didn't see the body. I did. And she definitely looked like she'd been murdered.'

'How would you know?'

'Well, from work...' I say, then immediately wish I could

take the words back. I've never told Dionne about my Company days, mainly to give her plausible deniability in case any of my old foes ever turn up at our door, hell-bent on revenge.

'And how exactly does a career as a hotel inspector qualify you in the finer points of forensic science?'

That stumps me for a moment. My fabricated occupation was always great for explaining my regular mission-dependent absences from home, although now I can see the flaw in my plan, so I have to think on my feet. 'Well, sometimes, in the course of my, um, *inspections*, we'd find, you know, *dead people.*'

'At the hotels?'

'Yes. In their rooms. And you can tell, can't you? If they've been bumped off. Once you've seen enough of them.'

'I should be so lucky. This is St Leonards, Dad. We've a distinct lack of murdering.' She jabs a thumb in the direction of the Garden Lounge. 'Except of the occasional song at those singalong mornings of yours.'

'Well, you *can!*' I say, a little belligerently. 'And there's another thing. Apparently if someone's on their last legs, a family member or perhaps one of the staff will sit with them. All night, if necessary. Whereas nobody saw it coming. In each case. All three of the victims died alone...' I click my fingers, then wince at the pain it causes in my arthritic knuckles. 'Like that!'

'How old was...?'

'Elsie? Ninety-three,' I say, happy I don't have to refer to my notebook for that particular fact. 'But that's not the point! Besides, people don't just die from old age. They die from some-thing *caused by* old age. Elsie appeared fighting fit to me.'

'Apart from being ninety-three and... what was it? Spending a lot of time asleep in her room?'

'Exactly!' I say, before realising Dionne's being sarcastic. 'Just because you enjoy regular naps, it doesn't mean you're at death's door.' I nod towards a loudly snoring Custard. 'That dog would have shuffled off this mortal coil long ago if so.'

Perhaps because he knows I'm talking about him, Custard suddenly snorts himself awake. He raises his head, and peers disgruntledly at me, as if I'm somehow being unreasonable.

In much the same way as Dionne appears to be doing.

4

———

'But what motivation would anyone in here have for...?' Dionne draws her finger across her neck exaggeratedly, and I get the distinct feeling she's teasing me.

'You're the policewoman. You tell me.'

Dionne shrugs, then stands up and goes to look out of the window, though she soon sits back down again. While Twilight Lodge occupies as prime a seafront location as it's possible to have in St Leonards, overlooking the promenade at the western end of town, my room's at the rear of the building, so my view's just the back wall of the neighbouring block of flats.

'But what if I'm right and someone *is* killing off the residents?' I say, adding, 'One by one,' in an attempt to imply that it could be me next.

Dionne takes my hand. 'Who would possibly want to do a thing like that?'

'Well, there's Shane, for one. He's got it in for us all.'

'I'm sure he hasn't.'

'I'm sure he *has*.'

'What would he possibly stand to gain by killing you all off? He'd be out of a job, for one thing!'

'A job he clearly detests. So there's your motive!'

Dionne raises both eyebrows. 'Are you sure this isn't because you thought he was stealing your sweets?'

'He *was*!' I insist. I'd been so convinced of this I'd set a trap, replacing the Mint Imperials in the bag in my bedside table drawer with copies I'd whittled out of the white toilet freshener cakes from my en-suite loo. Though one day, a little dopey from my afternoon nap, I'd forgotten I'd done this and ended up nearly breaking my dentures, not to mention almost poisoning myself.

Dionne gives me a look. 'You'll be telling me it's one of the other residents next.'

'Unlikely,' I say, as I've already considered this. 'Most of them are too frail to be able to exert the necessary deadly force, even if they knew how.' I'm not sure *I* still can, although that may simply be because I'm out of practice. 'You couldn't, you know... *look into it* for me, could you, love? Maybe find out the cause of death?'

Dionne sighs. 'Dad, even if I could, there's no way they'd do a post-mortem. And without any evidence...'

'Can't you at least find out what the national averages are for nursing home deaths? For my peace of mind, if nothing else. Just so I can be sure there's nothing untoward going on in here.'

I've tried to make my voice sound a little frailer than my normal booming baritone, and Dionne suddenly looks concerned. 'You can always come home early, you know?'

I shake my head. I'm convalescing at Twilight Lodge because I insisted on it, rather than Dionne having me committed, or whatever the term is. Not that it's stopped her feeling guilty. 'I told you – I don't want to be a burden while I'm recuperating.'

'You're hardly a burden.'

'Well, I don't want to become one. Just because I used to

wipe your backside, you shouldn't feel you'll have to do the same for me one day.'

Dionne shudders. 'Thanks for the imagery.'

'You know what I mean. You've got your own life to live. Without your old dad cramping your style!'

I grin at her, although Dionne doesn't return it. 'Okay,' she says after a moment, then she looks at me earnestly. 'Seriously, though. You're not worried, are you?'

'About my own safety?' I let out a short laugh. Even if there is a serial killer on the loose here at Twilight Lodge, I've got myself out of tighter scrapes in the past. 'Not at all.'

'Good.'

'But you'll check this place out? See how it compares?'

'We already did, remember? And Twilight Lodge gets virtually all five-star reviews. It's why we chose it.'

'Yes, well, nobody's going to review the place from beyond the grave, are they? It's a little too late by then to go on Google and say, "Murdered in my bed – one star". Besides, I meant on the "deaths" front. Statistics, and the like.'

Dionne opens her mouth as if to say something, then she sighs. 'Fine. Anything to make you forget all this "murder" nonsense...' She stops talking and clasps a hand to her mouth – my potential mental decline is a bit of a sensitive subject. 'Dad, I'm so sorry.'

'Forget about it,' I say, nudging her with my elbow, then doing it again for good measure.

Dionne smiles, then she looks at her watch, pats my arm, and stands up. 'Well, I'd better be on my way. Custard will be wanting his dinner.'

At the word 'dinner', and even though he appears to be fast asleep, Custard's ears prick up, which brings a smile to my face too. 'I hope it's tastier than mine was!' I say. 'Although that wouldn't be difficult.'

'What was it?' Dionne says cheerfully.

I stare at the empty plate sitting on the wheeled table to my left, though the answer as to what this evening's particular culinary delight was eludes me. 'A "TV" one,' I say, nodding towards the television, where a muted episode of *EastEnders* appears to be playing.

Dionne looks concerned. 'You can't remember, or was it hard to tell?'

'The latter,' I say, not only because it's the answer Dionne probably wants to hear.

'But you ate it anyway?'

'The evidence – or lack of it – would suggest I must have. Whatever it was.'

Dionne smiles, though it seems a little forced. 'I'm sure it's just because it wasn't memorable.'

'Shepherd's pie!'

'Pardon?'

'It was shepherd's pie! Tonight's meal.'

'Your favourite!'

'Well, your mum's version was.' I sigh. 'She was a great cook.'

Dionne can't meet my gaze, and to tell the truth, I'm glad. Her mother's passing hit us both hard. And even if I am starting to forget things, I know I'll never forget her. 'She was,' she says, after a moment, and I clear my throat, though it takes two goes to get rid of the lump that's formed there.

'Anyway, you get going. I've got things to do.'

'What things?' asks Dionne suspiciously.

'Jigsaw puzzles to solve, for one thing.' Jigsaws are one of the more popular activities here at Twilight Lodge. Although my suspicion is that Shane likes to pinch a random piece from each box just to frustrate us.

The smile returns to Dionne's face. 'As long as that's *all* you try and solve.'

I nod, trying to look as innocent as possible. 'But you'll do some digging? About the numbers?'

'I will.'

'Oh, and maybe check that Shane out? See if he's got a criminal record?'

Dionne purses her lips, then she stands up smartly. 'I'll see what I can do,' she says, leaning down to kiss me on the forehead, though given her tone I don't hold out much hope. 'But bear in mind I'm in London until Friday night, so...'

'London?'

'I told you, Dad. On a course. Interrogation techniques.'

'Oh. Yes. You said.' And she did. It's another reason why I checked myself in here. On top of the bathroom arrangements, four days of being home alone with a new hip and a dog with a penchant for getting under my feet at mealtimes probably wasn't the best of ideas. Not if Dionne didn't want to come back to find my half-eaten corpse next to an even fatter pug. 'No rush, love. What are you doing with...?' I nod towards Custard, who – sensing it's time to go – has hauled himself to his feet, performed what's known in our house as a 'big stretch', and is currently regarding me disdainfully, as if it's my fault he's late being fed.

Dionne shrugs. 'Julie. From work.'

I make a face. 'Does she know what she's letting herself in for?'

Dionne rolls her eyes, then reaches down and scratches Custard affectionately between his ears. 'He's not that bad.'

'He is with *me*.'

'It's only because he misses Mum.'

'He's not the only one,' I say, before I can stop myself, and Dionne smiles flatly.

'Anyway,' she says, after a moment. 'So I'll see you at the weekend?'

'Fingers crossed!'

I've not meant it as a reference to any reunion being subject to my surviving any deadly activities here at Twilight Lodge, and it's evident Dionne hasn't taken it that way, because she holds both hands up and crosses her fingers. So, fixing a smile on my face, I do the same.

Then keep them crossed until long after the two of them have gone.

5

There's a woman in Elsie's room when I take the scenic route back from breakfast the following morning. My first thought is that she's somehow involved in the murder, given the way she's stuffing all of Elsie's belongings into a large holdall, and I'm about to barge in and order her to stop because she's simultaneously removing evidence and contaminating the crime scene, when I decide I'd better do some investigation of my own first. Although it doesn't take long for even my rusty deductive powers to work out she must be a relative, given her appearance in at least two of the framed photographs on Elsie's shelves, not to mention the way she's sobbing. Quickly deciding on a change of tack, I knock softly on the open door, then say, 'I'm sorry for your loss,' when she looks up.

'Thank you.'

'Was Elsie...' I peer at the woman – she's sixty if she's a day, which I immediately realise gives me an 'in'. 'Your *grandmother?*'

'Mother,' says the woman, with the briefest of smiles, which lets me know my attempt at flattery has hit home. I pretend to be suitably surprised for a second or two, then shuffle into the room.

'I'm Martin,' I say. 'From Room Seventeen.'

'Yvette. Elsie's...'

'Daughter. I worked that out from what you just said.' I tap a finger against my temple to indicate there are no marbles missing. 'Nice to meet you. And again, my condolences. Elsie was well-liked here.'

'Thank you.' Yvette's eyes light up, in sharp contrast to the mascara streaks down her cheeks. 'That means a lot.'

'We...' – I think for a moment, wondering how to work the conversation round to a subtle line of enquiry, but in the absence of anything leaping to mind, decide to stay on what's probably safe ground – 'shared a mutual enjoyment of jigsaws.'

'Mum did like her jigsaws,' Yvette says, then her top lip begins to tremble, and she sits down heavily on the bed. 'I'm sorry. It's just such a shock. I mean, I knew she was old...' Her eyes flick briefly up at me, though I'm relieved to see I appear to pass some sort of test, as she carries on speaking without apologising. 'But she seemed fine. Good, actually.'

Conscious that my window of opportunity might not last that long, I raise an eyebrow. 'Your mother wasn't ill, then?'

Yvette shakes her head rapidly. 'Not at all. Mum sailed through her recent appraisal here with Gemma. You'd hardly say she was steady on her feet, of course, but she'd been talking about her birthday next month. How much she was looking forward to turning ninety-four. We were so sure she'd have many more years here. Just the other day I told her she'd probably keep going until she got a telegram from the King. Which is why I can't believe she's just...'

As Yvette's voice trails off, I stand up a little straighter at the reference to the Crown. Despite the clandestine nature of the Company's existence, 'For Queen and Country' was our motto.

I even took a bullet for her once. Before it was fired, but still. That was one red-faced assassin, I can tell you.

'I'm sorry to pry. I'm as surprised as you were. Your mother seemed so...' I stop talking, not sure how to end that sentence without giving away the fact that I hardly knew Elsie at all, then venture the obvious: 'Alive.'

'Wasn't she?' Yvette nods, on the verge of tears again. 'At least she didn't suffer, I suppose.'

I open my mouth, then close it again. I've never seen anyone die who didn't appear to be suffering at some point during the process, and if my suspicions about Elsie are true, she'll hardly have had the most relaxing of demises. But running my theory past Yvette when she's clearly so emotional probably isn't going to get me anywhere.

As she resumes her collecting, picking up photo frames, staring at them wistfully, then slotting each one into the holdall with an agonised sob, I realise if I'm going to get to the bottom of Elsie's death, I need to speak to other people who knew her, a bit like when we'd compile a dossier on the targets we were sent after. I need to work out why someone might want to kill her, which might then lead me to 'who?'. And there's only one way I can think of to do that.

'At the risk of asking an indelicate question, do you know when the funeral might be?'

Yvette stares at me blankly. 'Funeral?' she says, after a moment.

'Only I'd like to come, if you don't mind? Pay my respects properly.'

'Of course,' says Yvette, then her shoulders begin to heave. 'I'm sorry,' she says, in between sobs. 'I've just... I mean, there's so much to do, and I don't know where to...'

'I understand,' I say, passing her a tissue from the box on the bedside table. 'But if it's not too much trouble, could you let me know? Once *you* do?'

Yvette blows her nose loudly. 'Of course,' she says, dabbing at her eyes with the tissue. 'It would be good to have some of her friends there.'

'Thank you. Perhaps you'd be so kind as to call one of the staff here and ask them to pass the information on?'

Yvette nods, so I congratulate myself on a job well done, and I'm just about to make my escape when the unmistakeable waft of too much deodorant assaults my nostrils, and there's a loud 'All right?' from the doorway, which can only mean one thing.

The murderer has returned to the scene of the crime.

6

'Oh, *Shane*,' says Yvette, rushing across to give him a hug, which he endures awkwardly. He's not the most approachable of men, something hardly helped by what seems to be a permanent scowl on his face, and with a thickset physique that suggests he once spent a lot of time in the gym but has recently swapped that for the pub. What's more, he sports what I understand from Dionne are known as 'sleeves' of vividly inked tattoos on both arms which – though I consider myself fortunate not to have seen him with his shirt off – apparently extend across his torso, given the identical designs that poke up above his collar.

As I check his face for any signs of remorse, he frees himself from Yvette's grasp and narrows his eyes at me. 'What're you doing in here, Double-O Seventy?'

I shake my head at Shane's insult, though it's my own fault. Despite a lifetime of carefulness around Dionne and Madeleine, I must be getting a bit slack in my old age, because I made the mistake of letting slip my espionage past to him the other day, and now he won't let me forget it.

'Always turning up where you'd least expect him, that one,' Shane tells Yvette. 'Aren't you?'

He's raised his voice to direct the final two words at me as if I'm a pre-schooler or even a family pet, and the temptation to teach him some manners courtesy of the sharp end of my walking stick is one I only just manage to avoid. 'I'm here to pay my respects.'

Shane frowns, as if the concept is alien to him. 'Yeah? Well, I'm sure Mrs Rogers could do without you bothering her while she...'

He steps between us and nods towards the holdall, and Yvette looks up at him. 'Oh, it's not a problem,' she says.

'Even so,' says Shane, taking hold of my arm a little more firmly than necessary.

I consider expertly slipping out of his grasp, judo-sweeping him to the floor, and putting him in a headlock for good measure, but I don't want to over-tax my new hip. Besides, even if arthritis hadn't decommissioned my hands from their former 'deadly weapons' classification, I'm not yet at the stage where violent lashings-out can be explained away by any age-related condition, so instead I allow myself to be escorted towards the door, giving Yvette a little salute with my free hand on the way out.

'Lovely to meet you, Martin,' she calls after me. 'I'll be in touch about the, you know...'

I can tell the word is hard for her to say, so I give her a flat-lipped smile and a nod of encouragement. 'The pleasure was all mine. And thank you.'

As Yvette returns to her clear-out, Shane stares at me suspiciously, then virtually frog-marches me along the corridor until we're out of earshot. 'What was all that about?' he growls.

'All what about?'

Shane brings his face uncomfortably close to mine, revealing that his oral hygiene is just as repulsive as his personality. 'Her in there. Saying she'd be in touch.'

'In touch about what?' I say, aware sometimes playing the

'old' card can work in my favour, though Shane doesn't seem to fall for it.

'You *know* what. What did she mean?'

I shrug as nonchalantly as I can, though it's one-shouldered, given how my other arm is still in Shane's clutches. 'Elsie's funeral. I thought I might go.'

Shane does a double take. 'What would you want to do *that* for? You a relative?'

'Aren't we all, if you go back far enough? At least according to a certain fossil discovered in Ethiopia. Lucy, I believe, was her name. Well, probably not her *actual* name, if she even had one, given how *Australopithecus* didn't have the capacity for language. But it's what the palaeontologists named her.'

Shane looks at me strangely for a moment. 'So, no, then?'

'No, but...' I lower my voice, and decide attack is the best form of defence – maybe putting Shane on the back foot might not be a bad idea. 'Quite frankly, I think there's something suspicious about her death. And going to her funeral might reveal exactly what that is.'

I peer at him intently, looking for any kind of tell or nervous tic that'll let me know he's the guilty party, just like I've done a hundred times while holding suspects at gunpoint. But instead of the expected shifty reaction, or perhaps even some idle boast about his part in Elsie's demise, Shane lets my arm go and begins to laugh. 'You what?' he says, once he's finished. Which takes a while.

Unlike many of the residents here at Twilight Lodge, Shane doesn't have a hearing problem, so I refrain from repeating myself. 'You heard me.'

'Seriously? Elsie must have been a hundred years old! Who'd want to do her in?'

'You tell me.'

Shane shakes his head slowly. 'Oh, *mate*...' he says, though it doesn't sound like a term of endearment. Then he taps a finger to his temple. 'You're worse than I thought.'

'The feeling's mutual,' I mutter.

'Elsie's funeral!' he says, shaking his head as though it's the punchline to a clever joke he's just been told. 'What makes you think they'll let you out to go?'

'Let me out?' I gesture towards him with my stick. 'This place isn't a prison, you know?'

Shane neither confirms nor denies that. Instead, he just winks at me, spins round on his heel, heads off along the corridor, and disappears into the staffroom.

7

———

With Dionne away – not to mention the absence of her taking me seriously – I suspect I'm going to need a little help, not only because I don't have long to find out what's going on, but also because I want to avoid the same fate as Elsie.

Although I flew solo on countless missions for the Company back in the day, the past is a foreign country, according to the saying. Almost too many foreign countries to recall, in my case, though what I do remember is how an extra pair of eyes and ears could make the difference between life and death. Which is why I decide to take the once-unthinkable step of recruiting my one-time colleague, friend, and – in what's an almost unbelievable incidence of happenstance – my current next-door neighbour here at Twilight Lodge, Albie, back into the fold.

While I've braced myself for a less-than-generous response, his weary 'Bugger off, Martin!' when I clear my throat from his doorway certainly wasn't what I'd expected. Though perhaps I should have, given the somewhat acrimonious way we parted.

'Still mad at me, eh?' I say. 'Even after fifty years?'

Albie rolls his eyes, perhaps at my temerity for suggesting he should have forgiven me by now for my part in sending him to prison for the best part of half a century. 'Not *this* again?' he says, wheeling his wheelchair across the carpet from where he's been sitting, gazing out of the window. Albie gazes out of the window a lot. Possibly because if he squints at the potted palm trees that have been placed there to mask the view of the recycling bins, he can just about imagine he's back wherever it was in Central America he'd attempted to disappear – a suitcase stuffed full of Company funds under one arm, some drop-dead-gorgeous woman he'd met on a mission there on the other – all those years ago.

'It wasn't personal, Albie. I had my orders. Don't think I took any pleasure from that' – I wave my hand vaguely in the air in an attempt to encompass our brutal tussle, followed by my subsequently holding him in his beachside villa until the extraction team arrived, before bundling him into the boot of a car for the perilous drive to the jungle landing strip where one of the Company's jets was waiting to repatriate his traitorous self to face justice – '*business* a while back.'

'Martin, for the thousandth time, none of what you seem convinced happened actually happened. At least, not to me. Or *with* me.'

'It *did*,' I insist. 'Miriam told me you don't remember much from before your stroke last year. Maybe this is one of those things?'

Albie sighs exasperatedly. 'I think I'd remember being James bloody Bond!'

'I can understand you preferring to block those memories out, but you've paid your dues. And there are certainly no hard feelings on my part for what you did. Despite the fact we used to be partners.'

'I *didn't do anything*! And we were never partners. I'd never even met you before you arrived here the other week.'

'Sure,' I say sarcastically. Though he hid it well, I don't

think he could believe it when he first laid eyes on me here. And he still doesn't, judging by his repeated denials.

Albie's eyes flash with anger. 'Will. You. Just...' He glares at me for a moment longer, then sighs. 'Forget about it.'

'That's big of you, Albie,' I say, offering him a conciliatory handshake, though I'm a little hurt when he refuses.

'That's not... I mean, you're confused. Or confusing me with someone else. Either way, you're...' Albie pauses, makes a pistol with his hand, raises it to his temple as if he's about to shoot himself in the head, and circles his index finger there. Then he wheels himself straight past me and into the corridor, and I have to step back to avoid him running over my toes. Something I'm sure he's tried to do on purpose.

'It's okay,' I say, pursuing him along the corridor in a slow-motion chase that would probably appear quite comical if anyone who knew us from old was watching. 'I appreciate you might not want anybody here to know. And I haven't told them a thing.'

Albie stops abruptly and performs a quick about-turn, and it's all I can do to keep myself from toppling into his lap. 'That's because there's nothing to tell. All this "the Company" business you keep going on about... It's got nothing to do with me! I've never even been to Nicaragua...'

'*Nicaragua!*' I exclaim, with some relief. The name – like Albie back then – had temporarily escaped me. 'Thank you.'

Albie shakes his head, then starts off along the corridor in the other direction, and I do my best to fall into step beside him, though given that my new hip's not quite bedded in yet, he's a lot quicker on wheels than I am on my feet. In desperation, I reach out with my walking stick and, with a swift tap on the relevant lever, manage to engage the brake on his left wheel, which makes his wheelchair perform the equivalent of a hand-brake turn.

He growls in frustration, then looks crossly up at me. 'What do you *want*, Martin?'

I rest a hand on his shoulder, and he looks at it as if it's infected. 'Your help, Albie,' I say, as earnestly as I can.

'With what?'

I look to my left and my right to check the coast is clear, something which at my age now requires me to turn my whole body rather than just my head, then lower my voice:

'Murder.'

8

Albie widens his eyes. 'Who are you planning to kill?'

'Oh, no!' I break into a grin. 'Not committing. *Solving.*'

Albie looks relieved for a split second, though his expression quickly morphs into bewilderment. 'Who's been murdered?'

'Three of Twilight Lodge's residents, by my estimation.'

'Same question.'

I pull my notebook out of my cardigan pocket and turn to the appropriate page, hoping the fact it's in writing – albeit *my* writing – will give my claims more credence. 'George. Then Diana. Now Elsie.'

'They were *murdered?*'

'Seems that way.'

Albie looks even more confused. 'What on earth makes you think that?'

'Well, for one thing, I saw Elsie's body yesterday. And like they say, when you know, you know.'

'I don't think that's what that phrase refers to.'

'Come on, Albie. Three already this month? Bit suspicious, don't you think?'

Albie stares at me, looking for all the world like he doesn't think that at all. Something that he backs up a moment later by saying, 'Not really, no.'

'Did any of them look ill to you?'

'Not particularly,' he concedes. 'But they were *old*...'

'So are we. And we're not dead.'

'More's the pity.'

I roll my eyes. Back in Nicaragua, he'd told me I should have killed him rather than brought him in, and judging by his last statement, it's clear he still feels that way. 'Don't be like that.'

Albie nods down at his wheelchair. 'That's easy for you to say.'

'Come on, Albie,' I say, though I suppose spending the best part of your life in solitary confinement at Her Majesty's pleasure can really take away your will to live. And your ability to walk, in Albie's case, though he insists that's also a result of his recent stroke – which is pretty good as cover stories go. 'Twilight Lodge isn't so bad.'

Albie sniffs the air, then makes a face. Today's lunch preparation has started, judging by the cooking smells wafting from the kitchen. 'Oh yes,' he says flatly. 'Every day here is like being on a luxury cruise.'

'There are worse places!'

'Than St Leonard's? Not exactly St Lucia, is it?'

While true, that shouldn't be a surprise. The pension plan at the Company was almost as non-existent as the organisation itself was supposed to appear; certainly not generous enough for a retirement sipping martinis on some Caribbean island – perhaps because our particular line of work meant they didn't expect you to reach retirement age.

'Granted, but there's still a lot to live for. Even with our advancing years there are things to look forward to.'

'Such as?'

I hesitate. As far as I can deduce, given his lack of visitors,

Albie doesn't have a family, or if he does, they've probably disowned him due to his criminal record, so he has no one like Dionne, and he's not exactly a willing participant in any of the daily activities here. 'Okay. Perhaps you're right. But even if you *are* just waiting to die, don't you want something to help pass the time until you do? You had one of the most inquisitive minds at the Company. Wouldn't it be good to get the old brain cells firing again?'

Albie turns to look out of the window, just in time to catch Shane lighting a crafty cigarette in the garden. 'I just want to be left alone,' he says, slumping miserably in his wheelchair. 'Especially by you.'

'Right. Well, help me with this and I will.'

'What?'

'Do this one thing, and I won't bother you again.'

Albie seems to perk up a little. 'You promise?'

'Scout's honour!' I say, attempting the hand signal, despite my arthritic fingers and the fact I was never *in* the Scouts.

'No more talk of Nicaragua and all this "spy" nonsense?'

'Got it.'

Albie sighs. 'Fine!' he says reluctantly. 'Though it's just to get you off my back.'

'Understood.'

'I help you, and then you...' He gives me a hand signal of his own, and it's certainly not 'Scout's honour'.

'Deal.'

Albie shakes his head slowly, as if in despair at what he's just agreed to. Then he freezes, and his eyes seem to focus on something in the distance. For a moment I fear he's gone and died right in front of me – a pretty dramatic and selfish way of getting out of assisting me, in my opinion – but before I can summon a member of staff for assistance, there's a playful, 'Afternoon, boys!' from somewhere behind me, and Albie's cheeks turn a shade of red that proves he's still very much alive.

9

'Barbara,' Albie says weakly, almost as if he's informing me he's been fatally stabbed, and I turn round to see the aforementioned Barbara walking along the corridor towards us. She's what you'd describe as a handsome woman, her hair always so immaculate you'd think she owned a collection of expensive identical wigs rather than this being simply a result of regular visits to Twilight Lodge's 'salon'. Her wardrobe, too, is apparently designer rather than the usual High Street collections sported by most of the other residents. And what's also apparent is that Albie has the hugest of crushes on her.

'Good afternoon, Barbara,' I say formally, as she draws level – I'm aware of my magnetic attraction to the opposite sex, and the last thing I want to do is give Albie more of a reason to dislike me.

'Martin,' she says, followed by a slightly more flirtatious, '*Albert*,' then she frowns. 'You two look like you're up to no good.'

I give Albie's shoulder a squeeze in an attempt to encourage him to reply, but he's doing his best impression of a rabbit caught in the headlights. 'You know us,' I say, after a moment where it's clear he's not capable of responding. 'Where are you off to?'

Barbara indicates a few doors along. 'The Garden Lounge,' she says. 'There's a jigsaw there with my name on it.'

I'm just about to say, 'Have fun,' when Albie suddenly – and uncharacteristically – bursts out laughing. 'I don't...?' I say instead, unsure what he's finding so hilarious, and Barbara rests a hand on his arm.

'Thank you, Albert,' she says, then she turns back to me. 'My surname's "Ravensburger", you see...'

'... and that's also a popular make of jigsaw!' Albie blurts out, like a schoolboy swot desperate to tell the whole class he knows the answer.

'Aha,' I say. 'Very good. Both of you.'

Barbara smiles at me, then she winks at Albie. 'Well, whatever mischief you're involved in, make sure you involve *me* next time,' she says, resuming her journey along the corridor.

I wait until she's out of earshot, then open my mouth to say something to Albie, but the look he gives me makes me think better of it. 'So,' he says, evidently keen to steer the subject away from Barbara. 'Got any suspects for these "murders" of yours?'

'Oh yes.' I ignore both the fact he's made air quotes around the word 'murders' and referred to the crimes as mine, and turn to the most recent page in my notebook. 'Shane.'

'Anyone else?'

'Not yet, no. But it's still early days in my investigation.'

Albie looks at me warily. 'What makes you think it's him?' he says, his voice nearly a whisper, even though Shane's still visibly puffing away outside and therefore well out of earshot. Like most residents here, Albie's a little scared of Shane. No one likes being bullied, especially when you can't stand up for yourself, and even more especially if you're Albie and you can't actually stand up.

'Well, for one thing, because he's a nasty piece of work.

Elsie didn't look to me like she'd passed away peacefully, and Shane's the one who found her body.'

'So you're basing your theory on: "he who smelt it, dealt it"?' Albie says. 'That's hardly grounds to accuse the man of murder.'

'No, but it puts him at the murder scene.' I check my notebook again. 'Elsie died sometime on Sunday night. Diana on the seventh, around lunchtime. And George...' I leaf back a page or two. 'The morning of the second. So all I need to do is check the staff rota to see if Shane was working at those particular times, and if he was, he goes straight to the top of the list of suspects.'

'A list which currently has how many people on it?'

'Including Shane?'

'Including Shane.'

'Well, one.'

Albie snorts derisively, in the same way Custard does when his bowl isn't quite as full as he'd like. 'I'm no expert, but even if Shane was working, that's not exactly proof he killed them, is it?'

'It's circumstantial evidence. And if there's enough of that, I can build a case against him.'

'And then what?'

I hesitate. It's a good question. Back in the day, with enough evidence, even of the circumstantial variety, we'd be given the green light to take someone like Shane out *just like that*. But with all my old skills as rusty as they inevitably are, and without my gun – not to mention the fact that Shane's antics aren't exactly a threat to national security – I might just have to let the formal justice system take over. 'You leave that to me.'

Albie gives me a look that implies he'd like to leave *every-thing* to me. 'And how exactly do you plan to check the rota?'

I hesitate for a bit longer. Short of breaking into the staffroom, where I assume it's hanging on the wall, I can't think of another way to check it, so that's exactly what I decide to do. Though when I repeat my plan to Albie, he looks horrified.

'What if they – *he* – sees you? You'll be for it!'

'Maybe,' I say. 'Although age is on my side.'

'Huh?'

'There are advantages to being old enough to be labelled "forgetful",' I tell Albie. 'If I'm challenged, I'll just "realise" I'm in the wrong room and head back out again. Besides…'

'Besides what?'

'It's not going to come to that.'

Albie groans. 'I suspect I'm not going to like the answer to this question, but why not?'

'Simple.' With a deft tap from my stick, I release his brake, grab his wheelchair by the handles and push him along the corridor towards the staffroom. 'Because you're going to be my lookout.'

10

———————

From what I can make out through the door's frosted glass, no one's in the staffroom when we get there – perhaps not surprisingly, given that it's afternoon rounds time – a task that presumably includes checking whether anyone's pegged it, given recent events. Though knowing Shane, that still only gives me a window of a few minutes at most, as he's hardly the most thorough.

'Shame,' says Albie, though without a lot of conviction, as he peers up at the keypad lock on the door. 'Now you're stuffed.'

'Hardly,' I say, tapping four zeros in quick succession, then doing my best not to look smug as the lock buzzes.

As if in sympathy with the door, Albie's jaw drops open. 'How on earth did you...?'

'I've seen the staff go in. They think we're all too senile to notice so they don't bother with anything more complicated. Plus, it's probably the only code Shane's got a chance of remembering.' I give the door a slight push, and it opens easily. 'Now keep an eye out, will you?'

Albie squirms uncomfortably in his wheelchair. 'How do I let you know if someone's coming?'

'Oh yes. Our signal.' I think for a moment. 'Remember that mission we did together in the Western Congo?'

'*Martin...*'

'I was on lookout duty that time. And we'd decided if anything was up I'd make the call of the mountain gorilla – a smart move, because Western Congo only has *lowland* gorillas. The layman couldn't tell the difference, but for us, it was the difference between life and rotting to death in some hellhole of a prison. So if you see a member of staff, fire off a couple of pant-hoots, and I'll be out of there quicker than you can say...' I stop talking, partly because I can't think of anything that's quick to say, but also because I'm conscious I'm delaying things while I'm trying to come up with something that's quick to say, which is ironic if you think about it. 'Sound like a plan?'

Albie raises his eyes to the heavens. 'For the *millionth* time, Martin. Not to mention the fact that me grunting like a gorilla might sound a bit out of place in a nursing home in St Leonards...'

'Fine!' I say, getting a little fed up with Albie's constant denials of our shared history. 'You think of something appropriate. We're wasting time.'

I manoeuvre his wheelchair and park it strategically, both to give Albie the best view up and down the corridor and also so Shane won't be able to get past him that easily if I need to buy myself a few extra seconds. Then I re-enter the door code and make my way inside. The room's a bit of a mess – a few ramshackle lockers against the far wall, a kettle and one of those new-fangled pod coffee machines on a table by a sink full of dirty crockery, and a random assortment of chairs that look like they've been pinched from various residents' rooms. It also smells a little too strongly of Shane's deodorant. Next to the window there's a whiteboard, and taped to the middle of it appears to be exactly what I'm looking for.

Hurrying as quickly as I can over to the board, I peer at the rota, but the print's so small I can't make any of the entries out, so I delve into my pockets in an attempt to locate my reading glasses – then discover to my horror I've forgotten them. I squint at it a little harder, then take a step backwards to try and bring it into focus, but with no success. I curse my absent-mindedness under my breath. Imagine if this had been me in my younger days – whole missions foiled because I'd left my spectacles back at base! I'd have been laughed out of the Company!

I check the table, but there's nothing I can use as a magnifying glass. I wonder if Albie has better vision than me, but I don't want to remove him from his lookout position. Which means there's nothing for it but to take the mountain to Mohammed.

'Finally!' he says, when I crack the door open, quickly followed by, 'Well?'

'I forgot my glasses.' I hold up the rota, which I've removed from the whiteboard. 'So I can't read it!'

'Well, I don't have mine either, so don't look at me!'

'It's not you I want to look at. It's the rota. And I can't.'

'Because you forgot your glasses. You said.' Albie shakes his head in disbelief, then he freezes. 'Shame,' he mumbles, almost under his breath.

'Isn't it just? Oh well. You wait here while I go back to my room and...'

'What?'

'You're right, it is a shame, but...'

'Not "shame"!' Albie says, sounding more than a little concerned. '*Shane!*'

'What about him?'

'He's walking towards us!'

'What? Why didn't you say something?'

I glare at Albie, a little irritated that his lack of ape-isms has put us in this predicament, then peer round the door jamb to be greeted by the sight of Shane ambling along the corridor. Fortunately, he's too fascinated by something on his phone to notice me. Trouble is, with my hip the way it is, there's no way I'll get back over to the wall, reattach the rota, and make my escape before he reaches us.

In desperation, I take a couple of paces back through the doorway and stuff the rota down the back of my trousers, and by the time an irritated-looking Shane's barged his way past Albie's wheelchair and into the staffroom, I'm doing my best to look bewildered.

'Oi! Sean Coronary!' Shane glares at me. 'What're you doing here?'

'This isn't my bedroom,' I say, peering confusedly around the room.

Shane tuts loudly. 'It's the staffroom. How did you get in?'

I let out a short chuckle. 'Well, I'm hardly likely to have climbed in through the window, am I?'

'No, but...' Shane nods towards the door. 'How did you know the code?'

'What code?'

'For the door.'

'There's a code?'

Shane gives me a look as if to say, 'Life's too short to waste any more of it on this conversation.' And because that's a lot more relevant for someone of my age, I stare at him blankly for just long enough, blink a couple of times for good measure, and make for the door. Then, as if I've simply been interrupted mid-stroll, I grab Albie's chair by the handles and wheel him back into his room, occasionally glancing over my shoulder as we go, to make sure Shane hasn't realised the rota's missing and put two and two together.

Though knowing Shane, even that simple act of addition's probably beyond him.

11

———

'Well?' says Albie, a little impatiently.

'Well what?' I say, waiting for a moment to ensure we haven't been followed, before pulling the door firmly shut behind us.

'The rota!'

I stare at him for a moment before I remember what I've got and, more importantly, where I've got it. Slowly, not to mention carefully, given its sharp edges, I extract the document from my trousers and hand it to him.

'Here!'

Albie recoils. 'I'm not touching that after where it's been!'

'Lend me your reading glasses, then!'

Begrudgingly, Albie nods towards his bedside table, where a pair of red spectacles are lying on top of some novel which, although I can't make this out until I'm wearing them, seems to be of the spy variety. It's a bit of a giveaway if you ask me, despite his protestations, but now's not the time, so I file my observation away for future reference and hold the rota up to the light, as if it's some kind of secret document. 'Here goes. For your eyes only.' I tap the frame of Albie's glasses. 'Or should that be "for four eyes"...?'

Albie tuts at my attempt at a joke. 'Well?'

'Hold your horses,' I say as – pleased to see it covers the whole month – I scan through the rota and locate the night Elsie was killed. While Miriam, Joy – an older Spanish lady who works on reception and I'm pretty sure has the hots for me – and Philip – who's from the Philippines, a fact he regularly takes great pleasure in reminding us of, as if the coincidence of his provenance and his name is the best joke in the world – appear to have been on duty, there's no sign of my chief suspect until the morning shift.

'Any joy?' says Albie impatiently.

'Yes. And no.'

'Pardon?'

'Joy was working. But Shane only started at eight the following morning, which was when he apparently discovered the body.'

'That's it, then,' says Albie, looking a little relieved, perhaps at the fact that I'm not going to rope him in with any further shenanigans, particularly involving Shane.

'Maybe not.'

'What?'

'Maybe that's not "it". Maybe Shane killed Elsie as soon as he arrived. Or perhaps he even came in just before his shift started to do the deed, then *pretended* he'd discovered the body, thus giving himself an alibi.'

'Unlikely,' says Albie. 'From what I've seen of him, Shane never comes in early. On the odd occasion he's on time, most of the first half hour or so of his shift seems to be taken up with having a sneaky coffee or cigarette out in the garden. So the idea of him hitting the ground running, particularly if he was going to, you know...'

'Let me check the other dates,' I say, a little miffed Albie is shooting my theory down in flames so soon.

I scan through the older entries on the rota, cross-checking them with where I've written the details of George and Diana's demises in my notebook, though I'm disappointed to see no reference to Shane on the days in question. 'Conspicuous by his absence,' I say, in response to Albie's raised eyebrows.

'So that's Shane in the clear.'

'Not necessarily. He might have come back in specially. And could be using the rota as an alibi.'

'Martin, Shane doesn't want to be here even when he's supposed to. He's hardly going to choose to come back in on his day off.'

'Even if he's planning to "off" someone?'

'Especially then. It'd look too suspicious, him being here.' Albie pulls a handkerchief from his pocket and blows his nose loudly. 'Besides, why would he want to kill anyone? Especially Elsie.'

'Because he evidently hates old people. And if we're all out of the way, then he doesn't have to come into work, does he?'

'There's easier ways to quit your job than murdering all your customers.'

'Yes, but Shane's not very bright, is he? So he might not realise that.'

Albie looks at me as if that's the first plausible thing I've said, then he points a bony finger at the rota. 'Are there *any* overlaps?'

I check again. 'Just Joy,' I say, and Albie laughs.

'There you go! It's Joy!' he says. 'Case closed!'

'Perhaps I'm looking at this the wrong way,' I say, ignoring him. 'Remember what they taught us at the Company?'

'Taught *you*, you mean?'

I give him a look. 'Instead of trying to find who killed the three of them, perhaps first of all, it makes more sense to look at

what links the murders. And the easiest way to do that is to
work out what Elsie, George and Diana have in common...' I
stop talking. Albie's got his hand up. 'Yes, Albie?'

'Had.'

'Right. Sorry. "Had".'

'Which is?' says Albie, when I don't say anything further.

'You knew them better than I did.'

Albie puffs air out of his cheeks. 'Well, they're all dead...'

I check my notebook again, peering at the various snippets
of information I've jotted down, then sigh exasperatedly. 'Okay.
From what I saw in the visitor's book, they all had family
members coming to see them regularly. They were all in their
nineties...'

'...which probably makes them more likely to die of natural
causes.'

'They all lived on the ground floor. Elsie was in Room
Three, George in Room Twenty-Three, and Diana in Room
Thirteen.' I hesitate for a moment, sure there's something in
that, then it comes to me. 'Aha!'

'Aha?'

'Maybe the killer has triskaphobia...'

'Ri-i-ight.' Albie elongates the word, uttering it as if I've just
gone and solved the murders, though he quickly follows it up
with a sarcastic, 'Which is?'

'Fear of the number three.'

Albie frowns. 'That would surely make them less likely to
go into those particular rooms, given the room numbers on the
doors?'

'Good point.' I take my glasses off and absent-mindedly
suck on the end of one of the arms, then wonder why Albie's
scowling at me before I remember they're his. 'In that case,
there must be something else...' I say, wiping them carefully on
my sleeve before handing them over.

Albie begins wheeling himself towards his bedside table,

perhaps to put his glasses back where I found them, though he stops in his tracks before he's able to. 'Sea views!' he announces suddenly.

'Sorry?'

He points at the laminated fire exit diagram fixed to the wall above his bed, where all the rooms are clearly numbered, then spins round to face me. 'Rooms Three, Thirteen, and Twenty-Three are all at the front of the building. And have sea views.'

'Albie, you're a *genius*!' I say.

Albie allows himself to look smug for a moment, then his usual scowl returns. 'Still doesn't explain why anyone would want to kill them, though. It's the English Channel. Hardly a view to die for.'

'No, but at least we have something to go on.'

'*We?*' Albie shakes his head rapidly. 'You said you wanted my help. I've helped. The only "we" here is "we" had a deal.'

'Come on, Albie,' I say, my heart sinking. 'Don't be like that. You and me. Back together again. It'll be just like the old days. The *good* old days.'

Albie lets out an exasperated moan. 'For crying out loud, there were no old days! And even if there were, with you involved, I very much doubt they'd have been good!'

'Albie, please.' I sit down heavily on the chair in the corner of the room, putting myself at his eye level. 'I can't do this on my own. *No man is an island*, and all that.'

'What about the Isle of Man?'

I ignore what's admittedly a pretty good riposte. 'Help me out here.'

'With what?' Albie almost shouts. 'You've no proof anyone's been murdered, and even if they were, your prime suspect has an alibi! In fact, *three* alibis!'

'But what if I'm right, and they have? And okay, maybe it isn't Shane, but isn't that all the more worrying?' I lean forward and lower my voice. 'Anybody here at Twilight

Lodge could be the killer. And any one of us could be next. Me...'

'Not exactly motivating me to help you, that prospect.'

'...or even *you*.'

'Now *there's* a bright side.'

Frustrated, I haul myself to my feet, walk across to the wall and stare at the fire exit plan. Then something occurs to me. And although it's a little mean, it's something I'm sure I can use as leverage to ensure Albie's continuing assistance.

'Of course, you know who else has a sea-view room?' I say, as I make for the door.

'Who's that?' says Albie suspiciously.

'*Afternoon, boys!*' I say, doing my best impression of Barbara earlier.

Albie doesn't respond, though he turns even redder than before. And just like all those years ago in Nicaragua, I know I've got him.

12

The next couple of days are a bit of a mixed bag, but at least no one gets killed, although Olga comes close when – under the pretext of my ongoing physical therapy – she manipulates my hip into the kind of impossibly painful positions the Geneva Conventions were surely intended to outlaw. Miriam completes my fortnightly assessment, and even though I try not to show off too much on the aptitude tests, when you've been trained to defuse bombs and crack safes it's hard not to sail through the basic tasks I'm set. Albie's retreated back into his room, so I leave him to it while I try and work out what my next steps should be, but as hard as I rack my brains I can't seem to find a link between the deaths apart from the 'sea view' element. Which, as Albie pointed out, doesn't seem much of a motive for murder.

I do my best to keep tabs on Shane too, utilising several pretend naps in the various armchairs strategically placed around the building to covertly monitor his interactions with the other residents, but while he lurches around Twilight Lodge like he couldn't care less, he's not careless enough to give anything away. Given his complete lack of any kind of guilt or remorse, coupled with his absence from the crime scene at the times in question, I reluctantly concede he might not be my man.

Faced with no new leads, I throw myself into 'home' life in the hope that if the killer strikes again I'll be there to catch them. But no matter how many jigsaws I piece together or how much daytime television I watch, how often I take part in the kinds of arts and crafts activities I remember Dionne doing at primary school or how many brisk patrols of the building I perform under the guise of exercise, nothing seems amiss.

By Friday morning, though the thrice-weekly singalong is about to take over the Garden Lounge, I decide to give it a miss. It's a bit of a hardship – although a roomful of people who rely on electronic assistance to hear aren't exactly note-perfect vocally, what they lack in musicality they make up for in enthusiasm, making it one of my favourite activities – but I need to be able to hear myself think. And be more proactive with my detective work.

Under cover of Miriam doing her best to lead the room in a version of 'Unforgettable', I make my way through the happy crowd, slip out through the double doors, sweet-talk my way past Joy at reception and make for Elsie's room. It's still unoccupied, which strikes me as a little strange – you'd think management would want to minimise any downtime and the corresponding shortfall in revenue – but at least that provides me with the perfect opportunity to go in and look for clues. Though when I get there, the door's slightly ajar, and by the sound of things, there's someone poking around inside already.

Stealthily, hoping my sphincter won't give me away this time, I creep closer and peer through the gap. The interloper's a man, perhaps mid-forties, heavyset, unshaven, and wearing a blue polo shirt with POLO written on the front in large white letters – a labelling system a few of my fellow Lodgers could perhaps utilise, given the number of embarrassing wardrobe malfunctions I've observed since I arrived. My first impression is he's definitely the murdering type. But if so, why has he returned to the scene of the crime?

I don't have my gun, so forward-rolling in through the doorway and segueing straight into a half-kneeling firing position would be pointless, not to mention painful, so instead I do the next best thing, which is to hurriedly collect a loudly protesting Albie from his room for backup. Pausing for a moment outside to catch my breath, I push the door wide open, wheel him inside, and clear my throat loudly.

'Can I help you?' I say, fixing a steely focus on the intruder, and he spins around.

'Whassat?'

'To put it another way, what are you doing in Albie's room?'

The man looks at me with the air of someone who's been caught red-handed doing something he shouldn't be doing, but doesn't actually give what someone like Shane might refer to as 'a monkey's'. 'Who's Albie?' he says, so I quickly clamp a hand over Albie's mouth.

'Don't tell him, Albie,' I say.

As Albie bats my hand away angrily, the man looks confusedly at him. 'This is *your* room?'

'S'right.'

'They said it was empty.'

I fold my arms and bring myself up to my full height, doing my best to look as authoritative as possible, though that's difficult in baggy velour sweatpants and a cardigan, not to mention a pair of novelty pug slippers – a Christmas present allegedly from Custard, though I suspect Dionne was actually behind it. 'Who's "they"?'

'The girl at reception.'

It's hard not to react with incredulity, not only at the amount of heavy lifting the term 'girl' is doing where Joy is concerned, who's fifty if she's a day, but Albie beats me to it, as he snorts derisively.

'Well, it isn't,' he says, reluctantly getting into character. 'It's mine.'

The man frowns, then opens the wardrobe door, revealing a telltale lack of contents. 'Sure about that, are you?'

Albie stares at the wardrobe, then looks up at me helplessly. 'Someone's stolen all my things!' he offers feebly, and I tut loudly.

'Sorry,' I say, nodding down at Albie. 'Albie. For the millionth time. Why did you make me push you all this way if this isn't your room?'

As Albie sits there open-mouthed, the man looks at us as if we're some kind of comedy double-act, though one he'd be booting off stage if he were judging us in a talent show. In an attempt to find out who he is, I extend a hand for him to shake, and introduce myself with a friendly, 'Sorry about that. I'm Martin.'

'Right,' says the man, shaking it rather firmly given my obvious age, though he doesn't respond in kind. I'm a little disappointed my plan's fallen at the first hurdle, but I soldier on regardless.

'And this is Albie.'

'I worked that out already.'

'Right. Of course.' I let out a friendly chuckle. 'You didn't answer my question.'

'What question?'

'What you're doing in this room.'

The man sighs, then evidently decides that humouring us isn't worth his while. 'Maybe I'm checking it out,' he says, his tone only a notch or two up from 'none of your business'.

'For?'

'For living in.'

Albie snorts again. 'You're a little young for that.'

'Maybe it's for my mum.'

'She's thinking of coming here, is she?' I say.

'Maybe,' says the man. 'Maybe I'm thinking of sending her here. When the time comes.'

I narrow my eyes. 'That's a lot of maybes.'

'Maybe,' says the man. 'It's all right, is it? Twilight Lodge?'

'Maybe,' Albie says sarcastically.

There's an awkward pause that lasts so long I'm acutely aware I might need the toilet soon, before the man says, 'Right then, gents,' though it's not clear whether he needs the conveniences too or if he's paying Albie and me his respects. Then with a wink, he strolls nonchalantly past us, out of the door and back towards reception.

13

———

As quickly as I can, I wheel Albie over to the window, just in time to see the interloper crunch his way across the gravel to an expensive-looking Range Rover. It's painted in a strange matte grey, of the type favoured by premiership footballers and other people who have more money than style, and who are often pictured in the comics that laughingly pass for newspapers here at Twilight Lodge. If that wasn't enough, it's parked in one of the disabled bays in the car park – not that I can make out any kind of blue badge on display in the windscreen, or any visible disability on the man himself. Back in the day I'd have been tempted to go out and make sure he had a disabled badge. Instead, I settle for jotting down the car's registration number in my notebook.

As the Range Rover speeds out through the gates, sending a shower of gravel into the ornamental pond – which no doubt concusses a few of the resident goldfish – I narrow my eyes at Albie. 'What do you suppose that was all about?'

Albie wheels himself away from the window. 'Well, I may not quite have your level of deductive powers, but I'd say he was in here checking the place out for his mother.'

'Unaccompanied? This place has a higher level of security than the Pentagon. They're hardly likely to let anyone just wander round on their own.'

'They might have just left him to it. Or got called to some emergency.'

'Come on, Albie. Doesn't it strike you as a little suspicious? Poor old Elsie's body's barely cold, and someone's here, poking around in her room?'

'Was he poking around?'

'He knew the wardrobe was empty.'

'He might have been looking to see if there was space for his mother's things.'

'Why wouldn't he tell us his name, then?' I say, grabbing Albie's wheelchair by the handles and steering him out and along the corridor.

'Why *would* he?'

'Manners? Or even simply respect for his elders.'

Albie lets out a bark of a laugh. 'Good luck with both of those things nowadays!'

'More's the pity!' I say, as we draw level with the reception desk. Joy's on the phone, but when she covers the mouthpiece with her hand and looks quizzically at the two of us, I nod down at Albie as if I'm taking him somewhere important, which seems to do the trick, as she returns her attention to her call.

'What does it say in the visitor's book?'

'Eh?'

I direct Albie to the book on the small table next to the front door, where every arrival's supposed to sign in and out. 'It'd look too obvious if I checked it. You're already down at that level, so...'

Not for the first time, Albie glares at me. Then he pulls his reading glasses from his pocket – a different pair from the other day, perhaps as a result of my absent-minded sucking – slips them on, and peruses the last few entries. 'Nothing.'

'At all?'

After a moment's deliberation, Albie passes me his glasses. 'See for yourself,' he says, so I hurriedly put them on and check the relevant page. Apart from Barbara's daughter an hour or so ago, there's no one else signed in this morning. And when I flick back to the date of Elsie's demise, it's a similar story.

'Interesting,' I say, pointing out the lack of entries. 'Perhaps even the act of a guilty man, desperate to cover his tracks.'

'Not exactly proof, though, is it?'

'Unless it's the *absence* of proof that's the proof.'

'Whoosh!' says Albie.

'What?'

'That was the sound of what you just said going over my head.'

'Very funny, Albie. Though you must admit he was acting suspiciously.'

'Maybe,' Albie concedes. 'So how do we find out who he was?'

I note Albie's 'we', guessing my observation about Barbara potentially being in the line of fire has secured his involvement. 'Watch and learn, Albie,' I say, sidling up to the reception desk. Once Joy has put the receiver down, I give her my best full-beam smile.

'Martin,' she says, then she peers over the desk at Albie. 'You two look like you're up to something.'

'Just taking Albie for a walk,' I say, ignoring Albie's muttered 'I'm not a dog!'

'Lucky you, Albie,' she says, and nods towards the double doors, through which there's a panoramic vista of St Leonard's seafront. 'Although I can't complain, given the view.'

'And what a magnificent one it is,' I say, letting my eyes linger on her for just a moment too long. 'A question, Joy, if you don't mind?'

Joy looks a little flushed, and I'm pleased to see I've still got it, as the saying goes. 'Fire away,' she says.

'That chap who just left.'

'What about him?'

'I recognise him. At least, I think he might be one of my daughter Dionne's former *gentleman callers*, and I can't quite...' I tap my index finger to my temple, and Joy gives me a sympathetic look.

'I don't know his name, I'm afraid,' she says. 'Though I think he might be a friend of Nigel's?'

I frown, unsure if Nigel's an actual person, or if this is some slang or derogatory phrase. 'Nigel...?'

'Montfort.'

The name rings a bell – although not quite loudly enough for me to remember why. 'And Nigel Montfort is?'

'He owns Twilight Lodge.'

'Oh. Yes. Of course,' I say, retrieving my notebook from my pocket and flicking back to the first page, where I've jotted down *Nigel Montfort* – probably upon my arrival, when I'd insisted on knowing what the chain of command was. 'Might Nigel be available, by any chance?'

Joy regards me as if I've asked the oddest question. 'He's in his office, but...'

'And where might that be?' I say, upping the amperage of my smile.

Joy's eyes flick towards the far end of the corridor, down past Elsie's room. 'Martin, you can't just...'

'I'm a paying guest here,' I say as sweetly as possible, though the reminder of the several thousand pounds my sojourn at Twilight Lodge is costing me rankles slightly. Grabbing Albie's wheelchair, I spin the two of us in a smart one-eighty. 'So actually, I believe I *can*.'

14

Nigel's a large man, about Dionne's age, and dressed in smart grey trousers and a white button-down shirt with 'TLC' embroidered on the breast pocket. I imagine it stands for something along the lines of 'Twilight Lodge Care', though over the years, I've learned not to make assumptions.

His office is rather fancy – plush-carpeted, with an antique desk and expensive leather armchairs that put the ancient plastic-upholstered ones in our rooms to shame. The shelves are filled with golfing trophies, alongside gold-framed photographs of him posing with various people I assume must be more important or famous than he is, given how inanely he's grinning in each one, not to mention several photographs of him either sitting in or leaning smugly against the expensive Aston Martin motorcar that I've seen here in the car park. He's noisily shredding some documents with a machine by his desk when we arrive at his open doorway, so without waiting for him to finish, I park Albie outside, knock loudly on the doorframe, then march inside and lower myself into the armchair in the corner.

Nigel looks at me, seemingly a little alarmed, and for a moment I fear he's going to call security. Then I remember

Shane's off today, and while it might be a close-run thing, I'm sure I could still get the better of Joy if it came to it. With a terse, 'One moment,' he feeds the last sheet through the shredder and forces a smile. 'Martin, isn't it?'

'It is.'

'Here on a month's convalescence, if I'm not mistaken?'

'I am. So you're not.'

'And how are you finding it here?'

'I've stayed in worse places.' And I have. Compared to one particular assignment in Uzbekistan, where the 'toilet' for my communal yurt was nothing more than a shallow hole in the ground outside and a bit too communal for my liking, Twilight Lodge is virtually The Ritz. With prices to match, now I come to think of it.

'That's... good to hear,' says Nigel, though he doesn't sound sure if it is. 'So...?'

'So?'

'Can I help you?'

'You can.'

'How exactly?' asks Nigel, when I don't say anything further.

I shift position in my chair, then hope the noise I've just made is a result of the friction between my velour sweatpants and the plush leather. 'It's about Elsie's passing.'

It's almost imperceptible, but to my trained eye, Nigel seems to stiffen slightly. 'Such a sad business,' he says.

'What happened to Elsie? Or running nursing homes in general?'

'Elsie's passing,' Nigel says, glancing at his watch, an expensive-looking, chunky gold one, the kind that glossy gentleman's magazines might describe as a 'timepiece'. It looks incredibly heavy, and I find myself wondering whether Nigel's left arm is more muscled than his right as a result of wearing it, like that young Spanish tennis player Dionne had something of a crush on a few years back. 'So, um...' Nigel pulls his cuff down, perhaps fearing I've designs on stealing his watch, given the way I'm staring at it. 'What about it?'

'What about what?'

'Elsie's passing,' he says, sounding slightly irritated.

'Oh yes! So I was wondering. Does this mean her room's now available?' I may have fallen short on finding out who the interloper is, but perhaps at least a temporary move to Elsie's room might provide me with an insight as to why she might have been killed. Even though that might put *me* in danger.

Nigel visibly relaxes, then smiles at me across the desk. 'I'm afraid not.'

I frown. 'But just now I saw someone looking at it. A man, probably in his forties. Unshaven. Drives a Range Rover that's had all the shine taken off it. For his mother, he said. The room, not the Range Rover. A friend of yours, apparently.'

'Oh?' Nigel hesitates. 'No, he... That was a local builder. I'm thinking of having some alterations done, so he was giving me a quote. For the, you know, *alterations...*'

He stops talking, perhaps realising he's spilling the beans needlessly, so I arch my left eyebrow. 'Why would he have told me something different?'

Nigel looks like he's genuinely considering the question, though the conclusion he seems to come to rather quickly is that I don't deserve an answer. 'I can't imagine.'

'So, you're not friends?'

'Whyever would you have imagined we were?'

I shrug, and decide not to point out the framed photograph visible behind Nigel's left shoulder of the two men posing by some golf course, which would suggest exactly that. 'Is it available *until* the alterations?'

'No. Not for you, in any case.'

'I'll try not to take that personally!'

'Please don't,' says Nigel, though he almost looks like he

wishes I would. 'It's one of our Premium rooms, what with the sea view. You're here on convalescence...'

'Which the sea air might help with?'

Nigel half smiles. 'It's the same air wherever you are in Twilight Lodge. Whether or not you can see the sea.'

I refrain from pointing out how that's not strictly true, particularly in the case of the Garden Lounge on a Sunday afternoon if the roast lunch has included Brussels sprouts. 'Even so – perhaps in the meantime?'

'I'm sorry, but no.'

'But no one else is using it!' I say.

Nigel folds his arms. 'Like I said, it's a Premium room. Which means it's only available to long-term residents on a special scheme.'

'What kind of special scheme?'

Nigel unfolds his arms, but only so he can open one of the drawers in his desk, retrieve a glossy leaflet and hand it to me. 'You might want to give this a read. It'll explain everything.'

I'm still wearing Albie's reading glasses, so I make myself comfortable and turn to the first page, though I'm only a few words in when Nigel clears his throat loudly. 'Perhaps you could do that on your own time?' he says.

'What? Oh. Of course.' I make a 'silly me' face and slip the leaflet between the final page and the back cover of my notebook for perusal back in my room.

Nigel smiles again. 'Now, if there's nothing else?'

I know when I'm being dismissed, so with a curt, 'Nigel,' I haul myself up from my chair and make my way out into the corridor. Perhaps not surprisingly, Albie's nowhere to be seen, but I'm not suspecting foul play – at our age, any sudden disappearances are usually explained by pressing bladder issues.

Though Elsie, George and Diana's deaths are still very much a mystery.

15

It's Friday afternoon, and a sunny one, so Albie and I are out in the garden where we're hoping we won't be overheard. But once I've finished expounding my theory that Nigel's somehow involved in what's going on, given his evasiveness about knowing the interloper, Albie sighs so loudly I'm sure it must be audible inside the house.

'I'm sure if you looked up all the murders that have ever been committed in the history of the world, there wouldn't be that many committed by Nigels,' he says.

'I'm not saying Nigel actually does the murders,' I say, as I push Albie's wheelchair along the garden path. 'He probably just pays someone to do them out of the proceeds.'

'What proceeds?'

'Well, from the money he makes as a result,' I say, biting off the word 'obviously' from the end of that sentence.

'And he makes that how, exactly?'

'By renting their room to someone else. For more than they were paying, I'd imagine.'

'Bumping someone off so you can re-let their room at a

higher rate?' Albie squints up at me. 'It's not exactly the most compelling motive.'

'Perhaps not,' I say, parking him by the ornamental pond, then lowering myself onto the concrete bench in front of it. 'But it's *a* motive, nonetheless.'

'Why not just put their prices up? Save yourself the bother of killing them?'

That stumps me for a moment. 'That would make more sense, yes.'

'I mean...' Albie angles his head like Custard does when I'm explaining something to him – except he's the one giving the explanation. 'Say Elsie was paying, what, five grand a month? Even if you do her in and re-let the room at a twenty per cent uptick, it still only works out at an extra...' He peers off into the distance, I suppose either because he's doing the maths or because he's spotted Barbara elsewhere in the garden, though luckily it proves to be the former, as I don't have to wait too long. 'Twelve grand a year. I've no idea what the going rate for a murder is, but I'd be surprised if it's that low.'

'I disagree. One of those a month and it soon adds up to a tidy little sum – especially when you consider we've had three this month already. And I don't know about your pay grade, but I certainly wasn't earning that for doing something not that dissimilar all those years ago!'

Albie ignores my comment. 'But if Nigel's not the actual killer, who is?'

'The man we saw poking around the other day – you know, the one who drove the Range Rover like he'd stolen it. Or...' Despite our distance from the main building, I lower my voice, just in case. 'Someone like *you-know-who.*'

Albie looks at me in a decidedly doesn't-know-who way.

'*Shane*, I mean. You look in the dictionary under "henchman" and you'll find someone who matches his description to a T.'

Albie rolls his eyes. 'The same Shane who wasn't on duty when any of the victims died?'

'Maybe he was in doing some overtime? *Special* overtime, I mean, on Nigel's behalf. After all, a share of twelve thousand pounds is quite compelling, particularly if you're a minimum-wager like Shane probably is.'

Albie shakes his head. 'Doubtful. From what I've seen since I've been here, there's no love lost between the two of them. Shane mopes around like he'd rather be anywhere else – and Nigel lets him. Besides, Shane's hardly smart enough to cover his tracks.'

'What tracks? As Miriam pointed out to me, people die all the time in places like this and nobody's ever suspicious, for precisely that reason. And because they're not suspicious there's never a post-mortem or any kind of investigation. Even the families seem to be half expecting it. Let's face it, it's what they check the likes of us in here for.' I lean in, and lower my voice. 'To die.'

'I wish!' says Albie, pulling a packet of cigarettes from his pocket, sticking one in his mouth, and lighting it with the lighter he's secreted in the packet.

I look at him disapprovingly. 'Those things will kill you, you know.'

Albie inhales deeply. 'Why do you think I smoke them?'

'That's not funny.'

'It's not supposed to be.'

'You don't want to spend your final days in hospital.'

'There's only one medical establishment I want to spend my final days in, and that's a certain clinic in Switzerland.'

I open my mouth to admonish Albie further, then something occurs to me. 'Maybe that's it!'

'Maybe what's it?'

'The reason behind all of this.'

For a moment, Albie looks torn between his desire to hear

my theory and his yearning to smoke his cigarette in peace. He takes another long drag, then exhales in my direction. 'Go on then,' he says, as I wave the smoke away from my face.

'It could be some sort of "assisted-dying" type of offering. At least, from what I saw of Elsie, she'd certainly had some assistance!'

Albie's ears almost visibly prick up, then his face falls. 'But that's illegal. Here, at least. Unfortunately.'

'Exactly. So what if you really wanted out but you didn't have the wherewithal to get yourself to Switzerland? A word in the right ear here, accompanied by a cash "donation"...' I make air quotes like Albie's the other day to reinforce my point. 'Shane pays you a visit, a few moments with your face the wrong side of the pillow... nobody's any the wiser.'

'One question,' says Albie, taking a final drag on the cigarette, and despite myself, I'm impressed he's finished it in three. 'Is that still classed as murder?'

'If a tree falls down in the forest and no one's there to hear it, does it still make a sound?'

'Eh?'

I narrow my eyes and decide my analogy's probably not that appropriate. 'Sorry. To answer your question, yes. Like you said, it's illegal, even though you may have requested it. But think about it – somehow the staff get wind of the fact that someone's getting a little... *frustrated* with being old. Maybe they don't want to be what they see as a burden anymore, or fritter away all their offsprings' inheritance on care fees. Nigel learns about this and goes and has a quiet word. Tells them there's this hush-hush under-the-counter off-the-books service they offer here at Twilight Lodge, if you've got the money...'

'He hasn't had a quiet word with me!'

'Yes, well, you *haven't* got the money, have you?'

Albie glowers at me, perhaps because I'm the reason he hasn't, following our Nicaragua incident – although we both know it wasn't his money in the first place, which is why I'm guessing he doesn't bring it up. 'But you said Elsie looked like she'd been murdered,' he says instead. 'Which might suggest she wasn't a willing subscriber.'

'Maybe she changed her mind at the last minute. Or perhaps the way they killed her didn't turn out to be quite as painless as she'd been led to believe. Especially if Shane's the one doing the deed.'

'You're telling me – I've still got the bruises from the last bed bath he gave me.' Albie grimaces at the memory. 'But if that *is* what's going on, how do we prove it?'

'Good question,' I say. In our former line of work, proof was a subjective concept – we just had to witness whatever nefarious activity we'd been sent to investigate, then mete out justice as we saw fit. But I don't have that luxury anymore, and if I'm going to involve Dionne – and that's the only way I can see of bringing whoever the perpetrators are to justice – then I'm going to need proof.

Though right now, short of putting myself or Albie directly in the firing line, I don't have the faintest idea where to find it.

16

Albie's right – it's unlikely anyone's going to be murdering the likes of Elsie, George and Diana for financial gain instead of simply putting their fees up. Which means that right now, my 'assisted dying' theory is the only one I've got that provides a motive for the murders – unless it *is* Shane doing them on his own and it's simply down to the fact that he hates his job. There have been documented cases of serial killers who've murdered for the same reason – I've spent the afternoon looking them up on the ancient computer in the residents' library, if a room with a couple of dozen well-thumbed paperbacks on a rickety old shelf justifies the description – so it's not beyond the realms of possibility. Though when I present these two options to Dionne when she calls in that evening, her 'Pack your bags, then!' isn't quite the reaction I was hoping for.

'Pardon?'

'If you don't want to stay here to do your rehabilitation you just have to say so, rather than persist with this theory you've dreamed up about how residents are being bumped off. We'll manage at home. Especially since I'm back from my course now. Your physio can come to the house. Though bear in mind you've paid up front to be here, and I'm not sure they'll give you a refund.'

Dionne looks disappointed in me, and if I've given her the wrong impression then I feel doubly bad. 'No, love, it's not that. I do want to stay here until the end of the month. Really I do. Look!' I get up to do some enthusiastic stretches to demonstrate how well I'm getting on with my new hip, and almost end up injuring the other one. 'It's just...'

'...that there's a killer on the loose systematically murdering the elderly population of Twilight Lodge despite the fact that they're on their last legs anyway, either because they're asking for it, or because someone's not happy at work?'

I nod, pleased she's finally cottoned on, then realise her tone's more cynical than anything else. 'Elsie *was* murdered. I'm sure of it.'

'How?'

'I don't know yet. I'm guessing suffocation, perhaps with a pillow, but...'

'No, Dad. How are you sure she was murdered?'

I retrieve my notebook from my pocket and flick through to the latest page, but apart from the word SHANE written in capitals and underlined three times, there's nothing in there helps me. 'Like I said the other day, you can tell.'

'Can you?'

'Yes!'

'No, Dad – can *you*?'

'I can.'

'How?'

'Well, because...' I stop talking. Dionne doesn't need me to lecture her, not only because she's had someone else doing exactly that on her course for the last few days, and I realise if I want her to take me seriously, I'm at the point of no return.

'Because?' repeats Dionne, when I don't say anything more.

'Sit down, will you?' I hoist myself upright in my armchair

and pat the edge of the bed, although Dionne evidently decides she'll remain standing. 'Okay. Well. Listen. There's something I haven't told you.'

'About Elsie?'

'About me. Or rather, about my past.'

'Your *past?*'

I nod. 'It's something your mother didn't know either. *Couldn't* know.'

'Dad, you're scaring me a little.'

'It's nothing to be scared of. Not now, at least.' I pat the edge of the bed again, and Dionne sits down after a moment, as if she's doing me a favour. 'You know how I used to be away a lot when you were growing up? For work?'

'Inspecting hotels.'

'I wasn't really.'

'Inspecting hotels? Or away?'

'The first one.'

'I hope this isn't going to be one of those stories where you have a whole other secret family, and I'm about to discover I've a half-sister or brother somewhere?'

I let out a brief laugh, then realise Dionne's not meant that to be funny. 'Nothing like that. I worked for, well...' I lever myself up from my chair, amble over to the door, and push it shut. 'For the government.'

'Which government?'

'Ours, of course!' I say, perhaps a little sharply. 'For a... special branch.'

'Special Branch? As in the police?'

'No, *a* special branch. Of the government.'

Dionne frowns. 'I don't understand.'

I amble back to my chair and sit down. 'A *secret* one.'

'Secret how?'

'As in *service.*'

'You mean MI6?'

'A bit more secret than that.'

'So a *secret* secret service?'

I nod. 'We referred to it as "the Company". We did the jobs MI6 wouldn't – or couldn't be seen to – do. Covert operations. The kind that – if we got caught – they'd deny all knowledge of our existence.'

Dionne stares at me until the penny drops, which takes a good few seconds. 'You're trying to tell me you were a *spy*?'

'Something like that, yes.'

'You?' she says incredulously, and I nod briefly.

'That's right.'

'A spy,' she repeats, though her incredulity seems to have turned into sarcasm.

'Keep your voice down.'

'Like *James Bond*?'

'Not exactly. Okay, perhaps a bit. But without the gadgets.'

'Seriously?'

'Seriously,' I say, wondering whether I should add, 'Or the womanising,' but that might be what I understand is known as 'too much information' right now.

'Dad, I'm sorry, and please don't take this the wrong way, but if I were to picture a spy, the last person I'd think of would be you.'

'No offence taken. And that was the beauty of it, you see? No one ever expected, well, *me*.'

'O-kay,' says Dionne, in that way people do when they actually mean the opposite. 'And these missions you went on were what, exactly?' she continues, though the look on her face suggests she might as well be asking what next Saturday's winning lottery numbers are going to be.

'I'm afraid I can't tell you much about them.'

'Because then you'd have to kill me?'

'No!' I say, quickly, the thought of Dionne's demise abhorrent. 'Because I signed the Official Secrets Act.'

'I see,' says Dionne. 'Can you at least tell me where these missions took place?'

She looks as if she's choosing her questions carefully, and I realise I owe it to her to answer in the same way. 'All over the world. The Middle East. China. Russia more times than I care to remember – though of course it was called the USSR back then. East Germany, before the wall came down. The Caribbean. Wherever the bad guys were. And there were a lot of bad guys.'

'It's a wonder you survived,' says Dionne, flatly.

'I nearly didn't on a couple of occasions,' I chuckle. 'One time I took a bullet in Belize, and I thought I was a goner!' I wince at the memory. 'I was okay, though. It didn't hit any vital organs!'

'You were *shot?*'

'That's right. Hurt like the dickens, I can tell you!'

'Where?'

'I told you. In Belize.'

'No – where were you shot?'

I'm about to say 'Belize' for the third time, then it sinks in that Dionne means where on my body. Grateful for the chance to show her some proof of my admission, I unbutton my shirt. 'This is the scar from where they removed it after they'd medevaced me back to Blighty. It's not pretty, but...'

'Dad, that's...' Dionne puffs air out from her cheeks. 'You had an aneurysm.'

'What? When?'

'That scar. It's from the operation to repair your aorta.'

Puzzled, I peer at the five-inch 'zipper' on my chest, wondering if I've picked the wrong scar, though I'm relatively sure which is which, and I've no memory of ever undergoing any kind of heart surgery. 'That was probably what the doctors were instructed to tell you,' I say, buttoning up my shirt. 'As a cover story.' I grin. 'I mean, *aorta* know if I'd had an aneurysm or...'

'I was nine. Mum had a call saying you'd fallen ill at work and were in hospital, so she rushed round to pick me up from school. I sat outside intensive care for hours, praying you wouldn't die.' Dionne stands up, paces round the room a couple of times, then sits down smartly on the chair in the corner, before realising it's a commode and standing up again just as quickly. 'It was the worst day of my life, up until Mum died. And now you expect me to believe it was due to...?'

'It's true!'

'It can't be! For one thing, you've never even been to Belize.'

'Well, it is!' I say, as I consider telling her to ask Albie, but even though he's the one who got me out of there alive, he's unlikely to back me up. 'I don't know how else I can prove...' I stop talking. Dionne's eyes have misted up, and I suddenly feel terrible.

'Listen,' she says, walking back over and crouching down in front of me. 'You were a hotel inspector.' She takes my hands and clasps them tightly. 'A *hotel inspector*.'

I shake my head slowly. 'I had to hide it from you and your mum. The less you both knew, the less you'd worry about me. Besides, knowing the truth might have put you in danger. And that was the last thing I wanted.'

'Dad, I'm sorry, but...' Dionne sits down on the bed next to me, then reaches over and rests a hand against my cheek. 'All this. These... stories. And these murders. Recently, you seem to have developed a tendency to... exaggerate. Even – I don't know – make things up.'

'I'm not making this up, love.'

'Do you *seriously* expect me to believe you were a...?'

Before she can get the word out, we're interrupted by a knock on the door, so I quickly put my finger to my lips. While they come in and sweep my room daily, it's not for listening devices, so it's just occurred to me someone might be monitoring our conversation, and now they've come to put the frighteners on me for spilling the beans to Dionne.

'Come,' I say, bracing myself for a couple of no-neck goons with matching earpieces and telltale shoulder-holster bulges beneath their jackets to come bursting in. But instead, a petite, attractive, dark-haired woman, probably early thirties, smartly dressed in a white blouse and black slacks, and carrying a clipboard, opens the door tentatively.

'Mr Maxwell?' she asks cheerily, and perhaps a little loudly, as if I'm half deaf. 'It's me. Gemma?'

I haul myself to my feet as one is supposed to – unless you're Albie, of course – whenever a lady enters the room. 'Of course you are,' I say, though I'm grateful for the reminder. 'This is my daughter, Dionne. And please – call me Martin.'

Gemma smiles. 'Martin it is. And nice to meet you, Dionne,' she says, though Dionne doesn't respond in kind. She's still staring at me, and I can't quite fathom her expression, although at least she hasn't yet rolled her eyes, which I'm counting as a win. I'm sure it'll take a while for what I've just told her to sink in, so I'm grateful for the interruption.

'Gemma's the nice young lady who did my assessment when I arrived,' I say.

'That's right,' says Gemma, as if it's something I might have forgotten, then she turns to Dionne. 'I'm the head nurse here at Twilight Lodge.'

'You mean "head" nurse, as in...?' I tap a finger twice on the side of my skull, and Gemma laughs.

'As in "senior".'

'You don't look that senior,' I say, switching tack to an offensive of the charm variety, though it seems to fall a little flat, as Gemma suddenly looks stern. 'Sorry,' I say, hurriedly. 'I meant "senior" in the, well, *my* sense. And you're so *young.*'

The smile returns to Gemma's face. 'He's a charmer, isn't he, your dad?'

'Something like that,' says Dionne, still not looking best pleased, and Gemma frowns.

'I'm sorry,' she says, clearly picking up on the atmosphere. 'I just popped by to see how your physio's going, among other things, but I get the feeling I might be interrupting something?'

'Not at all,' I say quickly, keen to keep my recent revelation strictly between Dionne and me, but Dionne doesn't seem to be on my wavelength.

'Why don't you tell Gemma what you just told me?' she says, her tone verging on the hysterical.

'Don't be like that, love,' I say, mainly because if I did tell Gemma then I *might* have to kill her, but Dionne evidently decides 'like that' is *exactly* how she'll be.

'Dad used to be a secret agent.'

Gemma makes a face that's a little hard to read. 'That must have been... interesting for you, growing up?' she says, eventually.

Dionne shrugs dismissively. 'Actually, it's the first I've heard of it.'

'Ah.' Gemma consults her notes, then she frowns. 'But it says here you worked as a...'

'...hotel inspector,' I interrupt. 'That's right. Or at least, that's what I told Dionne and her mother.' I tap my index finger to the side of my nose, realising now Dionne's blown my cover, I might as well be honest. 'As a cover story.'

'Off saving the world, while Mum and I thought he was checking bedsheets for thread count and rating breakfast buffets,' says Dionne, giving me the side-eye. 'Would you believe it?'

Gemma doesn't respond, though she looks as if the answer to that question is a definite 'no'.

'Oh yes,' continues Dionne, getting to her feet and putting

an arm around my shoulders. 'He even got shot once. In the line of duty. But as you can see, he lived to tell the tale.'

Dionne sounds like she believes telling tales is exactly what I'm doing. 'It's true!' I protest, as the two women exchange not-so-subtle glances.

'I see.' Gemma smiles, though a little patronisingly, then she looks at her watch. 'Perhaps, if you've got a few minutes, you might prefer to continue this conversation in my office?' she suggests.

And while, quite frankly, something about the way she's directed the question at my daughter rather than me means I'd probably prefer not to, Dionne's vice-like grip as she escorts me towards the door doesn't offer me much of an alternative.

17

Gemma's office is a small, windowless room directly opposite the door to the Garden Lounge, presumably so she can be on hand if someone has a funny turn during the musical entertainment or while watching a particularly exciting episode of *Bargain Hunt*. I've never been in here before, and to be honest, I'm glad – it reminds me of some of the interrogation rooms I've spent time in. Though instead of a set of thumbscrews or a car battery attached to a pair of jump leads, the only items on display are a distinction certificate from the Royal College of Nursing hung proudly on the wall, along with a framed photo of a young, plump-faced astronaut on her desk which suggests that both age requirements and recruitment standards at NASA have dropped somewhat since its Apollo heydays.

'Milo. My sister's youngest. As Buzz,' Gemma says, as I peer at it.

'Ah,' I say, though it takes me a few seconds to work out she's just identified the subject of the photo as her nephew rather than blurted out the same sort of random vocabulary some of the older individuals here at Twilight Lodge are prone to.

'You know – Lightyear?' continues Gemma. 'From *Toy Story*? It was a contest. At Center Parcs. Everyone had to dress up as their favourite character. He won a trophy!'

I'm aware of the film – I watched it during one of the recent movie afternoons here – so make a suitably impressed face, though Dionne seems too preoccupied to respond in kind.

'Do you have any?' Gemma asks her.

'Trophies?'

'Children.'

'No,' Dionne says abruptly, evidently not keen to get into the story of her personal life, and I can see her mentally counting hippopotami during the awkward silence that particular question-and-answer routine usually provokes, given she's well into her forties now.

'Right,' says Gemma, after four and a half of the ponderous African beasts, then she places her clipboard on the filing cabinet in the corner and indicates the two chairs in front of her. But Dionne looks like she'd prefer to remain on her feet, and I don't want to sit down if neither of the two of them are, which leads to a bit of an awkward stand-off until Gemma perches cross-legged on the edge of her desk.

'So I understand your father's been at Twilight Lodge since...?'

'I'm here in the room too, you know?' I say pleasantly, as Dionne takes a seat, and I follow suit.

'Sorry, Martin.' Gemma's cheeks colour a little. '*You've* been at Twilight Lodge since...?'

'Since just after I got my new hip.'

'Which means?'

I glance cluelessly at my watch for some reason, and when I don't answer, Dionne clears her throat. 'Two weeks ago,' she says.

'And this hip replacement came how long after his...'

Gemma seems to remember something. 'Sorry, Martin – after *your* – dementia diagnosis?'

'I don't recall any dementia diagnosis,' I say, though neither of them seem to appreciate my attempt at humour.

'Dad hasn't been diagnosed,' says Dionne. 'Officially, that is.'

'But – and excuse me, Martin – he is showing signs of forgetfulness?'

Dionne looks at me as if she's about to betray me and feels awful about it, so I give her an encouraging smile. 'On the odd occasion,' I say, to put her out of her misery. 'It's why I began carrying this notebook with me.' I pat my pockets to locate it, then realise I must have left it in my room due to our hasty exit, which doesn't do my cause a lot of good. 'Usually.'

'And do you remember how long you've been doing that for?' asks Gemma.

'A good six months or so?' says Dionne, looking at me for confirmation.

'That long?' I say, though I shouldn't be surprised. The notebook was a present from Dionne for the first Christmas after my wife Madeleine's passing. And *everything* got worse after that.

The two women exchange glances, then Gemma takes a deep breath. 'Okay then,' she says cheerily. 'I don't know how much you know about the seven stages of dementia, so I'll just launch in, and if you've got any questions...' She pauses, though I don't have any as yet, so I sit quietly to indicate she should continue. 'To give you some background, every person with dementia experiences the disease differently, but people tend to follow a similar trajectory from the beginning of the illness to its conclusion. Which means we can generally break down the development of the disease into a number of more detailed stages.'

Gemma pauses again, perhaps to make sure I'm following, so I nod, adding, 'With you so far,' to leave her in no doubt.

'Good. So – stage one, it's not detectable, and no memory problems or symptoms are evident... Yes, Martin?'

I pull my hand down almost as quickly as I've just raised it. 'What's the point of that, then?'

'The point?'

'It's not really a "stage", is it?'

'I don't...'

'That's like me saying stage one of the desk you're sitting on is when it's a tree, but it could go on to be any item of wooden furniture really, whereas stage one should *actually* be after you've chopped the tree down and cut it into desk-sized planks. Why don't they just start at stage two, and call that stage one?'

'Well, I suppose they could...'

'Otherwise you're just wasting time, aren't you?'

'I didn't come up with the classification.'

'No, but...' I stop arguing, having recognised I'm 'doing it again', as Dionne calls it. 'Sorry. Go on.'

Gemma frowns as if she's lost her thread, and I find myself wondering whether dementia is in fact contagious, though I decide to save that question for now. 'Okay,' she says after a moment. 'The other stages get progressively worse, from stage two – very mild decline, to stage three, mild decline, where perhaps sufferers forget words, or can't remember peoples' names, or are constantly losing items, or getting things wrong. And the past seems a little... hazy.' She smiles kindly at Dionne. 'Perhaps you've seen some of that in your father?'

'Now and again,' says Dionne, though as if she means more often than that.

'Next is stage four,' Gemma continues. 'Where your short-term memory starts letting you down – for example, you might not be able to remember what you've had for breakfast, or indeed if you've had any. Maybe your memory's hazy about significant events in your life too. Things like simple arithmetic become difficult. As does managing your own finances or paying bills.' Gemma uncrosses her legs, then crosses them the other way, much like Sharon Stone in *Basic Instinct*, another – and a rather awkward – movie afternoon selection, and one I imagine was probably Shane's. 'Then things start to get serious. Stage five is known as moderately severe decline, where you forget personal details, perhaps your own phone number or even where you live, and you get confused all the time. Maybe you even stop dressing appropriately. Then there's stage six, which we call severe decline. You can't recognise anyone apart from those closest to you. Most of your past life's a blur. You need help with almost all of your daily activities, including bathing and toileting. You might even become doubly incontinent.'

I make a face to get Gemma's attention. 'And you said there were seven stages?'

'That's right,' says Gemma. 'In the final one, it's almost as if the brain's lost its connection to the body and becomes incapable of telling it what to do. You progressively lose your motor skills and the ability to speak. Perhaps you're only able to utter unintelligible sounds or words, if at all. I've seen it too many times in here.' Her eyes mist over, and she takes a moment to collect herself. 'My grandmother, too.'

'Does everyone make it to stage seven?' says Dionne, a hint of panic in her voice.

Gemma shakes her head slowly. 'Sometimes they'll pass away from other health complications first,' she says, though as if she wants to add the words 'thank goodness'.

Dionne swallows loudly. 'Are you saying it's almost better if you don't, you know...?'

'Make it that far?' I suggest.

Gemma smiles sympathetically, then she nods. 'Sometimes death can be a blessing,' she says.

18

As I find myself wishing I'd kept my Company-issue firearm rather than throwing it off the end of the pier a few years ago, Dionne clears her throat. 'But dementia is a disease, right?' she says anxiously. 'Which means you can treat it?

'I'm afraid not.'

It evidently takes a good few hippopotami for Gemma's words to sink in, although I'm too worried about how this is affecting Dionne to count how many.

'While there isn't a treatment,' Gemma continues, 'and your father's coping relatively well at present, if and when he does begin to develop symptoms and you decide to choose Twilight Lodge for his care, we can *manage* his condition.'

'How?'

Dionne and I have spoken at the same time, and Gemma's glance flicks between the two of us, though she decides to address Dionne. 'By making sure your father's comfortable. And that all his needs are taken care of.'

I move both eyebrows up and down like a ventriloquist's dummy, and Dionne shoots me a look.

'We pride ourselves in being able to keep our residents

safe,' adds Gemma. 'Our older residents receive twenty-four-seven care, where they're constantly monitored so they can't hurt themselves. The beds are specially designed so they can't fall out, with mattresses made from memory foam... Yes, Martin?'

I lower my hand back down. 'That helps with the dementia, does it?'

'Sadly not,' says Gemma, not acknowledging what I think is another pretty good joke, especially under the circumstances. 'But they do alleviate bedsores if you become bed bound. As you're probably aware, all the rooms have pressure mats by the beds, which are linked to an alarm so we'll know if you've got up in the middle of the night and might need help.' Gemma pauses, and looks at the two of us as if she's weighing something up. 'But, um...'

'Um?' I say.

'Can I be frank?'

She's addressing me now, a serious look on her face.

'Please.'

'You understand that if you do receive a dementia diagnosis, it's, well, somewhat of a one-way street?'

I pretend to be shocked. 'Sounds like more of a dead-end one to me!'

Gemma leans forward and gives my arm a brief, comforting squeeze. 'I'm sorry, Martin.'

'Don't be. It's not your fault.' I smile at Gemma, then at Dionne, though she seems unable to meet my gaze, and I can understand why: I've faced down death a hundred times, so the prospect of my own demise doesn't really scare me, but she's only seen it with her mother, and let's face it, no one wants to become an orphan. Even in their forties.

As Dionne stares down at her shoes, evidently doing her best to process all of this, I pat her lightly on the knee. 'Don't worry, love. Like Gemma here says, even if I do get diagnosed,

I've got ages yet. In the meantime, your old dad's not going anywhere! Besides, I've had a good life.'

Gemma folds her arms. 'Which brings us neatly back to the subject of this... *work* of yours?'

It's not exactly a question, and yet it quite evidently *is*, and so I take a deep breath. Without a copy of the Official Secrets Act to hand for Gemma and Dionne to sign, at least getting them both to promise will be something. 'Can you assure me this stays between these four walls?'

'*Dad...*' says Dionne, though I shush her by putting my finger on my lips.

'Everything we discuss is confidential,' says Gemma.

'Right. Well, as I said, I wasn't really a hotel inspector. I worked for a clandestine department...'

'As a spy!' interrupts Dionne, in a 'don't be ridiculous' way.

'We preferred the term "operative",' I say, and Dionne throws her hands up in the air.

'Excuse *me*!' she says sarcastically.

'Dionne,' says Gemma, softly but firmly. 'Why don't you let Martin tell us in his own words?'

Dionne opens her mouth as if to say something, then closes it again, before muttering, 'Fine!'

'Thank you,' I say, then realise I've lost *my* thread now. 'Where was I?' I ask, hoping Gemma doesn't read too much into the question.

'You were telling us about your former employment,' she says.

'Oh yes! Although that's all I *can* tell you, really. I shouldn't go into detail. Like back then. The less Dionne and her mother knew, the better. For their sake and mine.'

'I see,' says Gemma, noting something down on the clipboard. 'But might that be because there isn't, actually, any detail to go into?'

'I don't understand.'

Dionne rests a hand on my arm. 'She's saying she doesn't believe you, Dad. And she's not the only one.'

'Love, I know this must have come as a bit of a shock to you, but...' I wonder how I can prove it to them, but I'm reluctant to bare my chest again, and especially in front of Gemma – apart from anything else, I don't want her swooning and perhaps injuring herself in the fall. But aside from my scars, I've no other physical evidence. Nothing I ever did ever made the papers, for obvious reasons. And given the fact that the one other person in here who could corroborate my past appears to be in complete denial of his, I'm out of ideas. 'You'll just have to take my word for it.'

Gemma smiles, though whether it's patiently or patronisingly, I can't work out. 'There's something else you need to know about dementia,' she says. 'In particular, the way it affects your state of mind. And perhaps... *distorts* your recollections of past events.'

'How do you mean?' says Dionne.

'Well, for example, some people might start believing what they see on the television is real. As if they've actually lived it rather than simply watched it. Then they project that onto the present day, along with a series of quite elaborate, although fabricated' –

Gemma pauses, though it's only to make a set of air quotes – '"memories".'

'Are you calling me a liar?' I say, bristling slightly at the implication.

Gemma holds her hands out, palms forward, as if trying to halt an oncoming train. 'Not at all, Martin. Lying would be if you told me something you knew to be untrue. Being a spy...'

'An operative!'

'Sorry – an *operative* – is something you seem to genuinely believe you once were. So you're not actually lying.'

'But I'm making it up.'

'All I'm saying is, given what we know about your condition, it's possible.'

'Sounds impossible to me!' I say.

'Like your "missions", Dad!' says Dionne, making air quotes herself.

As I try to work out whether that's a compliment or a joke, Gemma turns back to Dionne. 'We had one resident here who became scared to go into the garden. Would you believe she was worried she was going to get eaten by lions? In *St Leonards*, of all places!'

Dionne looks like she doesn't know whether to find that amusing. 'And what...?'

'It turned out she'd simply been watching *Big Cat Diary* on the television.' Gemma smiles, although it's full of pity. 'Does your father have any favourite films? Or books?'

'Did you want to answer that, or shall I?' Dionne says, and I give an aggrieved snort.

'So what if I like espionage novels, or spy films? Call it a professional interest. You like your police procedurals. And as for you...' I turn my attention back to Gemma. 'Don't tell me you've never watched an episode of...' I rack my brain for a name of one of the many medical dramas that appear with alarming regularity on the television in the Garden Lounge, but all I can come up with is *Doctor Who*, which I'm fairly sure isn't right. 'Something with nurses in it.'

'Perhaps,' admits Gemma.

'Proves my point.' I glare defiantly at her. 'I'm hardly that far gone to start dreaming up that kind of thing.'

I turn to Dionne to back me up, but judging by her expression, Gemma's theory seems to be making sense to her, so instead I haul myself out of my chair to go and look out of the window, before remembering Gemma's office doesn't have one, which leaves me staring at the wall – though quite frankly, that's preferable to seeing the disappointed look on Dionne's face. Then I'm conscious there's someone standing behind me, and I don't like to turn round in case it's the men in white coats coming to take me away.

Just as I remember Dionne would never let that happen – as if *I* would – I hear her say, 'Dad...?' tenderly, and turn round to find her standing there, her hands in her pockets.

'What?' I say, crossly.

'You have to admit, it's a little far-fetched.'

'I don't have to admit anything!' I snap. 'I'm not imagining my past. And I'm certainly not imagining these murders!'

Gemma nearly falls off the end of the desk. '*Murders?*'

'Never mind,' I say, glaring at Dionne, who looks as if I've just given her some sort of gift.

'My father also seems to think there's something suspicious going on regarding the lady who passed away the other day.'

'She had a name, you know?' I mutter, adding, 'Elsie Watson!' when it fortuitously pops into my head.

'And the other two who died since he got here,' says Dionne, warming to her task.

'Diana. And George,' I say, though right now – something that doesn't exactly help my case – their surnames escape me, and trying to recall either one without my notebook would be a stab in the dark. Which, incidentally, I'm reasonably sure isn't how any of them met their ends.

'I've told him he's mistaken, but...'

'I'm *not* mistaken!'

'Okay...' Gemma takes a deep breath and huffs it out. 'Please, both of you, sit down.'

Dionne looks pleadingly at me, and I scowl back at her, then like a pair of gunfighters reluctantly agreeing to holster their weapons, we lower ourselves back into our chairs.

'Martin,' Gemma continues. 'I can assure you there's nothing suspicious going on here at Twilight Lodge. You're an intelligent man. You accept you might be showing signs of dementia.'

'*Early-stage* dementia,' I say. 'Very early if you factor out that ridiculous first stage.'

'Even so.' Gemma gives me a flat-lipped smile. 'Surely you have to concede there might be something behind what I'm saying?'

I look at her, open-mouthed, and I'm about to protest, to tell her she's got it completely wrong and explain more about what I did for this country. But then I see something in Dionne's expression, the way her eyes seem to be pleading with me to agree with Gemma and to put an end to this, and it causes a pain in my chest much worse than any bullet ever did. So I do the only thing I can do.

'Amazing!' I say, doing my best to look suitably amazed.

'What is?' says Dionne hesitantly.

'Who'd have thought?' I rap my knuckles on the side of my skull. 'How this thing can play tricks on you.'

'Oh, *Dad!*'

The relief on Dionne's face is palpable as she reaches across and takes my hand. And though it's strange to think she gets more comfort from the idea her old man might be going senile than that he had a clandestine career in the intelligence services, needs must, and all that.

'I mean! Me – a spy!'

'Don't you mean "operative"?' Gemma says, with a wink, as if we're all in on one big joke, so I make my fingers into a pistol and 'shoot' her with it in acknowledgement.

'Exactly!' I say, letting out a chuckle, though I don't have to fake my good humour. Because now I think about it, it's better this way, having them believe I'm just a silly old fool. Preferable, too, where investigating the murders here at Twilight Lodge is concerned, as it enables me to do something I always excelled at.

Working undercover.

19

'Dad?'

It's the following morning, and Dionne's come back in to visit, Custard in tow, though she's looking a little trepidatious – she's knocked on the door frame, which is a first, and seems to be waiting for permission to come into my room. I'm not sure whether she's feeling a little guilty after yesterday's encounter with Gemma or is just testing to see whether I still recognise my own name – and perhaps my own daughter – but I give her the kind of smile that gets us past both those things.

'Last time I checked!'

'We were just passing,' she says, walking over to where I'm sitting in my armchair reading the newspaper. 'Thought we'd pop in. Didn't we, Custard?'

'That's nice,' I say, careful to address both of them despite Custard's lack of response. I doubt he had a lot of input into the decision, though to my surprise, the brief sniff-and-lick he gives my hand when I reach down to scratch him under the chin is followed by a slightly-more-friendly-than-last-time snort.

'You see?' says Dionne. 'He misses you.'

'Misses someone to emotionally blackmail into giving him

biscuits, more likely,' I say. 'Besides, dogs only lick us because they know we've got bones inside.'

'I'm sure that's not...' Dionne narrows her eyes at me, then she smiles. 'Yes, Dad. Good one. How are you doing?'

'Pretty well,' I say, putting my newspaper down on the bed. And I am. I sailed through this morning's physio session with only a handful of out-loud curses, and to tell the truth, I'm enjoying the prospect of flexing my old espionage muscles too. Secretly I think Albie's feeling the same – not that he'd ever admit it.

'Pleased to hear it.'

'Oh. What with everything yesterday, I forgot to ask. How was the course?'

Dionne sits down next to me. 'Good, thanks,' she says, as Custard heads off to lie in a patch of sunlight on the carpet beneath the window.

'What was it on again?'

'Interrogation techniques.'

'I could tell you a few things about those!' I say, then as her face falls, I wink. 'Too soon?'

'Dad!' Dionne tries – and fails – to stifle a smile, so I take her hand and give it a squeeze.

'Sorry, love.'

'Very funny,' she says, squeezing my hand back, then she reaches into her pocket and retrieves a folded sheet of paper. 'Oh, I printed off those figures you asked for.'

'Figures?'

'For Twilight Lodge.' She lowers her voice. 'The, um, *death rate*.'

'Which is?'

Dionne unfolds the printout and hands it to me. 'Pretty much the national average, you'll be pleased to hear. Just over it, in fact, but only by a per cent.'

'Good,' I say, though more as a placeholder as I try and make sense of what I'm looking at. 'I'm sorry, I don't...'

She takes the printout back and scans through it. 'Eleven per cent, give or take. Compared to a national average of ten.'

'Oh,' I say, not quite knowing what to make of this new information. 'And where do these figures come from?'

'The Care Quality Commission. They're the people who rate places like Twilight Lodge. Now obviously these are last year's figures, seeing as this one hasn't finished yet, but hopefully they'll put your mind at ease.'

'Sure.' I retrieve my notebook and – under the guise of jotting this down, flick back to where I've made some recent notes. From what I've been able to work out on my patrols, Twilight Lodge has around thirty rooms and therefore the same number of residents. Although I'm no maths genius like Albie, if I'm interpreting this correctly, a death rate of eleven per cent would mean we're likely to lose three people a year, not in a *month*. Though for now, I decide to keep my powder dry where this particular piece of information is concerned – I might need Dionne's assistance at some point in the future, and I don't want to jeopardise that by sounding like a ranting old fool again. Especially so soon.

Dionne waits until I've put my notebook down, then she smiles. 'Does that make you feel better?'

'What, love?'

'The figures.'

'Much better,' I say, because it does. In that it means my suspicions must be true.

'That's good.'

'Isn't it? And any luck regarding you-know-who?'

'Shane?' Dionne rolls her eyes theatrically. 'Nothing serious in his past. Certainly not anything to suggest that he's, you know...'

'A murderer!'

I've said it in my best Inspector Clouseau accent as if it's a joke we're both in on, and Dionne chuckles. 'Exactly. A few minor run-ins for drugs when he was younger...'

'Drugs?'

'Dealing. To be honest, I'm surprised he's employed here, given that's on his record, but...' She shrugs. 'Certainly nothing more...'

'...Sinister?' I say, arching one eyebrow, then I realise it's probably time to change the subject to avoid raising Dionne's suspicions, and I'm just working out a subtle way to ask if she met any eligible men on her course when there's a knock on the open door, and Philip appears in the doorway.

'Morning, Martin,' he says, in his usual upbeat way, his smile amping up when he spots Dionne. I've often wondered whether the two of them might hit it off, but so far, and despite my constant attempts at 'bigging her up' – as I believe modern parlance would have it – whenever I see him, my subtle attempts to set them up have fallen on deaf ears. Mainly because Philip seems to lose his ability for coherent speech whenever he addresses Dionne directly. 'And who's this cutie?' he says, spotting Custard on the carpet.

'My daughter Dionne?' I say, as quick as a flash. 'I thought you two had...?'

'Ignore him, Philip,' Dionne says, in a long-suffering way, as Philip blushes. 'That's Custard.'

'Custard?' Philip laughs a little too hard. 'And he'd be a...?'

I'm about to say 'dog', but Dionne gets there before I can. 'He's a pug. He's... sorry, he *was*, my mother's.'

'Ah,' says Philip – I've briefed him about Madeleine, how Dionne and I miss her terribly, and the awkward silence he leaves is perhaps understandable.

'Philip's from the Philippines,' I say, mindful how mentioning an interesting fact about someone often promotes conversation, but Dionne looks like she's heard that particular snippet of information before.

'So I understand,' she says.

There's another awkward silence, then Philip seems to remember why he's here. 'Oh. I have a message for you,' he says, stepping tentatively into the room.

'Coded?'

'Pardon?'

'Never mind,' I say quickly. 'Who from?'

'Yvette Rogers.'

I stare at him blankly for a moment, then pick my notebook back up and hurriedly flick through the pages.

'Elsie Watson's daughter?' says Philip.

I speed up my flicking until I reach the relevant note. 'Oh yes. I mean, *oh*. Yes?'

'She asked me to tell you the funeral will be on Tuesday.'

'*This* Tuesday?'

Philip nods, and I widen my eyes.

'That was quick.'

'Apparently there was a cancellation at the crematorium.'

As I wonder what reason someone might have for cancelling a cremation – unless the deceased has come back to life – Philip hands me a yellow Post-it note. 'I've written down the details for you.'

'Thank you,' I say, squinting at the note. Given how undecipherable Philip's handwriting is, it's almost as if it *is* in code. 'I'm sorry,' I say, not wanting to insult his calligraphy. 'My eyesight's not quite what it used to be...'

It's a white lie, especially since I'm wearing my reading glasses, but it does the trick. 'Three p.m.,' he says. 'At Hastings Crematorium. Then back to the house, 4 Court Close, for the wake.'

I'm not sure I'll be *a*-wake given how that's nap time, so I make another note to switch to black coffee rather than my

usual cup of tea on Tuesday lunchtime. Then, as I stick the
Post-it in my notebook below the information I've just entered,
Dionne clears her throat.

'Are you thinking of going?' she asks, though in a way that
suggests the word 'seriously' is missing from the third position in
that sentence.

'I thought I might pop in. Pay my respects.'

Dionne opens her mouth as if to talk me out of it, then
apparently changes her mind, and shakes her head slowly
instead. 'Suit yourself.'

'I shall,' I say defiantly. 'Which reminds me. I'll need my
black one.'

'Your black one what?'

'Suit.'

'Which black suit?'

'In the suit carrier in my wardrobe. I'm sure I kept it.
For... occasions like this.' By 'occasions like this', I also mean my
late wife's funeral, but I don't want to upset Dionne. 'If you'd be
so kind?'

There's a pause, then Dionne sighs. 'Fine,' she says
resignedly.

'Great!' I say, then notice Philip's still hovering in the room,
so I give him a brief salute. 'Thank you, Philip,' I say, and he
returns the gesture.

'Did you want me to book you a taxi?' he asks, and I peer up
at a random spot on the wall, as if I'm lost in thought.

'I suppose you could,' I say – Hastings and St Leonards are
as next to each other as it's possible for two towns to be,
although the crematorium's on Hastings' far side and a bit of a
trek away – then I let my gaze slowly drift across to Dionne.
'Though taxis are expensive. And notoriously unreliable. Plus,
you never know if the driver's some escaped lunatic who might
just...'

'Fine!' she says again. 'I'll pick you up at a quarter to.'

'*Us* up,' I say, and Philip looks alarmed – perhaps concerned I'm trying to set him up on the world's worst date – until I say, 'Albie and me.'

Dionne frowns. 'Albie?'

'My next-door neighbour.' I jab a thumb at the wall, then at the other one, when Philip's side-eye subtly lets me know I'm jabbing the wrong way.

Dionne smiles sympathetically. 'Were he and Elsie close?'

'Closer than she and I, certainly,' I say. Which is true. Geographically, at least, given the relative locations of our rooms. 'So if you wouldn't mind driving the two of us?'

'No problem,' says Dionne, and I mentally high-five myself, though I suspect getting Albie to agree to go might not be quite so simple. 'Right,' she says, checking her watch. 'I'm off. But I'll call in this evening?'

'Lovely,' I say. 'See you later.'

'See you later,' says Dionne, and as she stands up, I'm conscious my matchmaking window is in danger of closing.

'Are you working this evening, Philip?' I say hurriedly.

'Um...' Philip glances shyly at Dionne, and just about manages to force out a mumbled, 'Yes.'

'You hear that, Dionne? Philip will be here later too.'

Dionne looks at me strangely. 'O-kay,' she says. 'In that case, I guess I'll see *you* later.'

As Dionne turns to go, I give Philip a look to imply, 'go on, say something', and though my message evidently gets through, his desperate 'Alligator!' wasn't quite what I had in mind.

'Pardon?' says Dionne, and Philip looks mortified, as if he's overstepped some mark, and I know if he and Dionne are going to have any kind of future together – or even just one date – I need to jump in and rescue him.

'Which isn't as frivolous a phrase as you might think,' I say quickly. 'Because alligators are one of the few creatures that don't actually have a finite life span. Unless affected by a lack of food, disease, accidents, or attacked by another large predator, they don't die, but just continue to grow...' I stop talking. Dionne's regarding me strangely, and so is Philip – though at least I'm happy they have something in common. 'So given their longevity,' I continue, 'statistically an alligator *is* therefore more likely to "see you later" than most other things that might, you know...' I smile, happy I've both educated the two of them *and* transferred Philip's awkwardness onto me. 'See you.'

Dionne waits for a moment, perhaps to be sure I've finished, then she and Philip exchange glances. 'Good to know, Dad,' she says, though I suspect she thinks it isn't.

With a brisk, 'Come on, sweetie!' she heads out through the door, and as Custard trots off after her, Philip's face falls.

Possibly because he's just realised she was talking to the dog.

20

In the end, Albie's attendance at Elsie's funeral is surprisingly easy to secure. Perhaps it's because of the prospect of food other than the standard Twilight Lodge fare, which isn't exactly Michelin-starred, though it's more likely to be the possibility of alcohol at the wake. And while I've asked him not to overdo it on either front – we'll both need our wits about us if we're going to glean any important information from the assembled mourners – he's told me in no uncertain terms he's allowed to eat and drink what he wants, or words to that effect. *Two* words, to be precise.

In the meantime, and with two days to kill before we'll get the chance to question Elsie's nearest and dearest, I decide Albie and I had better review where we're 'at', and the noise coming from the Sunday tea dance in the Garden Lounge provides us with the perfect cover. As I wheel him out into the garden, jauntily foot-stepping in time to the beat of the music, Albie looks at me disdainfully.

'So, who's on the suspect list?' he asks, as I park him up under the pergola.

I lower myself onto the bench opposite, take a sip from one

of the two cups of tea we've purloined from the dance's refreshments table, then surreptitiously check my notebook. 'Well, there's Shane. Obviously.'

'Despite having an alibi.'

'Just because he wasn't officially on duty doesn't mean he didn't sneak in and do the deed.'

Albie takes a mouthful of tea. 'I suppose not. Though we still don't have a credible motive.'

'Apart from the "mercy killing" theory.'

'In which case, given how he probably can't even spell "euthanasia", he's Nigel's henchman.' Albie sticks his lower lip out and angles his head. 'Which means Nigel's a suspect too.'

'Along with that chap we caught poking around in Elsie's room,' I say, checking my notebook again. My eye catches my jottings from yesterday evening. 'Oh. Did I tell you? Shane's got a couple of cautions for dealing drugs on his file, according to Dionne.'

Albie raises both eyebrows. 'The hard stuff?'

'You mean like Viagra?'

Albie shakes his head, though slowly, letting me know in no uncertain terms he's dismissing my joke. 'Doesn't make him a killer, though.'

'I don't know,' I say. 'I've had dealings with a few drug dealers in the past, and they were particularly nasty individuals. Mind you, this was in Colombia and...'

Albie holds up a hand, and I stop talking obediently. 'Maybe we're looking at this the wrong way,' he says.

'How so?'

'Assuming it's one of the staff. When it could just as easily be one of the residents.'

'Such as?' I say, taking another sip from my mug. It's got a version of the Aldi supermarket logo printed on the side, though the 'A' has been changed to an 'O', and the graphic edited to resemble a bent-over pensioner with a walking stick, which I can only imagine is someone's idea of an attempt at humour. Either that, or it's another passive-aggressive insult courtesy of Shane.

'Well, the killings started just after you moved in, so…'

I almost spit my tea out. 'If you're trying to imply…'

'Reel your neck back in!' growls Albie. 'Though now I think about it, might someone be trying to frame you?'

'Who'd be trying to frame me?'

'That's what I just asked you.'

'No you didn't. You asked if someone might. Not who it might be.'

'It's pretty much the same thing.'

I'm about to protest, then I realise bickering with Albie won't actually get us any closer to finding out who the killer is. 'Okay – *why* would someone be trying to frame me?'

'Someone from your' – Albie looks like he's battling not to make air quotes – '*past* might hold a grudge.'

I think for a moment, then for a bit longer. It's possible, of course, given my background, that somebody might want revenge. But surely there's no one left who may wish to do me harm, and certainly nobody knows I'm here at Twilight Lodge. Unless… I narrow my eyes at Albie for a moment, then file the suspicion away almost as quickly as it's occurred to me. He might have been festering for the past fifty years and may blame me for all his current ills, but unless he's been lying about being at Twilight Lodge for years and has somehow engineered coming here just in time for my post-hip-operation recuperation…

I shake my head to try and clear it. He's hardly likely to suggest such a motive if it's *his* motive – unless it's a clever double bluff. And while the old Albie might just have been resourceful enough to make such a thing happen, the current *actually* old Albie doesn't have the wherewithal, or the physical ability.

'How long did you say you'd been here at Twilight Lodge, Albie?'

'What's that got to do with anything?' says Albie crossly.

'It's a simple question.'

'A year, give or take. Since I had my stroke. So what?'

'Calm down!' I say, dismissing my suspicions almost as quickly as I came up with them. 'I just meant that you must know most of the other residents – at least, better than I do. So are any of them capable of murder?'

Albie lets out a short laugh. 'Most of them aren't capable *full stop.*'

'Okay. Well, is there anyone else here like me? Perhaps newly arrived, or here to recuperate, and with all their faculties?'

Albie looks like he's considering this – or perhaps he's considering the state of *my* faculties. 'Stanley!' he announces, after a second or two.

'Stanley?'

'You know – the old guy with the white hair...?'

'That doesn't exactly narrow it down in here.'

'Quite tall.'

'Doesn't everyone look tall from your perspective?'

'He was at the tea dance just now. From what I heard from Miriam, his family told him he was coming in for a couple of weeks' respite care, but that was over a month ago, so it looks like they've dumped him in here under false pretences. Always looks a bit angry to me.'

'Perhaps not surprisingly, if he's been abandoned like that.'

Albie nods. 'I tend to stay out of his way.'

'You tend to stay out of everyone's way. Except for Barbara's!'

As Albie looks like he wants to snap off the finger I've just poked him with, I jot down Stanley's name, along with the word 'angry', in my notebook. 'And where does Stanley live?'

'What am I – the Yellow Pages?' Albie glares at me. 'Room Six,' he says, after a moment, so I turn to where I've sketched the fire escape plan in the front of my notebook.

'That's a sea-view room too!'

'I know.'

'So is Stanley the last surviving resident in a sea-view room?' I say, wondering whether that makes him more or less of a suspect. 'On the ground floor, at least?'

'Um, not quite...' Albie looks shiftily at me. 'Barbara's on the ground floor too, remember?'

'Interesting,' I say, arching one eyebrow teasingly, and Albie suddenly seems fascinated by the contents of his mug.

'Some things don't mean anything,' he says. 'They're just a coincidence.'

'And some things are too much of a coincidence,' I say, trying – and failing – not to think of the fact that of all the nursing homes in all the world, Albie's in here with me. 'But dismissing Barbara from our list of suspects – although what a way to go, eh? – what on earth would Stanley's motive be?'

'Abandonment issues? Problems with anger management?' Albie counts them off on his fingers. 'Noisy neighbours?'

I drain the rest of my tea and indicate Albie should do the same. 'Let's just hope he doesn't have the same problem with nosey ones,' I say, levering myself up from the bench and grabbing the wheelchair by the handles.

'Where are we going *now*?' he says, giving me a look, and I smile archly down at him.

'Dancing, Albie,' I say.

21

While it's hardly the Grand Ballroom at Claridge's, the Garden Lounge has been transformed for this afternoon's tea dance. The tables have been moved to one side to clear a sizeable section of the wooden floor, with half the chairs stacked in the corner, leaving just enough handy seating for those residents who've pasodoble'd a little too strenuously. There's even a rotating mirrored ball hanging from the ceiling, casting the assembled dancers in a flickering light which I'm sure must be playing havoc with their balance. As is probably the noise coming from the karaoke machine, which is currently blasting out a fuzzy version of 'Begin the Beguine' at top volume.

At first glance it appears to mostly be women partnering each other, partly I'm sure because the fairer sex outnumber us menfolk at Twilight Lodge by perhaps two to one, but also I imagine, with males of our age, hips and knees aren't really up to the job unless you've a titanium replacement like mine. And even then, whatever agility we might have had is generally a distant memory, as are our reactions. Not a good thing when dancing with a partner whose tendency to dip is more often accidental than planned.

Smiling at the scene, I glance down at Albie, though he doesn't seem to share my appreciation. Instead, he's glowering at the tall, dapper, white-haired gentleman currently whirling a flushed-looking Barbara around the dance floor at what appears to be a dangerous speed.

'Which one's Stanley?' I ask, perhaps a little unnecessarily.

'The one with his hands where they shouldn't be,' Albie growls, probably because Stanley's holding Barbara a little closer – and a lot lower – than is appropriate. While I recognise him, I don't think we've spoken before, so I take the opportunity to size him up. He's well over six feet tall, dressed smartly in a white long-sleeved shirt and beige slacks, and while he's perhaps Albie's age, he looks like he's in decent shape. Certainly fit enough to kill someone. At least, someone like Elsie.

'Come on,' I say, grabbing Albie's wheelchair and steering him towards the dance floor, prompting raised eyebrows from the refreshments table, where Miriam is manning the tea urn, but before I've made much progress, Albie reaches down and abruptly flicks both brakes on.

'If you think I'm dancing with you, you've got another thing coming!'

'*Think* coming, Albie.'

'What?'

'It's "another *think* coming". It's referring to what you think I think.'

'Whatever!' says Albie exasperatedly. 'I'm still not doing it.'

'Hardly!' I say. 'You're going to cut in.'

'Why?'

'One of us needs to question Stanley.'

'I'm not dancing with him either!'

'That wasn't what I was suggesting.'

'You want me to...' Albie swallows so hard I can hear it above the music. '*Dance with Barbara?*'

'Come on, Albie. For Queen and Country, remember? Needs must, and all that.'

'No!'

'Whyever not?'

Albie indicates his seating arrangements. 'It may have escaped your attention, but I'm stuck in this... contraption.'

'That doesn't stop all those competitors at the Paralympics.'

'That's hardly the same thing.'

'You do know how to dance?' I ask, though I already know Albie does. No one conducts a successful espionage career without an ability to cha-cha-charm on the dancefloor – the Company even gave us lessons.

'In theory,' Albie begrudgingly admits. 'Although I've always had two left feet.'

'Which, may I remind you, don't currently work, which is surely a good thing. Or at least, some sort of double negative making a posit—'

'*Martin...*'

'Okay.' I think for a moment, though it's difficult given the volume level. 'How about I cut in and you question him?'

Albie looks torn for an instant, then perhaps realises he'll make an enemy of Stanley either way, and while I suspect his motivation might be more to do with freeing Barbara from Stanley's clutches than anything to do with identifying Twilight Lodge's killer, after a moment he reaches down and petulantly releases his brakes.

'Fine – I'll do it.'

'Do what, exactly?'

'Dance with Barbara.'

'Good man!' I say, patting him on the shoulder.

Then before he can change his mind, I give his wheelchair a firm shove, timing it just so he runs into the back of Stanley's knees.

22

Stanley spins round, seemingly mystified at what's just happened, until he lowers his gaze and spots Albie, and they exchange a few words. While Barbara looks delighted at Albie's suggestion, Stanley doesn't seem to share her enthusiasm. As he stalks angrily back to his seat, glaring back over his shoulder at Albie as he does so, I take the opportunity to sidle across the room and sit down next to him.

'Stanley, isn't it?' I say, after the three throat clearings it's taken to get his attention.

Stanley looks at my outstretched hand as if it's radioactive. 'What's it to you?' he says, his heavy Scottish accent almost impenetrable.

'I just wanted to introduce myself.'

'What for?'

'I believe we're both the new boys here?'

'Is that right?'

'It is.' I nod, conscious I've been holding my hand out for longer than is comfortable. 'Martin.'

Stanley peers at me suspiciously. 'Nice to meet you,' he says, finally shaking my hand in a way that suggests it isn't.

'And how are you finding life here at Twilight Lodge?'

Stanley folds his arms and focuses his attention on the dance floor, where Barbara's currently shimmying in front of a wide-eyed Albie, who looks like a naive groom getting his first ever lap dance on his stag night – if Saga ran strip clubs. 'You really don't want me to answer that,' he says, after a moment.

I fold my arms too, in an attempt to gain his confidence using what body language experts would call 'mirroring' – something I hope Dionne learned on her recent interrogation techniques course. 'You're in one of the sea-view rooms, I believe?'

Stanley turns and glowers at me. 'So what if I am?'

'I was just wondering. What's it like?'

'It's a room with a view of what passes for the sea around here,' he barks. 'What do you think it's like?'

'Well, yes, of course, that's exactly what I think it's like,' I say, the smile on my face being harder and harder to maintain, and certainly not something Stanley's making any attempt at mirroring. 'I meant more along the lines of what the neighbours are like. How's the soundproofing? Is the bed comfortable? That kind of thing.'

'Thinking of moving, are you?'

'Perhaps,' I say, as Philip waltzes carefully by with a lady at least my age, and I make a mental note to tell Dionne what a good dancer he is. 'I'm here on a month's recuperation at the moment. Hip replacement.' I tap my left hip, then realise that's the wrong one, although it's unlikely Stanley's going to know the difference. 'So I'm going home in a fortnight or so. But you never know.'

'Well, you'd better keep the noise down if you do!'

I'm at a bit of a loss as to what to say next. Albie's right – Stanley's evidently an angry individual, and while he's perhaps not as obviously psychotic as some of the baddies I've come across in the past, that doesn't mean he isn't capable of murder.

'Oh, don't worry. I like it quiet.'

'So do I,' says Stanley. '*Dead* quiet.'

As I try to work out whether that's a Freudian slip or simply him trying to tell me to shut up, Stanley holds my gaze for just long enough that I suspect it's the latter. Then he pointedly turns his attention back to the dance floor, where Barbara's holding Albie's hand while spinning him round on the spot, his expression equal parts elation and terror, like a child riding a rollercoaster for the first time.

'So,' I say, wondering whether Stanley's past might give me any clue to his relevance as a suspect. 'What did you do? Before this?'

I wave a hand around loosely to indicate the wider goings-on at Twilight Lodge, and Stanley glowers at me, either because I've ignored his request for silence, or for reminding him that 'this' is what he does now. 'Civil servant,' he says gruffly.

I sit up a little straighter in my chair as the emergence of some common ground gives me something to work on – though he's the least 'civil' civil servant I've ever encountered. 'What department?' I ask, and Stanley looks me up and down for a moment.

'What's it to you?'

'Oh, just...' I stop talking. *Trying to find out if your former occupation means you might be capable of murder* possibly isn't the best of conversational gambits. But before I can think of an alternative, the music finishes, and Stanley almost leaps to his feet. As Barbara and Albie applaud each other politely, he leans down towards me.

'Give your four-wheeled friend a message from me, will you?'

'Happy to oblige,' I say.

'Tell him...' Stanley looks across at the two of them, evidently not at all pleased that Barbara's now perched on Albie's lap as he wheels the two of them towards the refreshments table. 'Tell him if he dances with her again, he's a dead man!'

'Will do!' I say, taking out my notebook and pen, and Stanley looks at me strangely, perhaps because he feels I should be able to remember that kind of message without having to jot it down.

Although what I'm *actually* doing is crossing his name out at the bottom of my suspect list.

And rewriting it right at the top.

23

I'm enjoying a leisurely breakfast, holding court at a sunny window table with a pair of charming ladies who – fortunately, given my powers of recall aren't at their best first thing – are both called Shirley, when there's a commotion from somewhere along the corridor. My first thought is the murderer's been caught in the act, though when I excuse myself and reluctantly leave a plate of scrambled eggs that actually taste like eggs to follow the sound of the shouting, I find it's coming from Nigel's office.

The home's staff are all gathered nervously by the reception desk, while Joy appears to be hiding behind it, so I push my way between Philip and Miriam to see if I can be of any assistance. Evidently Gemma's got there before me, as when I emerge from the throng, she's already shepherding an unhappy-looking Shane from Nigel's office.

Surreptitiously, I unclench my fists, but not before – in lieu of Shane's mid-section – I've furtively punched the air, pleased my instincts haven't failed me, and my initial suspicions have turned out to be true. Though in an instant my face drops, as Gemma releases her grip on him, and I'm astounded to see that instead of delivering Shane to a waiting police car, they seem to be letting him go. I'm just about to protest when Miriam turns to me and answers my unasked question.

'They've just fired Shane,' she says, trying – and failing – to conceal the look of pleasure on her face.

'What for?' I say, then mentally face-palm myself. Of *course* murder's a sackable offence. As, probably, is not being able to carry out your duties because you're subsequently banged up for it.

'For being rubbish at his job, I'd imagine,' says Philip, which throws me a bit. But before I can ask anything further, a nervous-looking Nigel emerges from the safety of his office, and Shane's face turns even darker than before.

'You won't get away with this!'

'Get away with what?' says Gemma, and Shane glowers at her.

'I'd advise you to be careful with what you come out with next,' says Nigel. 'Especially in front of witnesses. And even more so if you want to keep that generous severance package we've just offered you.'

Shane opens his mouth as if to say something else, then evidently thinks better of it. Instead, he turns and scowls at the rest of us, and while I'd like to give him a cheery wave goodbye, something tells me now might not be the time.

'Yeah, well. Just remember, I know what the two of you've been up to,' he says, as Gemma steps past him and opens the front door.

'Shane?' she says, in an 'after you' kind of way, though I doubt she's intending on following him. Particularly after the look he gives her.

'You can stick your job!' he says, then he makes a less-than-friendly gesture towards Nigel and storms out of the building. For a moment, it occurs to me to go after him. But even though my new hip appears to be bedding in nicely, I doubt I'd be able to catch him given the rate at which he appears to be traversing the drive. Besides, there's an unfinished plate of scrambled eggs with my name on it.

As Nigel and Gemma return to their respective offices and the other carers go back to their duties, I begin making my way back along the corridor. But I can't have gone more than a couple of steps before I nearly collide with Albie.

'Well, well, well,' I say. 'If it isn't Fred Astaire!' and Albie gives me a look. He doesn't say anything, though he doesn't have to, given the colour his cheeks have turned. 'Where are you off to?'

'Breakfast,' replies Albie gruffly.

I look theatrically back over my shoulder. 'Now I know I haven't been here all that long, but isn't the dining room in the other direction?'

Albie gives me another look. 'Came to see what all the fuss was about, didn't I?'

'Oh.' I squint down at him, doubting he'd pass a lie detector test right now – especially since Barbara's room is in this direction too. 'Shane's been fired.'

'Excellent!' Albie beams up at me. 'For being a complete and utter b—?'

I hold my hand up to silence him – it's a little early for profanities, and there are ladies present. 'I'm not sure. Philip said it was for being a terrible carer, but there was something else.'

'What do you mean?'

I grab Albie's wheelchair by the handles and begin steering him back down the corridor. 'Just as he was leaving, he told Nigel and Gemma they wouldn't "get away with this".'

'With sacking him?'

'That's what I assumed, initially. But now I think about it, it almost sounded like he was accusing them of something. And they told him to keep quiet. Especially if he wanted to keep the "generous severance package" they'd offered him.'

'Why would you offer someone like Shane a generous severance package?'

'Hush money, maybe?'

'For what?'

'Traditionally, it's for hushing.'

Albie gives me the latest in a long line of looks. 'Hushing what, exactly?'

'He did say he knew, and I paraphrase, what the two of them had been up to. So I suppose it could be that.'

'What does *that* mean?'

'That's the question,' I say, steering Albie into the dining room and over to where I'd been sitting earlier. To my relief, my scrambled eggs are still there – perhaps because the staff have been too embroiled in the Shane incident to clear the tables – though they appear to have congealed somewhat. 'Surely he was referring to the murders. Although it didn't sound like he was accusing them directly.'

'Do you think Nigel and Gemma know there's something strange going on but they've been covering it up?' says Albie, once I've parked him next to me.

'Maybe. And maybe Shane found out?'

'But why would you want to cover up the fact that your residents are being murdered?'

I pick up my knife and fork and slice off a section of egg, which now appears to have the texture and consistency of polystyrene, suggesting there's not a lot of *actual* egg in it. 'Not exactly good for business, is it?'

'I suppose not.' Albie grunts his thanks at Miriam as she deposits his usual full English in front of him, then notices the expression on my face. 'What?'

'Hardly the healthiest of breakfasts, Albie.'

'My body is a temple,' he says.

'Of doom, perhaps?' I suggest, mindful of this week's 'starring Harrison Ford' movie afternoons as advertised on the residents' corkboard in the corridor.

Albie ignores me as he picks up his knife and fork and regards his plate thoughtfully, like a sculptor wondering where to start chipping away. 'So,' he says. 'Does that make them accessories, do you think?'

'After the fact, possibly,' I say. 'That's something I'll be able to check with Dionne. Not that we know what the fact is yet.'

'Although I think we can be sure Shane's not the murderer,' Albie says, skilfully assembling a forkful that appears to consist of a piece of everything on his plate.

'Unless he *is*, and the three of them have been running this "mercy killing" racket we discussed, but Nigel and Gemma have decided enough is enough.'

Albie shoves the forkful into his mouth, but not before liberally coating it in brown sauce. 'Why would they have suddenly decided that?' he says – or at least, that's what I interpret, given his mouth's full of food.

'Maybe someone voiced their suspicions about Elsie's death, so they've got cold feet.'

Albie pauses, mid-chew. 'Who on earth would have...?'

'I may have blurted something out to Gemma the other day,' I admit sheepishly.

Albie's eyes widen. 'What?'

'Don't worry. I kept your name out of it. In any case, I don't think she thought I was serious. In fact, I think she felt I might actually be a little...' I rotate my index finger next to my temple, and Albie gestures towards me with his fork.

'Demented?' he suggests, as if Gemma's not the only one who feels that way.

'Anyway.' I take a sip of my tea, then spit it back into the mug, as perhaps not surprisingly, it's now stone cold. 'If that *is* what's been going on, I reckon they've given Shane his share of the profits and told him to keep schtum.'

'The severance package.'

'AKA hush money.'

'Maybe. But why risk firing him? Why not keep him close so they can keep an eye on him?'

'That's not something I know the answer to – yet. Besides, he's not our only suspect.'

'Meaning?' says Albie, assembling another forkful.

I turn to my left, then my right. The dining room's empty apart from a couple asleep at their table in the far corner, but I lower my voice anyway. 'Stanley.'

Albie looks a little alarmed. 'Where?'

'Not here. I mean, he might be our killer.'

'Because?'

'Well, because of what he said to me yesterday.'

Albie sighs, then puts his fork back down. 'Let me get this straight. You think Stanley is the killer because he fancies Barbara.'

'In a roundabout way, yes. Don't forget he as good as threatened you with death for dancing with her.'

Albie butters himself a piece of toast. 'So he's been killing off his dancefloor rivals? Talk about marking their dance cards!'

'Maybe. Maybe George was sweet on Barbara too. Perhaps he danced with her once too often for Stanley's liking.'

'Okay.' Albie frowns. 'But, um...'

'What?'

'*Diana?* And *Elsie?*'

I throw my hands up in the air, painfully aware this whole situation isn't getting any clearer – in fact, if anything, the opposite is happening. 'I don't know,' I say, trying desperately to conjure up scenarios. 'It's possible Elsie was sweet on Stanley, and she and Barbara were friends, so Barbara wouldn't have anything to do with him because of it. Maybe he saw Barbara dancing with Diana and Elsie and somehow got it into his head that there was something going on there. Perhaps he simply killed her to throw everyone off the scent. All I know is, from what I saw of him yesterday, Stanley's perfectly capable of killing someone. *Three* someones, even.' I give Albie a meaningful look. 'Perhaps even four...'

Albie pales, then puts his toast down and slides his plate away. 'I'm sure I'm not going to like the answer to this question, but how do we check that particular theory out?'

'All in good time, Albie,' I say, reaching across to help myself to a rasher of bacon from his discarded breakfast. Though as far as I'm concerned, tomorrow – and in particular, Elsie's funeral – can't come around quickly enough.

24

It's Tuesday, and I'm as excited as it's reasonably acceptable to be when one is on one's way to a funeral. The only slight problem is, Dionne's brought the wrong black suit, so instead of my Savile Row 'funeral' two-piece, she's accidentally picked up my dinner suit. Something I only discover as I'm putting it on ten minutes before we're due to leave, so it's too late to call by her house and exchange it.

'Blimey,' says Albie, when I collect him from his room. 'Here's me thinking you've been making all that spy stuff up. Next you'll be telling me that Aston Martin parked outside's yours too.'

I shush him, hoping Dionne hasn't heard, then remember she's waiting for us outside. 'My daughter brought this suit by mistake, if you must know,' I say, doing my best to look suitably embarrassed, though secretly, I think I look rather dapper. I can't remember the last time I wore this ensemble – quite probably on official business, as I seem to recall the number of black-tie occasions in St Leonards for Madeleine and me to attend was rather limited – but I'm pleased I can still fit into it. If anything, it's a little loose – though that may be because it was originally tailored to hide an underarm holster for my handgun and a stiletto dagger strapped to my leg, as opposed to any age-related shrinkage on my part. Or rather, parts.

Albie nods at the rather wide lapels. 'A little dated, isn't it?'

'I think you'll find the word you're looking for is "classic".'

'Another word I'm looking for is "inappropriate". Especially for a funeral.'

'Rubbish. Besides, a funeral's like a wedding.'

'How d'you work that one out?'

'In the sense that everyone's too busy looking at the bride to notice what anyone else is wearing.'

Albie shudders. 'Only if it's an open casket.'

'That's not what I meant. And at least it's black.' While Albie's in a suit too, it's a light grey one, and by the looks of it, borrowed from someone somewhat larger than he is, though at least he's changed out of his usual jogging-bottoms-and-jumper get-up, so I decide not to pass further comment.

'Well, don't you look suave?'

I turn to see Gemma standing in the doorway, so I shoot my cuffs and give her a little salute, then spot Nigel behind her, also dressed in a black suit. Apparently he's planning to put in an appearance at Elsie's funeral too. He's even offered to take us in the Twilight Lodge minibus on account of the vehicle having ramp access for Albie's wheelchair, but I've politely declined. Dionne's a strong girl and more than capable of loading it – and Albie – into her car. Plus, I've the feeling we may need to hang around a little longer than Nigel might be planning to.

There's a mirror on the wall next to Albie's bed, so I go to check my reflection one last time to ensure the ends of my bow tie are perfectly aligned, though the moment I do, there's a loud beeping sound from somewhere behind me.

'Is that you reversing, Albie?' I say, which provokes the usual two-fingered response from him, before Gemma steps smartly into the room and presses a button on the console on the wall, silencing the noise.

'Albie's pressure mat,' she explains, pointing to a rubber contraption on the floor by the bed. 'To let us know if he's had a tumble during the night.'

'Chance would be a fine thing,' Albie mumbles to me.

'You stepped on it,' explains Gemma.

'Aha,' I say, then I check my watch. 'Speaking of which, we ought to do exactly that.'

'Okay. Well, have...' Gemma hesitates, perhaps wondering what word comes next, given the occasion.

'Will do,' I say, to put her out of her misery, then I wheel Albie out into the corridor, along through reception, and out onto the drive, to where Dionne's leaning against her Volvo, engrossed in something on her mobile phone. 'Dionne, Albie,' I say, and Dionne slips her phone away and smiles warmly at him.

'Pleased to meet you, Albie.'

'Excuse me if I don't get up,' Albie says, shaking the hand she's extended.

I open the Volvo's rear door for him, but before he can climb in, there's a loud snort from the back seat. 'Yikes!' says Albie, as Custard regards him suspiciously. 'What's *that*?'

'Custard,' I say, and at the sound of his name, Custard hauls himself stiffly to his feet. 'Dionne named him. He was my late wife's.'

Albie regards him suspiciously. 'And he's a...?'

'A *dog*, Albie.' I rest a concerned hand on his shoulder. 'That stroke really has messed with you, hasn't it?'

Albie shakes my hand off angrily. 'What *make*?'

'A pug,' I say. 'Interestingly, most people think the breed's name came from marmoset monkeys, also known as Pug monkeys, which were popular pets in the eighteenth century. Their faces look similar, you see. But it's actually from the Latin word "pugnus", meaning "fist". Hence the term "pugilist", for a boxer. The fighter, I mean, not the *other* breed of dog.'

Albie looks like he's considering engaging in some pugilism himself to shut me up, though fortunately, Dionne's 'Shall we be off?' puts paid to that. Instead, he grabs the handle attached to the roof and swings himself deftly into the back of the car – not that I should be surprised given his past record-breaking performances on the obstacle course at Company HQ. Then – pausing to collect Custard so he can travel up front with me – Dionne and I manhandle Albie's wheelchair into the boot.

'Seatbelts!' she commands, once we're all in, so we buckle up accordingly, then she steers us through Twilight Lodge's red-brick gate pillars and along the seafront, Custard sitting on my lap, peering excitedly out of the window like a newly adopted pet en route from the shelter to its new home following a last-minute reprieve.

And to my delight, when I turn to look at Albie, he's doing exactly the same.

25

Once we're safely on our way, Dionne looks in her rear-view mirror and catches Albie's eye. 'Are you from around here, Albie?'

I peer round, keen to see how Albie responds, in time to see him shake his head. 'Up north,' he says.

'Fancied a bit of better weather in your retirement?'

There's a flash of annoyance on his face, though I'm assuming Dionne means coming down south to St Leonards rather than his attempted escape to Central America five decades ago. 'Something like that,' he mumbles, and Dionne smiles.

'So, what made you choose Twilight Lodge?'

Albie gives me the briefest of looks. 'A series of unfortunate events, culminating in a stroke which robbed me of my memories, my ability to walk, and my will to live.'

'I'm sorry to hear that,' says Dionne, after an uncomfortable moment. 'And do you like it? Twilight Lodge, I mean.'

'Not much,' says Albie abruptly, then he gives me another look. 'But then again, it wasn't my first choice.'

'No?' says Dionne.

'No,' says Albie, in an end-of-conversation way, perhaps because his first choice would be to not be living *full stop*, though Dionne doesn't take the hint.

'I'll tell you where I'd like to go when I'm your age,' she says cheerfully, doing her best to make conversation. 'One of those places abroad.'

'What places abroad?' I say, suspecting this is a discussion Albie might not want to contribute to.

'It was on television the other day,' she says excitedly. 'A group of, ahem, *older* celebrities went on a trip to India to see if they could retire there. Not that I'd heard of any of them, mind you, except for the newsreader and that woman from the *Harry Potter* films. It was one of those fly-on-the-wall things.'

'I watched that,' says Albie. 'Some of those places they stayed in had a *lot* of flies on the wall.'

Dionne chuckles at Albie's comment, and deservedly so, though she's on her own there where he's concerned.

'Though they didn't, did they?' he asks, after a moment.

'Didn't what?'

'Retire to India.'

'Well, no. I think it was more to show how it's cheaper there. I don't believe they were ever planning to. Celebrities probably don't need to watch the pennies. Even so, it's an idea.'

There's a moment of silence that extends into an awkward one, so I decide it's time to change the subject, and the large Victorian building at the far end of the street provides me with the ideal opportunity.

'That place looks familiar,' I say, pointing at it through the windscreen, and Dionne sighs.

'It's my old school, Dad. St Saviour's. Remember?'

'Oh yes,' I say, although I don't. Though in my defence, I was away saving the world for most of Dionne's childhood. And while her mother did a good job going to all the carol concerts, school plays and sports fixtures I missed, I still feel a little guilty. 'Did you want to call in? For old times' sake?'

'No,' says Dionne, sounding about as enthusiastic as Albie a few moments ago.

'Or you could go and give a talk. Tell the kids all about a career in the police.'

Dionne slows to briefly look at the building, then puts her foot down again. 'Most of the kids who came out of there seem to be making a career trying to *avoid* the police. And anyway, there's no point. It's flats now.' She points to a Portakabin with a fabric SALES OFFICE sign hanging loosely above the door in what appears to have once been the playground. 'Hence that monstrosity.'

'Flats?' I say, absent-mindedly stroking Custard, who already appears to be dropping off to sleep in my lap. 'Did you ever think of buying one? That might have been fun, living in your old school. You could run along the corridors as much as you like without being told off.'

Dionne shakes her head. 'I couldn't afford it. They're high-end, apparently, starting at three, maybe four hundred thousand. And on a police salary...'

'You might have got a discount, seeing as it's your alma mater.'

'Doubtful, given who the developer is,' Dionne says, before slamming her foot on the Volvo's brakes to avoid a Range Rover that's just hurtled out through the gates. 'Speak of the devil.'

'Who's the devil?' I say, repositioning an indignant-looking Custard, who's almost been catapulted off my lap and into the footwell by Dionne's emergency stop. I peer at the Range Rover. Something about it – perhaps the grey, matte-painted exterior, not to mention the fact it's being driven at break-neck speed – rings a bell, and of the 'alarm' variety when I recall it's the same one I saw at Twilight Lodge the other day.

'Tommy Walker.' Dionne flashes her headlights at the

rapidly departing vehicle, only to receive what I believe is known as 'the finger' from the driver's side window. I find myself hoping she's about to stick a blue light on her roof and set off in pursuit, before remembering that kind of thing only happens in the movies. Besides, it's too late – the Range Rover's already speeding off round the corner, and Dionne's ageing Volvo would be no match for it even if it weren't weighed down with Albie and me.

'Who's Tommy Walker?' I ask, and Dionne harrumphs.

'I went to school with him,' she says, turning off the seafront road and into Hastings. 'Nasty piece of work.'

'When you say "nasty piece of work"...?' pipes up Albie from the back seat, and Dionne smiles humourlessly.

'He was a bully. Still is, evidently, given how he managed to convince the council to grant him planning permission in record time. We thought there was something fishy about it, particularly after the way he acquired the building. We even had a file on him for a while down at the station, but no one from the council would talk about it. Not to me, at least.'

It takes a big effort not to reach for my notebook, which I've secreted inside my jacket pocket, but the last thing I want is for Dionne to suspect I'm still investigating. Instead, I console myself with the fact that Albie's here, and his short-term memory – if not his attitude – is still first-rate. 'How did he acquire the building?'

Dionne glances across at me as if reluctant to share the information, then evidently decides it's not exactly a state secret. 'There were lots of problems with it, apparently. Asbestos, lead pipes, that sort of thing. Not great for a school.'

I raise both eyebrows. 'Apparently?'

'It was Tommy Walker who did the initial investigation. Or rather, one of his construction companies. Though god only knows how he got the contract in the first place. Friends in high places, perhaps.'

'Or low ones,' suggests Albie.

'Exactly,' says Dionne. 'So of course, they deemed it unsafe for the kids.'

I let out a short laugh. 'That kind of stuff that never did us any harm, eh, Albie?'

Dionne looks at me as if that's debatable. 'Anyway, as a result, they moved the whole school to some temporary buildings up the road. Then while it was closed and awaiting repairs, there was a fire. Not a big one – just enough to make it not economically viable to repair. At least, according to the company that did the survey.'

'Which was?' I say, mindful of a potential pattern emerging.

'T. Walker Surveying. Another of Tommy Walker's companies.'

'I worked that out already, thanks, love.'

Dionne gives me the side-eye. 'Anyway, the building went up for sale, and of course, no one wanted to touch it given the problems. No one, that was, except for a company called T.W. Developments.'

'Tommy Walker again?' I say, making eye contact with Albie. In return he gives me a 'not as stupid as you appear' look, which I try not to take offence at.

'Exactly,' says Dionne. 'So they get it at a knock-down price, mainly because the council are assuming they're actually going to have to knock it down, but all of a sudden it seems the structural issues aren't in fact as severe as first thought, and like I said, planning permission is virtually rushed through. A year or so later, it's twenty-one luxury flats, each one selling for almost what he purchased the whole building for.'

Albie whistles from the back seat. 'And there was no comeback?' he asks.

'For what? Tommy had obtained the building legally, plus he had planning permission. And with no one prepared to say anything about any of it...' Dionne sighs, then stares out through the windscreen, and I can sense her frustration.

'I bet you'd like another crack at him,' I say, as we reach the crematorium, and Dionne looks at me strangely.

'How?' she says, as she flicks the Volvo's left indicator and steers us in through the imposing iron gates. 'With no evidence and no one prepared to go on the record, it's pretty much case closed.'

'You could always reopen it? Or get him for something else.'

'Such as?' says Dionne, as she parks the car in front of the building.

I shrug as Custard jumps down from my lap, then climb out of the passenger seat and brush the dog hairs from my trousers. While in reality I've got an answer, it's not one I'm prepared to give Dionne just yet. And it's obvious Albie's thinking what I'm thinking, given the look he gives me as I help him out and into his wheelchair.

Murder.

26

Hastings Crematorium hasn't changed since I was last here. Though I suppose these places don't, really, except for a few additional headstones signifying the presence of more occupants in the graveyard.

Although this was where she was cremated, my wife's not one of them. Madeleine had wanted her ashes scattered from the end of Eastbourne pier – the same pier where we'd first met, a little way along the coast, at a dance in the ballroom some sixty years ago. Back when Eastbourne was still a glamorous resort and not the subject of the joke about how, if the south coast of England is full of old folks, then Eastbourne's where their parents live.

It's strange, given all the things I've forgotten, how I still remember our first encounter as if it were yesterday – the stunning red dress she wore that matched her equally striking hair, the heels I'd thought it must have been impossible to walk in, let alone dance, the scarlet lips I'd dreamed of kissing the moment I'd laid eyes on them, and more than anything, the courage it took for me to walk across the ballroom and ask her to dance. Nothing in all my days at the Company had ever made me that nervous again. And never – no matter how serious the consequences of me failing a mission – had there been a more important outcome than getting Madeleine to say 'yes' on that magical night.

It had taken months after her passing before I'd been ready to fulfil her wishes, and although her ashes are gone, I still carry a big part of her in my heart. And, I suspect, in the seams of my other black suit, seeing as there had been quite a blustery onshore breeze the day Dionne and I had uncapped the urn and said a final, painful goodbye. Why Madeleine had chosen her final resting place to be at sea, I still don't know – not that I suppose it mattered by then, but Madeleine was never a keen swimmer, especially in the chilly waters of the English Channel. She loved the warmth. So I suppose electing to depart here at the crematorium at least made some sense.

Dionne's refused to come in, preferring to wait in the car. She's said it's because she doesn't want to leave Custard on his own, but secretly I suspect the memories of her mother's funeral are still too raw, despite the fact it's been a year. Instead, she's left me to wheel Albie across the grass – not an easy task, as it could do with mowing – and in through the large wooden doors. I've taken a seat at the back of the chapel, strategically positioning Albie's wheelchair to block off the rest of the row so we can observe our fellow mourners without raising suspicions, though the view this affords us of the backs of people's heads hasn't proven to be all that enlightening so far. Still, it's a good enough vantage point until we get to the house, which is where the real investigation can begin.

There's a few minutes to go until 'kick-off', as Albie's unceremoniously termed it, but the room's almost full of hushed mourners, and Elsie's coffin – lid firmly on, thankfully – is already front and centre. While we wait, I lean across to nudge Albie, then point to it.

'Buried or cremated?'

Albie frowns at me. 'What are you going on about?'

'Buried or cremated?' I say again.

'Duh!' says Albie, rather childishly, I feel, before indicating where we are with a sweep of his hand. 'She's being cremated. Obviously.'

'Not Elsie. *You.*'

'As long as I'm dead first, I won't give a flying—'

'Okay, okay,' I say, keen to cut him off before any profanities can leave his lips – we're here to pay our respects, after all, though I could do with this part of the procedure getting going. And it's not just that I'm anxious to get on and start quizzing the other mourners. I'm an old man, and my bladder capacity isn't what it used to be.

Fortunately, Yvette chooses that moment to appear at the microphone at the front of the chapel, though she's a little overcome with emotion, and struggling to even get started on the tribute I imagine is written on the index cards she's clutching like a lifebelt. As she blows her nose noisily on a tissue she's just removed from her sleeve, dropping the cards on the floor in the process, I turn back to Albie.

'I think I'd like to be buried,' I say.

'Good for you,' says Albie, peering absent-mindedly up at the ceiling.

'Cremation's so final, after all,' I say, as a few of the assembled mourners almost fall over each other in an attempt to help Yvette pick the cards up. 'Whereas a burial... At least if they've made a mistake...'

'What sort of mistake?'

'If you're not actually dead.'

'That happens, does it?'

'It could,' I say. 'Which reminds me of that old chestnut about a hunter out in the woods with his friend, phoning for an ambulance and telling the operator, "I think my friend has died. What should I do?" The operator thinks for a moment, then says, "First thing is to make sure he's dead." There's a pause, then the operator hears the sound of a gunshot, and the hunter comes back on the line and says, "Okay. What now?"'

I nudge Albie again and raise both eyebrows, though he doesn't seem to want to acknowledge the brilliance of my joke – possibly just as well, seeing as Yvette's retrieved all her index cards and sorted them into some sort of order.

As she launches into her eulogy, I do my best to concentrate on what she's saying, just in case it bears any relevance to our investigation, although, between her intermittent sobbing and our positioning at the back of the chapel, it's hard to hear her. As she refers unintelligibly to the second of what appears to be a considerable number of index cards, I give up, and nudge Albie again.

'It's not actually ash, you know?' I whisper.

'What isn't?' asks Albie, at the same volume.

'The ashes.'

'What are you...?'

'The urn you get at the end. The contents aren't technically ash.'

Albie lets out a quiet but long-suffering sigh. 'I'm sure I'm going to regret asking this, but what exactly is it, then?'

'It's the bits that don't burn. The skeleton, mostly. They grind it up.'

Albie makes a face. 'How is it you need to write down everything that happens right in front of you in your notebook so you won't forget it, yet you manage to remember stuff like that?'

'Therein lies one of life's mysteries, my friend.'

Albie rolls his eyes, turns his attention back to Yvette, then does the slowest of double takes. 'Why is it called "ashes", in that case?'

'The appearance, I'd imagine,' I say, adding, 'and the feel,' and I'm transported back to the end of the pier and my final farewell to Madeleine. Albie catches my eye, and I have a sudden urge to change the subject. Besides, with Yvette getting up a head of steam on the eulogy, it occurs to me we ought to try and get our ducks in order. 'Anyway, perhaps now might be a good time to go through where we're at.'

'There you go with that "we" word again.'

I ignore what I'm sure is his good-natured jesting. 'So what do you think about that Tommy Walker?'

Albie looks across at me. 'What about him?'

'You recognised the car?'

Albie nods. 'The same one we saw at Twilight Lodge. When he was there checking out Elsie's room.'

'Exactly! So how do you think he's involved?'

'What makes you think he's involved at all?'

'Come on, Albie. You heard what Dionne said about her old school. A suspicious fire, Tommy Walker gets it at a knock-down price, then builds all these luxury flats and makes a fortune.'

Albie narrows his eyes, then suddenly widens them. 'You think he's got the same plans for Twilight Lodge?'

'Why not? It's a prime seafront location, and given the number of rooms and the size of the communal areas, if you convert it, you're going to get, I don't know, twenty or so apartments? If they all go for around the same price the ones in the school did, more even, given the location, that's...'

'Six or seven million quid,' announces Albie, before I've even begun to get my head around the multiplication.

'Exactly,' I say, taking Albie's word for it. He always was the numbers man – at least until his number was up. 'And if that's not motivation for murder, I don't know what is.'

'And you think it's Tommy Walker who's actually committing the murders?' Albie whispers, as Yvette pauses to collect herself.

'Perhaps. Though they all seem like inside jobs to me. Especially given the level of security.'

'Unless, of course, someone's letting him in unnoticed. Like the other day.'

'Nigel?'

'Possibly. But a bit too suspicious. For a one-off, perhaps. But time and time again? Increases your chances of being seen. Then all you need is someone to put two and two together...'

'Though those sea-view rooms do all have windows that open out to the front of the building. Easy for someone to climb in.'

Albie lets out a short laugh, causing a middle-aged couple sitting in front of us to swivel round to shush him, though they quickly turn back again when they catch sight of his expression. 'If they're Twiggy, maybe. Those windows only open a tiny bit to stop us falling out. Or making a break for it.'

'So Tommy Walker has a motive, therefore he could be the killer...' I think for a moment, then something occurs to me. 'Hang on. Tommy might have a motive, but he might also *be* a motive.'

Albie frowns. 'I don't understand.'

'Like you said, Tommy stands to make millions if he turns Twilight Lodge into flats. Which would also lead us to assume that Nigel will make a decent amount from selling him the building. Which he can't do if it's full of the likes of us.'

'So he's just going to kill us off one by one?'

I shake my head. 'Way too suspicious. Not to mention time-consuming.'

'Even though that's what appears to be happening?'

I nod, then shake my head again. 'I just don't get it. Surely it'd be a lot easier to just announce you're closing. Move the remaining residents somewhere else.'

Albie opens his mouth to say something, then stops himself. Yvette's begun speaking again, though she only manages half a sentence or so before collapsing heavily against the lectern. As someone who I assume is another relative leads her back to her seat, and a man dressed in a black suit with lapels almost as wide as mine takes her place, Albie elbows me.

'If it were me, I'd burn the place down. Gets rid of any remaining residents, allows me to sell it, clears the site for redevelopment *and* gives me a sizeable insurance payment.'

'True. Although from Tommy Walker's perspective, he could get away with one fire. Two is a big-time red flag leading to a potential investigation for arson.'

'Maybe,' says Albie thoughtfully.

We sit through the remaining tributes, then watch in respectful silence as someone presses a button and Elsie's coffin disappears from view to a soundtrack of 'My Way'. As the assembled mourners begin filing past us, I turn back to Albie. 'So the one thing we do agree on is that Tommy's involved?'

'Though perhaps unwittingly.'

'That remains to be seen.'

'So how do we prove it?'

'You leave that with me,' I say.

Albie's stomach rumbles loudly, his mind evidently already on the forthcoming buffet. 'Happy to,' he says. 'No rush, mind.'

Which is just as well. Because right now, I don't have the faintest idea how I'm going to prove anything at all.

27

The journey to Yvette's house doesn't take long – at least, not long enough for Custard to fall asleep on my lap again. Dionne doesn't ask us how the ceremony went, perhaps because she's mistaking our quiet repose for reflection on the emotional farewell we've just witnessed rather than the two of us trying to get to the bottom of the intricacies of a multiple homicide. By the time we arrive at the smart 1960s bungalow, I'm still no clearer as to who our main suspect is or how they're currently getting away with it – although if property development is the motive behind all of this, then that means we've got to eliminate any other possible reasons. Which, I remind Albie as we file politely inside, is why we're here today.

'So,' I say, as we keep ourselves to ourselves respectfully in the corner. 'Any thoughts regarding tactics?'

Albie looks to his left, then to his right, and finally nods towards the buffet table, which is currently being mobbed. 'I'll get a bit of speed up and see if I can clear a route to the vol-au-vents. You grab a couple of plates and back me up...'

'I meant to find out about Elsie!'

'What? Oh. Yeah.' Albie looks sheepish. 'Me too. I just thought we'd blend in more easily armed with finger food.'

I shake my head disdainfully for a moment or two, then decide perhaps he has a point. 'Okay. But I've only one pair of hands. You're effectively a trolley. So you get the plates and the food, and I'll organise us both something to drink.'

Albie's eyes light up, and he peers towards the table in the corner that's replete with bottles. 'You mean a *drink* drink?' He surreptitiously looks across at Nigel, who's standing a little awkwardly near the door, as if he's waiting for an appropriate moment to do a runner. 'Do you think we're supposed to?'

'I don't think we're supposed to be here full stop, so in for a penny...'

'Fair point.'

Under the guise of admiring the rather horrid abstract artwork on Yvette's walls that looks both expensive *and* like the kind of thing you see as the last 'amusing' story on the television news about how a chimpanzee's revealed an ability to paint, I mosey over to the drinks table, help myself to a couple of plastic cups, and splash a healthy measure of wine into each of them. I'm not sure if Albie's a red or white man, and when I think about it, I can't remember if I am either, so I get one of each. I'm about to elbow my way back through the crowd when there's a parting of the waves, and Albie – two plates piled high with assorted savouries balanced precariously on his lap – emerges from the throng.

'Red or white?' I say, holding out the drinks.

'Do I look like I mind?'

'Red it is, then,' I say, handing him the appropriate cup, and taking a sip of mine. It's lukewarm and rather sweet – hardly a Bollinger, not that that was ever allowed on the Company budget – but there's a lot of it on the table. While I'm fairly immune to its effects – back in the day, my once-legendary capacity enabled me to drink many an opposite number under the table in order to elicit state secrets – hopefully it'll help loosen a few tongues around here. 'Did you leave anything for everyone else?'

Albie shrugs. 'You snooze, you lose,' he says, popping a cocktail sausage roll into his mouth, then washing it down with a large gulp of wine.

'Keep drinking at that rate and snoozing is exactly what we'll be doing.'

'Best we get going, then,' says Albie.

'Quite,' I say, taking one of the plates, more for a prop than because any of the sausage-heavy fare appeals. 'Now remember, we need to find out if there's anyone here who'd benefit from Elsie's death – financially, I mean. So that means asking about her will. What happened to her house. That sort of thing.'

'Gotcha.'

'And do it subtly.'

'Subtly is my middle name,' says Albie, downing the remainder of his wine, then burping loudly before heading over and helping himself to a refill.

I shake my head as I watch him, though with a smile on my face. It feels good being on a mission again, especially with Albie. Just like old times. I suspect he feels the same. Not that he's likely to admit it.

As Albie strikes up a conversation with Yvette, who's perhaps understandably drinking at an even faster rate than he is, I circulate in the opposite direction to the buffet, exchanging the odd pleasantry in between mouthfuls of vol-au-vent, concentrating on the people who look genuinely upset, as they're the ones likely to have known Elsie better. Aside from one embarrassing incident, when one of the mourners seems to assume I'm a waiter, based on my attire, people seem happy to talk – something that increases the more depleted the bottles on the drinks table become. Though I'm three cups in myself and still haven't come up with a single lead when Albie almost crashes into me from behind.

'Sorry,' he says, nodding at his cup, which now looks suspiciously like it's full to the brim with whisky. 'Not used to drinking and driving.'

'How are you getting on?'

Albie shrugs. 'I reckon I've got a good couple of days' supply of sausage rolls,' he says, patting his now-bulging jacket pockets. 'But I'd stay away from the sandwiches if I were you. I still haven't identified the filling.' He stifles another burp. 'Even though it's doing its best to remind me on a regular basis.'

'And in terms of identifying anyone who might have a reason to want Elsie dead?' I say, doing my best to keep my voice level as I remind him why we're here.

'Eh? No. Nothing. Everyone here seems to have loved her. Not that you'd necessarily expect her killer to come to her funeral.'

'Unless they're trying to put us off the scent?'

Albie nods. 'Possibly. And Yvette seems genuinely shocked.'

'I think she felt her mum would go on and on.'

'A bit like you do, you mean?'

I take another sip of wine as I peer around the room. 'I just don't get it.'

'When you talk incessant—'

'No, Albie, I don't get what's going on here. From what people have told me, Elsie wasn't ill, her estate wasn't large enough for there to have been any feuds over it – and in any case, as the only child, it all goes to Yvette, who by the looks of this place doesn't seem to be desperate for the inheritance.'

'The euthanasia thing?'

'Not according to what Yvette told me the other day, about how Elsie was looking forward to her birthday.' I look up to the heavens for inspiration, but all that reveals is that Yvette's elaborate light fitting has a bulb out. 'There's got to be another explanation.'

'Yeah.' Albie thinks for a moment. 'Unless the explanation is that Elsie *wasn't* murdered.'

'You wouldn't be saying that if you'd seen the body, Albie,' I say, reluctant to entertain the fact that I'm wrong about this. 'And how else do you explain her death?'

'By saying that she just... died?'

'I just don't believe that. My instincts—'

Albie holds up his index finger. 'Martin, I'm sorry to break this to you, but we're getting old. And at our age, I'm afraid things certainly don't start improving. Our joints wear out. Some parts of our bodies stop working for no apparent reason. Our memory starts playing tricks on us. Who's to say that doesn't happen to our instincts too?'

I open my mouth to challenge him, then stop myself. He's got a point. But at the same time, I know what I saw, and I saw a murder victim. 'Maybe. Though I'll tell you one thing I've noticed that's a little strange.'

'What's that?'

'Despite making the effort to be here today, Nigel doesn't seem to be very popular.'

'Why do you say that?'

'He's hardly spoken to anyone. And no one seems keen to talk to him.'

'No one except for Yvette!' says Albie, drawing my attention to where the two of them are currently locked in what seems to be something of a heated discussion in the corner of the room. As quickly as I can, I grab Albie's wheelchair and push him across towards the altercation, stopping at the nearby buffet table where we can eavesdrop without suspicion.

'It just doesn't seem right!' Yvette says rather loudly, possibly due to a combination of grief and what appears to be her umpteenth glass of wine.

Nigel looks around awkwardly, evidently embarrassed at being the centre of a disturbance at a sombre occasion like this. 'I'm sorry, Mrs Rogers,' he says. 'But there's nothing I can do.'

'But Gemma said Mum might have *years...*'

'*Might*,' says Nigel, resting a placatory hand on Yvette's arm. 'It's not an exact science, especially when dealing with someone so elderly.'

'So there's no chance?'

Nigel shakes his head slowly, as if he's a surgeon delivering bad news following a lengthy yet unsuccessful operation. 'I'm afraid not. I did explain the risks to you at the time. It's all in the small print.'

Yvette shakes Nigel's hand off. 'Even so. It's just not fair!' she says, before stomping off towards the kitchen.

Sensing this is my moment, and with Nigel looking like he's about to make a hasty exit, I'm aware there's not a second to lose. 'Quick, Albie,' I say. 'You intercept Nigel, and I'll go and ask Yvette what that was all about.'

'How do I intercept...?'

'Use your initiative! This could be key to finding out who the murderer is!'

Albie peers up at me, then suddenly looks like he's seen a ghost, and it doesn't take long for me to work out why. Especially when from behind me, a voice that sounds suspiciously like Dionne's says crossly, 'You'll do no such thing!'

Though my stomach's just done a somersault – although that might be down to the vol-au-vents – I fix a smile on my face, turn around, and manage a sheepish, 'Hello, love!'

But Dionne's not having any of it. 'What's going on?'

'Nothing.'

'It doesn't look like nothing to me.'

'We're... Ow!' I reach down and rub my side, where Albie's just poked me. 'I mean, *I'm* just trying to find Elsie's killer. And Albie's been helping me.'

'Snitch!' hisses Albie.

'Have you been... *questioning* people?'

'I'd go with "interviewing".'

'At a *funeral*?'

'Technically we're now at the wake, so...'

'Right!' she says, confiscating Albie's whisky like a headmistress might seize a contraband packet of sweets from a naughty schoolboy. 'The two of you. Outside, now!'

While in the past we've talked our way out of the unlikeliest of situations with the odds massively against us, and although I've seen Albie face off the scariest of heavies, even he knows Dionne's not to be argued with. So outside is exactly where we go.

Now.

28

It's an awkward journey back to Twilight Lodge. Dionne's... well, 'seething' probably describes it best, particularly because she's 'wasted a rare afternoon off under false pretences' – a fact she's reminded me of three times during the first three minutes of the trip. And while she's polite enough to Albie, helping him into the car and carefully stowing his wheelchair in the boot, perhaps assuming he's been cajoled into all of this, the force with which she pulls the seatbelt tight around me before angrily clicking it into place suggests I'm not going to be allowed to forget this for a while.

'And it's not just me you lied to!' she says, as we head back past her old school. 'That poor lady. How you could have the cheek to go there, pretend to be mourning, even eat her food...?'

As Albie sits mutely in the back seat, perhaps reflecting on the afternoon's events, though more likely not wanting to upset the applecart further, I can't meet Dionne's eyes. Partly because she's not the best of drivers and I don't want to distract her, but also because it's actually worse than she thinks, given the egg mayonnaise rolls wrapped in a napkin and hidden in my jacket pockets that I appropriated on the way out, the smell of which appears to be making Custard drool.

'I'm just trying to get to the bottom of Elsie's murder.'

'*Death*, Dad. Elsie's death. In the absence of any hard evidence, that's all it is. And I don't see any hard evidence. Do you?'

'No, but that's only because we haven't found any yet!'

'Perhaps because there isn't any *to* find.'

I fold my arms petulantly as we stop at a pedestrian crossing, waiting for a couple of school children to cross, and when they seem in no particular hurry to get out of the road, Dionne angrily beeps her horn at them.

'What were you saying about your old pal?' I say, as the school children infinitesimally pick up the pace.

'What old pal?'

I blink a couple of times, the name escaping me for a moment, and turn to Albie for assistance, although he doesn't seem particularly keen to contribute. 'Whatsisname. Who did the thing.'

'I'll need a bit more to go on than that.'

'With your old school.'

'Tommy Walker?'

'That's the one. You said you knew there was something funny going on even though there was no proof. This is the same thing.'

Dionne sighs loudly. 'Dad, I'm a police officer. I've got experience in these things. You were a hotel inspector.' Albie snorts from the back seat, and Dionne gives him a look in the rear-view mirror. 'You don't.'

I open my mouth then close it again, fearful of upsetting Dionne even further by not only admitting again that I have been lying to her all her life, but that I've also been lying to her since I pretended I hadn't been lying. Then an alternative occurs to me. 'Actually, as a' – I clear my throat – '*hotel inspector*, you learn to notice things. Small details, which add up to a larger overall picture. Or when people are trying to pull the wool over your eyes. And that's what's going on here, which makes me think there's just something not right about all of this. Did you see those two people having an argument in the corner just now?'

'It's a funeral, Dad. People get upset.'

'Maybe so. But when the daughter of the deceased is furious with the owner of the nursing home where her mother's suddenly and unexpectedly died, you've got to wonder why.'

'Do you?'

'Yes!' I say, wondering why Dionne's not seeing this. 'You saw how shocked Yvette was by her mother's death. How angry she was with Nigel just now. You can't tell me there's not a small part of you that doesn't think I might be right.'

'You're right, Dad. There's not a small part. There's a whole big part that tells me you're seeing things where there's nothing *to* see.' Dionne stares ahead through the windscreen. 'People die. At all ages. And nine times out of ten, even though they might already be at death's door, it's still a shock. Look at Mum. Remember how we blamed her doctors when she eventually passed? How angry we were with them, even though it was nobody's fault? It's called "grieving" – or at least, it's part of the process.'

I swallow hard at the reminder of my wife's untimely passing, and though it may mean disregarding one of the few leads we've got, I have to concede Dionne might be right. Back then it was all I could do not to take my anger out on Madeleine's whole medical team – which with my particular set of skills wouldn't have been pretty. 'But three deaths in...' I pat my pockets in an attempt to locate my notebook, but all I can feel is the telltale bulge of the food I've appropriated. Mouthing a silent prayer that the egg rolls are still protected by the napkin –

otherwise this jacket's going straight to the dry cleaner's – I look to Albie for assistance.

'Nine days,' he says.

'Nine days! You hear that? That's ten per cent of Twilight Lodge's residents. And in less than two weeks.' I swivel round in my seat so I can make my point more forcefully, a task made more difficult with Custard on my lap. 'Remember when I asked you to bring me those figures for the Twilight Lodge death averages? Eleven per cent, you said. In a home this size, that means around three per year. We've had three this *month*!'

As Custard sighs loudly, perhaps with frustration at being unable to locate the source of the food smells, Dionne does the same. 'That's how averages work, Dad. Maybe you've just had your year's allocation already.'

'Unlikely,' I say, as I've been reading up on this courtesy of the home's computer. 'Deaths do sometimes spike in nursing homes, but that's usually just during the winter with all the associated illnesses and so on, and right now we're in the middle of summer.' I glance through the windscreen and up at the sky. It looks like the heavens are about to open, which I hope isn't some kind of omen. 'Compare it to the figures from previous years. Not to mention the national average, which is...' I frown again, but I don't need to look round at the back seat this time.

'Ten per cent,' says Albie. 'And not that I've been paying attention, but I think if you ask, you'll find these three aren't the first deaths we've had this year.'

Dionne stiffens her grip on the steering wheel, and for the first time, I detect the slightest hesitation in her response. 'This might all just be happening together by chance. Coincidence.'

'That's too much of a coincidence, if you ask me.'

'Well, I didn't ask you,' says Dionne, as she turns onto the seafront road. 'You need to promise me you're going to drop this.'

I can't meet her gaze. And I can't lie to Dionne. But at the same time, I'm conscious I've only a couple of weeks left at Twilight Lodge to find out what's going on, and I can't afford to take my foot off the accelerator.

As Dionne steers the car back through Twilight Lodge's gates, I let out a weary sigh. 'How can we prove it to you?'

'I don't know,' she says, shaking her head slowly. And then, as if she's thinking out loud, 'Perhaps if there was another death. But even then...'

She stops talking and narrows her eyes towards the front of the building. When I turn my head, I can see what's caught her attention. It's an ambulance, although its lights aren't flashing, and there's a reason for that.

Because parked behind it is a small white van with blacked-out windows, and it's unmarked. So as not to attract attention, I suppose.

Since it's the kind of van undertakers use to take bodies away.

29

I've never seen Albie move this fast – or at least, not since I was pursuing him along a beach while dodging gunfire a good fifty years ago. And he's moving *so* fast that while Dionne's just managing to keep up with his frantic wheeling, despite the recent progress I've made in terms of my new hip, I'm a good thirty seconds behind him by the time I get in through the front door. The reception desk's unmanned, which only serves to increase Albie's agitation, and when a flustered-looking Miriam appears at speed from the direction of Gemma's office, I'm convinced he's going to launch himself from his chair and rugby tackle her to the floor.

'What's happened?' he calls desperately, and Miriam almost skids to a halt.

'I'm afraid another of the residents has... passed,' she says.

'Oh dear.' I rest a reassuring hand on Albie's shoulder, which he doesn't immediately shake off. 'Who was it?' I ask, just managing to keep the words 'this' and 'time' from escaping my lips.

Miriam looks from Albie to me, then at Dionne, then me again, as if she's about to share some classified information. 'Mr

Faulkner,' she says, before our blank expressions prompt her to add, 'Stanley?'

There's a not-so-muffled 'Yes!' from Albie, who's evidently relieved by both the fact that Barbara's not the latest victim and that his rival for her affections – not to mention his potential assassin – is now out of the picture.

As Miriam looks at him strangely, I pretend to be confused, though it's only so I can deflect her attention from Albie's celebration. 'Remind me who he was again?' I say. 'Only it's hard to remember who's who, sometimes. At our age.'

Miriam's expression softens as she turns her attention back to me. 'Sorry. Yes. It must be a bit confusing. Room Six?'

'Which is where?' I say, though I already know the answer.

Miriam points towards the far end of the corridor. 'At the front. Philip went to get him when he hadn't appeared for lunch and found him slumped in his chair.' She makes a face. 'Not the nicest way to begin your shift.'

'Room Six – that would be one of the Premium rooms?' I say. 'With a sea view.'

'That's right,' says Miriam. 'Why?'

'Just checking,' I say, though I don't let on what exactly it is I'm checking. 'Thank you, Miriam.'

Miriam stands there for a moment, then perhaps realises she's been dismissed, and as she heads off to do whatever it was we interrupted, Dionne gives me a look.

'Well, *that* was tactful,' she says.

'Pardon?'

'They haven't even removed that poor man's body yet, and you've already got dibs on waking up to a better view!'

'It's not that,' I say.

'Well, what is it then?' says Dionne, looking and sounding very much like she's reached the end of her tether with my behaviour.

'We're just trying to establish if there's a pattern.'

'A pattern?'

'With the deaths,' I say.

'I didn't think you meant "knitting",' says Dionne, sitting down on the sofa next to the desk. 'But – and I can't believe I'm asking this – is there?'

I lower myself into the adjacent armchair, then glance across at Albie, though he shakes his head almost imperceptibly, as if to suggest now isn't the right time to share our 'sea view' theory. 'We're not sure.'

'Yet,' says Albie.

'Although there must be, or at least some kind of link, given how they've all happened in such a short space of time. We just don't know what it is.'

'Yet,' repeats Albie.

Dionne leans back in her seat, looking like she's not buying any of this, a fact borne out when she says, 'I'm sorry, I just don't buy any of this.'

'But you must admit, four deaths in a little over a fortnight is a bit suspicious.'

She shrugs dismissively. 'Or like I said in the car, coincidental. Besides, why on earth would someone want to kill them?'

'We haven't worked that out.'

Albie leans forward, then raises his index finger. 'Yet.'

'Okay, then. *Who* would want to kill them?'

'Same answer,' I say, hoping Albie's not going to add yet another 'yet'. 'At first, we thought it might be Shane, but then they fired him, and subsequently there was another death.'

'Today,' says Albie.

'Which kind of rules Shane out as a suspect.'

Albie nods. 'Plus, he wasn't working when any of the other three died. We checked.'

Dionne rolls her eyes. 'I won't ask how you found *that* out.'

'Then we wondered if it was Stanley.'

'The one who's just died?' Dionne puffs air out of her cheeks. 'Why ever would you think that?'

'Because the murders began just after he arrived.'

Albie clears his throat awkwardly. 'And because he threatened to kill *me*,' he says.

'What?' Dionne looks shocked. 'Why?'

'Over a woman,' I say, grinning as Albie turns a deep shade of red. 'But unless he's just killed himself in a fit of remorse provoked by Elsie's funeral, I think we can remove him from our list too.'

Dionne widens her eyes in disbelief. 'You've got a *list*?'

'A short list,' I say, not wanting to admit there are only two other names on it, and certainly not wanting to tell Dionne who they are until we've got some actual proof – or at least, a stronger theory to base our accusations on. 'We hoped we might narrow it down a bit at Elsie's funeral.'

'But you came away empty-handed?'

'Not entirely,' says Albie, though I'm assuming he's referring to his plundered party food.

'Come on, love,' I say. 'You said yourself as we drove in that if there was another death, and...' I stop talking, interrupted by a noise from the far end of the corridor. A moment later, as if on cue, two gentlemen in grey suits appear, wheeling a trolley that can only contain one cargo – Stanley, I imagine – encased in a body bag. Dionne stares at it as it passes, then side-eyes me, and although I don't like to say 'Ta-da!' given the subject matter, Albie evidently has no qualms.

'Ta-da!' he says.

I don't volunteer anything further, though to my surprise, Dionne seems unmoved. 'I said *perhaps* if there was another death,' she whispers, as Stanley's entourage heads out through the entrance. 'In any case, I'm sure these things are monitored. There must be checks that would flag up anything untoward.' She sighs, then takes my hand. 'Whatever you imagine might be going on here, that's all it is. Your imagination. Just like the other day when we had that little chat with Gemma about you believing you used to be, you know...?'

'What?' says Albie, mischievously.

Dionne looks me up and down, perhaps realising how what she's about to say chimes with the fact that I'm dressed in a tuxedo. 'Dad thinks...'

'*Thought*,' I correct.

'Sorry. Dad *thought* he used to be a... well, you know, a *spy*.'

'*No!*' says Albie, looking at me incredulously, and – in a piece of what's perhaps the worst acting I've ever seen – trying to appear as if it's the first time he's heard this particular snippet.

'And this is the same thing,' she says, turning her attention back to me. 'This is St Leonards-on-Sea, Dad. We don't have a serial killer on the loose. And certainly not one with' – she lets go of my hand and gestures vaguely in the air – '*you lot* in their sights.'

Dionne looks like she's slightly disappointed by her own opinion, and I understand her frustration. From her point of view, this is the kind of case that can make a career, which is another reason for us to catch the killer – or rather, unmask the killer, so *Dionne* can catch them. So again, I do the only thing I can do, which is make a suitably doolally face, then reach over and pat her on the knee.

'Whatever you say, love.'

'So you'll leave it alone?' she asks, and I smile archly.

'Scout's honour,' I say.

But as I may have already pointed out, I was never *in* the Scouts.

30

———

It's the following afternoon, and Albie and I are sitting in the Garden Lounge, half-heartedly doing a jigsaw as cover while we discuss the latest developments. It's a seascape, and fiendishly difficult, with the sea so undecipherable from the sky, Albie's resorted to hammering unmatched pieces together with his fist. And though I'm trying to ignore it, I can't help thinking that's a metaphor for our efforts in trying to solve these murders.

'So, Shane's not our man, then?' I say, preparing to cross his name off from the list in my notebook. Despite my promise to Dionne to leave it alone, I've resolved to do anything but, and Albie's on board with that, given the particular living arrangements of his intended squeeze.

Albie shakes his head. 'I suppose not, seeing as you probably have to be present to actually kill someone, and he's not allowed in the building any longer.'

'True,' I say, drawing a deliberate line through Shane's name. 'This is progress, Albie. Firstly, eliminating Shane from our list of suspects, then Stanley being eliminated too, in both senses of the word.'

Albie lowers his voice. 'We're sure Stanley was murdered?'

'He must have been. He certainly didn't look like he was on his last legs on Sunday, either when he was dancing with Barbara or when he threatened to kill you.'

Albie makes a face. 'Don't remind me. Of either of those things.'

'Though of course that makes you a suspect. Attack is the best form of defence, and all that. Getting your revenge in first...'

Albie gives me a look. 'Except I was with you when he was killed.'

'I'm kidding, Albie,' I say, randomly picking from the box a jigsaw piece that's an identical colour to about half of the other nine hundred and ninety-nine pieces, and placing it down on the table.

Albie studies the piece, then flips it a hundred and eighty degrees. To my eye it looks the same either way up. 'And we're not suspecting any of the other carers?'

'Such as?'

'Have you still got the rota?'

I check the coast is clear as I extract the previously purloined rota from where I've secreted it inside my shirt. 'Here,' I say, presenting it as if it's a classified document.

'Well, George died on the second,' says Albie, pointing a gnarled finger at the relevant section. 'Diana on the seventh. Elsie on the eleventh. Factor in Stanley yesterday, and it could have been any of them, either alone or working together.'

'Especially if you consider they might not have been there at the death.'

'Huh?'

'We're assuming they killed them there and then. They could have used other methods – poison, for example – that might not have taken effect until the perpetrator was long gone, thus leaving them in the clear.' I wave the rota in the air. 'At least as far as this is concerned.'

'Are any of them even capable of murder?' Albie consults the rota again. 'Philip, for example? He's the one who apparently found Stanley's body.'

'I can't even get him to take Dionne out, so it's unlikely he'd be able to take anyone else out, if you see what—'

Albie shuts me up with a long-suffering look. 'Miriam?'

'Too nice.'

'Joy?'

'She's the only one who was working every day a murder took place, but could you picture her killing anyone?'

Albie thinks for a minute, evidently trying his best to do exactly that, then shakes his head. 'I just can't see it.'

I take a sip of tea as I run through the others in my head, from Gemma to Marie the cleaner, even the nice young chap – Baz, I think he's called, or it could be Gaz – who drives the minibus, though decide to discount them all. And not just because I can't be sure of their names. 'Nor can I. With any of them.'

'Doesn't mean they didn't do it. Although what on earth would their motive be?'

I sigh dejectedly. 'I've no idea, Albie. And thinking about it, I can't see any of them teaming up on this. After all, what are the chances of more than one homicidal maniac – which is what you're going to have to be to murder someone of our age, and then do it again and again – getting jobs at the same nursing home?'

'Probably quite low.'

'Agreed.'

Albie scratches his head. 'What about Tommy Walker?'

'The builder?'

'That's the one.'

I retrieve my notebook and flick through to my most recent set of notes. 'Well, we still don't know what he was really doing in Elsie's room the day after she was killed. And where was he going in such a hurry when we saw him on our way to the funeral?'

'Off to commit murder while the coast was clear, perhaps?'

'When Nigel conveniently wasn't at Twilight Lodge. And in fact, had several witnesses to prove it.'

'True,' says Albie.

'But what's his connection to this whole sorry affair?'

'Like we said yesterday – he makes money from buying old buildings and converting them into flats.'

'So the question is...?'

'Is he looking to do the same thing he did with Dionne's old school to Twilight Lodge?'

'There's only one way to find out,' I say, randomly selecting another apparently identical jigsaw piece from the box and placing it on the table next to the first one.

'Whaddaya know?' says Albie, triumphantly slotting the two together. 'It fits!'

And though I don't really believe in omens, I have to think this might just be a good one.

31

The Garden Lounge is packed to the gills this morning. It's almost as if Ol' Blue Eyes himself has turned up and word's got round, rather than Miriam merely playing the *Simply Sinatra* CD from the *Karaoke Klassics* collection at full volume. Either way, there's not a seat that isn't occupied by a smiling, singing-at-the-top-of-their-voice pensioner – myself and Albie included, a radiant Barbara sitting next to him – conducted enthusiastically by Miriam and Philip at the front.

Of course, it could also be that people are worried about the recent deaths and seeking safety in numbers, like wildebeest herding together on the Serengeti whenever a pride of lions approaches, but whatever the reason, it's perfect – both in terms of cover to ensure I can execute my plan to question Tommy Walker, and so neither Albie nor I will be missed.

I've told him to locate himself as close to the door as possible, and when the time comes – Miriam having her usual trouble with the harsh feedback whistle between the wireless karaoke microphone and the speaker, so all her attention is on that – I grab his wheelchair by the handles and, resisting the temptation to chorus-line kick in time to the music, surreptitiously reverse him from the room.

Once we're safely in the corridor, Albie reaches up and switches his hearing aids back on – evidently Barbara is perfect in every way except 'pitch' – then he swivels round and frowns at me. 'You're not planning to push me all the way there?'

'Nothing like that,' I say, steering him out into the garden, checking the coast is clear, then darting along the side of the building. It's a sunny day, providing us plenty of opportunities to hide in the shadows cast by the trees as I sneak us towards my goal: the Twilight Lodge minibus. Though once we reach it, Albie's jaw drops open.

'You're not serious?'

'Why not?'

'This is stealing!'

'We're only going to borrow it, so no, it isn't.'

'Yes, it is! They'll throw me out. Or into prison.'

'Don't you mean *back* into prison?'

Albie glares at me. 'Martin, for the *billionth* time...'

'Relax. They'll never notice we're gone. And even if they do, and raise a fuss, I'll just draw their attention to the brochure.'

'What brochure?'

'The Twilight Lodge one.'

'Got it on you, have you?'

'Well, no. But I distinctly remember it mentioning a minibus for residents' use. Or something along those lines.'

'You *distinctly* remember?'

'Distinctly enough to know it's open to interpretation. And like I said, it's only stealing if we don't bring it back.'

'*We?* Don't expect me to drive! *Or* take the blame.'

'All right – if they catch us, I'll tell them I kidnapped you. Which won't be the first time. Happy?'

Albie appears anything but. 'Are you planning to hotwire it?'

'No need.' I wheel him round to the driver's door, pull it open, and indicate the key, which is conveniently already sitting in the ignition. 'It's just like the staffroom door lock code. They don't think anyone's going to steal... I mean, *borrow* it. Now are you coming or not?'

Albie looks at me as if 'not' is his preferred option, though I choose to ignore this. Instead, I wheel him round to the rear of the vehicle, throw the doors open, lower the ramp, and – though it requires a bit of a run-up to give me the necessary momentum, which tests my new hip somewhat more than Olga's physio has – propel his wheelchair up and into the back.

'When was the last time you drove?' Albie asks, securing his chair extra carefully as I clamber up into the driving seat. I have to think for a moment, then for a moment longer when I realise I can't be sure of the answer, which I suppose is an answer in itself.

'That's on a need-to-know basis.'

Albie opens his mouth to say something, then closes it again, as if, while he might need to know, he's suddenly decided he'd be better off without. Before he can change his mind and unbelt himself, I do my best to ignore how tightly he appears to be holding on already and fasten my own seatbelt.

'Shall we?' I say, more confidently than I feel, but when I consider some of the vehicles a person with my background is supposed to be able to jump into and drive *just like that* – a JCB digger, for example, or a Russian T-72 tank, or even an invisible car (and how on earth you're supposed to parallel park something like *that* is beyond me) – I wonder how difficult a Ford Transit minibus can be. Though the answer to that question soon proves to be 'quite', as when I adjust the mirrors, then turn the key in the ignition, nothing happens.

'What's wrong?' pipes up Albie, as I tut loudly.

'I'm not sure,' I say, trying the key again. 'It won't start.'

'Oh well.' Albie reaches down to unbuckle himself, and I glare at him in the mirror.

'Not so fast.'

Albie sighs resignedly. 'Fine,' he says, refastening his seatbelt. 'Maybe it's one of those vehicles where you need to depress one of the pedals first.'

I frown down at the footwell. 'How is making any of them feel miserable going to make a difference?' I say, then look round at him and raise both eyebrows, but my joke seems to have fallen as flat as I'm hoping the minibus's battery isn't.

'I'm serious!'

'Fine! Which one's the clutch pedal again?'

'The one on the left!' says Albie, sounding a little more anxious.

'There are three.'

'Three what?'

'Pedals. Which means there are two on the left.'

'So go for the left one of those.'

'Will do. And the left is...?'

I look at him again, though it's evident Albie's not finding my attempts to put him at ease amusing, so instead I try his suggestion, and to my relief, the engine roars into life. Hoping that everyone inside will be too involved in – or deafened by – the singalong to notice, I gun the throttle a couple of times, and when the engine doesn't die, move the gear lever to where I hope first must be. Then – though it's hard to resist the temptation to floor it – I steer the minibus slowly across the gravel drive and head out through the gates.

32

———

Cautiously, I check the mirror. Nobody's following us, which is a good sign – particularly since after a quick perusal of the dashboard buttons and switches, I can't see a toggle marked 'rear flame-thrower' anywhere. Nor has anyone come running out through reception to see what's going on.

'Right,' I say, as I begin retracing our trip with Dionne from the other day as best as I can remember. 'By my calculations, the singalong finishes at eleven, which means we've got' – I peer at the various displays and dials on the dashboard and – unless we happen to be travelling at ten miles per hour – locate what I assume is the clock – 'an hour to get to Tommy Walker's office, grill him, and deliver the minibus back.'

'Assuming he's there.'

'You'd better hope he is,' I say, pulling up at the last second at a red traffic light. 'Otherwise, we're going to have to break in.'

Albie looks horrified. 'And do what?'

'Look for evidence?'

'What kind of evidence?'

'Proof he's planning to redevelop Twilight Lodge.'

'Like what?'

I think for a moment. 'I'm sure we'll know it when we see it,' I say, though in truth, short of some sort of correspondence saying exactly that, or even a set of building plans, I'm not sure what the evidence might look like.

My musings are interrupted by a frantic beeping from the car behind us, and Albie digs me in the shoulder blade, then indicates the lights have changed with a sarcastic, 'What shade of green were you waiting for?' so I set off again, and we head along the seafront road in silence for a while, Albie probably not wanting to distract me while I'm concentrating. Though it's been a while, I do my best to drive as smoothly as possible, in particular ensuring I keep to the speed limit to avoid attracting attention. If we're stopped by the police, while informing the officer that my daughter's one of them will probably get me off any speeding charge, Dionne finding out what we're doing will probably have worse consequences for me than any fine or points on my licence.

Eventually, we reach Dionne's old school, and not without some relief, I pilot the minibus through the gates. 'We're in luck!' I say, nodding towards the matte-grey Range Rover parked in front of the sales office. 'He's here. Or at least his car is.'

'Oh, goody,' says Albie, unenthusiastically.

'Now when we get in there, just follow my lead.'

'Do I have a choice?'

'We always have a choice, Albie. Free will is what separates us from the rest of the animal kingdom.'

'I thought it was opposable thumbs?'

'Maybe it is,' I say, not wanting to get into a debate right now, mainly as I've got more important things to concentrate on. Like trying to reverse park the minibus in the space next to Tommy's car without denting either vehicle, which means I have to come out again and perform a three-point turn – though it turns into more of a nine-point turn when I forget I need to leave enough space at the back for the ramp. Getting Albie out proves a little more difficult, and though I suggest it'd be easier to just position him at the top of the ramp, line it up with the door and let him go, Albie refuses to release his brakes until I promise I'll wheel him carefully down.

'Ready?' I say, once we're standing outside the office.

'S'pose.'

'Just like old times, eh?'

'If you say so, Martin,' says Albie resignedly. 'What's our cover story?'

'Leave that to me,' I say, as I fix a smile on my face and steer him towards the door – mainly because I'm planning to come up with one on the hoof, depending on what we encounter. I take a couple of deep breaths and exhale loudly. 'Do you feel that?'

'Feel what?' says Albie suspiciously.

'Your heart beating? The adrenaline coursing through your veins? It's called being *alive*, Albie. And it feels good, doesn't it?'

'Better than being dead, I suppose.'

'That's the spirit,' I say, wondering if this is what's known as a 'breakthrough'.

And though it may not be much of one, I'll absolutely take it.

33

The moment I open the door, my training kicks in, and I take in my surroundings, careful to note escape routes and anything I can use as a weapon if things turn nasty. There's a girl sitting at a desk with a phone and a laptop computer in front of her – a computer I might have to ask Albie to purloin if Tommy's not around. In the corner, there's one of those large drinking fountains with an upside-down bottle of water on the top – potentially an item I can upend if I need to spoil a foot chase. Next to it, there's a gleaming coffee machine sporting so many knobs and dials it looks like it's been designed by NASA for a moon landing, something that – before I've even said a word – Albie makes a beeline for.

'These free, are they?' he says, helping himself to a mug, and the girl stares at him for a moment, then nods mutely. She looks about sixteen years old, which means my intended charm offensive will probably come off as simply offensive, so instead, I go for 'friendly'.

'The boss around?' I ask, in as amiable a tone as I can muster.

The girl drags her eyes away from where Albie's randomly

jabbing buttons on the coffee machine, then glances over her shoulder towards a separate office, the door to which is firmly shut. 'Do you have an appointment?'

'Do we need one?'

The girl looks confused. 'I'm... not sure.'

'Okay then,' I say, and there's something of a standoff for a moment or two, punctuated by Albie's triumphant 'Yes!' followed by the sound of coffee pouring into his mug, though fortunately it's ended by Tommy Walker emerging from his office. When he sees Albie and me, he does a double take.

'Christ – debt collectors are getting older and older!' Tommy grins at me, then he frowns. 'Hang on – you two look familiar?'

It's not strictly a question, but it sounds like one, so I decide to take his lead. 'We met the other day,' I say. 'At Twilight Lodge.'

If the mention of the scene of his crimes registers with Tommy's guilty conscience, he does a good job of hiding any reaction. 'Oh yeah,' he says. 'What can I do you for?'

'For you.'

'What?'

'It's "What can I do for you?". Not "do you for". What you said sounds like you've got something nefarious in mind.'

Tommy scratches his head. 'Eh?'

'You are Tommy Walker, I presume?'

'Guilty as charged!' Tommy holds both hands up, as if I've got a gun pointed at him, and for the second time in a week, I miss my firearm – he's a sizeable fellow, and I'm not sure I could take him at my age, even with whatever help Albie can give me.

Tommy peers out through the Portakabin window and notices the minibus, though I've parked it especially to obscure the TWILIGHT LODGE logo on the side. 'You on your own, are you?'

'As opposed to?' growls Albie.

'All right,' says Tommy, in a 'keep your hair on' tone. 'How can I help you gents?'

'Well, I was wondering...' I say, and Albie grunts, then takes a sip of coffee, so I start again. '*We* were wondering. About these flats of yours.'

'What about them?'

'We might be interested in buying one.'

'You? As in...' Tommy nods at us both in succession. 'Both of you?'

'That's right.'

'So, two flats?'

'No. Just the one.'

'But don't you both live at...?'

'Twilight Lodge?'

'More's the pity,' mumbles Albie, who's searching the area by the coffee machine, and if I know him, it'll be for biscuits rather than clues to Tommy Walker's involvement with the murders.

'We do. I mean, *he* does. I'm only there temporarily. New hip, you see...' I tap the right side of my pelvis, happy I've remembered correctly, then decide Tommy doesn't need my life story. 'But the flat's, um...'

'For his daughter,' says Albie, wheeling himself over to join us, his coffee balanced precariously between his knees. As he picks it up and takes another sip, I rest a hand on his shoulder.

'*Our* daughter,' I say, unable to think of another reason to be bringing Albie along.

As Albie almost drops his mug in shock, Tommy widens his eyes. 'Right!' he says. 'Good for you!' and Albie glowers at him.

'What's that supposed to mean?'

'Nothing.' Tommy stuffs his hands in his pockets self-consciously. 'Anyway, if it's a flat you're after, you've come to the right place.'

'Actually, we haven't,' I say.

'Huh?'

'Like I said. It's for my... I mean, *our* daughter. Trouble is, she went to school here. Didn't have the best of times. Got a bit bullied, you know how it is. Albie here wanted to come down and sort them out, but there are laws against that sort of thing... Anyway, that's another story. My point is, for her to come and live here might be a bit...'

I let my voice tail off, and Tommy's face falls. 'Triggering?'

'I'm afraid so.'

'You're sure?' Tommy sniffs. 'These flats are very popular. I could have sold the penthouse five times over.'

'Wouldn't that be illegal?' suggests Albie.

'That's not what I...' Tommy points at him, then winks. 'Good one,' he says.

'Anyway,' I say, trying to bring the conversation back to the matter at hand. 'For that reason, unfortunately, it's a "no" from us for anything in this particular development.'

Tommy shrugs. 'Say no more,' he says, and Albie looks at me as if he also wishes I wouldn't. But we're at crunch time, and I can't wimp out now.

I take a deep breath. 'So, I was wondering if you had anything else. Or rather, any*where* else. You know, in the pipeline?'

Tommy narrows his eyes, looks from me to Albie, then back to me again, then he smiles flatly. 'I'm sorry. Not right now, no.'

'Oh,' I say, feeling like I've just been punched in the stomach. If Tommy's not redeveloping Twilight Lodge, then he'll have to be crossed off my suspect list, as probably will be Nigel, which leaves me not only without a carrot with which to tempt Dionne to get involved, but also another theory that's gone out of the window. Not to mention a suspect list that features, well, *no one*. 'You're sure?'

'Sorry,' says Tommy. 'Not if you aren't interested in something here.'

'We're not,' says Albie, glancing at the coffee machine again, perhaps wondering whether he's got time to go and make himself another. Although Tommy puts paid to even that when he steps across to the door and pointedly hauls it open.

'I'm sorry you've had a wasted journey,' he says.

'Me too,' I say, a little stunned by this latest twist, and it's all I can do to grab Albie's wheelchair by the handles and aim for the doorway. But before I get there, Albie slaps one of his brakes on and spins round.

'Don't worry, erm, *Marty*,' he says, addressing me, but loudly enough so Tommy can hear. 'We'll just have to take our million quid and see what else is available.'

I'm a little shocked – not at Albie's genius brainwave, but by the fact he's addressed me just like he used to back in the day – but not as shocked as Tommy Walker. As if someone's just switched him off and on again, Tommy freezes, then hurriedly shuts the door before we can make our escape. 'You know what, gents?' he says, in a much more respectful tone than a few moments ago. 'This might just be your lucky day.'

'How so?' I say.

'How soon did you need somewhere?'

'No rush,' says Albie, perhaps assuming it'll take a while before Twilight Lodge can be redeveloped, though I don't want to let Tommy off the hook.

'Actually, there is a bit of a rush,' I say. 'Seeing as we're not getting any younger.'

'Right. Well, between you and me...' Tommy taps a finger to the side of his nose conspiratorially, then he lowers his voice. 'There is one... *project* I'm working on right now that might be right up your street.'

I catch my breath. If it's Twilight Lodge he's referring to, then it couldn't *be* more up our street. Certain he's got our full attention, and perhaps dazzled by pound signs, Tommy beams at the two of us. 'Lovely old building. Sea views, too.'

Albie and I exchange glances. 'Sea views, was that?' I say, and Tommy does a good impression of those nodding dogs you used to see on the rear parcel shelves of cars.

'Oh yeah. To die for!'

Albie swallows so loudly I'm sure everyone in the Portakabin can hear it. 'And where is this, exactly?' he says.

'I'm not at liberty to say,' says Tommy. 'But it's not a million miles from here.'

'How many miles, exactly?' I ask, knowing it's something I can check via the minibus's odometer on the way home, but Tommy purses his lips.

'I can't tell you any more than that right now,' he says. 'But suffice to say, you won't be disappointed.'

'*She* won't be disappointed,' I say.

'What?'

'My daughter.'

Albie reaches up and gives my hand a squeeze. '*Our* daughter, Marty.'

'Oh. Yeah.' Tommy grins. '*Your* daughter.'

'And when do you think the apartment might be available?' I say, gently but firmly removing my hand from Albie's.

Tommy shrugs. 'Hard to say. It's just, the deal's not quite done yet. So I can't go into detail. Don't want someone coming in and pinching it from right under my nose. You know how it is.'

I nod. 'When might you be able to give us some more information, do you think?'

Tommy looks at his watch for some reason, though whether that's because the deal is imminent or we're keeping him from something, I'm not sure. 'Shouldn't be too long,' he says. 'There are just a few... obstacles I have to deal with before I can sign on the dotted line. But if you wanted to give Britney here your details?'

The girl at the desk – Britney, I'm guessing – looks up from where she's been engrossed in something on her mobile. 'Whassat?' she says, and Tommy rolls his eyes.

'You can get hold of us at Twilight Lodge. But don't worry,' I say, collecting a business card from Britney's desk before Albie and I head out of the Portakabin. 'We've got your number.'

34

Because that statement might well be true, I shush Albie as I load him back into the minibus, pretty sure Tommy's watching us from inside. It's only once we're driving back along the seafront that I feel confident to broach the subject. But not before I've dealt with something else.

'*Marty*?' I shake my head. 'Really, Albie?'

'You told me to follow your lead.'

'*That's* where it came from?'

'Where else?' says Albie, crossly. 'In character, wasn't I?'

I'm a little disappointed Albie still can't remember anything about our former lives, or at least, still won't admit to remembering anything, though the fact our meeting with Tommy Walker couldn't have gone any better mitigates that somewhat. 'That went well, then?'

I can feel Albie's eyes drilling into the back of my head. 'Are you being sarcastic?'

'Not at all! He as good as admitted that he's going to be turning Twilight Lodge into flats. Expensive ones – and with sea views! And those "obstacles" he's got to deal with first...'

'Us?'

'Exactly.'

Albie doesn't say anything for a moment, then he clears his throat. 'Don't you think it's a little far-fetched to be murdering the occupants of a building you don't already own?'

'Not if that's part of the deal. After all, he set fire to the school, and he didn't own that.'

'Arson's different. This is murder we're talking about. Cold-blooded and systematic. Like I said the other day, setting fire to Twilight Lodge would be easier. Get rid of all the "obstacles" in one full sweep.'

'Maybe he wants the building as intact as possible. Why give yourself extra construction work and therefore additional costs if you don't have to? And by the way, it's "fell swoop".'

'What is?'

'You said "full sweep". It's "fell swoop".'

'Don't be ridiculous!'

'I'm not being ridiculous.'

'Yes you are!' spits Albie.

'Okay, clever clogs. What is a "full sweep", exactly?'

'It's where you do everything in one go, like a sweep...' Albie makes an appropriate gesture with his hand, grand enough that I can see it in the rear-view mirror. 'And because you've done everything, it's a full one.'

'Don't you mean "clean sweep"?'

'No!' says Albie, testily. 'Well, yes. That as well.'

'So why didn't you say that?'

'Because the phrase is "full sweep".'

'No, it *isn't!*' I insist. 'It's f-e-l-l. And "swoop". Like a bird might.'

'Why isn't it "fowl swoop", then?'

'Well, because...' I give him a look over my shoulder, wondering whether to concede he might have a point, and Albie rolls his eyes, and I grin, and we both already know we've moved past our disagreement. This used to happen a lot in the field – when you're on surveillance duties, usually stuck in cramped quarters, sometimes for days, and quite possibly without access to proper sanitary facilities, even the lightest of remarks or most innocuous of habits can become the most ridiculously frustrating annoyances. But you just can't let these things get to you, especially when you're on an important mission. And both armed.

Surreptitiously, I glance at Albie in the rear-view mirror, happy to see what's almost a smile on his face. 'So Tommy Walker's a suspect?'

'He's got the motive. He also seems like the kind of person who'd sell his own grandmother.'

'So it's entirely possible he'd have no qualms about killing someone else's?'

Albie nods. 'And the fact that Nigel isn't re-letting the rooms, but instead he's getting Tommy to refurbish them, thus maybe giving him a head start on his renovations...?'

'... suggests Nigel's in on it.'

'Probably.'

'Or at least, possibly,' I say, then I frown. 'Although one thing puzzles me. If you were Tommy Walker, why do the dirty work yourself? Why not just get Nigel to arrange it?'

'Good question,' says Albie. Which is a good answer, if you don't know the *actual* answer.

'So, how are we going to prove any of this, Albie? Because at the moment all we've got is a theory, and two suspects who appear to be excellent at covering their tracks.'

'Maybe we just wait. See if one of them slips up. And then...' There's a pause, possibly because he's just mimed pouncing – though I'm concentrating too hard on driving to look – then Albie says, 'Pounce!'

'You mean wait until someone else gets murdered?'

'Maybe.'

'But that means someone else has to get murdered.'

'Collateral damage, isn't it?'

'It might be Barbara,' I remind him, then glance up at the rear-view mirror again, noting how white he's suddenly gone. 'Perhaps she could do with some protection in the meantime.'

'What are you inferring?' says Albie gruffly.

'Just that perhaps you should be keeping a closer eye on her.' I check the rear-view mirror a third time. Albie's just-whitened complexion has now turned a shade of red. 'And speaking of keeping an eye on people, have you ever heard of the observer effect?'

Albie sighs. 'I might regret this, but I'm going to say "no".'

'It's a thing in physics. I learned about it from one of the Royal Institution Christmas Lectures I used to watch on the BBC with Dionne when she was growing up... Anyway, that's not important. Essentially, it's where the act of observing something influences whatever it is you're observing. Like when you use a thermometer to take someone's temperature, the material in the thermometer has to absorb some thermal energy to get a reading, and therefore changes the temperature of the body it's measuring.'

'And your point is?'

'What we need to do is let the murderer know someone's on to them,' I say. 'Then hope the *effect* of that is that they'll make a mistake. Or even crack.'

'How on earth do we do that without putting ourselves in danger? Not to mention the fact that we're not actually sure who the murderer is.'

I flick the indicator and steer the minibus back in through Twilight Lodge's gate, happy I've got it – and us – back home without a scratch. According to the clock on the dashboard, the singalong's due to finish in five minutes – just enough time to park the minibus where we found it and get back inside before we're missed.

'You leave that to me, Albie,' I say.

And not for the first time, Albie seems happy to do exactly that.

35

———

It's the following day, and I'm making the short walk from Twilight Lodge to Hastings police station. In stark contrast to yesterday, it looks like it might rain, plus the wind's a little stronger than an old man with a new hip might want to have to battle for very long. To cover my tracks, I've slipped out via the garden rather than arouse any suspicions by marching out through reception or telling anyone where I'm going, though I have left a note on my bedside table saying I've gone for a 'recuperative walk' in case they decide to send out a search party.

The police station's a concrete monstrosity, reminiscent of the kind they used to put up in the fifties in East Berlin – a place I know all too well from numerous missions, or what I referred to as 'work trips' – and located next to the equally ugly magistrate's court, which I suppose makes for efficient prisoner processing. Parked outside are so many police vans and squad cars that even if I wasn't a highly trained observer, I'd be sure I must be in the right place, though what their drivers are doing here and not out on the street stopping crimes, I can't imagine. Though I *can* imagine it's possibly why there's a serial killer free to go about their business virtually under their noses.

I've not been here before – Dionne's never invited me, perhaps because there's not been a 'bring your dad to work' day, as far as I'm aware, and I've never been arrested – at least, not in this country. Dionne's not on duty until later this afternoon, but even so, I linger outside for a moment, wondering whether this is in fact the right step to take, as the last thing I want to do is embarrass her. But better she's a little red-faced than someone gets away with murder, I suppose, so I straighten my clothing, brush my hair to the other side in an attempt at a makeshift disguise, push my way in through the heavy swing door and march up to the desk. It's evidently a slow crime day as there's no one else waiting, and the rather bored-looking desk sergeant looks as if I've just interrupted his nap.

'Can I help you, sir?' he asks, sitting up stiffly. He's rather overweight, probably close to retirement age, and I'd guess has been stuck behind this desk for a while. I want to tell him he ought to do something about it, have some fun or excitement in his last few years on the job, as before he knows it, he'll find himself in that weird twilight zone before he gets to go some-where like Twilight Lodge and this mundane desk posting will seem like high times. But then I remember what I've come in for and realise it might just do the trick.

'You can if this is where someone comes to report a murder,' I say, and the desk sergeant nearly falls off his chair.

'I beg your pardon?'

'Assuming I've come to the right place, I'd like to report a murder. Four murders, actually, Sergeant...' I retrieve my glasses, slip them on, and peer at his name badge. 'Dawkins.'

When you're as skilled at reading people as I am – you have to be in my line of work, whether you're negotiating for state secrets or simply playing in the weekly poker game with your fellow operatives – you can immediately tell if someone doesn't believe what you're saying, and that's certainly the case now, as something in Sergeant Dawkins' demeanour changes.

'Is that so?'

'It is.'

'And where did these murders take place?'

I can almost hear the air quotes around the word 'murders'. 'At Twilight Lodge.'

'Twilight Lodge? The old fogey's... I mean, the nursing home on the seafront?'

'That's right.' Careful not to make any sudden movements, I reach into my cardigan pocket and retrieve my notebook. 'One on the second of this month, the next on the seventh, one on the eleventh, then the last one just two days ago.'

My eyes flick down to the pen and pad on the desk in front of him, and I wonder why Sergeant Dawkins isn't writing any of this down. Instead, he sits back in his chair and folds his arms. 'That's a lot of murders.'

'Par for the course when there's a serial killer on the loose.'

'At *Twilight Lodge?*'

'That's right. Assuming you haven't had reports from other similar establishments.'

'So the victims are all... residents?'

I sigh. If this is indicative of the deductive powers on tap here at Hastings police station, then I don't hold out much hope of a speedy arrest. Although on the plus side, Dionne's career prospects don't appear too shabby if this is the level at which the bar is set.

'They are. Or rather, were.' I say. 'Did you want their names?'

I turn to the relevant page in my notebook, and Sergeant Dawkins smiles patronisingly. 'Perhaps I could start by taking *your* name, sir?'

'*My* name? It's Mar...' I hesitate, wondering whether giving my real name is wise, what with my daughter working here, but what else to say? I've worked under so many aliases in the past I know how hard it is to come up with a plausible-sounding one –

probably why James Bond doesn't seem to bother most of the time, now I come to think of it.

Sergeant Dawkins frowns. 'Mar...?'

'That's right. But with, um, a "k".'

'Eh?'

'No, a "k". As in "Mark".'

'Mark...?'

'Just Mark. Call this an anonymous tip-off. Well, strictly speaking it's semi-anonymous, seeing as I've told you my first name.'

'Right,' says Sergeant Dawkins, though he's still made no move to make any notes. 'And these... victims?'

'What about them?'

'What makes you think they were murdered?'

'Because they were alive, and now they're dead.'

'And you don't think they might have just... died?'

'They might have. But they didn't. Or rather, they did, but at someone else's hands.'

Sergeant Dawkins looks like he's having a hard time believing me. A fact backed up when he says, 'Don't you think this all sounds rather... unlikely?'

'That's the thing with murders – they *are* unlikely, thank goodness. It doesn't mean they don't occur, you know?'

'Not in St Leonards, they don't.'

Like Dionne the other day, Sergeant Dawkins sounds a little disappointed, and I can understand why. It must be extremely disheartening to join the constabulary as an eager teenager hoping you'll get to spend your days solving juicy crimes, but all you actually end up doing is reuniting lost children with their parents or adjudicating disputes over deckchairs on the beach. Though if that *is* the case, I can't understand why he's not biting my hand off for the lead I'm giving him.

'Listen, Sergeant, you look like you run a tight ship here,' I say, aiming for the flattery approach that's worked so well for me so far. 'So tell me something. What was the overall crime rate here last year?'

'Officially? Ninety-five per thousand of the population.'

'So just under ten per cent,' I say, not needing Albie's help with the maths for once. 'And this year? So far?'

Sergeant Dawkins smiles proudly. 'Around the same.'

'And if all of a sudden that rate went up to, say, forty per cent, what would you think?'

'Well, I'd think there was something wrong.'

'And that's exactly what's happened at Twilight Lodge. Last year there were around three deaths all year. So far this month we've already had four. Doesn't that strike you as a little suspicious?'

Sergeant Dawkins furrows his brow, perhaps as he does the maths, and I can tell I've got his attention. 'It could just be coincidence, you know? Most of them just happening to die this month.'

'It could,' I say, wondering whether this is a standard excuse for crime waves from the police playbook, seeing as it was Dionne's first reaction too. 'But it isn't.'

Sergeant Dawkins regards me for a moment, then – though possibly it's because he's decided it's the quickest way to get rid of me – he reaches for his notepad and pen and begins to jot a few details down. 'Four, you say?'

'So far.'

'*So far?*'

'Like I said, it might be a serial killer. So who knows where it'll end?'

'What do the staff at Twilight Lodge think?'

'I'm not sure they're paid to think. Besides, I haven't asked. Especially since one of them might be the killer. As I'm sure you can understand, the last thing I want is to raise my head above the parapet unnecessarily and risk becoming their next victim.'

Sergeant Dawkins nods in a 'fair enough' kind of way. 'What makes you think it might be one of the staff?'

'Because it's highly unlikely to be one of the residents, given that they're mostly – how did you put it earlier – "old fogeys"?'

'Good point,' he says, without a trace of embarrassment. 'And what's your connection with all this?'

'I don't have a connection. Apart from being a concerned resident.'

'Of Twilight Lodge?'

'If I were resident anywhere else, I wouldn't be concerned, would I? Unless, like I said, it's happening elsewhere too?'

'Right. No. Of course.'

'So you'll look into it?'

'Well, we're very busy at the moment, so...'

At my widened eyes, Sergeant Dawkins' voice trails off, particularly when I make a point of peering through the internal window and into the room behind him, where several police officers seem to be sitting at their desks drinking tea, or eating biscuits, or even in one case, soundly asleep on his computer keyboard, leading me to think that perhaps Custard's employment prospects here are better than I'd thought.

'Look, Sergeant. You might think that I'm just a foolish old man who's come in here crying wolf about some "murders"' – I do the 'air quotes' thing myself – 'at his nursing home when there could be a perfectly ordinary explanation for the sudden rise in the number of deaths there. And it's true – I might be. So yes, you could dismiss all of this as some senior-moment rambling, wait until I've left, then rip that particular page out of your notebook, ball it up, and throw it into your wastepaper bin. But imagine if I'm right? What if there *is* something untoward happening? And if that's the case and there's another murder and you did nothing to stop it because you didn't even bother to check out what I was saying, and then someone finds out that actually, somebody had come in to report the goings-on at Twilight Lodge, but you'd just filed the report under "R" for "rubbish"...' I shake my head. 'And imagine if that someone was the son or daughter of the killer's next victim, mourning the loss of their dear father or beloved mother. Would you be able to look them in the eye, or even look at yourself in the mirror, knowing that it was your fault? That you could have prevented all that pain, all that suffering, all that misery.'

Sergeant Dawkins stares at me for a moment, then he sits up a little straighter. 'Okay,' he says, as if he's doing me the biggest of favours. 'I'll send someone to check it out.'

'You will?'

'I've just said so, haven't I?'

'Excellent!' I say. 'When?'

'As soon as we can, sir.'

'*Today* soon? Because there doesn't seem to be any pattern to these murders. And with the last one happening just two days ago, the killer might be poised to strike again.'

'Fine!' says Sergeant Dawkins, like a petulant child reluctantly agreeing to tidy their room.

'Thank you,' I say, happy I seem to have put the cat among the pigeons – and anonymously, at that, as the last thing I want to happen is for the perpetrator to find out it's me and Albie who are investigating and deviate from their normal pattern of 'sea-view' victims to stop us from interfering further. Hopefully the notion that the police are aware something funny's going on will at least make the killer take stock, or even put the killings on hold until we've had a chance to make further enquiries. And who knows – the police might even uncover something themselves and prove there *is* something untoward happening – though given the general levels of activity I can see here, that might be a big ask. But either way, I've achieved what I came here for.

With a brief salute, I spin round smartly, and – ignoring the twinge in my 'old' hip – make my way back outside. And maybe it's my imagination, but compared to when I walked here, the sky seems like it's becoming clearer.

If only I could say the same thing about the goings-on at Twilight Lodge.

36

It's late afternoon, and I'm relaxing in the armchair in my room, enjoying a wonderful dream about Madeleine back before she became ill, when I become aware of someone clearing their throat from the doorway. I start awake, swallow the pang of disappointment that my wife of fifty-nine years is now my *late* wife, and smile up at my daughter as she walks in. Unusually, there's no sign of Custard, and more importantly, Dionne's in uniform, but in my half-asleep state, I don't realise what this means until it's too late.

'Hello, love. Here to arrest someone?'

I grin at her, but Dionne's not looking particularly amused. 'I ought to be arresting *you*.'

'Me?' I say, my smile faltering slightly. 'On what charge?'

'Wasting police time. Specifically, mine.'

'How's that, love?' I ask, though I already know I'm not going to like the answer.

'I had an interesting conversation with the desk sergeant when I arrived at work this afternoon.'

'Oh yes?'

Dionne walks over and perches on the end of the bed.

'Apparently someone came into the station this morning to report a murder. Four murders, actually. Here at Twilight Lodge, would you believe?'

'Oh.' I look sheepishly up at her. 'Did they leave a name?'

'Half of their real one,' she says. 'But even if they hadn't, I'd have known who it was.'

'I see,' I say, cringing a little at what's not the best bit of thinking on my feet I've ever done.

'So now I've been sent round here to see if there's any truth in these – and I'm quoting directly from Sergeant Dawkins here – "preposterous suggestions".'

'That's good, isn't it?'

'How is it possibly good, Dad?'

'You've always said you wanted to work on something a bit meatier. This is a murder enquiry, so now's your chance. I'd have thought it would make a nice change from the normal—' I stop talking, as Albie's just appeared at the door. He begins wheeling himself into the room, then catches sight of the implied warning in my expression – but before he can throw himself into reverse, Dionne spots him and fixes him with a glare.

'In here, you!'

As Albie does what he's told, I continue my protest. 'Besides, you didn't leave me a lot of choice. People are dying here.'

'It's a nursing home, Dad. That's kind of what happens.' She glances briefly at Albie. 'No offence, Albie.'

Albie shrugs. 'None taken!'

Dionne gets up from the bed, though it's only to take up what's possibly a more official position on the chair in the corner, and as she folds her arms, I brace myself. 'Right,' she says. 'I'm going to ask this just the once. Have the two of you got anything?'

'Such as?' I say, presuming she doesn't mean 'dementia'.

'Any evidence – *concrete* evidence – that these deaths are anything more than just... deaths.'

'Oh yes,' I say, giving Albie my best 'feel free to jump in at any time' look, before reaching for my notebook and frantically flicking through the pages. 'For one thing, from what we understand, all four victims...'

'Victims?' says Dionne, raising one eyebrow.

'Deceased, then,' says Albie.

'All the *deceased*,' I say. 'Are connected.'

'Connected?' Dionne raises both eyebrows.

'Or at least, they've all got something in common,' says Albie.

'Apart from being dead, obviously,' I say.

Dionne raises both eyebrows even higher. 'Which is?'

'A sea view,' I say.

'What?'

'Their rooms,' I explain. 'They all had a view.'

'Of the sea,' says Albie, and Dionne rolls her eyes.

'The building's on the seafront. I'd imagine the majority of the rooms have some sort of sea view?'

'You'd think,' I say. 'But it doesn't work like that. Only the rooms at the front look out over the promenade towards the channel. The rest...' I hesitate, not having been in all of the others, so I can't be sure what exactly they look out on. 'Well, *don't*.'

'Exhibit A', says Albie, pointing at the distinctly sea-free vista that's visible through my window. 'And Martin's Exhibit B, seeing as he doesn't have a sea view, and he's still alive.'

'As does – or rather *doesn't*, and is – Albie,' I add, not wanting to call him 'Exhibit C', which might confuse the issue.

Dionne gives me a look, then does the same to Albie. 'Even so, that doesn't mean there's anything odd going on. For example, there's a high correlation between people wearing jeans and dying of cancer, but that doesn't mean wearing jeans *gives* you cancer.'

'We're not saying it's the view that's killing them,' I say, as Philip walks past the open doorway, catches sight of Dionne in her uniform, and is so distracted as a result, he almost bumps into Miriam coming the other way.

'Just that there's a link,' says Albie. 'After all, there are thirty rooms here at Twilight Lodge. Twelve of them are Premium rooms...'

'With a sea view,' I add helpfully.

'And so far this month, one third of the occupants of those rooms have died.'

'In suspicious circumstances,' I suggest.

Albie nods. 'Occupants with no apparent illnesses. All on the ground floor, too. Which *does* seem a little odd, to use your word from a moment ago.'

Dionne looks at me, then Albie. 'So what are you saying? That someone's climbing in from the front of the building and randomly killing anyone they find?'

'We considered that, but the windows don't open wide enough. Besides, these are targeted killings. They have to be.'

'Why?'

'At the risk of repeating myself,' I say – which is a risk nowadays, I have to admit – 'because everyone who's died has a sea-view room.'

'No.' Dionne shakes her head. '*Why* are they targeting the sea-view room occupants?'

'We don't know yet,' says Albie.

As I gratefully acknowledge both his use of the word 'we' and the word 'yet', Dionne takes a deep breath, then exhales loudly through her nose. 'I'm sorry, but I really can't see why anyone would want to kill someone who's probably – again, no offence, Albie – going to die of natural causes in the not-so-distant future anyway.'

'But that's the beauty of it,' I say. '*Because* they – yet again, no offence, Albie – might be likely to, *you know*, then there's no suspicion. It's the perfect murder. Murders.'

'But *what for?*'

Albie and I regard each other helplessly, then something occurs to me. 'Maybe it's not about the sea-view rooms. Maybe the killer's targeting them to throw us off the scent.'

Dionne looks at me blankly. 'You're going to have to explain that one.'

'Maybe they're killing those residents in the sea-view rooms to make us think the killings are all about the sea-view rooms, when in fact, they're planning on killing everyone. Or at least enough of us so the remaining residents start to believe it's not safe here, and they leave.'

Dionne takes her hat off, though it's only so she can scratch her head. 'So now you're suggesting the murders are in fact a decoy for more murders, all so they don't have to murder everyone?'

'Eh?' I say, not exactly following Dionne's logic, then I realise it's my logic that she's batted back at me.

'All we're saying,' says Albie, 'is that the higher-than-normal number of deaths here recently would indicate there's something untoward going on. And that our preliminary investigations would suggest there's a link between the victims. Surely that's enough to raise some sort of enquiry, if not a formal investigation?'

'Couldn't you at least say something?' I implore, gesturing towards the door. 'And make a show of it. If the killer finds out you're asking questions, thinks the police are involved – or at least have some suspicions – it might make them slip up, or even call a halt to things for now. For my sake. And for Albie's.'

'You're not in a sea-view room. Neither is Albie.'

'No, but my' – Albie turns the deepest shade of red I've ever seen – '*girlfriend* is.'

He puts on his most pleading puppy-dog eyes, but Dionne's evidently immune, as she hauls herself to her feet and straightens her jacket.

'Where are you going?' I say, hopefully.

'Back to the station.' Dionne smiles flatly as she puts her hat back on. 'I'm sorry, you two, but there's just not enough here to...'

'Tommy Walker!' says Albie, loudly and suddenly enough to make me jump.

And by the looks of her, it's had the same effect on Dionne.

37

'What about him?' Dionne says, and I catch my breath, hoping we might have finally piqued her interest.

'We think he might be involved.'

'You think Tommy Walker could be the killer?'

'We're not sure if he's the *actual* killer,' says Albie.

'Though we're pretty sure he's – what do you call it – a person of interest?' I add.

'What possible reason would Tommy Walker have to be involved in a series of murders in a place like Twilight...?' Dionne stops mid-sentence – though only because she's apparently putting two and two together. She looks around briefly, as if sizing up the building's development potential, then sits back down again. 'You've got my attention,' she says.

'So, as you may have guessed.' Albie reverses over to the door, bumps it shut, then wheels himself back to where we're sitting. 'We think he's got designs on this place.'

'Like he did with your old school,' I say.

Albie nods. 'In that he wants to turn it into flats.'

'*Luxury* flats,' I say. 'With sea views.'

'Which he can't do if it's full of old folks.'

Dionne does a double take. 'So he's killing them off one by one?'

'Maybe,' I say. 'Though maybe not all of them. Like I said, perhaps just enough to make the rest run scared. Well, not *run*, given their ages, but you know what I mean.'

Dionne considers this for a moment, then puffs air out of her cheeks. 'I'm sorry, but there's a huge difference between setting fire to an empty building like he did...'

'*Allegedly* did,' I say, then realise the reason Albie's glaring at me is because he thinks the comment hasn't exactly helped our case, though I've a longer game in mind. 'But only "allegedly" because you couldn't prove it.'

'Quite,' says Dionne. 'Even so, arson's one thing. Whereas multiple murders...'

'Granted. And we've no proof he's the murderer. Just that he might stand to benefit if he gets his hands on the place.'

'But what makes you think he's interested in Twilight Lodge?'

Albie and I exchange nervous glances. 'We saw him here,' I say.

'Last week,' adds Albie.

'Snooping around Elsie's room.'

Dionne angles her head. 'Elsie being one of the ones who...?'

'Was murdered. Yes,' I say, pleased to note Dionne doesn't correct me this time. 'And when we confronted him...'

'You *confronted him*?'

'We, um, might have done,' I say sheepishly. 'Just to see why he was in there.'

'And?'

Albie and I play 'After you' with our eyes for a moment, then Albie pipes up.

'He said he was checking it out.'

'For his mother.'

As I wonder whether it's a good or bad thing Albie and I are finishing each other's sentences like an old married couple, a strange look passes across Dionne's face. 'Tommy Walker's mother died when he was at school.'

'Maybe he killed her!' suggests Albie. 'Got a taste for it. And now...'

'Hardly,' says Dionne.

'Still,' I say. 'That proves he's involved. With what's going on here, I mean. Not with, you know, his mother's demise.'

Dionne holds both hands out, as if warming them on a fire. 'Steady on,' she says. 'All it proves is that he's a liar.'

'Maybe,' says Albie. 'But when we went to see him yesterday, he said...'

'*You went to see Tommy Walker?*' says Dionne, incredulously.

'That's right,' I say. 'We pretended we wanted to buy a flat.'

'For you,' says Albie, as if that'll mitigate our actions, although Dionne still looks angry, so it evidently doesn't.

'You went to see him on your own, even though you suspected he might be a murderer?'

'We weren't on our own,' I say.

'Technically,' adds Albie. 'Seeing as there were two of us.'

'You know what I mean.'

I do my best to look suitably sheepish – that we were putting ourselves in danger hadn't really occurred to me. Even though Albie's admitted he wants to die, I hadn't appreciated it was perhaps a little selfish of me where Dionne's concerned, though fortunately, she seems a little too wrapped up in the possibility Tommy Walker might be involved in more criminal activity to worry about that right now.

'We didn't think he'd murder *us*,' I say, though, at this moment, Dionne's looking like *she* might.

'And we were right,' says Albie, a little unnecessarily, I feel.

'What did he say?'

'He was quite cagey, as you might expect. Although he did admit he had a potential new project he was attempting to secure. A new development. High-end flats.'

'With sea views,' adds Albie.

'Though he couldn't tell us any more about it right now. He said he had a few... What was it, Albie?'

'Obstacles.'

'*Obstacles* to deal with first.'

'Meaning the likes of us,' says Albie. 'Or so we assumed.'

'Which is just charming!' I say.

Dionne stares at me for a moment, then sighs, and it's a long and loud one. 'So let me get this straight. You think Tommy Walker is planning on acquiring Twilight Lodge so he can turn it into expensive flats...'

'*Sea-view* flats,' interrupts Albie.

'...but before he can do that, he's killing off a few of the residents in order to promote some sort of mass exodus?'

'Or arranging for them to be killed,' I say. 'Or at least, he's party to it.'

'After all,' says Albie. 'He's got history.'

'Not murderous history, though,' says Dionne.

'Perhaps not,' I say. 'Though he was prepared to set fire to your old school building.'

'Allegedly,' says Albie.

'And you don't do that kind of thing in the middle of a populated area if you're worried about potential loss of life as a consequence.'

Dionne scratches her head again, though she's forgotten she's put her hat back on so it takes her two goes. 'Why not just buy the building as is? Tell all the residents they've got to move elsewhere?'

I shrug. 'Maybe he'll get it cheaper this way. It'd be a failing concern by then, rather than a "going" one.'

'And the reason you didn't mention this when you reported these' – she clears her throat – '*murders*, is...'

'Because we've got no hard evidence,' says Albie.

'Yet,' I say. 'Which is where you come in.'

Dionne thinks for a moment, then shakes her head. 'I'm sorry, but as much as I'd like to collar Tommy Walker for this, seeing as how he squirmed his way out of any blame for the school debacle, I can hardly storm into his office and accuse him of murder. Not without any evidence, or anything to tie him to the killings, or even simply link him to this place – apart from the fact that you two saw him here. Knowing Tommy, there'll be nothing on paper about what he's up to. And he's hardly going to admit it.'

The three of us sit in silence for a moment, the impasse we've reached seemingly impossible to overcome. Then Albie suddenly sits up, and I can almost see the lightbulb that's appeared above his head.

'We're forgetting something,' he says, a grin appearing on his face.

'Which is?' Dionne says impatiently, when Albie doesn't elucidate.

'Wherever there's a buyer, there's a seller!' Albie says, and Dionne narrows her eyes at him.

'Which means?'

I flick back to the first entry in my notebook. 'Nigel Montfort,' I say, showing the page to Dionne, adding, 'He owns Twilight Lodge,' in response to her puzzled expression. 'He told me he and Tommy Walker aren't friends. Though photographic evidence in his office would suggest otherwise.'

'You've been in Nigel Montfort's office?'

'Only to establish whether Tommy Walker was a liar,' I say. 'And it turns out he was. *Is.* And don't worry. Nigel was in there at the time. It's not like I broke in. Or stole anything.'

'Unlike the staffroom. And the minibus,' mutters Albie, then his face pales. 'Sorry. Did I say that out loud?'

Dionne stares at him for a moment, then she stands up, looking like she's not sure whether to congratulate us or tear us off another strip. Instead, she just shakes her head as she walks to the door.

'Where are you going now?' I ask, although I suspect I already know the answer.

'To speak to Nigel Montfort,' says Dionne.

And for the first time since she arrived – and in fact, the first time in a while – there's a glint in her eye.

38

Dionne stops suddenly, wheels around, then puts both hands on my shoulders, bringing an abrupt halt to my attempt to follow her through the door.

'Where do you think you're going?'

'With you, of course.'

'What for?'

'To question Nigel.'

'I think you'll find that's my job.'

'But...' I glance across at Albie for support, but he's already making the 'don't look at me' face. 'How will you know what to ask him?'

Dionne takes a pace backwards, looks down at her uniform, then condescendingly up at me. 'I think I'll be able to come up with something.'

'We could double-team him. You know, good cop, bad cop?'

'I'd hardly be a good cop if I let you come in there with me, would I?'

'Okay then. I could offer some muscle. Strong-arm him if he's being evasive.'

'That's how you used to treat all those hoteliers you were inspecting, was it?'

Albie lets out a snigger, and I turn a shade of red. 'I just thought I could help.'

Dionne glares at me, perhaps at the implication she *needs* help, and when I take another step towards the door, holds a hand up. 'Stay!' she says, quickly followed by, 'Sit!'

As Albie gives me the side-eye, I reluctantly do as ordered. 'Fine,' I say. 'But you'll let us know how it goes?'

Dionne straightens her uniform. '*If* there's anything to report.'

'Great. Well then, good luck, love,' I say, as if Dionne's off to her first day at school. Once she's disappeared from view, I count to ten, lever myself out of my chair, and grab Albie's wheelchair by the handles with an urgent, 'Come on!'

'Where are we going?'

'To listen in on Dionne's interrogation of Nigel, of course,' I say, steering him out and along the corridor.

'How are we going to do *that*?' asks Albie, though in a way that suggests he's not expecting to like the answer.

'Watch and learn, Albie,' I say, as I skilfully weave past a few of the home's other, slower residents and make for the double doors that lead out into the garden. 'Watch and learn.'

As Albie theatrically clamps a hand over his eyes, I hurriedly push him outside and along the path, carefully counting the requisite number of windows that'll place us directly outside Nigel's office. I'm banking on his window being open, otherwise my plan will fail at the first hurdle, and fortunately – no doubt thanks to the fact that it's a warm day – it is.

Parking Albie strategically underneath it, I consider my options. Twilight Lodge is a Victorian building, so the window is of the sash variety, and rather tall, and given the fact that it's the top section that's been half-slid down, I estimate I need to somehow get around eight feet off the ground – some two feet higher than my official height before gravity and old age conspired to reduce it – in order to be able to listen in effectively. And I need to get there quickly.

There's a trellis running up the wall, but it doesn't look like it'd hold my weight, plus it's doubtful I've the strength and dexterity in my arthritic fingers to clamber up it anyway. I could abseil down from the window above, I suppose, but I don't have time to procure a suitable length of rope, and besides, the rather thorny-looking rosebush underneath would hardly give me the most comfortable of landings if I fell – not to mention the potential damage I could do to my new hip. Which means there's only one thing for it.

'Give me a leg-up, will you?' I whisper.

Albie stares at me in disbelief, then hisses, 'You're joking!' for good measure.

'I just need to get up onto the arms of your chair.'

'Where *my* arms are?'

'Well, tuck them in!'

'How can I give you a leg-up if my arms are tucked in?'

'Spread your legs, then.'

'What for?'

'So I can use your seat as a step.'

'No fear!' Albie looks horrified, though I don't blame him. One misstep on my part and that's him and Barbara over before they've even begun. 'Besides, what if someone sees us?'

'We can just pretend we're doing some exercise.'

'Sure,' says Albie sarcastically. 'Because that's exactly what it'll look like.'

I sigh loudly, then – using a combination of the wheelchair's footrests, frame, and my tenuous grip on the trellis – do my best to climb up into position. Apart from an awkward moment, when my groin is in Albie's face and his appalled rearing backwards almost causes me to lose my balance, I just about manage to get myself within listening distance.

'Right,' I say, holding on to the trellis for dear life, while praying it'll stay attached to the wall. 'Keep a lookout.'

'How?' hisses Albie. 'I can't see anything with your crotch obscuring my vision.'

'One second…' I shift to one side, then discover to my horror that Albie's not put his brakes on. Slowly, like some comedy circus balancing act, we start rolling away from the window.

It's all I can do to maintain my grip on the trellis, and while to anyone else this might appear an amusing spectacle, I suspect if I lose my balance and have to make a leap for it, the old parachute-roll landing might severely test the tensile strength of not only my new titanium joint but my old bone one too. And as fun as the last three weeks have been, a second recuperative stay at Twilight Lodge isn't exactly top of my bucket list.

'Hold on!' commands Albie, as he struggles to regain control of the chair and bring us to a halt before we hit the potentially lethal uneven surface of the lawn.

'Now *that* hadn't occurred to me.'

'Can you pull us back into position?'

'I'm trying, Albie!'

'Well, try harder!'

I brace myself for what will surely require a superhuman effort, not to mention the sternest test yet of how my physiotherapy's progressing, though when I begin to apply pressure, the trellis looks like it's about to come loose – and because I'm worried my new joint might as well, I'm forced to abort. 'No can do, Albie,' I say, conscious my forearms are beginning to tire too. 'You'll have to wheel us back.'

'I would if I could see where we were going!'

Albie's voice is a little muffled, and I don't like to think by what, so – careful not to set us off on the move again – I shift position slightly. 'You don't need to see. Just… reverse!'

'Fine!' snaps Albie. 'Again, hold on!'

'Already ahead of you there, Albie,' I say, as he does as he's told, and somehow, slowly, *miraculously*, like a spacecraft balletically docking with the mothership, we manage to get back to our original location. 'Put the brakes on this time, will you?'

'You think?'

As Albie reaches down to flip the lever, I tentatively peer around the window frame, coincidentally just as Nigel's showing Dionne into his office. As he bids her to sit down, I'm grateful both for the fact he's been rude enough to make her wait, and that the desk is side-on to the window, which means neither of them is likely to spot me. Even so, I decide to keep out of sight, though the trouble is, while my ear's now at the precise height for the gap in the window, I'm not close enough to hear more than the murmur of their voices. Frustrated, I look down at Albie for inspiration, to find him staring expectantly up at me.

'What's going on?' he says.

'I've no idea – I can't hear a thing!'

Albie thinks for a moment, then reaches up to his ear and removes one of his hearing aids. 'Try this,' he says, passing it up to me.

'You might have wiped it first.'

'Did you want me to release my brakes again?'

I bite off my reply, then take the tiny device and slip it into my left ear, and by some miracle, I can suddenly hear Dionne. 'Quick!' I say. 'Give me the other one,' and Albie does as instructed, making a show of wiping it on his handkerchief first. Ignoring his petulance, I insert it into my other ear, and to both my amazement and relief, Nigel's voice comes through loud and clear.

39

'Albie!' I stage whisper down to him. 'You're a genius!'

'Pardon?'

'Never mind!'

'What?'

Risking the briefest of let-goes from the trellis, I shush him with a wave of my hand and concentrate on the conversation coming from the office, just in time to hear Nigel say, 'I'm sorry, but is this an official visit?'

'Semi-official,' says Dionne.

'Oh yes?'

'I'm afraid so, Mr Montfort. There's been a... complaint.'

'What sort of complaint?' asks Nigel indignantly. 'And from whom?'

'I'm afraid I'm not at liberty to say.' Dionne's voice sounds friendly but formal. 'Although seeing as there has been, we have a duty to investigate it. I'm sure it's only routine.'

'Right,' says Nigel, as if he's not sure Dionne's sure. 'You mentioned to the receptionist that this was about a death?'

'Ssss.'

'I'm sorry?'

'Death-s,' says Dionne, enunciating the last letter carefully. 'Plural. The recent ones, in particular.'

'You mean...?'

There's the sound of Dionne flicking through her notebook, and I marvel at how good Albie's hearing aids are at picking up and amplifying everything. Certainly better than the old glass-against-the-wall trick I had to use during the early days of my professional career. And something to remember next time Albie pretends he can't hear me.

'Stanley Faulkner. Elsie Watson. Diana McGuire. And George Philips.'

I feel a sudden surge of pride. Despite Dionne's reticence with me and Albie earlier, she's evidently done her homework before coming here, and when Nigel swallows hard – surely a guilty sign if ever there was one – I hope Dionne hears it as well as I do. Then there's a tug on my left trouser leg, which almost unbalances me, and a loud, 'What's going on?' from below, nearly deafening me into the bargain.

'Be quiet!' I hiss.

'What?'

I put my finger on my lips, like you might when shushing an unruly child, and turn my attention back to Nigel's office. 'You have to understand,' Nigel is saying, 'these people are elderly. And quite poorly, in a lot of circumstances, as a result. And none of the permanent residents leave here any other way.'

'That sounds quite sinister to me.'

'Them's the facts, as the saying goes,' he says, the put-on poor grammar sounding insincere in his clipped, public-school accent. 'It's the sad nature of this business.'

'Tell me, Mr Montfort. How many deaths have there been here at Twilight Lodge this year?'

Though I can't see either of their faces, I can guess the expression on Nigel's right now. 'Among our residents?' he says, and Dionne clears her throat.

'Unless you've lost any staff members as well?'

'What? Oh, no! Not so far, at least!' Nigel lets out a short – and a little inappropriate, I feel – laugh, before he thinks for a moment. 'I'd have to check, but I'd say around... six?'

'Are you asking me or telling me?'

'Like I say, I'd have to check.'

'And that includes these last four?'

'Well, no,' says Nigel awkwardly. 'I thought you meant other deaths.'

'So, ten?'

'Again, like I say...'

'You'd have to check.'

'That's right.'

'Could you?'

'Now?' says Nigel, as if he's been asked to donate a kidney – and to someone he's never even met.

'Whenever you get a moment. Just call the station when you have. They'll pass on the information. Or if you'd prefer, I could come back?'

I can almost hear Nigel forcing a smile. 'No, that's fine,' he says. 'I'll get onto it. As soon as you've gone.'

If that's a hint, Dionne doesn't take it. 'Thank you. And do you know what the national average is for deaths in establishments of this nature?'

'Off the top of my head, no,' says Nigel flatly. 'But I'm sure you're about to tell me.'

'Ten per cent.'

There's a pause, possibly while Nigel works out what that should equate to here at Twilight Lodge, then the mood in the room seems to change. 'Constable...?'

'Maxwell,' says Dionne.

'Constable Maxwell.' Nigel takes a deep breath, then it catches in his throat. 'Hang on. Are you any relation to *Martin* Maxwell?'

'He's my father. Not that that has any bearing on why I'm here.'

'Right,' says Nigel, though he doesn't sound convinced, perhaps because Dionne's not quite developed my levels of subterfuge. 'That's as may be...'

'Or may not be...'

'I'm wondering whether we should be continuing this conversation with my lawyer present.'

Any semblance of friendliness has disappeared from Nigel's voice, whereas Dionne takes the opportunity to increase the level in hers – perhaps something she's learned in her recent interrogation techniques course. 'Why would you think that, Mr Montfort?'

'Because it sounds like you're building up to accusing me of something.'

'What does it sound like I'm accusing you of?' says Dionne, and I think to myself, *That's my girl!* Get him to admit it. After all, if he knows what's going on, his guilty conscience might just let it slip.

'Listen,' says Nigel, levelly, though it sounds like it's an effort to keep his composure. 'We've been audited by the powers that be. Vetted to the highest standards. Assessed every which way. On a regular basis. And I can assure you there's nothing out of the ordinary happening here at Twilight Lodge...'

'Apart from a mortality rate that appears to be considerably higher than the national average.'

'This year,' says Nigel. 'So far. Though may I remind you, the year isn't over yet.'

'So there could be more?'

'Or less.'

'Only if you're planning to resurrect the dead, Mr Montfort.' Dionne pauses, and I presume she's writing something down. 'And previous years?'

'Again, I'd have to check,' he says tersely, then he sighs

loudly. 'Look – you know the other thing that's higher than the national average here at Twilight Lodge? Our Google rating. Four point four, if you'd care to take a look. And that's out of five.'

'I do know how Google reviews work, Mr Montfort.'

'Of course you do,' says Nigel, adopting a friendlier – if also smarmier – tone. 'I just mean, I hardly think the score would be that high if we were doing something wrong. And remember, averages are just that – averages. Some years, you get more. Some less. It just so happens that this year...'

'Just so happens?'

'That's right,' says Nigel, a little testily. 'Besides, what would we stand to gain from our residents dying? We're not simply a conveyor belt here. When someone passes, it creates more problems than it solves. There are forms to fill in. Relatives to inform. We have to manage the impact on the other residents. And find new occupants to fill any dead space...'

'An interesting turn of phrase.'

'All I'm saying is, it's not good for business.'

'Unless you're able to re-let the rooms at a higher rate? The moment one of your longer-term residents passes away, I'd imagine you could put the price up and...'

'Aha,' says Nigel, triumphantly.

I can picture Dionne's frown. 'I'm sorry – what's "aha"?'

'We haven't.'

'Haven't what?'

'Re-let the rooms.'

'Because no one wants to take them, due to recent developments?'

There's a moment of silence, and I imagine Nigel's about to boil over, but instead, he adopts a patient tone. 'No. For the simple reason that I'm thinking of refurbishing them.'

'Refurbishing them?'

'It's the perfect opportunity. Like you said, some of these

residents who have… *unfortunately* passed away had been here for a long time. We don't like to move them when they're here – it upsets them, you see. Messes up the routines that give them comfort. And there's no way we could decorate around them, of course. So I've been getting some quotes in…'

'From Tommy Walker?'

Nigel's sharp intake of breath is probably even audible to Albie without his hearing aids. 'How did you know about…?'

'St Leonards is a small town, Mr Montfort.'

'Evidently!' says Nigel, then he stops talking, perhaps realising he's already said more than enough. After a long, awkward moment, Dionne clears her throat.

'Okay, then,' she says. 'But just for the record, you're saying you can think of no reason why the number of deaths here might have spiked so suddenly this past month?'

There's another, longer pause, though evidently not long enough for Nigel to come up with anything plausible. 'I suppose it's just one of those things,' he says. 'There have certainly been no changes in our care levels, or routines, or practices.'

'No other factors?'

'Such as?'

'You tell me.'

'Like I said, I'm just as mystified as you,' Nigel says, and through gritted teeth by the sound of it. 'But people do just… die. Especially old people. It comes with the territory of advancing years, and the development of dementia, or congestive heart failure, or any number of ailments associated with ageing. You must be concerned about your father, for example?'

Whether that's a veiled threat towards me, I can't tell, but Dionne doesn't latch on to it – or dignify it with a response if she does. 'And there's no one here who might have some sort of grudge, or any reason to…?'

'*Kill anyone?*' says Nigel, incredulously. 'They'd hardly be employed here as carers if that was the case, would they?'

'To be fair, they're unlikely to admit to any sort of murderous intent when you interview them.'

'True,' says Nigel. 'There was one member of staff who turned out to be a little, shall we say, careless. But he's been... terminated. If you excuse the phrase.'

'That would be Shane Watkins?'

'That's right,' says Nigel, sounding a little surprised Dionne knows so much about the goings-on here, though now he's aware I'm her father, I'm sure he'll soon put two and two together and realise where Dionne's information has come from. 'Listen, Constable Maxwell,' he says, adopting a friendly tone again. 'I'm sure this is just all a misunderstanding. You might as well suggest it's your father on some sort of killing spree, seeing as from what you're saying, this has all been happening since he moved in!' I almost lose my balance at the accusation as Nigel lets out a peal of laughter, though, to her credit, Dionne doesn't join in. 'Now if there's nothing else?'

'Nothing apart from those figures you promised me?'

'As soon as I can,' says Nigel.

There's silence for a moment, until Dionne says, 'Okay, then,' again, followed by the sound of a chair scraping across the floor – Dionne standing up, I imagine – and a moment later, a door being opened. 'You've been most helpful,' she adds, though there's no response.

Then the door shuts firmly, and the next thing I hear is Nigel's long, loud sigh.

And if I were a betting man, I'd put money on it being a sigh of relief.

40

———

While it's a struggle to clamber down safely from my elevated position, then get Albie and myself back to my room before Dionne returns, *and* in time to look like we've been there all along, somehow, we just about make it, perhaps because she gets held up by the snail's pace of the outflow from the weekly bingo session that's just finished in the Garden Lounge. Though when Dionne comes in and sees me flopped in the armchair, breathing heavily while dabbing at the perspiration on my forehead with my handkerchief, her voice takes on a concerned note.

'Dad? Are you okay?'

I wince at the sudden pain in my ear, then realise I've still got Albie's hearing aids in. 'Fine, thanks,' I say, as robustly as I can manage, almost deafening myself again. 'Just... hang on a minute...' I carefully extract the devices, give them a cursory rub on my sleeve, and pass them back to their rightful owner. 'No, Albie. They seem to be working fine to me,' I say loudly.

Albie frowns at me, then wipes the earpieces thoroughly with his handkerchief and puts them back in. 'Thanks?' he says hesitantly, finishing off our little charade, then the two of us turn expectantly to face Dionne.

'So?' I say. Obviously I've heard everything that went on, but Albie hasn't, and I haven't had time to brief him – especially given the fact that I've been too breathless to talk on the way back from our eavesdropping mission. And of course, *not* asking might suggest I've been up to something.

Dionne takes a seat on the end of the bed. 'Not much to report, really. Nigel was...vague. And it almost felt as if he'd been expecting me – or rather, someone like me – to come and ask him some questions. And he was prepared to get "lawyered up" very quickly.'

'And Tommy Walker?' I say.

'Here to quote for refurbishing a few of the rooms, apparently.'

'And not to buy the place for redevelopment,' I say dejectedly. If that's true, then there goes his motive – and it also leaves me without much of one for Nigel.

'Not according to Nigel.'

'So he's not in any kind of financial difficulties?' says Albie.

'The Aston Martin keyring on his desk, not to mention that expensive-looking watch he was doing his best to not keep glancing at, would seem to suggest otherwise.' Dionne shakes her head. 'Looking at him, it's hard to imagine. Surely he wouldn't be leaving those rooms empty if he was struggling for money. And especially not if he's thinking of revamping the place. Builders aren't cheap. Particularly if they're Tommy Walker.'

'And the excess deaths?' says Albie.

'"Just one of those things", he said.'

'So that's that, then?' says Albie, and I might be imagining it, but I think I can detect a bit of disappointment in his voice. 'Case closed?'

Dionne takes a breath. 'Not exactly,' she says, enigmatically.

'What do you mean by that?' I say, and Dionne pinches the bridge of her nose.

'I don't know. Call it a hunch, but there was something just not quite right about him.'

'I could have told you that for nothing,' mumbles Albie, and I shush him.

'In what way?'

'It's hard to put my finger on it. But when you do my job, you develop a bit of a sixth sense for when someone's not being entirely straightforward.'

'Really?' I say, suspecting Dionne might have inherited that from me. 'You felt he was lying to you?'

'Not lying. More like...' Dionne thinks for a moment. 'Withholding the truth.'

'What made you think that?'

'He just seemed a little...'

'Spooked?' suggests Albie, and Dionne shakes her head.

'The opposite, actually. Annoyed that an officer of the law had just confronted him and implied there was something seriously untoward going on here. Which is strange, don't you think?'

'Unless there isn't,' I suggest, despondently.

'But if you take a snapshot of the numbers, there certainly appears to be. If someone pointed out a potential issue with your business, wouldn't you at least show some concern?' Dionne exhales loudly. 'I've met a few men like him in my time. Men who think the normal rules don't apply to them – and who certainly don't like it when a woman calls them out.'

'It might just be arrogance?' I suggest, playing devil's advocate, and Dionne shrugs.

'Maybe. But it didn't feel like that to me – plus there's a big difference between arrogance and committing murder. Either way, I can't think of a motive for any of this. And without a motive...'

Her voice trails off, and the three of us sit there for an uncomfortable moment until Albie clears his throat. 'Follow the money?' he suggests, and Dionne frowns.

'But Nigel was getting the money anyway, and from people who looked like they'd be in a position to keep providing it for a while,' she says. 'So why would he – or anyone – want to kill these particular cash cows, if you excuse the phrase? You've got a paying resident in a room, they die, they're eventually replaced with another paying resident. Where's the upside?'

'That may be how it appears.' Albie peers off into the distance. 'But from what I understand, these kinds of crimes are always about either money or passion.'

'From what you understand?' says Dionne, a puzzled look on her face.

'Albie's a big fan of *Death in Paradise*,' I explain, which seems to do the trick, as Dionne's bafflement disappears.

'Sorry, Albie. Go on.'

Albie shifts awkwardly in his seat. 'Yeah, so the way I see it, given that the victims – if they *are* victims – are the age they are, and both male and female, that second motive is rather unlikely, particularly since there's been so many of them, which means that somehow, there's got to be money involved – more money than simply what Nigel makes from care fees. All we need to do is find where it's coming from, follow it and see where it ends up. If it's from the victims, if it ends up in Nigel's pocket, and if there's been something dodgy about how it got there...'

It's the longest speech I've heard Albie give since we started, and I'm impressed – not to mention a little surprised. And Dionne seems to be regarding him with a newfound respect too. 'That's a lot of "ifs", Albie,' she says. 'But I can't fault your logic.'

'Neither can I,' I say, clapping Albie proudly on the shoulder. 'So where do we go from here?'

For the first time, Dionne doesn't tut at my use of the

word 'we'. 'As Albie says, follow the money. Without any evidence of foul play from any exhumations or post-mortems...'

'Which we wouldn't get anyway, since the alleged victims were all cremated,' I point out.

'Conveniently,' says Albie.

'Except for Stanley. Yet...' I say hopefully to Dionne, but she shakes her head.

'We'd need a proper motive, not to mention some actual evidence, to even start going down that route,' she says. 'But in the absence of any kind of forensics, perhaps if we check the wills? See if there was any money there and, if so, what happened to it. Or whether any of the four changed their wills just before their deaths.'

'Good luck with that,' Albie says. 'Aren't wills only made public once probate has been granted? And it's a little too soon in the day for that.'

Dionne stands up and taps her badge. 'Not for a police offi-cer,' she says, making for the door.

'What about us?' I say, and she narrows her eyes at me.

'What about you?'

'What do you want us to do?'

'Nothing.'

'But...' I huff, and Dionne holds up a placatory hand.

'Doing nothing is still doing something, if you think about it.'

'That's hardly the best use of our resources.'

'Not to mention our position on the inside,' adds Albie.

Dionne folds her arms and regards us like she's a school-teacher and we're the two troublemakers at the back of the class. 'If – and it's a big "if" at the moment – there does turn out to be some substance behind any of this, then we'll open an official investigation, and... Yes, Albie?'

Albie puts down the hand he's raised. 'By "we", you mean

the police, right, and not...' He indicates the three of us, and Dionne nods.

'Exactly. So you two need to keep as low a profile as possible. If there is something strange going on here at Twilight Lodge, then the last thing you should be doing is drawing attention to yourselves. Understood?'

Albie and I exchange glances. 'Understood,' we chorus.

Though I suspect what we've understood – and what Dionne means – are possibly quite different things.

41

——————

The way I see it – or probably, the way I'm *choosing* to see it – is that Dionne's instruction for us to keep a low profile is as good as her telling us to continue our investigation covertly. So while she makes her official enquiries and waits for Nigel to supply her with the information she's asked for, Albie and I do our best to leave no stone unturned in terms of subtly questioning as many of Twilight Lodge's residents as we can, trying to uncover any piece of evidence, however small, that might incriminate Nigel, or Tommy, or Nigel and Tommy together, or failing that, point us in the direction of whoever else the killer might be. The trouble is, it's not easy to get information about things that happened weeks ago from people who have a job remembering what they've had for breakfast, and even if we do, the fact they have a tendency to misremember means they're not exactly what you'd call reliable witnesses.

By Sunday morning, and with Dionne due in with an update this evening – a fact I've shared with Philip in my ongoing attempt to get the two of them in the same room and hope some sort of magic happens – we've drawn a blank, which means we need to start taking some risks, and that starts with me trying to get my hands on a particularly small piece of evidence, or rather, several small pieces. And while on any other day that might necessitate breaking into Nigel's office, if my jottings regarding the usual working routines here at Twilight Lodge are correct, this particular morning's staff movements should mean I don't have to.

As nonchalantly as I can, I stroll across to the window and – as if I'm casually checking the weather – reconnoitre the car park. There's no sign of Nigel's Aston Martin, and it's a sunny day, so he's probably on the golf course, which means he'll be gone for hours. Although five minutes is all I need.

I check my watch – if things are running to schedule, we should be just in time for what I'm planning – then hurry back to where Albie's sitting, half asleep, in front of something on the television. 'Albie!' I say, making sure I'm out of arm's reach in case in his drowsy state he mistakenly thinks I'm an assassin sneaking up on him. Any memory of his past life may have gone, but his reflexes might be just as lethal as they always were, and the last thing I want to do is become a victim of friendly fire. Even though you'd be hard pushed to describe Albie as friendly.

'What?' he says, without taking his half-lidded eyes from the screen.

'Watching something interesting?'

'*Escape to the Country*,' he says unenthusiastically.

'Which country – Nicaragua?' I say, quickly followed by, 'Too soon?' and even though it's been the best part of fifty years, Albie's rather rude hand gesture tells me it is. 'Come on,' I say, grabbing his wheelchair by the handles, and for once he doesn't complain.

'Have you found something?'

'Not yet,' I say, pushing him towards the reception desk, answering Miriam's raised eyebrows with a nod down at Albie and a mouthing of the word 'toilet' when we pass her at speed in the corridor.

'So where are we going?'

'Nigel's office.'

'What for?'

'To look for evidence.'

'Please god!' says Albie, who I suspect is as frustrated as I am with our lack of progress. 'Such as?'

'Anything incriminating.'

Albie makes a face. 'Again – such as?'

'A written confession – or failing that, something that links him to the murders – would be nice!'

'Wouldn't it just? Although where are we going to find *that*?'

'Watch and learn, old boy!' I say, pausing as we pass reception. Joy's not there – I've already spotted her heading off to the ladies' – so quickly, I reach over and help myself to the contents of Nigel's in-tray – yesterday's post, apparently – provoking a look of horror from Albie.

'You can't just steal his private mail!'

'Albie, he might be a murderer. Postal theft pales into insignificance compared to that.'

Albie scans up and down the corridor, his earlier bravado evaporating. 'This is hardly keeping a low profile,' he says agitatedly.

'Albie, you can't even see over the desk. How much lower can you get?'

'But we might get into trouble!'

'With who? Nigel's not here. And nor is Joy right now, so we'd better get a move on if—'

'We might get into trouble with Dionne.'

'What's she going to do – arrest us?'

Albie glares at me. 'Quite possibly, seeing as she's a police officer.'

'We'll just plead diminished responsibility.'

Albie looks at me as if that goes without saying in my case. 'Even so. It'll be worse for me.'

'Rubbish!'

'It's not rubbish. It's all right for you. You're out of here in a week or so. I've got to spend the rest of my days here, and if they decide to kick me out for something you made me do which messes up my prospects...'

Albie stops mid-sentence, although he doesn't need to complete it for me to know what he's talking about, or rather, *who* he's talking about. And I can't jeopardise his chances with Barbara. Not if I want to be sure he's got a purpose after I've left.

'Fine,' I say, putting the letters back down – though only because I've already clocked the senders' addresses on the back, and unless Nigel's in league with either the Reader's Digest or the subscription department of *Golf Monthly*, there's nothing incriminating here. 'The last thing I want to do is put a spanner in the works with you and you-know-who. Which is why I've come up with a plan which helps both you and me, and you and *she*, out.'

42

Albie looks simultaneously intrigued and worried. 'Dare I ask?'

'Like I just said – rubbish. And Nigel's insistence his office is cleaned on a regular basis.'

'I don't...?'

'Remember,' I say, as I hover in the corridor, doing my best to look as innocent as possible. 'Just play dumb if we're caught.'

'I don't have to play dumb, seeing as I haven't the faintest idea what we're—'

'Shh!' I say, as right on schedule, Marie the cleaner emerges from Nigel's office, having just finished her usual Sunday morning stint. She's carrying a vacuum cleaner in one hand and – I'm happy to note – Nigel's wastepaper bin in the other. 'Right,' I say to Albie. 'You distract her, and I'll grab the bin.'

'Distract her how?'

'Pretend you're having a fit, or fall dramatically out of your wheelchair?' I sigh exasperatedly. 'Why do I have to come up with everything?'

'You said you had a plan!'

'Fair enough. Brace yourself!'

'What?' says Albie, sounding rather alarmed, but before I

can lift the back of his wheelchair and tip him over and onto the carpet, Marie puts the vacuum cleaner down next to an empty black plastic bin bag in the hallway, picks up the bag, shakes it open, then empties the bin into it.

'Even better,' I say as she heads back into Nigel's office to return the wastepaper bin – my cue to push Albie across to where she's left the bin bag, before picking it up and depositing it on his lap.

'What are you...?'

'Just check inside!'

Resignedly, Albie peers into the bag. 'It's just a load of shredded paper.'

'Exactly as I thought!'

'And that's good because?'

'It's what I saw Nigel doing the other day.'

'Same question.'

'Why would you shred anything?'

Albie's eyes widen. 'Because you don't want anyone else reading it!'

'And what on earth would the owner of a nursing home in a sleepy seaside town on the south coast of England not want anyone to read?'

Albie doesn't answer my question – not that he needs to, given the revelatory look on his face – so I say, 'Exactly!' then reach inside and extract a handful of the strips. They're only a couple of millimetres wide, and so thinly shredded I doubt I'd be able to make out what's on them even if I increased the prescription on my reading glasses to the maximum level, but before I even get the chance, Marie reappears from Nigel's office to find us going through her refuse. Perhaps not surprisingly, she seems a little puzzled.

'Can I help you gentlemen with something?'

'What? Oh. No. I'm fine, thanks. We're fine. Aren't we, Albie?'

'That's right, Martin. Fine,' says Albie. 'Tickety-boo, in fact.'

'Okay. Well...'

Marie moves to take the bin bag back, but faced with the prospect of losing what could possibly be key evidence, I'm not prepared to let her, so I make a grab for it. So does Albie, which leads to a rather comical tug of war until the bag bursts, covering Albie in shredded paper.

'What are you *doing?*' says Marie, looking at the two of us as if we've lost the plot.

Frantically, Albie gathers as much of the bag's contents as he can hold in his lap. 'We, er, need this,' he says.

'Need what?'

'These shreds,' Albie says, and Marie frowns.

'What on earth for?'

'Um...' I say, and it's as far as I get. The actual answer is 'to try and trap a killer', but I'm not sure that particular explanation will wash. Nor, apparently, is Albie, because he looks desperately up at me. Then something obviously occurs to him, and he smiles.

'It's for him,' he says, handing me the shreds. 'He needs stuffing.'

'Stuffing?' says Marie, sizing me up as a taxidermist might.

'That's right. Martin here has taken up crocheting, would you believe?'

'Oh, *that* kind of stuffing,' says Marie, though she sounds like she doesn't believe it at all.

'Yes,' I say. 'It, um, helps with the old arthritis.'

I crack my knuckles, making both myself and Albie wince.

'He's currently making a rather large teddy bear,' Albie says. 'As a present.'

'Who for?' asks Marie suspiciously.

'My daughter Dionne,' I say, before I remember Marie and Dionne were in the same year at school – though even if they weren't, I doubt she'd think someone like me would have a child of stuffed toy age.

Marie stares at me in disbelief. 'I didn't have Dionne down as the teddy bear type.'

'It's not *for* her,' says Albie quickly. 'It's for her to give to someone else.'

'That's right,' I say quickly. 'As a present, like I mentioned. And this shredded paper would be perfect.'

'For the stuffing,' adds Albie.

'Of the bear,' I say. 'The bear I'm crocheting.'

'For Dionne,' says Albie. 'His daughter.'

'To give to someone else,' I say. 'As a present. She's a police officer, you see? And bears are expensive. Especially if you're on a police salary. Which is why I'm crocheting one. For her.'

I've noticed that the older I get, the more rambling an excuse I give for any odd behaviour, the less anyone is likely to challenge it, and in fact, the more probable it is that someone's going to dismiss it as the musings of a mad old man and subsequently dismiss *me*. And that turns out to be exactly the case here, as Marie evidently decides calling time on this conversation is the easiest option, and picks up her vacuum cleaner.

'Knock yourselves out,' she says – something Albie and I almost take a little too literally, given how we just about manage to avoid head-butting each other when we simultaneously bend down to collect the shreds we've dropped.

As Marie locks Nigel's office then heads off along the corridor, I hold my share of the mix of shredded correspondence and scraps of bin bag triumphantly aloft, adding, 'Ta-da!' for good measure, and Albie squints up at me.

'Brilliant!' he says, bundling the strips on his lap into a loose ball. 'Although how do we...?' His voice trails off, and to illustrate his point, he selects two strips at random and lines them up together. Unlike my good fortune with the jigsaw the other day, they don't match. 'There must be hundreds of pieces here.'

'Albie, my friend, I don't have to tell you that ninety per cent of espionage work isn't martinis and microdots. It's grunt work. Data analysis. Doing the boring stuff.'

Albie snorts. 'And I don't have to tell *you* that trying to make sense of all this is going to take *ages*. I have neither the eyesight, agility in my joints, or years left on this planet to try and find the needle in the haystack among what's probably just going to turn out to be worthless rubbish.'

I shrug, careful to keep from dropping my precious cargo. 'It might be rubbish, Albie, but whether it's worthless or not remains to be seen. And anyway – you don't have to match all this stuff up. And nor do I.'

'Why not?'

'Because we know a woman who can.'

Albie selects another couple of strips and holds them up to the light, squinting at them as if he's not sure if he's got them the right way up or not. 'I hardly think Dionne's going to waste any time on this. And besides, it's illegally obtained evidence. Even if she could make head or tail of it, she couldn't use it.'

'She couldn't. But we can,' I say, wheeling him towards a particular sea-view room, and one that he's got designs on – or rather, designs on its occupant. 'And in any case, I wasn't referring to Dionne.'

Before he can protest, I knock smartly on Barbara's open door, and wheel him into her room. She's sitting at her dressing table, making adjustments to what appears to be an already immaculate hairstyle, and when she catches sight of me in the mirror, her eyes widen.

'Martin?' she says, swivelling round on her stool, then she breaks into a grin. 'And Albert! To what do I owe this pleasure?'

As Albie gazes up at me, evidently in need of the same question being answered, I push the door to behind me. 'You remember the other day, when you asked us to involve you in our next bout of mischief?'

'I do,' she says, excitedly clasping her hands together.

'Well, we need your help. Don't we, Albie?'

After a moment, Albie realises that's his cue to speak. 'Um, yeah.'

'With what?'

'Reassembling these,' I say. 'If you'd be so kind?'

I give Albie a nudge, and he wheels himself over to where Barbara's sitting and hands her the mangled plastic bag.

'Oh, Albert!' Barbara exclaims, at Albie's sorry-looking offering. 'You shouldn't have!'

Albie starts to protest, then perhaps appreciates she's teasing him, and his cheeks colour. 'They're documents,' he says. 'Or they were. They've been shredded. In a, you know...?'

'Shredder?' Barbara's grin widens as she inspects the bag's contents. 'I *love* puzzles!'

'That's probably why you're so fond of the enigma that's Albie,' I say, and as the two of them giggle like five-year-olds, I hand Barbara the roll of Sellotape I skilfully purloined from the arts and crafts box in the Garden Lounge earlier. 'And not a word to anyone, if you don't mind? This is top secret. Isn't that right, Albie?'

'What?' Albie frowns. 'Oh. Right. We're, ahem...' He clears his throat, then lowers his voice. 'Undercover.'

Barbara taps her index finger against the side of her nose. 'Say no more,' she says. 'Although there's a thought, Albert.'

Albie does a double take. 'I'm sorry. I don't...?'

'You and me,' says Barbara, then she rests a hand on his knee. 'Under covers.'

And by the look on Albie's face, it's all he can do not to wheel himself at top speed out of the room.

43

It takes Barbara just a couple of hours – though almost the whole roll of Sellotape – to reassemble what turn out to be a couple of documents. And when Albie and I examine them in the privacy of his room, they appear to be extremely interesting indeed.

'What do you reckon?' says Albie, holding one of them up to the light, then passing it across to me.

I push my reading glasses further up my nose and squint at the page. Some bits are missing, or shredded in a way that they're almost illegible, but even so, it's a marvel of reconstruction. No wonder Barbara's unofficial title here at Twilight Lodge is the Jigsaw Queen – and not just because of her surname. 'It appears to be a letter from a solicitor. Nigel's, I'd imagine. About his divorce.'

'What divorce?'

I read a little further. 'The one his wife's apparently filed for.'

'What does it say?'

'It's confirming the amount of the divorce settlement. Just shy of a million pounds!'

Albie's eyes go wide. '*A million pounds?*'

'Apparently so.'

'That he's got to pay his *wife?*'

If I were Dionne's age, I think the correct response to Albie might be 'duh', but I'm not. 'Not that I've ever been divorced myself, you understand, but I imagine that's how it works.'

Albie whistles. 'It'd have been cheaper to have murdered *her,*' he says. 'Now there's a reason to sell Twilight Lodge.'

'Quite. Although he appears to be doing the opposite by refurbishing the place.'

'Maybe he doesn't have to sell, even in light of this.' Albie takes the letter back. 'As your daughter pointed out, you've seen his car.'

'And his watch!'

'Exactly. He hardly looks like a man struggling for money. Plus, he does run a business with a turnover of...' There's a pause, presumably for Albie to make the calculation, which he does after only a second or two. 'Almost two hundred thousand a month.'

It's my turn to whistle. 'Even so, a million pounds is still a million pounds, so I'd say we have a potential motive. Wouldn't you?'

'Most definitely.' Albie nods at the other document Barbara's pieced together. 'What else have we got?'

I pick it up and scan through the first couple of paragraphs. 'Another letter.'

'From?'

'An insurance company, if I'm not mistaken,' I say, the hairs on the back of my neck standing up. 'This could be the proof we need. Maybe Nigel's over-insured Twilight Lodge, and if he and Tommy Walker are planning to burn it down, he'll collect a hefty payout.'

'Is that what it says?' says Albie. 'At least, the first part.'

'Hold on.' Excitedly I read through the remaining sections,

hoping my brain still works well enough to fill in any gaps or parts destroyed by the shredder, then my face falls. 'No.'

'No?' says Albie, disappointedly.

'It's an individual policy. Relating to...' I peer closely at a ragged section. 'A "Lifetime Car Plan".'

I pass Albie the second letter, and he scrutinises it carefully. 'It must be for Nigel's Aston Martin.'

'Well, if it is, it might not be insured.' I reach across and point at the relevant paragraph. 'It says here the premium's still outstanding, and unless it's paid, they won't be providing cover.'

Albie flips the letter over, then points a bony finger at a figure in a box. 'I'm not surprised he didn't pay it. Look how much the premium was!'

'A hundred and sixty thousand pounds!' I exhale loudly. 'Even if it is for Nigel's lifetime, and say he's in his fifties, which means he's possibly got another thirty years of driving, it still works out at...'

I wait for Albie to do his usual and supply me with the answer, which again, doesn't take him long. 'Over five grand a year.'

'Crikey!' I jot down the policy details along with the company's telephone number in my notebook. 'Another potential requirement for money, don't you think?'

Albie nods. 'An Aston Martin's an expensive toy. Though maybe he's paid it now. And with the proceeds he's making from these murders.'

I peer at the letter again, hardly daring to hope we might have finally uncovered some solid evidence. 'That's something we can easily check out courtesy of that marvellous invention known as "the telephone", I think. Though we ought to hide these first.'

'Good idea.' Albie takes both letters, propels himself across to the chest of drawers in the corner of his room, and slips them into the top drawer, hiding them beneath several greying pairs

of Y-fronts – probably as safe a place as any to conceal them –
then he stares at me. 'What are you waiting for?' he says impatiently.

'I don't have a mobile.'

'Why not?'

'I've never needed one,' I say, though I'm acutely aware I
need one *now*.

'There's a payphone in reception,' says Albie, wheeling
himself towards the door. 'We can call from there.'

'Best not, Albie.'

'Why not?'

'Walls have ears,' I say, then something occurs to me. 'And
they also make ice creams.'

'What?'

'There's a phone box on the seafront, right next to where
the ice cream van is normally parked. We can call from there.
And reward ourselves with a couple of cones afterwards if it
proves to be anything significant.'

'A celebratory ice cream,' says Albie, unenthusiastically.
'What a time to be alive.'

Without giving him a chance to moan further, I grab his
wheelchair by the handles, steer him into the corridor, dash into
my room to retrieve some loose change, then push him past Joy
at reception.

'You two look like you're on a mission,' she says, as we speed
by, and the irony's not lost on me.

'Just popping out for some recuperative exercise.'

Joy looks puzzled. 'With Albie?'

I look down, as if noticing him for the first time. 'Um, yes.
Olga's told me to pick up the pace and add some resistance
when I walk.' I make a show of gripping the wheelchair tightly.
'This makes the perfect go-faster Zimmer frame, given the
wheels. And Albie in it provides the resistance, you see?'

As Joy makes a 'can't argue with that' face, I ignore Albie's

'I'm not resisting!' and steer him out of Twilight Lodge, through the gates, across the zebra crossing, and onto the seafront. It's a sunny day, so the promenade's busy, full of an assortment of weekenders: shirtless young men, young mothers with toddlers in tow and tattooed midriffs on show, and older individuals like us, dressed as if they're off on an expedition to the North Pole despite the fact that the temperature must be in the mid-twenties.

The ice cream van's in its usual spot opposite the square, though when we get to the phone box, there's no sign of anything resembling a telephone in it – or even any glass, when I examine it closely. To be honest, it smells more like it's been used as some sort of public convenience. Which makes it rather *in*convenient for me.

'What's wrong,' says Albie, as I stand and stare blankly at it.

'It's been vandalised!'

'Typical. Where's the next nearest one?'

I peer helplessly up and down the promenade. 'I have no idea.'

'Wait a second.' To my surprise, Albie pulls what looks suspiciously like a mobile phone from his pocket, taps the screen a few times, then puts it away again. 'There's one by the pier,' he says triumphantly, then he gives me a funny look, though perhaps it's in response to the one I'm giving him. 'What?'

'You've just found the location of the nearest payphone.'

'That's right.'

'By using *your* phone.'

'So what?'

'Which you've had all this time.'

I can almost hear the penny drop. 'Um, yeah.'

'Well, let me borrow it, then!'

'No fear!'

'Why not?'

'I'm waiting for a WhatsApp,' Albie says sheepishly.

'What's that?'

'No – a WhatsApp.'

'And what's that, Albie?' I say, enunciating carefully.

'Oh. It's like a message.'

'Why didn't you just say "message"?'

'Because unlike you, I have my finger on the pulse of popular culture.'

I ignore what I'm sure is Albie's attempt at an insult. 'Who from?'

'Who do you think?'

I glare at him. This isn't the first time a woman's come between Albie and a mission. And while I couldn't dissuade him from staying in Nicaragua with one all those years ago without the use of force, this argument should be easier to win. 'Yes, well, if you don't let me borrow it, she might not be able to WhatsApp you, because she'll be dead. *Murdered* dead, in fact. All because we weren't able to find out who the killer was, which ringing the insurance company might just get us a step closer to. Did you think of that?'

Albie doesn't seem to have an answer for that one, so like a dog forced to relinquish its grip on a favourite bone, he reluctantly hands the telephone over. It's pretty old, but compared to the days they used to send us out into the field with just a gun and a radio transmitter, it's a godsend. Hurriedly, I retrieve my notebook from my cardigan pocket, turn to the page where I've copied down the details of the insurance policy from Nigel's shredded letter, and dial the number.

'Put it on the speaker!' says Albie.

I look around, but can't see a speaker to rest it on, though I've hardly had a chance to properly check my surroundings when Albie snatches the phone from me and jabs at one of the buttons. There's the sound of a ringing tone, then a voice welcomes us to the Carstairs Insurance helpline, but before I can launch into my questioning, the same voice starts repeating the office hours. Which don't, sadly, include Sundays.

'Not much of a helpline!' says Albie.

'My sentiments exactly,' I say. 'Who knew espionage would be so dependent on the nine to five, eh?' I stare out to sea for a moment, and something occurs to me. 'Though thinking about it, what on earth could Nigel's non-payment of his motor insurance policy have to do with him being a murderer?'

Albie slips his phone back into his pocket. 'It might prove he's a criminal. After all, if you're prepared to drive around uninsured...'

'It's a big leap from that to multiple homicide. Besides, all that letter really says is that he didn't take out a policy with Carstairs. He might simply have gone with another insurer. Which means we're clutching at straws, Albie. So what's the point?'

'Of?'

'Phoning them. Or Barbara's hard work.' I let out a frustrated sigh as I look at my watch, then notice the ice cream van out of the corner of my eye. Dionne's not due to visit for an hour or so, and even though we don't have anything to celebrate – quite the opposite, in fact – it's not as if we're in a rush to get back to Twilight Lodge. 'Oh well. Why don't we go and investigate Mister Softee in the meantime?'

'Is he another suspect?'

'Not exactly, Albie,' I say, then I point at the van. 'Ice cream time!'

44

———

Albie looks suspiciously at the van, then makes a face. 'I'm watching my weight.'

I narrow my eyes at him. Albie's always been built like a racing snake – though he's also always had what we used to refer to as short arms and deep pockets, which I suspect is the real reason for his reluctance. 'My treat!' I say, and Albie considers this for approximately a millisecond, then his face lights up, proving my theory.

'In that case, rude not to.'

'Rude not to indeed,' I say, as I push him over to the van and straight up to the window, using the fact he's in a wheelchair to jump the queue, although it gets me the evil eye from a couple of teenage girls who – given the number of brightly coloured tattoos they're sporting – wouldn't look out of place among Tokyo's yakuza.

'What would you like, Albie?'

Albie peers up at the pictorial menu on the side of the van. 'I don't suppose there's one with alcohol in it?'

'I doubt they have a licence,' I say. 'Apart from "to chill"…'

I'm quite pleased with my wordplay, but like most of my

bon mots, it seems to go over Albie's head – and not just because he's permanently seated.

'A ninety-nine, then.'

'Excellent choice!' I say, smiling up at the pasty-faced youth manning the van. 'Two of your finest ninety-nines, please.'

I can't remember the last time I had a ninety-nine – because it must have been *ages* ago, not due to the state of my memory – and a wave of nostalgia washes over me when I realise it was probably when Dionne was a child. I watch fondly as the youth fills a couple of cones with swirls of ice cream, then skewers each one with a chocolate flake. Though my good humour quickly fades when he says, 'Six quid, please.'

'*Six pounds?*'

'S'right.'

'For two ninety-nines?'

'Yeah.' The youth nods at the picture menu. 'They're three quid each.'

'Really?' I say, though I've already managed to work that out, and without Albie's help. 'They were a tenth of that in my day.'

The youth looks me up and down, perhaps trying to work out how many years 'my day' was before he was born, though he gives up rather quickly. 'You want them or not?'

I think about this for a moment, aware that – unlike a good bottle of red wine – ice creams don't improve with age, and while saying 'not' would be quite satisfying, seeing as he's already made them, it'd also be childish. Besides, I've promised Albie one. And I always keep my promises.

'I suppose so,' I say, fishing in my pocket for the appropriate change – though it seems my intention to pay with actual cash brings almost as much ridicule as my shock at the price.

'It's card only.'

'What is?'

'Payment.'

'I don't have a card.'

The youth sniffs dismissively. 'I don't have any change.'

I examine the handful of coins I've just retrieved from my pocket. 'Then today's your lucky day,' I say, counting out six pounds and placing the exact sum on the counter in front of him.

We stare at each other for a moment, unblinking, much like the time I engaged in a 'quick draw' with a Colombian drug lord, except for the fact that back then, one of us ended up dead. Then – possibly because the queue behind me is getting restless, and in a scene reminiscent of many a hostage exchange I've been involved in – the youth begrudgingly takes the cash with one hand and hands over the ice creams with the other.

'A pleasure doing business with you,' I say sarcastically, then I pass one down to Albie, and we make ourselves scarce. They're already beginning to melt, so I'm torn between telling him to make it last, given what it cost, or to wolf it down as quickly as possible. Though as it stands, he doesn't get the chance. Before we're even ten yards further along the promenade, a seagull – and one that surely proves the theory that dinosaurs evolved into birds, as it's the size of a pterodactyl – swoops down and relieves him of his flake.

As Albie fruitily curses the bird, causing a young mum next to us to cover her toddler's ears, I let out a brief laugh, then snap my flake in two and offer him half. 'Just like that night holed up in that *favela* in Rio, eh?' I say, referring to the time Albie was out of ammo, so I gave him one of my last two bullets, just in case we needed to avoid capture, torture and certain death by another's hand. But if he remembers, Albie doesn't let on.

'Nothing more we can do, then?' he asks, once he's devoured the last of his ice cream, waved away my offer of a handkerchief, then licked his fingers clean.

'Not until Monday, no, Albie,' I say, unable to keep the frustration out of my voice. 'Though on the plus side, it certainly looks like Nigel has motive.'

'Agreed,' says Albie, nodding for good measure as I reverse-park him next to the nearest bench.

'But I still can't see him committing the actual murders. Particularly because, in Stanley's case, he wasn't even at Twilight Lodge at the time.'

'He does drive an Aston Martin. Even though he was still at Elsie's funeral when we left, he could have overtaken us on the way back and got there in time to do the deed.'

'I doubt even Niki Lauda at the wheel would have beaten Dionne back to Twilight Lodge that day, given how angry she was,' I say, testing the graffiti on the bench with my finger to make sure the paint's not still wet.

'Don't remind me.' Albie eyes a circling seagull suspiciously, perhaps wishing he had his gun. 'Which means if he *is* involved, he most certainly has an accomplice.'

'Exactly.' I sit down on the bench next to him and stare at the passers-by. 'An accomplice who might be: A, Tommy Walker, or B, any of the Twilight Lodge staff, given as they're the ones with unlimited access to, well, *us*, or... Oh.'

'You've skipped around a dozen letters there.'

'Not "O", Albie. *Oh*.'

Albie looks as if he can't tell the difference, so I put a hand on the top of his head, swivelling it around so he can see what I can see, and he pales. Because walking along the promenade towards us, swigging from a can of lager and scowling, is none other than Shane.

45

It's too late to hide, particularly given the visibility and lack of manoeuvrability of Albie's wheelchair, and while I could probably scuttle off and lose myself somewhere in the crowds, I've never abandoned another man in the field, and I'm not about to start now.

'What if he blames us for him getting fired?' says Albie nervously. 'Thinks it was us who dobbed him in?'

'Keep calm, Albie. I'm sure he won't have a go at us. Not in broad daylight and with so many witnesses.' It's a white lie, especially since the relative protection you'd have hoped the employee-customer relationship afforded us didn't seem to stop Shane's brutish behaviour when he was employed at Twilight Lodge. I look around for a suitable weapon to defend ourselves with, just in case, but all I can lay my hands on is the biro clipped onto my notebook. And while I once helped Albie incapacitate an over-zealous North Korean border guard via a swift stab to the jugular with the sharp end of a pen cap, Shane's visible lack of anything you'd describe as a neck makes that a no-go.

'Perhaps if we keep still he won't notice us,' Albie whispers.

I give him a look. 'Even better, why don't we make for the beach and stick our heads in the sand?'

Albie appears to be actually considering that, then evidently realises I'm being sarcastic, given St Leonards has a pebble beach. 'What are we going to do?'

'Don't worry, Albie. I've got your back.'

'It's my front I'm more worried about!' he says, as Shane drains the last of his beer, burps loudly, then crushes the can against his forehead and lobs it towards the bin next to our bench. He misses, and it clatters noisily to the ground, though he looks like he's got no intention of picking it up. It's all I can do not to tut loudly, but I'm worried about Albie's safety so I resolve to let it slide. Though the mistake I make is to pick up the can and drop it in the bin myself, because when I do, Shane catches sight of us, and his eyes widen in recognition. But instead of the all-out full-frontal assault I've braced myself for, he simply marches over and plonks himself down on the bench between us.

'All right, Jason Eastbourne?'

'I believe that's your best one yet, Shane,' I say, simultaneously trying to flatter him whilst surreptitiously tightening my grip on my biro. The smell of beer on his breath is a little overpowering, and I suspect the can I just binned wasn't his first today.

'Yeah? I had "Codger Moore" too.'

'Again, another corker.'

Shane regards me for a moment, perhaps wondering if I'm being flippant, then he grins. 'Escaped, have you?'

'Only for an hour or so, sadly,' I say, and Shane lets out a short chuckle.

'Don't blame you,' he says.

As he stares out to sea, I clear my throat. 'I... I mean, *we*, were sorry to hear about your being let go. Weren't we, Albie?'

Albie glares at me, as if Shane might not have noticed him

but for my mention of his name, and Shane sighs. 'No you wasn't,' he says. 'Me neither, to be honest. I hated that stupid job.'

'We could tell,' says Albie, under his breath.

'I mean, no offence, but who wants to spend every day with a bunch of incontinent, braindead old geriatrics?'

I hesitate, not sure if that's an actual question, but Shane starts talking again before I get the chance to answer. 'Still, I s'pose it was only a matter of time, seeing as how I knew what was going on.'

I stiffen slightly – or at least, slightly more than normal for someone of my age. 'What did you say?'

'Oh. Right. Sorry. Forgot.' Shane taps his ear, then leans across and raises his voice. 'I knew what was going on!' he almost shouts.

I hold my breath, almost unable to believe what I'm hearing. This could be the key to everything. And although Shane strikes me as the most unreliable of unreliable witnesses, he may be the only one we've got. 'What was going on with what?'

'With Nigel?' says Shane, as if I should already know who he's talking about. I fight the urge to reach for my notebook, as I don't want to make any sudden movements, just in case. Again, I console myself with the fact that at least Albie's here and his memory's better than mine, and give him a deliberate side-eye, which I'm glad to see he returns.

'And what *was* going on with Nigel, Shane?' I say, as levelly as I can.

Shane looks round at me. 'Him and Gemma?'

'Him and Gemma...?'

I leave the question hanging, and Shane rolls his eyes, as if Albie and I are among the 'braindead' he's just referred to. 'Shagging, weren't they?'

'Were they?' I say, fearing Shane's habit of ending every

sentence with a question makes his statements less likely to hold up in court – assuming this ever gets that far.

'Like rabbits.'

'That's *it*?' says Albie, incredulously.

Shane folds his arms, making the tattoos on his biceps twitch. 'Well, yeah,' he says, sounding a little disappointed at Albie's reaction to his big reveal. 'But he's married, isn't he?'

'How did you know?'

Shane frowns. 'He wears a wedding ring, doesn't he? And she's been in, Nigel's missus. Playing Madam High and Mighty. Bossing everyone about. Including me.'

'No – how did you know Nigel was, ahem, *with* Gemma?'

'Saw them, didn't I?' Shane shudders at the recollection. 'Caught them in the act. In her office. So I told them I'd tell his wife unless my job suddenly became a lot' – Shane grins in a self-satisfied way – 'cushier.'

'Which I'm guessing it did,' says Albie, and Shane nods.

'Too right.'

'And how long ago was this?' I say.

'When I caught them?' Shane thinks for a moment. 'Christmas, give or take?'

'So what happened?'

'His wife found out, didn't she? A couple of months ago. Not through me. I dunno what happened. But anyway, I s'pose she told him she wanted a divorce, and...' Shane draws a finger across where his throat should be, in an attempt to mime slitting it. 'That was that.'

I sigh, disappointed this hasn't been the revelation Albie and I had been hoping for, but nevertheless, I'm sure it's still something. 'So when his wife told Nigel she was divorcing him, you lost your leverage.'

'My what?'

'Your ability to blackmail him.'

Shane looks at me for a moment, perhaps unsure if I'm

teasing him. 'Something like that. In any case, that's not why they sacked me – officially, like.'

'Well, why...?' I say, and Shane's expression darkens.

'Old no-Joy's fault, wasn't it?'

'By that, I take it you mean *actual* Joy?'

'Yeah.' Shane hits the thumb-side of his fist twice against his chest, and while for a moment I fear he's about to launch into a Māori-style haka, it's apparently just to help release some trapped wind. 'Always had it in for me, that one.'

Albie frowns. 'But she seems so... nice.'

'Yeah. Well.' Shane burps again. 'Looks can be deceiving. Turns out she'd only been compiling a list of complaints against me from the residents. Making most of 'em up herself, I reckon.'

'What sort of complaints?' Albie asks, despite my desperate telepathic attempts to warn him not to, and Shane shrugs.

'How long have you got?' he says, looking up at the heavens. 'One of them apparently accused me of nicking his sweets, would yer believe? I don't even *like* Mint Imperials.'

I grip the arm of the bench tightly, fearing Shane might suspect which of the residents this particular complaint came from, so it's a relief when Albie quickly changes the subject.

'Why would she want you gone?' he asks.

'I didn't ask. Mainly coz they said they'd use the drugs thing against me if I didn't go quietly.'

'*Drugs thing?*' I say, pretending Dionne hasn't told me anything about his past.

Shane shrugs. 'I used to deal a bit. When I was younger. Only the soft stuff, mind. But Nigel said if I made a fuss, they'd tell the police they'd caught me trying to sell gear to the residents.'

'You didn't!' I say, and Shane, to his credit, looks a little offended.

'As if! Most of you are on so many meds you're off your heads already!'

'But you do sell... *gear?*' asks Albie, leaning forward in his wheelchair.

'Not anymore,' says Shane, then he lowers his voice. 'Why – you after something?'

I chuckle at the prospect, but Albie seems deadly serious. 'Might be,' he says.

A look comes over Shane's face – and seeing as it's Shane's face, it takes me a moment to recognise it as *concern* – evidently, however many lagers he's consumed today has mellowed him. 'You're not still thinking of topping yerself, Albie?'

'What?' Albie avoids my gaze. 'No. Nothing like that. The opposite, in fact.'

'Huh?'

'I'm after something to...' He leans in so closely I worry he's going to tip the wheelchair over and land in Shane's lap. 'Perk me up.'

'Perk you up how?' asks Shane.

'Don't make me spell it out.'

'Or mime it!' I suggest.

Shane stares at him for a second or two, then his eyes widen. 'You randy old sod!'

'Can you help me or not?' says Albie, his expression somewhere between indignation and embarrassment.

'All right, all right. Keep your hair on,' says Shane, perhaps a little disrespectfully given Albie's lack of it. 'You should ask that Gemma. She seems to have a bit of everything in that medicine cabinet of hers.'

'Yeah, sure,' says Albie. 'I can just see *that* conversation working out well.'

Shane shakes his head slowly. 'Like I said, that's not been my thing for a while. But I might be able to help you out in another way. Point you in the right direction, so to speak. Have you got a bit of paper?'

Albie looks horrified. 'I hope you're not going to draw me a diagram?'

'Nah.' Shane takes the notebook and pen I've offered him and turns to the first blank page. 'Go to this place,' he says, scribbling something down. 'Ask for Asif. He's a mate. Tell him Shane sent you, and you're after some "blue diamonds". He should be able to help. But don't go overdoing it, eh?' Shane lets out a bark of a laugh. Then he sets the notebook and pen down on the bench, stretches exaggeratedly, and climbs to his feet. 'Anyway,' he says. 'As emotional as this little reunion has been, I can't hang around here all day with you two. Got my reputation to think of, haven't I?'

'Right. Well, best of luck with the job hunt,' I say, and Shane sniggers.

'Good one, Martin,' he says.

46

As Shane struts off along the promenade, Albie and I exchange bemused glances. 'Crikey,' says Albie. 'Are you sure that's the same Shane that used to work at Twilight Lodge?'

'Actually, no!' I say. 'Maybe they should have let him drink at work. But what do you make of his revelation?'

'Nigel and Gemma?' Albie sticks out his bottom lip thoughtfully. 'Happens all the time, workplace romances.'

'I'm flattered, Albie, and I'm very fond of you too, but speak for yourself,' I say, then I give him a wink, and he glowers at me. 'I meant, how does it affect our investigation?'

Albie frowns. 'At least we know why he got divorced now. And there's a reason to need money, if ever there was one.'

'The divorce settlement.'

'And to keep Gemma in the style to which she might want to become accustomed.'

'True. So Nigel's wife divorces him, Nigel has to find the cash to pay her off, he sells Twilight Lodge to Tommy Walker...' I puff air out of my cheeks. 'It still doesn't explain why anyone would be murdering the residents.'

'And why sell Twilight Lodge in the first place? We know

it's a licence to print money. So why kill the goose that lays the golden eggs?'

'And we also know Tommy Walker's not one to pay full price for anything if he can help it.' Fed up, I lean forward and rest my head in my hands. 'It just doesn't add up.'

Albie folds his arms and stares out to sea. 'Not much about any of this does.'

'Unless we're dismissing prematurely the one piece of evidence we do have.'

'Which is?' says Albie, evidently having dismissed it so prematurely he doesn't even know what I'm referring to.

'Who was the one staff member present in Twilight Lodge for every murder?'

'You're telling me *Joy's* the killer?'

'When you have eliminated all which is impossible, then whatever remains, however improbable, must be the truth.' I've hammed up my voice to sound like a Victorian gentleman, and Albie gives me an inquisitive look. 'It's my favourite Sherlock Holmes quote.'

'So it has to be her, simply because we've been unable to uncover any credible evidence incriminating anyone else?'

'Consider the following, Albie,' I say, preparing to count the facts off on my fingers. 'Joy's the only one who was on duty when all four murders took place. Shane apparently found Elsie's body, and according to him, Joy was the person who got him fired, so one might wonder whether he saw something suspicious.'

'Why didn't he say anything?'

'You've met him, Albie – he may simply not have realised. But why take the risk he might? And the other day she even said something to me about how nice Twilight Lodge's sea view was. Taken on their own, each of those things is circumstantial. Inconsequential, even. But when you look at the wider picture...'

'Which also includes the fact that it's *Joy*...'

'I know,' I say miserably. 'Not to mention the fact that she doesn't have a motive – or at least, not one we can think of.' I look at my watch, then stand up from the bench and take hold of Albie's chair by the handles. 'Anyway – shall we?'

'Where are we going now?' says Albie.

'Back to Twilight Lodge. Dionne will be there soon. Perhaps with the missing piece of this puzzle.'

Albie shuffles round in his chair and looks up at me earnestly. 'Can we make a stop on the way first?'

'You can't cross your legs until we get back?' I say, assuming Albie means the seafront loos, though it turns out I'm mistaken, as Albie turns a shade of red.

'I can't do *anything* from the waist down, Martin. Which is why I need to make a stop on the way.'

It doesn't take me long to put two and two together. '*Seriously?*'

'Yes, seriously. A woman like Barbara is bound to have' – Albie colours again – '*expectations*. And I'm not sure... I mean, it's been a long time since I had someone, you know, *pay me a visit. At night...*'

'Have you tried pressing the alarm button in your en-suite?'

'Not funny, Martin.'

As Albie's voice trails off, I can't say I don't feel for him. 'I'm sure it'll be fine,' I say, in my best reassuring tone. 'After all, I seem to remember you were quite the ladies' man.'

'If only!' says Albie. 'And even if I used to be, I suspect the only thing I can do three times a night at my age is *pee*.'

'Albie...' I say, preparing to give him a lecture on the dangers of drugs, and especially ones bought via what I'm sure are Shane's dodgy contacts.

But before I can, he fixes me with a glare and says simply, 'Don't!'

So – and though it's against my better judgement – I don't.

47

The address Shane's given us turns out to be a newsagent just around the corner from Twilight Lodge. Unless things have changed considerably since the days I used to pop into my local one for a paper and what used to be called a 'Marathon' – until this beloved country of mine decided to follow America rather than the other way round – it seems doubtful we're going to come out with anything that's likely to pep Albie up, apart from perhaps a magazine from the top shelf. Especially since, when we get there, Albie refuses to go in.

'Why ever not?' I say.

'I don't want word getting round.'

'Whereas it's all right if word gets round about *me*?'

'You're leaving Twilight Lodge in a few days, so yes!'

'Might I remind you my daughter's a policewoman?'

Albie glowers at me. 'Might I remind *you* that you owe me big time for all my help over the past couple of weeks?'

I stare at him for a moment, then realise he's got a point, so without another word, I park him up outside the shop, check the coast is clear, then march in. There's a large man behind the counter, removing items from an equally large display with the word VAPES written above it – the owner, I assume, unless I've made a mistake and he's robbing the place – so I clear my throat, and he looks round.

'Help you, mate?'

'Asif?'

'Well, what have you come into my shop for, then?' The man grins as if it's not the first time he's made that remark, then perhaps sees my bewilderment. 'Yeah. That's me.'

'Good. Well, um...' I hesitate – I haven't done a drug deal since the Eighties, and as part of a sting operation on a Russian ambassador rather than for any personal gain – and I'm a little nervous about the protocol nowadays. Though I remind myself that negotiating between trigger-happy Afghan warlords and Mossad agents was perhaps a bit riskier than facing down a St Leonards shopkeeper. 'Shane gave me your details.'

'Shane?' Asif raises one eyebrow. 'Oh yes?'

'He said you might be able to furnish me with... I mean, I'd like some, ahem...'

'Blue diamonds?'

'How did you know?'

Asif lowers his voice. 'We get a lot of gentlemen your age in here asking for the same thing. Some older ladies, too. I think they like to crush them up and sprinkle them on their husbands—'

'Woah, Asif!' I say, holding a hand up for good measure. 'I believe that's what's known nowadays as "too much information".'

'*Dinner*, I was going to say.'

'Oh. Right.' I cough awkwardly. 'Yes, then. Blue diamonds it is, please. Not that they're for me, you understand.'

'Of course not,' says Asif, sarcastically.

'They're not!' I say indignantly. 'Everything's in perfect working order as far as I'm concerned, I'll have you know! They're for my friend.' I jab a thumb over my shoulder, then –

when Asif stares blankly in that direction – turn around to indicate where I've left Albie in front of the doorway. Annoyingly,
he's nowhere to be seen.

'For your "friend". Sure,' says Asif, making the air quotes
sign I'm beginning to loathe. He reaches down beneath the till
and retrieves a small, clear plastic click-seal bag containing half
a dozen vividly blue pills. 'These what you were after?'

'I imagine so,' I say, then I reach into my pocket and fish out
the rest of my change, though there's not a great deal – the
ninety-nines have unexpectedly almost bankrupted me. 'How
much are they?'

'Twenty quid.'

'How many can I get for...' I swiftly count my remaining
coins. 'Four pounds ninety?'

Asif laughs. 'It's not pick and mix. Tell you what, though...'
He reaches back down beneath the till and produces a bag of
slightly less blue but similar-shaped tablets. 'I'll do you these
instead.'

'The real thing, are they?'

'For a fiver?' Asif laughs as he hands me the bag. 'Nah. Best
Chinese knock-off version, though.'

'And they're safe?'

'Safe enough. Although how does the joke go about the old
guy with the younger girlfriend – "if she dies, she dies"?' Asif
smirks, then he suddenly looks serious. 'At your age, given what
you're using them for, it won't be them that kill you, if you know
what I mean?'

Asif looks as if he's considering adding a nudge and a wink
to that sentence, so I can imagine exactly what he means, but at
the same time, I know I can't give these to Albie. I'm as strong as
an ox, but he's half the man he used to be. If something untoward happens to him as a result of taking them, I'd never forgive
myself, and – aside from the fact that it would make me an
accomplice to manslaughter – I'm rather enjoying having him

around again. It's not quite like the old days, but it's the best I'm going to get. Besides, we've still got a killer to catch.

In desperation, I scan the counter, and my eye falls on a box of something called 'Tic Tacs'. From what I can just about make out on the label, they appear to be mints, and 'frosty', whatever that means. While they're more capsule-shaped than diamond-like, what really appeals to me is their intense shade of blue.

'I've changed my mind,' I tell Asif, handing him back the bag. As he puts the tablets back underneath the counter, I stealthily palm a box of Tic Tacs. It's shoplifting, I suppose, but Asif's a drug dealer, and in my experience, if you don't play by the rules, karma's eventually going to get you.

I bid Asif goodbye, head out of the shop and peer up and down the street, eventually spotting Albie lurking behind a post box a little further along. Surreptitiously, I peel the label off the Tic Tacs as he wheels himself towards me.

'Did you get them?'

'I did,' I say, checking over my shoulder in case we're being watched, before realising I'm not actually involved in a drug deal now, given my recent sleight of hand. 'Here,' I say, handing him the box.

Albie peers at them suspiciously. 'I thought they were supposed to be diamond shaped?'

'These are the new smooth-edged version. Apparently they go down easier.'

Albie grins. 'Hopefully they'll have the opposite effect,' he says, then he pops the box open, and my eyes widen in alarm.

'You're not going to take one now?'

'Don't be daft.' He gives the Tic Tacs a cautious sniff, then wrinkles his nose. 'They smell minty.'

'What?' I feign surprise, then lean down and take a sniff. 'You're right. Two birds with one stone, I suppose.'

'Huh?'

'You don't want to put her off with a bit of the old bad

breath. Especially if you're, you know, *up for it* for a limited time. If you see what I mean?'

Albie looks like he sees exactly what I mean. 'Makes sense,' he says, swiftly pocketing the box. 'What do I owe you?'

I wave him away. 'On me,' I say, and Albie beams up at me.

'You're a lifesaver,' he says.

'I just might be,' I say under my breath.

48

Pleased I seem to have gotten away with my spontaneous subterfuge, I steer Albie back along the pavement, round the corner and in through Twilight Lodge's gates, just in time to see Dionne emerge from her car. She's early, and out of uniform this time, plus Custard's at her feet, making me fear she's not come up with anything, which is disappointing, to say the least. Even so, I fix a smile on my face, give her a wave, and indicate she should join us. Uncharacteristically, and with a turn of speed I didn't know he possessed, Custard beats her to it.

'Where have you two been?' Dionne says, as Custard yaps excitedly, then sits himself on my foot.

I bend down and scratch one of the rolls of fat on his back. 'Out for an ice cream,' I say hurriedly, reluctant to admit the real reason for our outing, let alone the encounter with Shane or our attempted drug deal. 'Isn't that right, Albie?'

'What?' Albie almost jumps, his mind evidently on other things, though I don't like to think what. 'Oh. Yes – a ninety-nine!' he says.

'All right for some,' says Dionne. 'While I've been hard at work.'

I give a brief salute. 'And thank you for your dedication to duty,' I say. 'Speaking of which, did you check out the wills?'

'As I said, I've been hard at work,' she says, making for the building, though I put a hand on her arm to stop her. I've just spotted Olga heading along the corridor, and the last thing I want is an impromptu run-through of the excruciating exercises I'll no doubt be set as homework.

'Shall we walk and talk?' I say, directing Dionne towards the garden. 'Or rather, push and talk?'

I make a face as if to infer Albie's heavy, and Dionne takes the hint – and subsequently the wheelchair – and steers him round the side of the building. Clicking my fingers at Custard – who, rather than simply getting up and off my foot, looks at me as if I've asked him to run a marathon, before reluctantly complying – I follow them both to the area under the pergola where we're sure not to be overheard.

'Okay,' Dionne says, parking Albie in a shady spot, before retrieving her phone and consulting her notes. 'George left just less than seventy thousand pounds, which all went to his wife. Diana's bungalow was sold last year, and the money all went on her care here, apparently, leaving not much left to speak of. Elsie's daughter got the balance of her estate, which amounted to some thirty-four thousand pounds. Stanley didn't have much to his name, but his son's something in the City and quite well off, so was paying for him to be here.'

Albie scratches his head. 'So of them all, the only relative who might have had a motive is Stanley's son.'

Dionne frowns. 'How do you work that out?'

'So he didn't have to pay for him to be here any longer. I'm sure there's lots of things he'd prefer to be spending six grand a month on.'

Dionne looks puzzled. 'Except it was Stanley's son who put him in here in the first place.'

'It's a good alibi,' says Albie, reaching a hand down to pat

Custard, who's sniffing his wheelchair tentatively, possibly catching the scent of the Tic Tacs. I find myself idly wondering whether the pug's olfactory abilities might assist us in tracking the murderer down. Though I dismiss the idea just as quickly – with no food involved in the crimes, he just wouldn't be interested.

'If he was only going to kill Stanley,' points out Dionne. 'There's still no link between the four of them.'

'No other link, apart from the "sea view" angle,' I interrupt, lowering myself onto the bench.

'Right,' says Dionne, following suit, then hoisting Custard up to sit between us. 'And until we have that...'

I smile to myself, happy that Dionne's use of the word 'we' means our investigation team now officially numbers three. 'Unless the link *is* Tommy Walker, killing off the residents here so he can get his hands on the place.'

As Custard rests a paw on my arm – not to contribute a theory, sadly, but just to request some attention – Dionne shakes her head. 'I can't see it. Tommy Walker's a lot of things, but a *killer*? I'm just not convinced.'

'But he's a suspect?'

Dionne gives me a look. 'Unofficially,' she says.

'And Nigel?' asks Albie.

'The same. Although with no evidence tying either of them into any sort of crime, and no proof any of the deceased were murdered...'

'You could always perform a post-mortem on Stanley,' I suggest, absent-mindedly stroking Custard on the very spot that makes his back leg twitch.

'On what grounds?' says Dionne. 'In any case, he's due to be cremated next week. So unless you've come up with anything concrete...?'

I open my mouth, then close it again. Even after all this digging, I have to concede we haven't. And while I'd normally add the word 'yet' to that sentence, seeing as I'm leaving on Wednesday, we don't have a lot of time left to do so.

Dionne looks at the two of us for a moment, then she takes a deep breath. 'I can't believe I'm about to say this, but...'

I pause mid-stroke, causing Custard to whimper in protest. 'But what?'

'Keep an eye out, will you? For anything suspicious that happens. Just in case. And I mean *anything*. Otherwise...' She throws her hands up in the air. 'That's it.'

Albie and I lock eyes, and I can tell he wants me to let Dionne know about the letters we found, what Shane told us about Nigel, how we've got circumstantial evidence that puts Joy in the frame, and perhaps even the fact that Nigel might be driving around uninsured, but I've not finished processing all of that quite yet so I keep schtum. Until I've worked out what's going on, giving Dionne that information – and maybe letting the killer know what we know – might do more harm than good to our investigation.

Not to mention the harm it might do to *us*.

49

The trouble is, nothing much happens *at all*. No one else gets murdered, Tommy Walker doesn't return to Twilight Lodge, Nigel swans around like he owns the place – which I suppose is justified – and despite almost constant surveillance by either myself or Albie, and sometimes the both of us in case he or I fall asleep, Nigel and Gemma behave so professionally towards each other you'd think Shane had been making things up. I have to conclude I've hit a dead end. And by Monday, with less than three days before I'm due to go back home, I'm all too aware that time's running out.

As Albie and I sit by the window in his room, pretending to do yet another jigsaw while we're actually keeping tabs on any comings and goings, Nigel pulls up in his Aston Martin. There's something different about the car, and while I can't quite work out what it is, Albie spots it straight away.

'Flash git. Or rather, flashier.'

'How do you mean?'

'Apart from the fact that he's driving a car that costs more than most people's houses?' Albie roots angrily through the jigsaw box and retrieves a piece of sky that looks identical to the one he's just put back in. 'Look at the number plate.'

I peer at the front of the car and make out an 'N' and a '1', followed by a 'G', an 'E', and an 'S', note the clever positioning of a black bolt-head as if it's an apostrophe between the last two letters, and conclude Albie's description is spot on. 'That probably cost him as much as the car did.'

'All right for some,' says Albie, as a smug-looking Nigel climbs out of the vehicle, before taking a step backwards to admire it. 'D'you think he'll let me have a drive, seeing as I've effectively bought it for him?'

'I thought the government were paying for your stay?'

Albie glowers at me. 'It's still six grand a month going into his pocket as a result of me being here.'

I stare out of the window at the car, then sit bolt upright, which causes my good hip to twinge – and I'm reminded that at my age, 'good' is a relative term. 'Hang on,' I say. 'It just doesn't add up.'

'Yes it does,' says Albie. 'Six grand a month is seventy-two a year. That car's the best part of a hundred and fifty thousand. I've been here two years, which means...'

'No, I mean...' Frantically, I leaf back through my notebook. 'He's getting divorced, right? And we've seen the settlement he's going to have to pay his wife. And if he is thinking about selling this place to Tommy Walker, surely he only gets the money when the deal is done?'

'So?'

I take a deep breath. 'Albie, did I ever tell you how I tracked you down to Nicaragua?'

Albie puts his head in his hands. 'Not *this* again...'

'We knew you'd gone to Central America, but then you disappeared off-grid. We'd completely lost you. You weren't using your credit cards, there were no bills in your name – *any* of your names, or rather aliases – or records of any of your passports being stamped anywhere in the world. Not so much as a peep. And we – I – almost gave up. Then I remembered something you told me back in the early days, when we were trying to catch that crooked arms dealer who was supplying those terrorists in… Where was it again?'

Albie looks up from where he's been examining the picture on the jigsaw box. 'If I only had the faintest idea…'

'Anyway, no matter. It was the same thing then. We had no evidence. Couldn't pin anything on him. His codename was "Teflon" because no matter how hard we tried, nothing would stick.'

Albie stifles a yawn, though I'm not convinced it's a genuine one. 'Are you going somewhere with this?'

'You said we should follow the money, then and now. But back then, we had no record of the transactions, because they weren't going through the normal channels, and were all happening in cash – although what we *could* see, when we looked hard enough, was the *evidence* of them. So when a battery of cruise missiles appeared in Afghanistan, or a consignment of Kalashnikovs turned up in Iraq, we just had to work backwards from that. And it was the same with you. Even though we couldn't see you buying anything, or detect any movement in your bank accounts – although that was probably because we'd frozen the ones we knew you had. Anyway, in the absence of that, we focused on the things we *could* see. So whenever a house was sold in the region, we'd investigate to try and find the buyer. Because we knew eventually, one time, it would be you.'

'What's your point?'

'You were tough to catch because you don't have an ego, and you wanted to keep your head beneath the parapet. Someone like him…' I nod out of the window, where Nigel is currently attempting to take a series of what I believe are known as 'selfies' with his latest addition – along with his grinning mug – in view. 'Someone who wants a personalised number plate on a flash car is desperate to show people how successful he is. Look at all the photographs he's got in his office of him with local celebrities.'

'Most of whom I've probably never heard of!'

'Me neither. But even so, while the sensible thing to do, if you're coming into a lot of money as a result of these murders, would be to stash it somewhere away from prying eyes, someone like Nigel just can't resist splashing it about. And you'd think right now, given what he's going through, Nigel can't afford to be spending. So the fact that he *is...*'

Albie stares at me for a moment as the penny drops. '... proves he's the one benefitting from what's going on here.'

'Unless he's won the lottery. Which is highly unlikely. More unlikely than me taking your mobile phone, dialling a random number, and the King answering, in fact. And not only because you hate me borrowing it.'

'So you think Nigel's our killer?'

'All we know right now is that Nigel's the beneficiary. Because all of a sudden he seems to have all the money in the world.'

'And just when you'd think he wouldn't.'

'Exactly.' I grin, then replace the expression with a frown. 'But where's he getting it from?'

'Like you just said. The murders.'

'I know that. Otherwise what would be the point of them? Why run the risk?'

'So, Tommy Walker?'

'Looking more and more unlikely, don't you think?'

Albie nods. 'Especially since, why would he be giving Nigel money *now?*'

'Quite. No, he's definitely getting it from the victims. But how? According to Dionne, none of them had any money to leave.' I stare up at the heavens for inspiration, then flick through my notebook for the umpteenth time. 'I'm sure there's something in here I've forgotten. Something I've overlooked.'

'Maybe you wrote it down.'

'Maybe. But it's not leaping out at me.'

'Shall I take a look? See if it leaps out at *me*?'

'Help yourself,' I say, handing Albie the notebook. As I pass it across, the cover falls open, and a leaflet drops out from between the back pages. With a groan, I bend down and pick it up from the floor.

'What's that?'

I peer at the front of the leaflet, recognising it from the other day. 'Just something Nigel gave me when I was asking about moving to Elsie's room,' I say, handing it over.

'Oh, the Premium Care Plan.'

'Which is?'

'Some kind of lifetime annuity thing. They asked me about it when I first arrived. Instead of the monthly fee, you pay a lump sum up front, and it guarantees they look after you for as long as you live.'

'You weren't interested?'

Albie lets out a short laugh. 'As you pointed out earlier, the government are paying for my stay here. They were hardly likely to cough up for something like this.'

'Why ever not?'

'I'm eighty-three years old, I like a smoke and a drink, and half of my body's already shut down. I'm not exactly a great candidate. And even if I was, it's not exactly what it says on the tin, is it?'

'How do you mean?'

Albie indicates the leaflet's title. '"Premium Care Plan". I'd hardly describe what goes on here at Twilight Lodge as premium care. I mean, I'm sure they do their best to take care of you, but...' Albie stops talking – perhaps because I'm gripping his knee rather firmly. 'Gerroff, will you?'

'Sorry, Albie,' I say, removing my hand. 'But what did you just say?'

'Gerroff?'

'Before that.'

'They do their best to take care of you. Why?'

'That's *exactly* what they've been doing. And not in a good way. Look here.' I reach over and point to the leaflet's first paragraph. 'Or rather, look what everyone on the Premium Care Plan gets.'

'A sea-view room,' says Albie, then his eyes widen.

'Precisely. How much is the premium?'

Albie scans quickly through the leaflet. 'It doesn't say.'

I get up and start pacing round the room, excited that things might be finally falling into place. 'This is it, Albie. Where the money comes from. Remember the letter from the insurance company?'

'About Nigel's Aston Martin?'

'Yes. Only it wasn't, was it?'

'Wasn't it?'

'No!'

'Why not?'

'Because it didn't say "Lifetime Car Plan".' I hurry over to Albie's chest of drawers, open his underwear drawer and – like a contestant on one of those television reality programmes asked to put his hand into something unpleasant – gingerly reach in and retrieve the letter from beneath Albie's Y-fronts. 'It said "Lifetime *Care* Plan".'

50

Albie slips the leaflet into his pocket, wheels over to me, and scrutinises the letter for a moment. 'The shredder's obliterated the "e" from the end of "Care",' he says, wide-eyed.

'Exactly.'

Wordlessly, he hides the letter carefully back in the drawer, then motions for me to follow him. We head through the door, along the corridor and out into the garden. Once we're safely ensconced beneath the pergola, he retrieves his mobile phone from his trousers, presses 'redial' followed by the speaker icon, and sets it down between us on the arm of the bench. After a moment, a friendly female voice welcomes us to Carstairs Insurance.

'Oh,' I say. 'Um, hello. I'd like to...'

'For policies, press "1". To make a claim, press "2". For anything else,' says the voice, 'press "3".'

I look at Albie, take a deep breath, then press the '3' key as if it's the last critical stage in an attempt to disarm a nuclear device. After a moment, a woman answers.

'Thank you for calling Carstairs Insurance,' she says, sounding suspiciously like the recorded message, so much so I think we must be on hold until she adds, 'This is Naomi speaking. Can I take your policy number, please?'

I wink at Albie, and smugly indicate where I've – *fortunately* – written this down, though in response, he hurriedly mouths 'disguise your voice'.

'Good idea,' I mouth back, then say, 'Of course, Naomi,' raising my normal baritone a few octaves while putting on my best approximation of a Scottish accent. 'It's four, four, two, seven, two, nine.'

'And if you could just confirm your full name and the first line of your address?'

I stare in wide-eyed panic at Albie, wishing I hadn't just done my best to sound like a woman.

'Hello?' says Naomi, though I'm a little too rabbit-in-the-headlights to respond.

'Sorry,' I say, as I frantically flick back through the pages. 'It's Nigel.'

'*Nigel...?*' says Naomi, though whether she's simply asking for a surname or has doubts that anyone called 'Nigel' would have a voice this high, it's hard to tell.

'That's right,' I say, playing for time as I flick back to where I've written this down. 'Montfort. And the address is Twilight Lodge, St Leonards-on-Sea, East Sussex.'

'Thank you,' says Naomi, and Albie and I punch the air in celebration that we're in. Though it's a celebration that doesn't last long when she says, 'Do you know the postcode?'

Albie and I look at each other, our relief at having seemingly bypassed Carstairs Insurance's security requirement evaporating somewhat suddenly. 'No,' Albie says, adopting a similar tone to mine. Though to our pleasant surprise, Naomi doesn't seem to see this as a problem.

'That's fine,' she says, perhaps keen to get us off the phone so she can deal with somebody normal. 'How can I help you?'

'You sent me a letter,' says Albie, still doing a good impression of me sounding like a woman. 'About this policy. And I just wanted to follow that up.'

'In terms of...?'

'You know. The letter.'

'What about it?'

'Well, um... I'm sorry,' says Albie, sounding more and more like Mrs Doubtfire – another recent movie afternoon pick – with every word. 'I'm actually Nigel Montfort's secretary here at Twilight Lodge. And I'm afraid I accidentally shredded it before he got a chance to read it. So I don't actually know what you were writing to me – I mean, my boss Nigel – about.'

There's a pause, and then Naomi says, 'I'm sorry, but I can't really discuss private correspondence with anyone but the addressee.'

I mime face-palming myself, but Albie doesn't look fazed. 'I understand that,' he says. 'But my boss...'

'Nigel?' says Naomi.

'Yes. Nigel. He gets very angry if I get something wrong. Even violent, on the odd occasion. And if he finds out about this...'

There's another pause, and then Naomi comes back on the line. 'That's awful,' she says sympathetically. 'Let me just check.'

'Thank you,' says Albie, rubbing his throat, as if the effort of speaking like this is painful, which I have to conclude, even after my brief attempt, it is.

There's the sound of someone – presumably still Naomi – typing something on a keyboard, and Albie and I hold our breath. 'The letter was regarding a Mrs Elsie Watson,' she says, after a moment, and the way Albie and I raise our eyebrows at the exact same moment, you'd be forgiven for thinking we'd been practising.

'Oh yes?' I say.

'Specifically, the non-payment of the premium for her Lifetime Care Plan. I'm assuming she decided not to take the policy out?'

'I'm sorry,' Albie says, in more of a squeak now. 'Could you just repeat that?'

'Mrs Watson's Lifetime Care Plan. We quoted you for this on May the twenty-third, but subsequently never received the payment. So I'm afraid the quote expired.'

Albie places his hand over the mobile's microphone. 'As did Elsie,' he whispers.

'I see,' I say, batting his hand away. 'So just to be clear, Mrs Watson didn't actually take the policy out?'

'That's right.'

'You're sure?'

There's the sound of a bit more tapping. 'Yes. There's a note on the account to say a message chasing this up was left with...' Naomi makes a few brief humming noises as if she's speed-reading something. 'A Joy Esperanza on the tenth. But there's no record of any subsequent payment. Unless Mrs Watson might have made it recently?'

'That would be difficult,' whispers Albie, and I shush him.

'Recently, as in...?'

'Well, if she's sent it in the last couple of days, then it might not be showing up in our system yet. Although the fact that we sent you that letter would suggest she hasn't. All quotes have a validity period, you see?'

I quickly jot this down. 'How long is the validity period?'

'A month,' says Naomi. 'And those letters are generally sent out a month after the quotation date. So...'

'I see. Thank you, Naomi.'

'Yes,' says Albie, perhaps forgetting he's me. 'Thank you.'

'I'm sorry,' I add quickly. 'I didn't mean to thank you twice.'

'But you've been doubly helpful,' says Albie, with a grin.

'Not a problem,' says Naomi. 'Is there anything else I can help you with today?'

'No. You've answered my question,' I say, doubtful I can maintain this elevated pitch much longer.

'And raised a load of others,' says Albie, once he's pressed the 'end call' button.

We sit there in stunned silence for a moment or two, then Albie picks his phone up and slips it back into his pocket. 'I don't get it,' he says, retrieving the leaflet and indicating the backdrop photograph, which shows a view of a sea so blue it must have been liberally photoshopped. 'Elsie had a sea view. Which means she was in a Premium room. Which also means she'd paid for a Premium Care Plan. Or, as Carstairs Insurance call it, a Lifetime Care Plan.'

'Except according to Naomi just now, she hadn't.'

'And yet she had,' I say. 'Otherwise why would her daughter Yvette and Nigel have been arguing about it at Elsie's funeral?'

'Were they?'

I nod frantically. 'What else could it have been about?' I stare at the leaflet again. 'Maybe Yvette was asking for a refund, and Nigel refused. "It's all in the small print", he told her. Why would he say that if Elsie hadn't taken the policy out in the first place?'

'So Nigel's in cahoots with someone at the insurance company?'

I shake my head. 'I doubt the money gets that far.'

'And the fact that a message was left with Joy?'

'Again, that could simply be coincidence. She's on reception, she answers the phone, maybe even deals with Nigel's correspondence.'

'I think this is something someone needs to check with Nigel,' says Albie.

'You mean Dionne?'

'Well, *I'm* certainly not going to.'

'Fair enough,' I say, getting up so quickly from the bench it makes me feel a little giddy – though that could just as easily be from my exhilaration at what I have to see as a major break-through.

'Where are you going?'

'To find out if we're right,' I say, patting my pockets to make sure I've got my notebook and pen with me.

'And how are you going to do that?'

'By being the someone who checks with Nigel.' I lean over and grab him by the shoulders excitedly. 'This could be it, Albie! What we've been looking for.'

'The money we should be following.'

'Exactly!' I say, making for the building.

Albie looks at me for a moment, and for the first time, I think I detect a bit of respect in his eyes. 'Martin...' he says, before I've made it more than a yard or two.

'Yes, Albie?'

'Be careful.'

I place a hand over my heart, touched by his apparent concern, and at that, he rolls his eyes.

'Yes, Albie,' I say, with a smile.

51

'She's a beauty!'

'What?' Nigel looks up with a start from where he's been rubbing at a non-existent smudge on the Aston Martin's paint-work with his sleeve. 'Oh. Thanks.'

'I used to have one of these.'

'A car?'

'An Aston Martin.'

Nigel's eyes go wide as he fails to hide his disbelief. 'Really?'

'Yes, really.' It's a blatant lie – and I very much doubt anyone in my line of work actually drove one either, despite what the films would have you believe – but I'm attempting to build rapport. 'Mine was a little older. Though I suppose that's no surprise, seeing as I am!' I lean down and squint in through the driver's-side window. The interior's quite space-age – I can't even see a gear stick, let alone one with an 'ejector seat' button on the top. 'What does it do?'

'Zero to sixty in under four seconds, with a top end just shy of two hundred.'

I actually meant in terms of gadgets, though I suppose civilians don't get to specify the kind of options that might get you out of the sort of trouble a certain 'Double-O' seemed to regularly find himself in. 'Must have cost you a pretty penny?'

Nigel waits until I'm fully upright again, then leans in to wipe off the handprint I've evidently left on the door. 'Oh, you know,' he says dismissively.

'Not really,' I say. 'Mine was actually a Company car.'

It's an uncharacteristic slip on my part, and for a moment I'm worried I've blown my cover, until I remember Nigel probably hasn't heard the capital 'C' in 'Company', or even if he has, most likely doesn't know its significance. Something he proves with his next statement.

'Whatever did you do for a living to get an Aston Martin with your job?'

'Hotel inspector,' I say automatically, and Nigel does a double take.

'At the *Savoy*?' He lets out a short laugh, and I smile politely. It's quite a good joke, but I don't want to over-acknowledge it, especially if Nigel *is* a killer.

'Listen,' I say, as he locks the car via the remote fastened to his rather unsubtle Aston Martin keyring and starts walking towards the building. 'I've been thinking.'

'Oh yes?' he says, as I hurry as fast as I can after him.

'About that leaflet you gave me. Regarding the Premium Care Plan.'

Nigel stops so suddenly in his tracks there's an accompanying scrunch of gravel. 'Oh yes?' he says again, though with about fifty times more enthusiasm than a moment ago.

'Because I'm due to go home in a couple of days, as you probably know. But I've had a lovely time here recuperating. And the last thing I want to do is be a burden to my daughter, Dionne. Who I think you've met?'

Nigel's smile wavers. 'The policewoman,' he says, the effort of keeping his voice level evident on his face.

'That's right,' I say. 'I live with her now. But I've been thinking recently that perhaps I shouldn't. And trying to cope on my own at my age isn't the easiest of things, I should imagine. So I was wondering how it would work, exactly. If I wanted to stay here. You know, *long term?*'

Nigel nods slowly until he's sure I've finished speaking, then indicates I should walk with him. 'Well, Martin, as the leaflet hopefully explained, instead of you paying for your stay on a monthly basis – with all the budgetary uncertainty that brings – our Premium Care Plan allows you to pay one lump sum up front that guarantees your expenses will continue to be met.'

'Forever?'

'Certainly, as far as you're concerned!' Nigel grins, then perhaps realises he shouldn't have. 'I mean, yes, up until the day you, you know...'

'Die?'

Nigel pauses to hold the front door open for me. 'That's right,' he says, waving me past before following me inside. 'It gives you and your loved ones—'

'Loved *one*,' I correct him. 'It's only my daughter and me left now.'

'Dionne, wasn't it?'

'That's right.'

'Well, in that case, it'll give you and Dionne peace of mind, knowing all your residential care costs will be fully covered in perpetuity, with no nasty surprises...'

I raise an eyebrow. 'What kind of nasty surprises?'

'Well, prices go up, don't they?'

'They do if you put them up.'

'Inflation, I'm afraid. Something we have no control over.' Nigel nods a curt hello to Philip, who's escorting one of the Shirleys towards the Garden Lounge. He then smiles at Joy at reception, before leading me down the corridor towards his office. 'Anyway, as I was saying, the last thing you want is to run out of money and be unable to afford to continue to stay here. Changes in later life can be extremely disruptive. Upsetting, even. And let's not forget about the fact that you can also make sure you're leaving your relatives – sorry, *relative* – something. Guaranteeing Dionne will at least receive some inheritance – perhaps even know exactly what she's getting, without having to go through the agony of seeing it dwindle away on a monthly basis. So she can plan for her future too.'

It's a convincing argument. And a well-practised one too by the sound of Nigel's smooth delivery. Though I'm conscious I need to drill down somewhat if I'm to work out exactly what's going on. 'So let me get this straight. I pay a one-off fee and never have to pay anything again?'

'That's right.'

'Even if your prices go up?'

'Correct.'

'And even if I live until a hundred?'

Nigel looks me up and down, the expression on his face implying the prospect of that is highly unlikely. 'In theory, yes.'

'In *theory*?'

'Yes.'

'What about in practice?'

'That too.'

We've reached his office now, and Nigel ushers me inside. 'And excuse my ignorance,' I say, trying not to wonder how many other people have come in here to have a similar conversation, not knowing they might have been signing their own death warrant. 'But how do you work out how much that one-off fee is?'

Nigel indicates the chair in front of me, then – once I've sat down – takes his usual one behind his desk. 'We have an algorithm. From the insurance company.'

'Insurance company?'

'That's right. Carstairs, they're called. They're our underwriters, you see, so the policy's actually with them and not us.'

'And how does the algorithm know how much I should be paying?'

Nigel puffs air out of his cheeks, as if the science behind it is beyond him, then goes on to explain it anyway. 'It guesstimates how long you're likely to live, based on factors such as your current age, medical history, pre-existing conditions, those sorts of things. So first of all you'd undergo a medical assessment...'

I pull out my notebook and pen and begin to jot this down. 'And who does that assessment?'

'That would be Gemma, our head nurse. Have you met...?'

'I have. A lovely young lady. Don't you agree?'

Nigel looks at me for a moment, perhaps trying to work out if I'm trying to imply something. 'Quite,' he says. 'Anyway, then we feed all the information we collect at the assessment – along with your personal details – into the algorithm and come back with a figure.'

'And that's it?'

'That's it. Then you do your sums, perhaps talk it over with Dionne, and assuming you decide you want to proceed, you transfer us that amount, we set you up in one of our premium sea-view rooms, and... bingo!'

'Right,' I say, assuming Nigel means the equivalent of *voilà*, and not that I'd have to play that dreadful game that seems to get everyone here so excited. 'So I pay you, and not the insurance company?'

'That's right,' says Nigel. 'We, of course, pass your premium on to them.'

'Why don't I just pay them directly?'

Nigel looks a little annoyed. 'Because the contract's between us and them. They reimburse us for your care on a monthly basis.'

'I see,' I say, being sure to jot this particular point down.

'And roughly how much might the fee be in my case, do you think?'

'I'm sure you understand, it's hard to give an accurate figure off the top of my head...'

'On average? Just so I know I can afford it. After all, I don't want to waste anyone's time.'

'Sure, sure.' Nigel thinks for a moment. 'Well, most people who come here are in their late eighties. And the average length of stay in a nursing home for someone that age is around three and a half years, give or take.' Nigel pauses while I make a note of these figures. 'And at our current level of fees, that would work out at around two hundred and forty thousand pounds.'

I let out a whistle. That's almost two Aston Martins. Though perhaps Nigel's planning to treat Gemma to one so they can drive his 'n' hers models. 'That's a lot of money!'

'It is.' Nigel smiles sympathetically. 'But you can't put a price on peace of mind.'

'And yet that's exactly what you're doing.'

'Yes, well, like I said, it's not actually us who comes up with the figure.'

'It's the algorithm.'

'Correct.'

'From the insurance company. Who underwrite the whole scheme.'

'That's right,' says Nigel, sounding pleasantly surprised that I've cottoned on.

As he leans back in his chair, looking pleased with himself, as if he's just delivered the perfect sales pitch, I pretend I'm writing all this down, but in reality, I'm doodling randomly while I try to get my head around all of this.

'So this insurance company – it's effectively betting we're not going to live that long. Or rather, not as long as their algorithm predicts. Otherwise what's in it for them?'

Nigel gazes at a spot somewhere on the wall behind me, as

if he's never thought about this before. 'I suppose, on balance, it must be skewed in their favour,' he says, after a moment. 'Though even if that's by as little as a month or so, I'm sure they provide a sufficient number of these policies to make it all add up to something worthwhile. And remember, they have all your money up front, so I'm sure they invest it wisely. Plus, I'd imagine they insure themselves. Sell on the risk to someone else, who then sells it on again...' He waves a hand vaguely in the air, as if to illustrate the confusing wizardry of the financial markets. 'You know how these things work. But the important thing is that from your point of view, you can be sure your needs are met for as long as *you* need. You can plan. In terms of your will, too. Like I said, this way you're able to guarantee that you'll leave something to Dionne. Maybe she can even start enjoying her inheritance early. Especially since...' Nigel hesitates, perhaps as he works out the best way to phrase what he's about to say. 'Well, you're not going to be needing it, are you?'

It's an interesting point. And perhaps one that's struck home with previous occupants of the chair I'm sitting in. After all, what loving parent *wouldn't* want their offspring to benefit from their inheritance while they could actually see the enjoyment they got from it? 'Makes sense,' I say, and Nigel nods.

'Perhaps even with your guidance.'

I let out a chuckle. 'As long as she doesn't blow it all on Custard, I wouldn't mind what Dionne did with it.'

'Is that... likely?' says Nigel, looking a little perplexed, and though it occurs to me that's probably because he doesn't know I'm referring to an already-pampered pooch and not the dessert sauce, I'd rather he thinks I'm coming out with statements like this because I'm mentally a few sandwiches short of a picnic, as the saying goes. He's less likely to have his guard up that way, and I'll need to rely on that being the case if I'm going to engineer him into a situation where he gives the game away.

'Stranger things have happened,' I say. As Nigel looks at me as if he doubts that, I frown. 'Why doesn't everyone do this?'

'Spend their inheritance on custard?'

'Take out one of these policies.'

'I'd imagine not everyone can afford it, for one thing. As you said, it's a lot of money. And a considerable sum for some people to find. Most often it comes from the sale of a house, which of course you no longer need if you're living here and not there. Plus, I assume that some people... Well, let's just say that by the time they move in here, three and a half years is a big ask. So they may decide that they're better off... *not*.'

'*Literally* better off!' I say, then something else occurs to me. 'And you said all residents on the Premium Care Plan get a sea-view room?'

'That's right.'

'What if there aren't any available?'

'There are.'

'But what if there weren't?'

'Why wouldn't there be?'

'If you had a run on them, for example.'

Nigel looks momentarily enchanted by the prospect. 'It's funny you should say that,' he says, and I catch my breath, though I quickly release it again. It's not as if he's about to admit he'd kill off an incumbent just to give their room to someone new.

'Funny how?'

'Well, between you and me, I'm thinking of adding some more.'

'Some more...?'

'Sea-view rooms. In fact, I've got someone coming in tomorrow to finalise the plans. But rest assured, Martin, there's a room with your name on it right now if you'd like one.'

'Stanley's, for example. Or Elsie's. Or Diana's. Or George's.'

Nigel looks at me strangely. 'Well, yes.'

'Excellent!' I say. 'I think you've answered all my questions. So, what's the next step?'

Nigel rests his elbows on his desk and his chin on his fists, though that's possibly only to stop him from rubbing his hands together. 'You're interested?'

'Definitely.'

'In that case, we should really book you in for your assessment,' he says, already getting to his feet. 'Let me go and see if Gemma's around. So we can find a date.'

'Great,' I say. 'Though I leave on Wednesday, and before I go would be preferable.'

'I'm sure we can arrange something.'

'For Wednesday morning?'

'I'll do what I can.'

'Say, eleven o'clock?'

'Eleven o'clock,' says Nigel, though I don't know whether that's a confirmation, or if he's just taking me literally. He hesitates, perhaps waiting to see if I've anything more to say, then almost sprints from the room, pausing only to squeeze my shoulder as he passes.

52

I wait for a moment, then haul myself out of my chair, walk round to Nigel's side of the desk and peer at his diary. Sure enough, he's got a ten o'clock meeting scheduled for tomorrow with a 'TW', and I hardly need the code-breaking skills of Alan Turing to work out this must be Tommy Walker. As quickly as I can, I note this down, and I'm back in my seat by the time he comes back in, followed by Gemma. He's looking a little red-faced, and I hope that's from the effort of his recent hasty exit rather than anything along the lines Shane was suggesting.

'Martin,' she says, perching on the corner of Nigel's desk. 'Nigel tells me you might be interested in one of our Premium Care Plans?'

'That's right. As I was telling him, I've had such a lovely time here these past few weeks that I'm thinking of making Twilight Lodge my permanent home.'

Gemma beams at me. 'That's wonderful news. Isn't it, Nigel?'

Nigel's *actually* rubbing his hands together now. 'Wonderful,' he says.

'In which case we'd need to book you in for an assessment.'

'So I understand.'

'Great. So when might you…?'

'As I mentioned to Nigel, I was thinking Wednesday morning. Perhaps around eleven o'clock? My daughter Dionne can come and collect me afterwards, you see. I think you met her a week or so ago.'

Gemma nods. 'Oh yes. When we all had that little… misunderstanding.'

I force a chuckle at the memory, and Gemma follows suit, although hopefully it'll be me who'll be having the last laugh if things go my way on Wednesday. 'I've already forgotten about it,' I say. 'In a "don't mention it" way, I mean, rather than, you know…' I make a 'doolally' face.

'Martin's daughter's a policewoman,' Nigel tells Gemma, though I'm not sure why, and Gemma doesn't seem to know either as her smile flickers for an instant, then she turns back to me. 'Eleven o'clock on Wednesday it is,' she says. 'And did Nigel mention the kind of figure you might be looking at?'

'He did.'

Gemma folds her arms. 'And did it sound… affordable?'

'Oh, don't worry about that!' I say, hoping it'll provoke the kind of reaction I'm expecting, which it does, as Nigel and Gemma exchange a look.

'Martin used to drive a car like mine,' says Nigel.

'An Aston Martin?'

I can't detect whether there's a comma between her second and third words, so I'm not sure whether that's a question directed to me or Nigel, but I nod anyway, enjoying playing the role, and Gemma leans forward and smiles warmly. 'Now, you're a good few years younger than most of our other residents on this kind of plan,' she says. 'And from what I've seen, you're in great shape for your age. So – fingers crossed – you'll probably be spending a little longer here than most. Though I have to warn you that may well mean your quote might come out a little higher.'

'How much higher?'

Gemma glances at Nigel again. 'That's hard to say until we've done your assessment and run the numbers through the algorithm.'

'And how long might that take?'

'The assessment? Perhaps half an hour. And then we...' Gemma mimes what I'd guess is typing something into a computer – either that or playing the piano, but that wouldn't really make sense. 'We'll be able to tell you there and then.'

'Great,' I say. 'Because I'm keen to get this all sorted out before I leave.'

Gemma and Nigel exchange glances for a third time. I may be mistaken, but it looks to me like Nigel licks his lips. 'And assuming everything goes satisfactorily, when might you be thinking of moving in?' he says.

I take that as my cue to stand up. '*Back* in, you mean?'

'Back in,' says Nigel. 'Of course.'

'That'll all depend on what happens on Wednesday,' I say, making for the door. 'So, eleven o'clock?'

'All will be revealed,' says Nigel.

'I'll look forward to that,' I say. Though I still don't quite know *how* it's going to be.

53

It's the spray of gravel bouncing off the window at five minutes to ten the following morning, no doubt caused by a high-speed circuit of the driveway, that alerts Albie and me to Tommy Walker's arrival as we enjoy a post-breakfast coffee in the Garden Lounge. Sure enough, when we look outside, his Range Rover's skidding to a stop dangerously close to Nigel's Aston Martin.

'See how he drives?' I say.

'As if he's fleeing the scene of a crime?' says Albie.

'Exactly. Except he obviously drives like that all the time.'

'Which means he probably wasn't on his way to murder anyone when we saw him on the day of Stanley's murder.'

'Quite,' I say, taking in the peaceful scene around me, where my fellow Lodgers are all chatting away, or napping, or, like us, happily making their way through plates of biscuits and hot beverages. My resolve to put an end to whatever's going on here stiffens. 'Although there's only one way to be sure.' Draining the last of my coffee, I wave away Miriam's offer of a refill, then stand up straight and adjust the cuffs of my cardigan. 'Ready, Albie?'

Albie angles his head to the left, then to the right, then winces, as I do at the popping sound coming from his vertebrae. 'As I'll ever be!'

'Now remember, this could be the final piece of the puzzle.'

'Gotcha!'

'Or rather, hopefully the piece that doesn't fit.'

'Sure.'

'We just need to eliminate Tommy Walker from our enquiries.'

'Yup.'

'Then work out how to get enough evidence to trap the real killer. Or killers.'

Albie glares impatiently at me. 'Which we can't do while you're standing here gabbing on.'

'What? Oh. Right. Sorry.'

Without another word, I nod my thanks to Miriam, grab Albie's wheelchair, and steer him out of the room and along the corridor. I had the last of my physio sessions with Olga first thing this morning, and my hip's going gangbusters – which is just as well, seeing as Tommy Walker's already walking in through Twilight Lodge's front door and I need to intercept him before he gets to Nigel's office. Though while my joint may be new, the rest of me isn't, meaning I'm not fast enough to close the ground between us. Fortunately I know a man who might be. At least, given a helping hand or two.

With a quick, 'Brace yourself!' I give Albie a hefty shove, setting him on a collision course before Tommy Walker can get past reception. I was always a top marksman, and fortunately that's no different whether it's lining someone up in the sights of a sniper's rifle at a mile or so's distance, or between the front wheels of Albie's wheelchair ten yards from the reception desk – something evidenced by the way Albie scoots as straight as a die along the corridor and smacks plumb into Tommy Walker's legs.

'What the...?' Tommy bends down and rubs his shin, then does a double take as he first recognises Albie, then clocks me hurrying towards him. '*You two?*'

'Mr Walker,' I say. 'Fancy running into you.'

'Literally!' grumbles Albie. The collision's nearly unseated him, though he waves away my attempt to help him re-site his backside in his wheelchair.

'Back here to check out another room for your mother?' I say, and Tommy stares vacantly at me.

'What? Oh. Yeah. That's right.'

'Well, you're a little late,' says Albie.

'About thirty years too late, according to my daughter.'

'Your daughter?' Tommy frowns. 'The one you're buying the flat for?'

'Dionne Maxwell,' I say. 'You may remember her. I think she was in your year at school.'

Tommy stares at the two of us for a moment, then shakes his head. 'Guilty as charged.'

'Why did you tell us that, when your mother died thirty years ago?' Albie asks, and Tommy shrugs.

'First thing that came to mind, wasn't it?'

I fold my arms. 'But you were checking the room out?'

'Might have been.'

'What for?' says Albie.

'Inspiration.'

'For what?' I say.

Tommy looks at the two of us, then evidently decides any secrets due to client-contractor confidentiality are by-the-by. 'He wants an extension,' he says, jabbing a thumb in the general direction of Nigel's office.

'An extension?'

'Yeah. Sixteen new rooms. On the side. Though that'll take out half the garden. I told him it'd be easier to build them round the back, but he was adamant they had to be there.'

'Why there in particular?' says Albie.

Tommy points out through the window. 'Something about them having sea views,' he says, and Albie and I exchange glances. If our theory is correct, then more sea-view rooms mean more murders – all the more reason to stop Nigel as soon as we can.

'And when is Nigel thinking of having this done?'

Tommy shrugs again. 'Soon as possible, he said. And as cheaply as possible. And as similar as possible to the existing ones.'

'So just to be clear,' I say. 'You were here the other day looking at Elsie's room so you could see exactly what Nigel wanted you to build.'

Tommy nods. 'Yeah,' he says. 'A room with a view. And an en suite. A loo with a view, too.'

'So you're not buying this place for redevelopment?' I say, ignoring his attempt at toilet humour.

Tommy glances around the spacious reception area. 'I wish!' he says. 'But nope.'

Albie and I exchange another look. 'So these new flats you mentioned...' I say.

Tommy's ears prick up. 'What about them?'

'Where are they going to be, exactly?'

'Exactly?' Tommy pulls his phone out of his pocket, opens the maps function, scrolls west along the coast, and jabs at a spot. 'Here,' he says, passing it to me. 'On King Edward's Parade.'

'*King Edward's Parade?*' I angle the phone's screen so Albie can see. 'In Eastbourne?'

'That's right.'

'Not here in St Leonards?'

'Nope.'

'So the other day, when you said it wasn't a million miles from here...?'

'It's not.' Tommy takes his phone back and presses a blue button with DIRECTIONS written on it. 'It's about eighteen, in fact. Which last time I looked was considerably less than a million.'

Albie angles his head up at Tommy. 'Why not here, out of interest?'

'This place?' Tommy shakes his head. 'It's not for sale, for one thing. We've had a couple of chats about it, Nigel and me, down at the golf club...'

'I didn't have you down as a golfer?' I say, and Tommy laughs.

'I'm not. But lots of people like Nigel are. People with money. And that's where they hang out, if you get my drift. At first, he seemed interested. But then he changed his mind. I suppose this place is too much of a good earner for him. Probably why he's looking to extend it.'

I nod sagely, then stick my hands in my pockets, although it's hard not to high-five Albie in celebration. With Tommy's potential motive off the table, that means we've narrowed our suspect list right down. And the works Nigel's asked Tommy to do are surely more proof, if any was needed, that we've got the right link too.

I'm just wondering whether there's anything more I can ask that might give us a few more clues or a bit more proof, perhaps something Nigel's let slip that Tommy's thought suspicious, but before I get the chance, Tommy looks at his watch.

'Right, well, I'd love to stay and chat. But time is money, and all that.' He takes a step in the direction of Nigel's office, then stops abruptly. 'By the way – are you two still interested in one of those new flats? I'd do you a good deal. Especially if you bought two.'

'Two?' says Albie.

'One for Dionne, one for the two of you. It's a lovely old building. And a lovely town.'

'*Eastbourne?*' Albie shudders theatrically. 'We're not dead yet,' he says.

Which reminds me – if we can't work out how we're going to get hold of some actual proof of what's been going on before Nigel gets wind of our investigation, then 'yet' might well be the operative word.

54

———

It's definitely Nigel who's behind the murders. I'm sure of it now. The trouble is, in the absence of any evidence, and with Dionne due to take me home tomorrow, I've only got a day to work out how to prove it – or at least find a way to extract some kind of confession. And while if this was a film, Nigel would no doubt take the time to politely explain his murderous scheme to me in great detail while he had me at his mercy, rather than using that time more efficiently to just murder *me* and ensure I wasn't ever going to be able to interfere and thwart his plans, real life *isn't* the movies, so I'm absolutely stumped as to how I can possibly get him to do that. And do it in a way I can use against him.

Albie's in the Garden Lounge when I wander despondently in, wave a half-hearted hello to the dozen or so other residents sat around the room, and take the chair next to him. In a change to his usual builder's tea with three sugars, there's a half-finished orange juice in a beaker with a straw sticking out of it on the table next to him. In contrast to my demeanour, he's looking particularly chipper, and I can only imagine why.

'On some sort of health kick, Albie?'

'Got to keep my strength up, haven't I?'

'For?'

Albie answers me with a grin, picks the beaker up, and drains the remainder of his juice.

'You're looking uncharacteristically upbeat?' I say.

'Yeah, well, you're going home tomorrow, aren't you?' He puts the beaker back down and elbows me in the side. 'Just kidding.'

I mime a belly laugh, then lower myself into the armchair next to him. 'Sorry to be leaving you on your own with all this.'

'Looks like I might not be on my own,' he says.

'What do you mean?'

He nods towards somewhere over my shoulder. 'Don't look, but...'

I swivel in my seat and spy Barbara sitting at the far side of the room. She's with a couple of her 'gal pals', as I might have referred to them sixty-or-so years ago, though every now and again she glances over in Albie's direction. 'Aha!' I say, then turn back round to find Albie glowering at me.

'What part of "don't look" didn't you understand?' he hisses.

'Relax! It's clear she's got the hots for you. And with Stanley out of the way...'

'God rest his soul,' says Albie, though not particularly convincingly.

'... I'd say it'll be plain sailing from now on.'

'Assuming neither of us gets murdered in the meantime.' Albie's eyes flick across to where Barbara's sitting, though he obviously mistimes it as there's a collective giggle from the women, and he turns a deep shade of red. 'Which is why we need to expose Nigel for the reprehensible git he is and put an end to these murders once and for all.'

'Yes, but how, Albie? And besides, I think it's pretty clear Nigel's not doing the killing.'

'Just because you're not the one who pulls the trigger, it

doesn't mean you're not a murderer. In any case, how do we know that for sure?'

'We don't. Yet. Although it seems highly unlikely, given that he owns the place. Not to mention the fact the two of us can provide him with an alibi for when Stanley was killed.'

'So Joy's still in the frame? As his henchman?'

'Can we really say that?'

'All right, Mr Woke!' Albie rolls his eyes. 'Hench*person*.'

'That's not what I meant, and you know it.' I harrumph exasperatedly as I turn to stare out of the window. 'What are we going to do?'

For the first time, Albie doesn't challenge my use of the word 'we'. 'The letter from the insurance company isn't enough of a smoking gun?'

'All that shows is that Nigel didn't pass on the premium Elsie paid. At best, that's a clerical error. At worst, it's embezzlement. Even if that's the case with the other three, it still doesn't prove they were murdered as a direct result. Or who murdered them.' I take a deep breath, then sigh it out slowly. 'And in the absence of finding something else that might corroborate...'

'What?'

'It means "confirm".'

'What does?'

'Corroborate. It means...'

'No, I know what "corroborate" means. I meant, what on earth might we find?'

I hold up an index finger. 'That's what I'm hoping to discover when I see Nigel tomorrow on my little fishing trip.'

'But what if you don't find anything?'

'That's why it's called "fishing" and not "catching", Albie.'

'Using yourself as bait?' Albie gives me a look. 'You do know usually the fish *eats* the bait?'

'What alternative do I have? Especially since I'm leaving tomorrow.' My voice catches, and I'm a little surprised by the lump I can feel in my throat. 'Speaking of which, I'll obviously come back and visit you. If you'd like?'

Albie pretends to consider this for a little too long. 'Better than nothing, I suppose. Not much better, but still...'

I clap him on the shoulder. 'Of course, we could be worrying about nothing.'

'How do you mean?'

'Maybe now Dionne's alerted Nigel to the fact that someone's on to him, it'll make him lie low for a while. Or even stop.'

'Why stop when it's such a good earner?'

'Good point,' I say. Albie knows this as well as I do – how, for many a bad guy, the lure of 'one last job' is too much to resist. And while, on the upside, the more murders there are, the more chance there is the murderer will be caught, that also brings a major downside. 'So how are you going to keep Barbara safe in the meantime?'

Albie turns an even deeper shade of red than a moment ago. 'Keep your voice down!'

'If I did that, you couldn't hear me.'

'Chance would be a fine thing.'

'Seriously, though?'

Albie leans in conspiratorially. 'Between you and me, we're planning to spend the night together.'

'When?'

'Tonight.'

'How on earth did you manage that?'

Albie looks a little offended at the inference it might have been difficult for him. 'My irresistible charm, of course. Plus the fact that I told her people were being murdered in sea-view rooms and it might be safer for her to stay with me for the time being.'

'Is that allowed?' I ask, though I'm secretly impressed at his resourcefulness.

'All's fair in love and war.'

'No – her staying in your room.'

He grins. 'Last time I checked, Twilight Lodge was a nursing home, not a monastery.'

'Fair enough. So it's going well, then?'

Albie taps his shirt pocket, and there's the unmistakeable rattle of the Tic Tac box. 'I'll let you know tomorrow,' he says.

And I can only hope I'll be able to do the same.

55

It's the morning of my last day here at Twilight Lodge, and after an unusually sleepless night, I get up to find Albie's not at breakfast. For a moment, I'm a little worried, until I realise there's no sign of any fluster at reception, the likes of which normally accompanies a death at the home. That, and the fact that Barbara's not appeared this morning either.

I wait for him until all the breakfast things are cleared away, then go for a contemplative walk round the grounds, primarily because the singalong's about to start in the Garden Lounge, and I won't be able to hear myself think. When I can't wait any longer, mainly because my meeting with Nigel is imminent, I make my way to Albie's room. His wheelchair's parked outside, which I assume means he's inside, so I knock lightly on the door.

'Albie?' I stage-whisper, and when there's no answer, I cover my eyes with one hand and prepare to open the door with the other – there are some sights you probably can't unsee, and a pair of cavorting octogenarians is one of them. But before I've even had the chance to turn the handle, a flushed-looking Barbara throws the door open. For once, her hair's a little mussed up, and she looks like she's just got dressed – and in a hurry, to boot.

'Good morning, Barbara!' I say.

Barbara smiles coquettishly. 'So far it's been *very* good, thank you for asking.'

'Is Albie...?'

'Choose your next word carefully, Martin.'

'Here,' I say, having quickly decided against 'up'. Although by the looks of Barbara, 'still breathing' might be appropriate.

'Very much so,' says Barbara, as she takes a step backwards and beckons me into the room.

'Is he decent?'

'I'll say!' she says, glancing back over her shoulder and blowing him a kiss, before heading out past me.

As she pulls the door firmly shut behind her, I turn to face Albie, who's sporting a grin that looks like it might have to be surgically removed. He's sitting up in bed, and dressed – thankfully – in his pyjamas, though on closer inspection, the buttons on his pyjama top appear to be fastened lopsidedly.

'You old dog!' I exclaim, and Albie's smile widens. 'I shan't ask you for a debriefing. Because given the state of Barbara this morning, that's already happened!'

'Might have done.'

'I take it from the look on your face all went well?'

'A gentleman never kisses and tells.'

'Quite right too. But...?' I give him a thumbs-up, and Albie rolls his eyes.

'Not that it's any of your business, but...' He gives me a thumbs-down, as a Roman emperor might when condemning a losing gladiator to death, then swivels his fist a hundred and eighty degrees to the vertical.

'Good on you!'

'Good on *these*,' says Albie, producing the Tic Tacs from his pyjama pocket. 'And the best part was, when Barbara asked what they were, I told her they were breath mints... And she believed me! I was a little worried when she asked for one, but...' He sets the box down reverently on his bedside table. 'Let's just say they're not unisex!'

'I'm very happy for you, Albie,' I say, stepping carefully over the pressure mat and sitting on the end of his bed. 'Anyway. I just wanted to check you were still alive.'

Albie lets out a short laugh. 'More so than in years,' he says, then he makes a serious face. 'What time's your meeting with Nigel?'

I look at my watch. 'In about five minutes.'

'How are you going to play it?'

'By ear.'

'Not the best strategy, perhaps?'

'Any other ideas?'

Albie thinks for a moment. 'Appeal to his ego, perhaps? Get him to boast about what he's done? You've seen his number plate – he wants everyone to know whose Aston Martin that is. So there's got to be a part of him that's tempted to crow about his crimes.'

'Perhaps,' I say. 'Though even if I manage to get Nigel to admit his guilt, and to confirm who his accomplice is, *and* if I manage to write it down in my notebook, he's hardly going to sign it, and what good is that going to be? Who's going to believe me?'

'He might let something slip that'll lead to some actual evidence. Something Dionne can use to pin these murders on him.'

'Maybe. Though now Tommy Walker's out of the frame, she might not be interested.'

'And his henchman... Sorry, hench*person*?'

I try not to smile at what's still admittedly a good joke. 'Remember those Company poker nights we used to have, back in the day?'

'No,' says Albie. 'But what's your point?'

'Just that sometimes, all you can do is play the cards you're holding.'

'What if it's not a winning hand?'

'Well, at least you get to see what the others have got.'

'That's *poker*, Martin. Your opponent *has* to show their cards when you do. Different rules apply here.'

I sit there miserably for a moment. The truth is, even if getting a confession out of Nigel might be a possibility, getting out of Nigel's office alive once I've obtained that might be a trickier prospect. And I suspect Albie knows this too, because he reaches over and squeezes my arm.

'You've done all you can, Martin. And look – no one's been murdered since you went to the police. So maybe that'll be the end of it.'

'Maybe,' I say again, though I'm sure I don't sound convinced, and Albie smiles.

'Anyway,' he says. 'What time is Dionne coming to take you home?'

'Any minute now.'

'When you're in with Nigel?'

'Hopefully,' I say – I'm banking on her coming in to rescue me if things turn nasty. Although at this rate, I can't imagine I'll be in with him for very long. 'I'll come and say goodbye before I go.'

'You do that.'

'I will.'

'And good luck!'

'Thanks,' I say – and I suspect I'm going to need it.

Levering myself up from the end of Albie's bed, I step back over the pressure mat and head for the door, although when I give the handle a tug, the door won't open.

'What's the matter?' says Albie.

I try the handle again, and while it turns, nothing else happens. 'Does it normally stick?'

'No. Never. I wonder what...' Albie's face suddenly falls. 'I gave Barbara the key to lock us in last night so we wouldn't be disturbed. She must have accidentally locked it on her way out.'

'You're joking!' I say, though Albie looks as if he's doing anything but, and I put my head in my hands. This is possibly my best and only chance to get Nigel to incriminate himself – save my actually coming back to live at Twilight Lodge full-time – and the fact that I've got him together with Gemma makes it extra important.

But none of that is going to happen if I can't get out of this room and to one with the two of them in it.

56

I glance across to the window, assessing it as a possible means of escape, but it looks to be the same as mine, with a limited opening span, and I'm well past the age and waist measurement where I could contort myself to get through the gap. In desperation, I try the door again, putting all my strength into it, but it won't budge. Back in the day I'd probably have been able to shoulder charge it down, or shoot out the lock, or even pick it. But I don't have those kinds of shoulders anymore, or my gun, or the manual dexterity – nowadays, opening one of those accursed black bin bags is tricky enough. Besides, it's fireproof, which means it's reinforced, and possibly soundproof too.

Hurriedly, I consider my options. I can't use Albie's wheelchair as a battering ram, since it's parked outside in the corridor, and besides, given the design of modern door frames, that would only be any good for breaking in, not out. Instead, I try banging on the door and calling out, hoping I'll be able to attract someone from outside, but by the sounds of things, the noises emanating from the singalong in the Garden Lounge are too loud for anyone to hear me. And even though it'll be finished in a few minutes, a few minutes are exactly what I don't have.

'You can't get it open?' says Albie, in what's possibly a contender for 'obvious statement of the year'.

'Yes, Albie. That's why I'm still stood here chatting with you rather than in Nigel's office doing my best to extract a confession. Come and help me, will you? Maybe between us we can break the lock. Force it open. Or at least make enough of a commotion that someone will hear us and—'

'I can't!'

'Why not?'

'Well, for one thing, I'm exhausted after last night. And for another, in case you'd forgotten, I *can't actually walk.*'

I stare at him in frustration for a moment or two, aware my window of opportunity is about to shut just as firmly as Albie's door appears to be. Then something occurs to me. And while it's a long shot, it has to be worth a try.

'Albie. Those "pills" you took.'

Albie peers confusedly at me, perhaps puzzled by the fact I've made air quotes around the word 'pills'. 'Martin, even if I took them all, I doubt I'd be able to…'

'No!' I shake my head, trying desperately to get rid of the mental image Albie's just conjured up. 'They were *breath mints.*'

'Pardon?'

'They're not *you-know-what.* They're breath mints. Tic Tacs, to be precise. I stole them from the newsagent's.'

'What?' Albie has the same incredulous look on his face I remember from when I apprehended him in Nicaragua all those years ago. 'Why?'

'I was worried the actual pills might kill you.'

'But…' Albie stares at the Tic Tacs with what I imagine must be the same level of betrayal he felt for me back then. 'They can't be.'

'Why not?'

'Because...' He turns a shade of red again, this time so quickly he'd put a traffic light to shame. 'They *worked*!'

'Have you never heard of the placebo effect?'

'Well, yes, but...' He frowns. 'Not for... *mechanical* problems. That's like saying if you fill a car's fuel tank up with water but think it's petrol, you'll still be able to start the engine and drive down the street. And believe you me, I drove down that street last night. And more than once.'

'But don't you see? This is good news. It means your problem isn't physical. It's all in your mind!' I tap the side of my skull for emphasis. 'And if that's the case, then so is your inability to walk!'

'Don't be ridiculous!'

'I'm not! Look at you. You're just as sharp mentally as you always were. And if last night proves anything, it's that all you lack is the motivation. So come on. Walk over here on your own two feet. And *help me get out of this room*.'

Albie stares at me in disbelief for a moment or two, then he retrieves the Tic Tacs from the table, sniffs the box, shakes one out and pops it into his mouth, and gives me the filthiest of looks. Then, with a wheeze I'm sure he's putting on for effect, he swivels himself round and dangles his feet off the bed.

'That's it, Albie!' I shout. 'Do it for me! Or if not for me, for Elsie, George, Stanley and Diana! And more importantly, for Barbara!'

At that, Albie appears to be psyching himself up to take the next decisive step, and I can't believe what I'm seeing. After all this time, he's going to stand up. Walk, even. And though I don't know if we'll even be able to get the door open between the two of us, I appreciate the effort perhaps more than anything he's ever done for me.

'You can do it, Albie!' I say excitedly. 'I believe in you. Even when no one else did, I believed in you then. It's why I spared you. Brought you back from Nicaragua. Because somehow I knew that someday we'd work together again, just like old times. So come on. On three. One, two...'

Albie gives me a look I'd rather not interpret, then with one final heave, pushes himself off the bed and onto his feet. Though my cry of triumph dies in my throat, as almost immediately he collapses heavily onto the floor.

Grateful that at least the pressure mat has cushioned his fall, I stand there abjectly for a moment, a wave of disappointment washing over me, sorry as much for Albie as I am for the fact that my chances of escaping in time are dashed. Then I'm aware of the beeping noise emanating from the box on the wall next to his bed, and I realise he's a *genius*.

'The pressure mat alarm! Well done, Albie! I knew you could do it!'

'Ouch,' groans Albie, from the jumble he's lying in, though he doesn't get the chance to say anything else, as all of a sudden there's a commotion from the other side of the door, followed by a jangling of keys. A moment later, Philip lets himself into the room.

'Martin?' he says, a puzzled look on his face. 'Why was that door locked?'

I shrug. 'Search me.'

'And Albie. What are you doing on the floor?'

'I'm wondering that myself,' says Albie, rubbing his elbow.

As Philip silences the alarm, I rush over to help Albie up, but before I can, he grabs my arm and pulls me down to his level. 'Leave me,' he says. 'And go and nail him, will you?'

'I will!' I say, though he doesn't immediately let my arm go.

'And that stuff I told you. About, *you know*?' He exhales in my direction, and the pleasant whiff of spearmint makes me smile.

'If you're referring to you and Barb...'

Albie silences me with a glare. 'That's the thing.'

'What about it?'

Albie lowers his voice. 'Just don't go broadcasting it round the Garden Lounge, will you?'

I stare at him for a moment, then stand bolt upright so quickly I almost crick my back. 'What did you say?'

'I said, don't go broadcasting it...'

'Albie, I could kiss you!'

'Wha...?' Albie looks even more scared than the time I asked him to dance with Barbara. 'Don't you dare!'

'Don't worry. I'm not going to. But I've said it before, and I'll say it again – you're a *genius*!'

'Tell me something I don't know,' he says, though it's quickly followed by, 'Although why?'

'I'll explain later,' I say, looking at my watch, knowing I've got to be somewhere. Two somewheres, in fact. 'In the meantime, do me a favour, will you? When Dionne gets here, tell her I'll meet her in the Garden Lounge. In fact, take her there yourself as soon as she arrives, will you? Make sure she stays there, along with everyone else. Then...'

'Then what?'

'Wait for my signal.'

Albie flexes his arms. Nothing appears to be broken, thankfully, though knowing Albie, he'd have already let us know if it was. 'Will do,' he says, then he looks at me blankly. 'Well, what are you waiting for?' he says. 'Off you go.'

And I can't think of anything. So off I go.

57

Thanks to my unplanned temporary detention in Albie's room, my subsequent ambushing and interrogation in the corridor by the two Shirleys regarding Barbara's discombobulation this morning, *and* the diversion via the Garden Lounge I've made en route to collect what I need now the singalong's finished, I'm running ten minutes late by the time I get to Nigel's office. Gemma's just leaving with what appears to be her medical kit, so I thank my lucky stars I've caught her.

'Martin?' she says, looking concerned, perhaps because I'm a little out of breath from my exertions. 'Everything okay?'

'Yes. I've been... working out.'

It's a bit of a white lie, in that the only thing I've been working out is how best to trap a murderer, but Gemma appears impressed, so I don't elucidate. 'I just have to attend to something,' she says. 'But I'll be back in a little while.'

This almost throws me, as I need the two of them together if my plan is going to work, and I have to think on my feet in order to get – and keep – Gemma in with Nigel, so I feign unsteadiness, extending a hand in an attempt at a feeble grab for the wall.

'Actually, could you possibly be a dear and help me?' I nod at Nigel's door. 'In there. And then maybe stay for a few minutes. Just until I feel a bit stronger.'

I make my voice tremble – the old man's equivalent of batting my eyelashes – and Gemma looks so concerned I almost feel a little guilty at the effectiveness of my acting skills. 'Of course!' she says, taking me by the arm and escorting me into the office. As she shuts the door behind us, Nigel looks up from his desk.

'Martin!' he says, looking genuinely pleased to see me for once. It's possibly because he's actually seeing pound signs instead, although I've a suspicion his good humour's about to change once I've said what I've come to say. He indicates the chair in front of his desk, and I lower myself down into it, careful not to disturb my precious cargo.

'Sorry I'm late.'

'We were beginning to think you'd changed your mind.'

'I had something I couldn't get out of.'

'I see.' Nigel smiles. 'So – the big question. Will we be seeing you again here at Twilight Lodge?'

I smile back at him, then round at Gemma, very aware she's still standing behind me and therefore between me and the door, which breaks one of the first Company rules we were taught about always making sure you have a clear exit. Unless that changes, if I'm right about everything and get the reaction I'm hoping for, but the rest of my plan fails, my most likely way out could be in a body bag like poor old Stanley the other day. Though I'm not sure I've any choice but to just go with it.

'Well, I've been giving a lot of thought to that Premium Care Plan you mentioned.'

'Oh yes?'

'And I'm afraid I won't be taking you up on it.'

Nigel's face falls as if a switch has been flicked. 'And why is that, if I can ask?' he says tersely.

'Because as attractive as the outlook from one of your sea-view rooms sounds, I don't think *my* outlook will be very promising if I do.'

'Pardon?' says Nigel, after a pause so pregnant you'd think it was expecting triplets.

'Let me put it in another way. I don't want to end up dead. At least not before my time.'

'Dead?' says Nigel. 'I don't...'

'*Murdered* dead, that is.'

There's a sharp intake of breath from behind me, while Nigel's double take is almost comical. 'Whatever do you mean by that?' he says, doing his best to regain his composure.

Gemma thankfully moves round the chair and into my eyeline, and I breathe a silent sigh of relief.

'Just that in my experience, everyone who seems to take out one of your Premium Care Plans appears to die. Rather soon after doing so. And in suspicious circumstances.'

Nigel swallows so loudly it's as good as an admission of guilt, but before he can say anything, Gemma perches on the corner of his desk. 'Martin?' she says, softly but firmly. 'We've talked about this. With Dionne. Remember?'

'You have?' splutters Nigel.

Gemma gives me a kindly smile, then turns to Nigel. 'Martin believes he used to be a secret agent,' she explains. 'Which is somewhat contrary to his daughter's understanding that he worked as a hotel inspector, to say the least. And may be why he's come up with this fanciful idea that—'

'It's not fanciful,' I say. 'First George. Then Diana. Then Elsie. Then Stanley. Each of them as fit as the proverbial fiddles. But it's you who's on the fiddle, isn't it? Which is why they all had to die.'

I've addressed the last sentence at Nigel, who appears to be clenching his jaw tightly. 'We've discussed this too, Martin,' says Gemma. 'They were *old*.'

'In that case, you need to look at that algorithm you're using, which convinced them that if they took out one of your Premium Care Plans, it would be money well spent. Little did they know it would be spent' – I turn my attention back to Nigel – 'on your divorce settlement and a new Aston Martin – with a personalised number plate, to boot. A bit of a giveaway, I have to say.'

As Nigel sits there, his mouth wide open, it's all I can do not to reach over and shut it for him. Instead, where once I'd have pulled out a gun to convince him to play ball, I pull out my notebook – although I've a feeling the contents are going to have almost the same effect. 'How do you...?' he starts to say, and I hold up a hand to silence him.

'I have to admit, we nearly didn't work it out.'

'We?' says Gemma, and I can almost hear Albie groan.

'I, I mean,' I say, mindful I ought to make sure Albie's in the clear in case I don't make it out of here – the last thing I want is for them to come for him next. 'It was such a clever scheme, I was convinced there was something else going on. Something involving your good friend Tommy Walker.'

'*Tommy Walker?*' says Nigel. 'I barely know the man.'

'That's not what it looks like from where I'm sitting,' I say, indicating the photograph on the shelf behind him, and Nigel swivels round in his chair and looks at the picture as if it's personally betrayed him.

'That was just...' he starts to say, then perhaps decides I don't deserve an explanation. 'Even if I do, what's that got to do with anything?'

'Just that I know you were considering selling Twilight Lodge to him. For redevelopment. So he could turn it into posh flats and make a killing. But it was actually you who was making a killing, wasn't it? Four of them, in fact. That I know about, that is. So far.'

Gemma leans over and rests a hand on my arm. 'Martin,'

she says, 'I can assure you...' But her voice trails off when she catches sight of Nigel's expression.

'No,' he says. 'Let him talk.'

'Thank you,' I say, then I lose my thread. 'Where was I?'

Nigel smiles. 'The part about me selling Twilight Lodge to Tommy Walker. So he could – what was it – turn it into flats?'

'Oh yes. Thanks. Only you realised you couldn't sell him the building if you still had residents here on Premium Care Plans, because where would they go? After all, you'd already taken their money. Promised them care for the rest of their days. Care that you couldn't give them if you'd sold the building where they were living. Which was why you started bumping them off.'

'Come on, Martin,' says Gemma. 'Don't you think this might all be down to that overactive imagination of yours? Dionne told me you weren't a spy. That you'd made it all up. Imagined everything. So this... *far-fetched theory* is just that. Imagined. In your head. Nobody's killing anybody here.'

'No it isn't. And yes they are.' I hold up my notebook. 'It's all in here, in fact. All the evidence I've collected over the past few weeks.'

Nigel regards me levelly from his side of the desk, as if he's not sure whether to be annoyed or to pity me. 'Well, it's certainly an interesting theory, though it does have one major flaw, in that I'm not planning to sell Twilight Lodge to Tommy Walker, or to anyone. Something he'll tell you if you ask him.'

'I know. Because I did. And yes, you're right. He told me you probably weren't selling because Twilight Lodge was such a cash cow. And you realised it could become much more of one once you'd added those extra sea-view rooms. Hold on...' I check my notebook just to be sure. 'Sixteen of them, I believe?'

Nigel's jaw drops again. 'Whatever Tommy Walker might have told you...'

'My memory might not be what it once was, but I'm not stupid,' I say. 'Although I must admit it threw me at first. But then I heard you arguing with Elsie's daughter at her funeral. About money, I believe. At the time, it struck me as strange, until I worked out why – that Elsie must have taken out a Premium Care Plan not long before she died. How unfortunate that a woman whose daughter you told could go on for years ended up meeting her end just a few weeks later. Not to mention you having the gall to turn up at her funeral, eat Yvette's vol-au-vents and explain how you were sorry but the insurance company weren't going to give her any kind of refund – though, of course, that was because they hadn't seen a penny of her premium in the first place. And *that* was because you'd realised that rather than simply killing off your existing Premium Care Plan residents so you could sell the building to Tommy Walker, if you sold new policies instead, kept the premiums, then bumped off the policyholders a few months later, that'd be far more lucrative. Partly because you wouldn't then need to sell the place. But mainly because you could do it again and again and again...'

'Martin...'

That's as far as Nigel gets, mainly because I've silenced him with a wagging finger. 'Stanley's son shut him away in here barely a month before his unfortunate demise, happy to pay up front to ensure his father's care would be covered *in perpetuum*. And I'll bet if we look at your records for George and Diana, we'll find something similar. Two old people in the best of health, who Gemma here quite rightly decides might well go on for ages, and whose nearest and dearest you manage to convince it's in their best interests to take out a Premium Care Plan. Whereas it's *your* best interests you're really concerned with.'

I pause for breath, though neither Gemma nor Nigel take the opportunity to interject when I do, so I take their nonresponse as my cue to carry on. 'Of course, I wouldn't have realised this if I'd just assumed you were passing the premiums on to the insurers. After all, what was in it for you then? But then I found proof you'd been pocketing the premiums yourself, a fact I'm sure Elsie's daughter would be interested to hear, as would – ultimately – a judge and jury. And I wonder, once the police get involved, how many others you'll be found to have convinced to do the same thing? How many other residents are enjoying their sea views, unaware they're on your kill list?' I shake my head disdainfully. 'It's a brilliant money-making scheme if you think about it. After all, what's more profitable than selling a high-priced service that you don't ever plan to deliver? And you can do it as often as you like, and no one will ever get suspicious – because that's the nature of the game, isn't it? George, Diana, Elsie and Stanley were simply unlucky because they were just old, weren't they? If they weren't exactly knocking on death's door already, they were certainly quite far down the ever-shortening corridor that led to it – something you perhaps exaggerated to their GP to avoid suspicion. Because of that, no one was likely to even consider calling for a post-mortem. And now I think about it, it wouldn't surprise me if you hand-picked those who'd put "cremation" as a preference for their funeral wishes, because then you'd have a natural way of getting rid of the evidence of your crimes without having to lift a finger.'

Because this has just occurred to me, I make a note in my notebook to check this when – sorry, *if* – I get out of here, but when I look up, Gemma's rolling her eyes to such a degree you'd worry she was possessed.

'Of course, now we come to the matter of who was actually doing your dirty work,' I continue. 'After all, it's highly unlikely someone like you would have the know-how or the stomach to actually carry out the murders. No offence.'

'None taken,' says Nigel, though he's still looking a little shell-shocked.

'Plus, the fact that you were at Elsie's funeral when Stanley was killed – a nice touch, by the way – gives you an alibi. One that I myself can vouch for.'

Nigel furrows his brow. 'Um, *thank you*, Martin?'

'And I realised the killer had to be someone with regular contact with the victims. Someone they trusted, which enabled them to administer whatever method you decided was best to get rid of them without arousing suspicion. At first I suspected Shane, but that was perhaps a little too obvious. And unlikely – after all, how could you rely on someone who had difficulty delivering even the most basic levels of care to carry out something as challenging as murder? *And* so skilfully it would go undetected time and time again, allowing them – and you – to get away with it? Furthermore, when I looked at all the evidence, it seemed to point to the member of staff the least likely to be the culprit.'

Nigel holds up his index finger, though I'm not sure whether it's to stop me or ask a question, until he says, 'Who on earth are you talking about, Martin?' When Gemma grips the edge of the desk so tightly her knuckles turn white, I recognise now's the time to play my hand.

'Joy, of course.'

'*Joy?*' Gemma visibly relaxes, so much so she looks like she's about to burst out laughing. 'As in Joy on reception?'

'That's the one.'

'I'm sorry, Martin,' says Nigel. 'But you if you think that *Joy…?*'

'I didn't say I thought it was her. I just said that's what the evidence suggested. I mean, it's more likely to be me, or even you, Gemma – though you've such a position of trusted responsibility here at Twilight Lodge, it's extremely unlikely you'd be the murderer. Which is why I didn't suspect you until I found out your link to Nigel.'

'My link...?'

'The affair you've been having. You might have been clever enough to conceal these killings, but you weren't smart enough to conceal *that*. And from *Shane*, of all people!'

'I don't see what that's got to do with anything,' splutters Nigel.

'Because while, in my experience, people will do almost anything for money, they'll go even further if it's for love.' I'm about to say, 'Just ask Albie', but remember to stop myself just in time. 'As to how Nigel convinced you, how perhaps you even justified to yourself what you were doing wasn't wrong – that had me stumped for a while, until I recalled something you said to Dionne and me that time in your office. Something so shocking I didn't need to write it down in my notebook to remember it.'

'Perhaps you could refresh *my* memory,' says Gemma tersely.

'Of course. It was about the final stage of dementia – stage seven, I believe, if you include that debatable first one – how awful it is, and how it was often better if sufferers didn't make it that far – and you said something about how death "can be a blessing". And that was how you saw it, wasn't it – at least, at the beginning? That you were doing them a favour. Putting them out of their misery. Sparing them from what you saw as a dreadful fate. Ending their suffering before it had even begun. *Years* before, in some cases, I'd imagine.'

'That's not...'

'But it has to be. Four people who your assessment said were likely to live at least another few years didn't even survive a few more months. So unless it's simply because you're not very good at your job – though the distinction certificate from the Royal College of Nursing hanging on the wall in your office is evidence to the contrary – there's definitely something reprehensible going on here at Twilight Lodge. And in the absence of any other explanations, not to mention your relief when I played my "Joy" bluff a few moments ago, I'm afraid, Gemma, the murderer has to be you.'

58

I stop talking and take a breath. Gemma's shaking her head in disbelief, and while that might be because I've got everything completely wrong, I suspect it's more because I've got it right.

'So,' I say, closing my notebook and putting it down on the desk in front of me, as if I've just read the two of them a bedtime story. 'In a nutshell, you've been presenting Twilight Lodge as the ideal place to spend one's twilight years, and offering to take all the worry out of those years by telling people that if they make a one-off payment they can live in the lap of luxury until their dying day. Then you realised if you kept the payment and brought that day significantly forward, you could pocket the difference, all with their devastated relatives too upset to raise a fuss... I mean, congratulations, Nigel. You're quite the criminal mastermind. At least you would have been – if you hadn't been found out.'

Nigel sits up straighter in his chair, like a child at the end of a telling-off. 'That's quite a nutshell,' he says, after a moment.

'More like a coco de mer,' I say, and Nigel and Gemma exchange puzzled looks, so I add, 'It's the largest nut in the world. Native to the Seychelles – somewhere you've possibly been considering as a holiday destination, given the amount of money you're raking in thanks to all of this?'

Nigel lets out a short laugh. 'Okay, Martin,' he says, holding both arms out, hands balled into fists, as if he's expecting me to put him in handcuffs. 'You've got me, guilty as charged. Gemma too.'

Gemma's eyes widen. 'Nigel!'

'What?'

'You just confessed!'

'To *him*?' Nigel withdraws his arms, links his fingers, puts his hands behind his head and leans back in his chair. 'So what? What's he going to do? It's his daughter who's the policewoman, and from what you've just told me, she probably already thinks he's crazy. Who cares if he leaves this office spouting all these theories about how you and I killed Elsie and Stanley, and... what were their names again?'

'George. And Diana,' I say, well past the point where I need to look it up.

'Thank you, Martin,' says Nigel, though I doubt he's being sincere. 'I have to hand it to you, you managed to work it all out despite... Where's he at, Gemma?'

Gemma peers at me as if she's doing my assessment there and then. 'He's not been officially diagnosed. But given the reliance on the notebook and – shall we say – the questions regarding his past, I'd estimate... stage two?'

Nigel sticks his lower lip out and nods, perhaps to indicate how impressed he is with my deductive powers. 'Impressive work, considering.'

'Thank *you*, Nigel,' I say. 'Though can I just add, shame on you. These were old people. Vulnerable people. They put their trust in you, and you betrayed them, and all for greed.' I shake my head, then turn to Gemma. 'And you! What about the Hippocratic Oath? How could you let him convince you to kill...?'

'It's the Nightingale Pledge for nurses,' says Gemma haughtily. 'The Hippocratic Oath is for doctors. And that's not the only thing you've got wrong.'

I fold my arms. 'Enlighten me.'

'None of this was Nigel's idea.'

'It wasn't?'

'No.' Gemma smiles proudly. 'It was all mine.'

I rock back in my chair as the cogs turn in my mind, and in a moment of clarity, the likes of which are sadly nowhere near as frequent as they once were, I understand everything perfectly. As Albie pointed out a while ago, your average Nigel's not that likely to be a murderer. But a Nigel infatuated with a young, attractive woman could probably be pillow-talked into turning a blind eye to what was going on. Especially if his head is also turned by the money. And even more especially, if he *needs* the money to pay off his ex-wife in order to indulge in what appears to be – given the Aston Martin and the younger woman – some sort of mid-life crisis.

'Aha,' I say. 'May I ask why?'

Gemma shrugs dismissively. 'You said it yourself earlier.'

'You think you're doing them a *favour*?'

She nods. 'Most definitely. If you'd seen what I've seen, you'd—'

'But it's *murder*.'

'In this country, maybe.'

'You're *in* this country,' I say, and while Nigel at least has the decency to appear a little awkward at that, Gemma is staring defiantly back at me. 'And what about the relatives?'

Gemma makes a face, as if I'm the one who's being unreasonable. 'You don't think I'm sparing them from something too?'

'You're taking their money while promising them the opposite.'

'I'm doing them a service. Something I'm sure most of them would secretly prefer if they knew the reality. Why shouldn't they pay for that? Or rather, why shouldn't *I* get paid for that?'

'Because it's wrong?' I suggest, noting for the first time the diamond earrings and necklace Dionne would no doubt refer to as 'bling', the Rolex on Gemma's wrist, and the expensive mani-cure – a combination that's surely way above her pay grade. 'And however you try and dress it up, it still makes you a murderer. Oh, and a thief!'

Gemma looks at me scornfully. 'That depends on your point of view, I suppose,' she says. 'So we'll just have to agree to disagree.'

'I suppose so,' I say, not because I agree, but because it's quite clear Gemma's a homicidal sociopath, and as I've seen many a time in my Company days, there's no reasoning with the likes of her. Nigel, on the other hand, appears almost as perturbed by her attitude as I am, and I have to wonder whether he might just be the key to my surviving our little tête-à-tête. 'Though there's one part I just haven't worked out yet.'

'Which is?' says Gemma accommodatingly. She's evidently taking some delight in humouring me, though I don't want to think too deeply about why that might be.

'How.'

'How?' asks Nigel.

'As in how you murdered them.'

'Gemma?' says Nigel, as if handing over to a co-presenter on a daytime television show, and she gives him the briefest of smiles.

'Old people can be surprisingly... fragile,' she says, and Nigel nods.

'Especially when it comes to ending their lives.'

'Have the decency to call it what it is, will you!' I say, my voice finding some of its old gravitas, and Nigel swallows hard.

'"Murdering" them, then,' he says, although he's mimed air quotes, which I still think is a little disrespectful.

'Thank you,' I say. 'So how did you do it?'

Gemma stares at me for a moment, perhaps surprised by my temerity, then she shrugs, either deciding she's in for a penny, in for a pound, or that Nigel's right and no one will take me seriously even if I somehow manage to get out of here. Though that's no doubt because she doesn't know what I know.

Slowly, carefully, I shift position in my chair, managing to avoid the embarrassing sound that movement produced last time I did it in here, and thrust my pelvis towards Gemma, answering her puzzled look with, 'New hip. Just getting comfortable,' and Gemma nods in acknowledgement.

'Simple, really,' she says. 'Three hundred millilitres of air injected at a hundred millilitres a second. Done correctly, that'll cause an embolism that's difficult to distinguish from a normal stroke or aneurysm. Half of the residents in here are getting regular injections for something or another, or flu jabs and vaccinations. Even if they weren't, it's easy to inject someone where it won't be detected. And like you said, certainly not after they've been cremated.'

'Ingenious,' I say, picking my notebook back up and jotting that down just in case. Then I look at my watch. It's eleven thirty – hopefully Dionne's arrived by now, and if so... Well, that's down to Albie. Not for the first time, my survival depends on him. I can only hope he's not seeing this as an opportunity for payback.

'Right,' I say, recapping my pen. 'I think that's everything.' I smile curtly at them both, as if I've just ended a formal meeting, and haul myself up from my armchair. 'Anyway, thank you both for all of this. As I said, my daughter's waiting to take me home, so I'd better be off. And I'm sure we'll be having a very interesting conversation on the way.'

'Not so fast, Martin!' says Nigel, rising to his feet.

'If only, at my age!'

'Just... your notes.'

Like a striking cobra – albeit one with a heavy gold watch around its neck – Nigel's arm shoots out, and he snatches the notebook from my grasp. Slowly, systematically, he tears each page out and begins feeding them into the shredder next to his desk, and as I watch my weeks of carefully gathered evidence being destroyed, I can only hope my wider plan is working.

'If only you were this easy to get rid of, Martin,' Gemma says. Then she locks eyes with Nigel, and I can tell I have to act quickly. I could still probably make the door, and I'm sure I can remember a move or two that'll let me bypass the two of them if not, but then I change my mind, wondering if this might be the one last act that'll guarantee their conviction. Though it means putting myself at risk, I'm no stranger to that.

I hesitate, pretending to be a bit unsteady on my feet again, allowing Gemma just enough time to block my route to the doorway. 'I'm sorry, Martin,' she says, though without a trace of regret in her voice. 'But I don't think we can let you leave. Not with you knowing all this.'

Nigel gets to his feet, and I prepare myself to judo-sweep him to the floor – though while I fear he's about to attempt to detain me, instead he puts a restraining hand on Gemma's arm. 'Let's not be hasty,' he says.

'Hasty?' Anger flashes in Gemma's eyes, and she pulls away from him. 'We wouldn't need to be if you hadn't been so sloppy.'

'How have I been sloppy?'

Nigel sounds genuinely hurt, and Gemma shakes her head in frustration. 'You must have been. Otherwise how would he have found everything out?'

'Well, because you just *told* him, for one thing,' says Nigel, bristling slightly.

'Only after you admitted it!' Gemma says, through gritted teeth. 'I warned you not to buy that stupid car.'

'*Darling...*'

'Don't you "darling" me!' snaps Gemma. 'You think I want to be working in a place like this for the rest of my life?'

Nigel looks like he's been slapped in the face. 'That's not a very nice thing to...' is as far as he gets, partly because he's perhaps realised chastising a murderer for uttering a few hurtful words is a little pointless, but mainly because Gemma's expression has darkened so quickly it's as if there's been a localised solar eclipse.

'*Nice?*' she says incredulously. 'None of this is about being nice, Nigel. We had an arrangement.'

'More than an arrangement, surely?' he says, though he doesn't wait for Gemma to respond. 'And we can still get away with it, if we stop now. Like you said, no one's going to believe him.' He tears the last page from my notebook and makes a show of feeding it through the shredder. 'Especially now I've destroyed all the evidence.'

'Evidence?' scoffs Gemma. 'Or simply the imaginary scribblings of an old fool? Either way, there's no sense in taking chances. It's just a pity we didn't get the chance to sign him up for one of our Premium Care Plans beforehand.'

'Beforehand of what?' I say, as much to remind them I'm still here as anything else, and Gemma looks at me strangely, though I doubt it's as a result of my questionable grammar.

'For someone who claims he used to work for the intelligence services, you're being a bit thick,' she says, reaching for her medical kit. 'Your tragic and untimely death, of course.'

Nigel stares in horror at Gemma for a moment, perhaps for the first time seeing a side of her he didn't want to acknowledge existed. Then he looks at me apologetically and hands what's left of my notebook back.

'That's okay,' I say, waving him away. 'I don't need it. After all, I have your confession.'

'My *confession?*'

'That's right.'

For the first time, Nigel looks at me as if I *am*, in fact, an old fool. 'But you're the only one who's heard it.'

'That's what you think.'

Nigel looks puzzled, then even more so, given the whooping noises I've just begun making. 'Are you all right?' he says, perhaps hoping I'm saving Gemma a job.

'I'm perfectly fine, thank you,' I say, as I sit back down to wait for the cavalry.

He looks at Gemma, though as experienced as she is with dementia patients, judging by her expression, I don't think she's ever seen anything like this before. 'It sounds like you might need a little injection of something,' she says, unzipping her medical kit. 'To calm you down.'

'Three hundred millilitres of air, you mean?' I say. 'Injected at a hundred millilitres a second, perhaps?'

'It's like you're reading my mind,' says Gemma menacingly, as I start whooping again, a little more urgently this time. 'Hold him down, will you, Nigel?'

Puffing my chest out, I give Nigel my best 'good luck with that' look, and it seems to do the trick as he remains rooted to the spot – though that only aggravates Gemma further. 'Do I have to do *everything*?' she sighs, but before she can retrieve her syringe, there's the sound of a commotion from the corridor. Then, to my relief, Dionne comes bursting in through the door, closely followed by Albie, then Joy and Miriam, with Philip blocking the exit.

'What the...?' Nigel looks flustered at the incursion, then does his best to regain his composure. 'I'm so glad you're here,' he says quickly. 'I think your father might be having a stroke.'

'Nah,' says Albie. 'That was the sound of a mountain gorilla. Which is definitely not found in the Western Congo, eh, Martin?'

Nigel gawps at him, then at Gemma, then at Dionne, and finally, at me. '*What?*' he says.

'Did you hear everything, Albie?' I say, and Albie breaks into a grin, and it's almost as wide as the one on his face earlier this morning.

'Loud and clear, Martin.'

Nigel shakes his head briefly. 'What are you talking about?'

'Like I said a few moments ago,' I say. 'Your confession.'

'What confession?' says Nigel, though not especially confidently.

'The one you've been broadcasting round the Garden Lounge.'

I haul myself back to my feet, carefully stand on one leg – proof, if it were needed, that my physiotherapy has been working – and approximate my best attempt at what I believe is known as 'twerking'. After a moment, the wireless karaoke microphone I've purloined from the singalong on my way here tumbles down the inside of my trouser leg and lands on the floor with a loud thump.

As Dionne begins reading Nigel and Gemma their rights, and Gemma's expression morphs from surprise into what looks a lot like anger, Albie reaches down, picks the microphone up, switches the button to 'off', then winks at me. 'I believe,' he says, 'that's what the youth of today would refer to as a "mic drop".'

And though – as Albie pointed out the other day – I don't quite have *my* finger on the pulse of popular culture, I think I can work out what he means.

59

The arrival of three police cars at Twilight Lodge is quite a sight, lights flashing and sirens blaring as they come flying through the gates and skid to a halt on the drive, sending more gravel flying than even Tommy Walker managed. But I suppose you can't blame them for their exuberance – as has been pointed out to me on more than one occasion, these kinds of crimes don't normally happen in a town like St Leonards.

The third police car parks strategically to block the exit, ensuring Nigel and Gemma aren't going anywhere apart from prison, which I think they both already knew, given the lack of any attempt to escape. Though I suppose it would be hard to stay inconspicuous if you went on the run in an Aston Martin, particularly one with your name on the number plate. And even more so if you don't have the keys to it, which I've slyly lifted from Nigel's desk in all the confusion. Not that I'm intending to take the car anywhere – after all, there's not exactly a lot of room for Albie's wheelchair in the back. But the keyring will make a nice souvenir. And besides, one never knows when emergency transport might be required.

We're quite the heroes, it appears. There's even a round of

applause and something of a guard of honour as I steer Albie through the assembled staff and residents in the driveway. It's not something I'm used to, given how all my missions had to be clandestine back in the day – the only time you got any kind of recognition was if you died in the line of duty – so for once, I allow myself the chance to bask in the adulation. And make sure Albie gets his moment in the sun too. After all, he's the one staying here.

And while the 'daggers' I get from Gemma as she's manhandled into the back of the leading police car isn't the nicest of farewells with which to be leaving Twilight Lodge, at least they're not *real* daggers. I'm not sure my reflexes are good enough to fend those off any more. Though the last month has shown I've still 'got it' – or at least a bit of it – especially with my old partner Albie by my side.

I clap a celebratory hand on his shoulder, more than a little sad I have to leave, and though he doesn't show it, I sense Albie feels the same. He glances across to where Barbara's gazing admiringly at him through the Garden Lounge window, unconsciously reaches for his shirt pocket to check he hasn't misplaced the Tic Tacs in all the excitement, then holds out a hand for me to shake.

'Thanks for everything, Martin,' he says.

'Does this mean you've forgiven me for Nicaragua?'

Albie sighs. 'Martin, I wish I could remember this incredible former life you seem convinced we both shared, but you know my memories of anything I did before my stroke are pretty much non-existent.'

'That's a shame. You were the best, Albie,' I say, shaking his hand warmly. 'Well, second best, perhaps. And still are.' I glance across towards the window. 'Although not as far as a certain lady's concerned.'

Not for the first time, Albie turns a deep shade of red. 'Perhaps,' he says, his usual glass-half-emptiness gone.

'No doubt about it.' I give his wheelchair an affectionate pat. 'And you'll be up and out of that thing in no time, I'm sure.'

'There's a different flavour of Tic Tacs to help me with that, is there?'

'I'll have a word with Shane.'

'You do that. And before next week's tea dance, if you wouldn't mind?'

I raise an eyebrow. 'Sounds like someone's rediscovered their zest for life.'

'Maybe,' says Albie, and I feel my chest swell with pride. He saved my life in Belize, and even though it's a little late in the day, the feeling I might just have returned the favour is a wonderful one. 'Although I won't be rushing to sign up for a Premium Care Plan just yet.'

'You never know, Albie,' I say, then I sigh wistfully. 'I just wish we could have worked it out sooner. Saved poor old Elsie. And Stanley.'

'I know,' says Albie, giving Barbara a little wave. 'Though maybe not Stanley.'

'Maybe not,' I say, with a chuckle, then I rest my hand back on his shoulder. 'I couldn't have done it without you, you know?'

'Get off, you soppy old sod!'

'Seriously. It's been just like old times. You and me, we're a *team*. Like... Robin and Batman. Or Hutch and Starsky. Or Watson and Holmes...'

'*Nursing* Holmes, you mean, Martin.' Albie winks exaggeratedly at me, then nods down at his wheelchair. 'Maybe not *just like* old times, I'd imagine. Still, these last few weeks have been an adventure.'

'Something to tell the grandkids.'

'If I had any.'

'You and me both,' I say, glancing across at Dionne, who, to my pleasant surprise, appears to be having something of a flirty conversation with Philip. 'Though watch this space,' I add, as after a moment's hesitation, she types what I presume is her number into his mobile. 'You see, Albie? It's never too late.'

'Until it is,' Albie says, as Philip takes his phone back, slips it into his pocket as if it's as valuable as the crown jewels, then hands Dionne my suitcase. 'Oh, and Martin...'

'Yes, Albie?'

'Don't be a stranger, will you?'

'Of course not,' I say, the words almost catching in my throat.

'Though having said that, don't make me regret it.'

'As if!' I say, mock-indignantly. 'In any case, what are the chances of another killing spree here at Twilight Lodge?'

Albie beckons me closer. 'Anyone gets in the way of Barbara and me, and you might find out!' he whispers.

I do my best to smother a laugh as Dionne approaches us. 'Here she is!' I say, standing up abruptly. 'The woman of the hour.'

Dionne deposits my suitcase at my feet and regards us suspiciously. 'Why are you two looking so secretive?'

'Just... reminiscing,' says Albie.

'About?'

I narrow my eyes. My mission's over, though technically I'm still bound by the Official Secrets Act. Besides, Dionne still thinks I've made up all these stories about my past, so probably best to keep things that way. 'Just the past few weeks,' I say, as I load my suitcase into the back of her car, pausing to scratch Custard – who's pacing around in the back seat, his tail twitching like the Volvo's windscreen wipers on their fastest setting – affectionately between his ears.

'Someone's glad you're coming home,' Dionne says.

'Thanks very much!' I say, pretending to be offended, and Dionne grins at me.

'We both are.' She steps in and gives me the biggest of hugs, then releases me, and though I don't point it out – perhaps because mine might do the same – I'm sure her eyes have misted over. 'Really glad.'

'Well, that makes three of us,' I say. 'I told you I wasn't going anywhere.'

Dionne fixes me with a steely look. 'You make sure you don't!'

'And leave you on your own?' I say, in mock outrage. 'Never. Especially since there's only the two of us now.' My voice cracks, though I just about manage to add, 'No offence, Custard.'

Dionne's smile reminds me of her late mother's, particularly when she couples it with a slow shake of the head, and it's a wonderful, if bittersweet, feeling. 'I still don't know how the two of you managed to work out what was going on.'

'Just lucky, I guess,' I say, and Albie snorts derisively.

'Speak for yourself!'

'I was,' I say, then I turn back to Dionne. 'Whereas Albie has, shall we say, a special set of skills.'

'Dare I ask?' she says, rolling her eyes. 'Though so do you, obviously, getting them to confess like that. So we could all hear it.'

'That was Albie's idea,' I point out, happy to see he doesn't dispute the fact – credit where credit's due, and all that.

'But to go in there with a microphone hidden down your trousers...' Dionne makes a face at the audacity of it all. 'Weren't you worried they might notice it, or that you might have been out of range?'

'Not really,' I say. In truth, given the positioning of the microphone, my biggest concern had been my sphincter letting me down again, meaning I'd have broadcast more than simply our conversation. 'Do you think it'll be enough to convict them?'

Dionne nods. 'A confession heard by thirty-odd people? Probably. Even though most of the witnesses might not be the most reliable, the staff all heard it. And I heard it – and I'm a police constable.' She pulls her mobile phone from her pocket and taps the screen. 'Also, I recorded it.'

'Good thinking,' I say proudly. 'Maybe not merely a constable for long after cracking this case, eh?'

Dionne smiles bashfully. 'I hardly cracked...'

'You're the arresting officer, and I'm sure that counts for a lot. Plus, you were the one who first interviewed Nigel and thought there was something fishy about him. And who knows? The more you investigate, the more victims you might uncover. Perhaps among the other six deaths Nigel told you about that occurred this year before I moved in.'

Dionne looks at me strangely. 'How do you know about those?'

I freeze, and wonder how to explain this without letting on about my eavesdropping outside Nigel's office. Fortunately, and not for the first time today, Albie comes to my rescue.

'There might have been even more,' he says, gazing long-ingly at Barbara. 'If you hadn't nailed the two of them today.'

'Including me!' I say.

Dionne takes my hand and gives it a squeeze. 'Which I still haven't forgiven you for, putting yourself in danger like that!'

'Of course, you'll still need to do a lot of follow-ups with the relatives. Cross-check who paid what, and whether Nigel passed on all those premiums to the insurance company.'

'Ahead of you there, Dad.'

'Oh, and the results of the post-mortem on Stanley should be the final, you know...' I hesitate, unable to think of another way to say, 'nail in the coffin', which seems a little insensitive. 'Assuming you're going to request one? Which I think would be a good idea.'

'Yes, thank you, Dad. That had occurred to me too.'

I hold both hands up. 'Of course. I don't mean to tell you your job.'

'So don't!' Dionne scolds, then she shakes her head slowly. 'Who'd have thought? A couple of cold, calculating killers in a nursing home in St Leonards-on-Sea!'

'You mean Nigel and Gemma, right? And not...' I indicate Albie and myself, and Dionne laughs.

'Right. Unless Albie used to be a secret agent too?'

Her tone suggests it's a joke, and Albie chuckles accordingly. 'Hardly,' he says.

'What was it you did for a living, if I can ask?' she says, and Albie looks puzzled.

'He had a stroke,' I remind her. 'And his memory...'

'No, hang on,' says Albie suddenly. 'It's all coming back to me...' He gives me the briefest of side-eyes. 'I was...'

'Yes, Albie?'

Albie thinks for a moment longer, then he makes the kind of face people do when they've finally remembered where they've left their missing bunch of keys. 'I was a *hotel inspector.*'

Dionne's jaw drops open. 'That's a coincidence,' she says, narrowing her eyes. 'Isn't it, Dad?'

'Isn't it just?' I say.

'It's a wonder you two never met before.'

'Oh, I'm sure our paths probably crossed in the line of duty,' I say. 'Isn't that right, Albie?'

Albie peers at me, as if my face rings a bell he can't quite hear. 'It wouldn't surprise me,' he says, as he begins wheeling himself backwards towards Twilight Lodge's main entrance, though he stops almost immediately and jabs a thumb in the direction of the building. 'That was brave, what you just did. You could have been killed.'

'Nonsense! If things had gotten nasty, I'd just have...' I demonstrate a karate chop, then wince at the sudden pain in my shoulder the movement provokes. 'You'd have done the same if the tables were turned.'

'Not on your life!' says Albie. 'No doubt about it – you dodged a bullet in there.'

'You reckon?'

'Yeah.' Albie nods as he performs a deft one-eighty and resumes his journey towards the building, though he turns back just before he gets there. 'Unlike that time we were in Belize, eh, Martin?'

I give him a farewell salute, hoping Dionne hasn't heard, though given her expression, my luck seems to have deserted me.

And as we clamber into the Volvo for the short journey home, not for the first time today, I suspect I've some explaining to do.

A LETTER FROM MATT

Dear Reader,

I just want to say a HUGE thank you for choosing to read *The Armchair Detectives*. If you'd like to keep up to date with all my latest releases, just sign up at the following link. Your email address will never be shared and you can unsubscribe at any time – although obviously I hope you won't!

www.bookouture.com/matt-dunn

It was so much fun to write my first murder mystery after fourteen (I know!) romantic comedies. Martin and Albie were such a joy to spend time with, and I'm so enjoying getting them into more and more trouble as the series progresses. It certainly puts a new slant on 'getting' the girl, and by foul means rather than fair – my internet (re)search history would definitely get me arrested nowadays!

If you enjoyed *The Armchair Detectives*, I'd be very grateful if you could find a few moments to write a short review. I'd love to hear what you think, and your review will make such a difference in terms of helping new readers to discover one of my books for the first time. I'd love to hear from you too – you can get in touch through any of my 'socials' (as the youth of today call them) or via my website.

Right – back to work for me. These books don't write themselves. Yet, anyway...

Thanks again, and all best wishes,

Matt Dunn

www.mattdunn.co.uk

instagram.com/mattdunnwrites

facebook.com/mattdunnwrites

x.com/mattdunnwrites

bsky.app/profile/mattdunnwrites.bsky.social

threads.com/@mattdunnwrites

ACKNOWLEDGEMENTS

Thanks, in no particular order, to:

Laura Deacon, Kim Nash, Hannah Snetsinger and the team at Bookouture.

The unmistakeable Gabbie Chant and Lynne Walker.

Kate Nash (my agent, not the "Foundations" singer), and everyone at the Kate Nash Literary Agency.

The Board. Has it really been twenty years?

Tina. Has it really been twenty-eight?!

And to you, dear reader(s). Without you, I'd have to get a proper job. And I fear that ship has sailed.

PUBLISHING TEAM

Turning a manuscript into a book requires the efforts of many people. The publishing team at Bookouture would like to acknowledge everyone who contributed to this publication.

Audio
Alba Proko
Melissa Tran
Sinead O'Connor

Commercial
Lauren Morrissette
Hannah Richmond
Imogen Allport

Cover design
Tash Webber

Data and analysis
Mark Alder
Mohamed Bussuri

Editorial
Laura Deacon
Imogen Allport

Copyeditor
Gabbie Chant

Proofreader
Lynne Walker

Marketing
Alex Crow
Melanie Price
Occy Carr
Cíara Rosney
Martyna Młynarska

Operations and distribution
Marina Valles
Stephanie Straub
Joe Morris

Production
Hannah Snetsinger
Mandy Kullar
Ria Clare
Nadia Michael

Publicity
Kim Nash
Noelle Holten
Jess Readett
Sarah Hardy

Rights and contracts
Peta Nightingale
Richard King
Saidah Graham

Dear Reader,

We'd love your attention for one more page to tell you about the crisis in children's reading, and what we can all do.

Studies have shown that reading for fun is the **single biggest predictor of a child's future life chances** – more than family circumstance, parents' educational background or income. It improves academic results, mental health, wealth, communication skills, ambition and happiness.

The number of children reading for fun is in rapid decline. Young people have a lot of competition for their time, and a worryingly high number do not have a single book at home.

Hachette works extensively with schools, libraries and literacy charities, but here are some ways we can all raise more readers:

- Reading to children for just 10 minutes a day makes a difference
- Don't give up if children aren't regular readers – there will be books for them!

- Visit bookshops and libraries to get recommendations
- Encourage them to listen to audiobooks
- Support school libraries
- Give books as gifts

There's a lot more information about how to encourage children to read on our websites: **www.RaisingReaders.co.uk** and **www.JoinRaisingReaders.com**.

Thank you for reading.